Race to Damascus

K. J. Maxwell

AuthorHouse™
1663 Liberty Drive
Bloomington, IN 47403
www.authorhouse.com
Phone: 1-800-839-8640

© 2010 K. J. Maxwell. All rights reserved.

No part of this book may be reproduced, stored in a retrieval system, or transmitted by any means without the written permission of the author.

First published by AuthorHouse 3/17/2010

ISBN: 978-1-4343-9634-1 (sc)

Printed in the United States of America
Bloomington, Indiana

This book is printed on acid-free paper.

Dedicated to CLM. Thank you for being my best friend.

Chapter One

Brandon Parkes had never been to Monte Carlo. Though he had traveled to Europe on half a dozen occasions he had never been to the one place he desired to visit most. As he boarded the flight to Paris, he wondered if the trip he was making to the tiny principality would be like the one he had always fantasized about, or just a disappointing waste of both time and money that he could ill afford right now.

As he settled in to First Class he looked no different than the other passengers who shared the cabin with him. Dressed in a dark gray Boss suit and wearing a silver Rolex Daytona watch, he seemed to fit right in. However, he could not have felt more out of place; in fact, desperate might have been a more accurate description of his feelings.

"May I take your suit coat, sir?" the female flight attendant asked him politely. "Sure", said Parkes as he removed his jacket and handed it to the attractive young woman.

"Can I bring you something to drink?" she then asked.

"I'll have a scotch and soda." he replied with a forced smile.

As he sat in down in his seat and fastened the belts he thought of the first time he ever had tasted scotch. It had been almost thirteen years ago in Carmel, California. That had been a pretty happy time in his life, if not the best time he had ever known.

Maybe going to visit the old friend who had introduced him to scotch and soda was exactly what he needed right now, he thought. He hoped that his buddy would be willing to help him out with a professional matter as well.

Finishing his drink, he reclined back for a quick nap before dinner. "Damn it!" he said under his breath. "Relax and enjoy yourself." He reminded himself that he was on his way to see his first Grand Prix of Monaco. A smile came to his face at that thought, and as soon as the plane was airborne he was fast asleep.

Not long after drifting off he began to lose the pleasant feelings and start having the same bad dream that had been haunting him for months. Like always, the dream started with him driving a rental car through the familiar gates of the Daytona International Speedway.

He had been to the famed track several times in his life. The first time as a fan in his late teens, and then as a professional road racer driving in the 24 hour sportscar race. However, this trip was different from his earlier visits. This time he would be testing a stock car on the oval track and the Daytona Speedway, at least in the fog of sleep, has a completely different feel to him.

The Impala SS race car that he is driving, on the two and one half mile oval, seems to be traveling at near supersonic speed. It soon becomes uncontrollable and slams hard into the turn three wall. The contrast between hurtling down the track and suddenly coming to a dead stop is both traumatic and terrifying to him.

It takes the rescue crew, what feels like an hour to reach him. The dream slows down even more as a rescuer attempts to cut him out of the car with the Jaws of Life. Trying to help them extract him, he attempts to get out of the driver's seat but finds that if he tries to move his reward is intense pain.

After finally being freed from the wreckage of his once pristine race car, he is transported to the Daytona infield hospital and told by a physician that his leg is badly broken and that the pain he feels in his chest is from a bruised sternum. The doctor's face is soon replaced by that of a pastor from Motorsport Ministries. The man keeps asking him if he wants to pray with him. His tone is serious and seems that his life might depend on it. Standing with the pastor is the team owner who says to him repeatedly, in a strong southern accent, "maybe these big super speedways just aren't your cup of tea, son."

He then awoke in a sweat. Just as he had every time he'd relived this surreal version of his real life experience.

Feeling anxious and a bit embarrassed, Parkes realizes where he is and quickly looks around to see if anyone seated near him on the plane has noticed his fitful sleep.

Checking his watch to see what time it was he realized that they were already almost halfway to Paris. He guessed that he had missed dinner, but took comfort in the knowledge that there was still plenty of time to get some good rest. After downing the emergency Xanax that he kept in his wallet with the leftover club soda on the tray table, Parkes turned his pillow over and soon was back to sleep.

His next dream was much better than his last. It was a pleasant fantasy located in the land of the rich and famous. He was enjoying it immensely when it all came to an abrupt halt.

The flight attendant woke him just as he was having a nice conversation with Monaco's Prince Albert while at a party that his friend Scott Battle was hosting the night prior to the Grand Prix.

Still groggy, he was slightly disappointed that the sleep induced delusion was not in fact reality. He followed her instruction to place his seat back into the upright position for landing and made sure his seat belt was pulled tight.

"Ladies and gentlemen, welcome to Charles de Gaulle airport", said the French accented female voice on the aircraft loudspeaker.

As the plane taxied to the gate, Parkes realized that he not only had missed dinner but also had managed to sleep through most of the Trans Atlantic crossing. He was actually feeling better now, than when he had started the journey, which was not at all normal for him. Often he became bored while flying long distances, so the fact that he was already in Paris and in such fine form was uplifting and caused him to feel a bit more optimism about his adventure.

After finding the gate for his next flight he saw that it was just a brief flight to Nice, and then a short helicopter ride to Monte Carlo, Monaco. Happily it would seem like no time at all compared to the long trip from America.

The next leg of his journey found him making up for having missed dinner. He not only ate his own meal, but shamelessly also ate that of his female seatmate when she had decided not to eat hers. The only negative on the flight had been the sudden realization that he'd forgotten the copy of AutoWeek magazine he had brought in the seat back of the plane he had been on from Indianapolis to Cincinnati. It wouldn't have been a big deal but for the fact it contained a great two page story on a new racing series that he was hoping to race in. He had wanted to share it with his friend, Scott. Because he wasn't sure if he could get another copy of the American magazine in Europe, he resolved to down load the article from their website once he was settled into his hotel room in Monaco.

Upon arrival at Nice, he hurriedly disembarked from the commuter jet and rushed toward the area where the commuter helicopters were located. Having never been on a helicopter, Parkes couldn't wait to get to the pad for the final portion of his journey. It felt strange as he found himself ducking to avoid the rotors as he boarded the aircraft.

As he looked out of the helicopter window, he soon began to see the familiar layout of the street race circuit where the annual Monaco Grand Prix was held. Advertising signs, flags and other decorations were already being displayed, and it looked to him as though the Formula 1 cars were on the track and at speed.

There was a man who looked to be in his sixties wearing a black suit who held a placard that welcomed him as he left the helipad. The man grabbed his bags and told him that he had been sent to drive him to Scott Battle's home.

"I had thought that my friend had made a reservation at the Fairmont" he told the limo driver. Before he shut the door the driver said that he had instructions deliver him to Scott Battle's home. "He insisted that you stay with him instead of at the hotel, Mr. Parkes."

After placing the luggage in the trunk the driver slid behind the wheel of the big Mercedes and turned back to look at his passenger. "Mr. Battle provided you with a card for the door" said the driver as he reached his hand back over the seat and handed him the piece of white plastic.

"That's all fine with me" Parkes replied with a smile as he took the key card and placed it in his jacket pocket. His host had just saved him a whole bag of money by deciding to let him stay at his place for the weekend instead of the four star hotel that he thought Scott had reserved a room for him at.

As the limo approached the condos where Scott Battle lived, he began to notice the Rolls Royce, Lamborghini and Ferrari automobiles that were as numerous here as Yellow Cabs in New York City. There clearly was no recession in the Principality. In a word, Monaco was just so... perfect.

Well, perfect if you were wealthy, or at least had a friend who was, thought Parkes as he entered Battle's two-bedroom condo. "So this is what $2.5 mil will buy you in the newer part of Monte Carlo" he said out loud as he took a quick look around his buddy's well appointed home.

"That was three years ago, I like to think it is worth more now, especially with all the improvements we've made" said a feminine voice from another room.

He turned toward the master bedroom and saw a slender woman with caramel skin emerge. "Hello, I am Michele, Scott's partner."

"Hi, I am Brandon, and …I'm just Scott's friend, but I am very pleased to meet you." Michele did not reply. She simply spun around on her heel and made her way back to the bedroom from which she had only just appeared.

"Scott will be home soon, so just make yourself comfortable; or if you prefer, you can go down to the track to watch practice. Your credentials to get into the garage area are there on the kitchen table," she said curtly as she shut the bedroom door.

"Sir, where should I place your luggage?" asked the limo driver. "Just leave it there by the door, and thanks for everything" he said as he handed him a folded twenty dollar bill.

The limo driver smiled. "Your fare, as well as a tip has already been taken care of sir."

He thought for a second about taking the money back, but Parkes quickly decided that he didn't want to look like a rube.

"Uh, then just keep that for bringing up my bags."

The man smiled again, nodded and then closed the door behind him.

As he thought about what he should do for the next couple of hours, he was once more beginning to get that feeling of being out place. He wasn't too jet lagged and quickly decided that what he needed was to go and pay a visit to the race track, the one spot where he felt the most comfortable of all.

He walked the short distance from his friend's place to the temporary street circuit where the race was held. As he approached the pit garage area the practice session for the Grand Prix had just ended and the drivers had returned their speedy mounts to their respective stalls on pit lane.

Standing just outside the Jamison Racing garage he heard a familiar voice. Given how loud and caustic it was there was no doubt in Parkes mind that his friend Scott Battle was not very happy with the current performance of the Jamison JR-1B Formula One racing car that he had just occupied a short time earlier.

"Anyone want to know why we did so poorly today?" Without pausing to get a response to his question he continued with his vocal outburst. "The damned car is pushing badly at every single corner!" he exclaimed. "I could hardly get it to turn in... and didn't I tell you that we needed to dial in more front wing or that we'd suffer from under steer?" he asked of no one in particular.

Battle made his way to the back of the Jamison Racing garage area, grabbed his drink bottle and took a quick swallow before throwing the clear plastic container in the direction of his team manager, Ian Walters. "I hope you are happy with fifteenth quickest because that is all that box of crap will do right now, barked Battle.

"Look Scott, I know the car is not spot on yet, but unloading your frustration on the crew isn't helping things" Walters admonished in a stern voice.

Team managers are ultimately responsible for the preparation of the car, so Ian was not any happier than Scott that things hadn't gone well.

"You were absolutely right, Scott. We all know how tight this circuit is, but we obviously underestimated the amount of aerodynamic down force that we would need. That said, it's more that aero changes that are called for. We also need a different suspension set- up than what we have on the car now to give us better mechanical grip." said Walters in a more mellow tone.

"Well, it obviously better be fixed by the time we go out to qualify tomorrow." Battle said with a frown.

He then snatched his dark gray carbon fiber brief case off the workbench and placed his blue Jamison Racing cap on his head.

"I'm going home now to try and forget about today. Be sure to tell the lads on the crew to have a good evening", he said with a sarcastic tone.

Just as he was walking out of his garage, Parkes greeted his friend with a warm smile and an outstretched hand. Like a chameleon, it seemed that Battle transformed from a Formula One prima donna back to his normal friendly persona, by which he was better known for among friends and fans alike.

The two men shook hands and then embraced like a pair of old war buddies, which in some ways they were indeed.

Both had started at roughly the same place in motorsports. They had been young men looking to become professional racing drivers when they first met. However, one had become a star, and the first African American to ever win in Formula One. The other was a journey man driver, and about as white as any corn fed Iowa boy could be. Despite differences in status and color, after seeing one another they acted no differently than they had years before as aspiring racers.

"Wow, you look like you own one of those big yachts out in the harbor wearing that outfit, said Battle with a smile. "Hey, I didn't want to embarrass you, Mr. F1 star." replied Parkes.

"The only reason I would be embarrassed today is because I didn't look like much of a star out there in practice, we are a long way off on the set-up", said Battle as he looked down at the ground; "I just can't get the damned thing to turn in properly and with the super tight corners on a street course like this it makes it kind of tough to be very quick."

"Cheer up, you will get it sorted, you always do. Heck, you used to get your car and mine right before every race we did together", he said in a reassuring voice.

"True enough," admitted Battle. "Anyway, let's go get you settled in and find both of us a good meal". "There must be least a couple places in this town that serve decent food," he said with a laugh.

Some of the Jamison mechanics, mostly young men in their twenties, were clearly giving Battle dirty looks as he and Parkes headed for the exit from the garage area.

"Are you doing alright here, Scott?" These guys don't exactly give me any warm, fuzzy feelings, you know what I mean?"

Battle, whose back was to his team's garage, turned his head to see that the crew had begun working on his car.

"Our other driver is an OK young guy, but the team manager and a few of his crewmen are typical British asses. But I guess they call it Grand Prix racing for a reason"

Parkes laughed at the fact that his friend had not left the x in the word Prix silent. He nodded. "I have experienced a few of the type myself".

"Why are you agreeing with me, BP? You are almost as British and just as white bread as these guys are!"

"Yeah, but I like to think I'm not quite as big of a jerk as those guys seem to be" replied Parkes with a smile.

The F-1 ace put his arm around his friend and patted him on the back.

"Man, it is good to see you, BP. Come on, let's hurry back to my humble abode and get ourselves cleaned up so that I can take you out on the town."

After getting back to Battle's home Parkes had showered and changed into his usual race weekend uniform of black slacks and a white oxford cloth shirt. Sitting down in the luxurious living room he began to roll up the sleeves of his long sleeved button down and then took in a deep breath as he tried to make himself relax. He checked the time and wondered what was taking Scott and his girlfriend so long to get ready for their night out.

He noticed that on the coffee table was the newest issue of the British publication, Autosport. It was of course the Monaco GP preview issue and inside was an article entitled "Battle in a Battle for his seat at Jamison?" When he saw the headline he understood why the guy was so worked up. Parkes knew how it felt to lose your ride, it had just happened to him a few months before. But at least his situation hadn't been speculated about in the press prior to it even taking place.

Just as he began to read the article, his host walked out and asked if he was ready to go. "Sure, let's do it" he said as he placed the magazine back on the table. "Is Michele joining us?"

"No, it's just you and me this evening. Michele is already sound asleep"

As Brandon stood up Battle asked him the question that he had hoped he wouldn't "Nice article about me in there, did you see it?"

"Uh, yeah, I guess. But hey, at least they are writing about you" replied Parkes, who was feeling like he had just been caught doing something wrong by even looking at the magazine.

Race to Damascus

"Don't worry, everything is fine, BP."

Nodding in the affirmative, he just smiled and followed his friend out the door. He sensed that things were a bit tenser than his host would care to admit to, both at home and at work.

It was obvious to Parkes that being a famous racecar driver was something that Scott Battle would never grow tired of. No matter how trying the day had been, he still had time for the fans. As he walked down the streets of Monaco this night, he was mobbed by people asking for his autograph and those wanting to shake his hand and wish him good luck. It took nearly an hour to walk the three blocks to the restaurant.

Not all Formula One stars were so friendly. That is part of why Scott had become so very popular. There were some who might be more successful on the track, but the current fan-favorite was the good-looking man from Georgia.

It was not just a matter of him being a nice guy, or even enjoying the attention that he received. This was more about something that tended to be very American. It was all about money. Seven figure money that made it easy for him to be interested in others and present a good image.

While his five million dollar retainer to drive was about average for a driver with his record, he now had nearly an additional six million coming in through endorsement deals with personal sponsors.

Some compared him to Tiger Woods, but in a Nomex racing suit. One big difference between them was that a golfer such as Tiger could have a dry spell or personal issues and then stage a career comeback starting at the very next tournament he entered. In Formula 1, a slump for a driver could mean getting sacked and finding one's self not getting another opportunity. Everything you had worked, risked and sacrificed for could disappear overnight.

Losing your life in a race car was of far less concern to most pro racers than losing your career, at least to those still in their prime. It was that important when you had reached the top rungs of the sport and Parkes felt that Scott Battle was still not exempt from that kind of thinking.

At 31, with four seasons on the Grand Prix circuit and 3 wins to his credit, Battle was at a point of moving up in F-1 or maybe moving on. So far this season had not been going at all well and the rumors about his demise were making the rounds. Just as it hurts an actor who reads a bad movie review, the negative stories had to be taking an emotional toll, thought Parkes.

However he clearly was not ready to give it all up, nor would Scott let anyone call time on his career but himself. Besides, unlike the other well paid racing drivers who called the tax haven of Monaco home, as a US citizen he was still required to pay far too close to half of his income out in taxes. The fact that he had forgotten this small detail over the past three years meant that he now owed Uncle Sam even more money with penalties and interest tacked on and the Feds wanted to be paid. In fact, Parkes had recently been told that the government was becoming very difficult as of late and that it was only the efforts of the Battle family attorney that had kept Scott from being arrested while visiting his family in Atlanta at Christmas.

There was no choice for his friend but to fight the good fight and try to keep his place in the Grand Prix circus, even if it was only to enable him to continue to be paid millions of dollars that would in turn allow him to make a viable settlement offer to his new friends at the Internal Revenue Service.

The walk down the street to the Italian restaurant seemed to uplift both men. Excitement about the upcoming race was already in the air. One young fan even asked Parkes for his autograph, but then wanted to know what team in Formula 1 he was driving for.

"This is my old friend from America, and yes, he is a racing driver as well" said Battle with a smile and a pat on Parkes back. "He's one of our top sportscar stars, so hang on to that autograph son, as it will be worth some money to you one of these days" he exclaimed.

Looking out for friends feelings was seemingly not something that the jet set, cutthroat world of international motorsport had yet exorcised from Battle's soul. Scott had never once treated him as anything less than an equal.

When the two men entered the eatery the easily recognized F1 driver waved to all he recognized and even to a few that he did not know. Making everyone feel important was just part of his charm.

Once seated at his favorite table he asked the waiter, in Italian, for his usual carb-up meal; but this time for two.

"Michele is doing the low carb thing so she would never order what we are having, but I think we will both need energy to burn- so I got you the pasta dish too. Oh, and I also ordered the drink that makes for better race drivers, just for old times' sake."

"Are we having scotch by chance?

"Dewars on the rocks" replied Battle with a grin.

With both of them in such good spirits, it crossed Brandon's mind to mention the opportunity he had for a drive and how Battle might be able to help him out in achieving that goal. Just as quickly he decided not to ruin the fun by discussing the business side of motorsports. Scott's situation was almost as delicate as his own right now. He would speak to him about his other reason for coming to Europe soon enough. Tonight was about reminiscing, talking about race driving and savoring some long overdue time with his very best friend.

Saturday afternoon - Qualifying for the Monaco GP

The dark blue Jamison Formula One car rolled slowly down pit lane and then stopped at its appointed spot in front of the garage. The open wheel car looked pretty much like all the other twenty-three cars on the track that day, but this car could be distinguished by the unique black and white checkered flag helmet design of its driver, Scott Battle.

As he stepped out of the seat, he thanked the crew for the improvements they had made and told them that despite only an eighth place spot in qualifying, he should be able to make the car as fast as any of the others, in the race itself.

Ian Walters nodded at Battle and then instructed his crew to go over the car inch by inch before they left that night. "We really need to have a good race this weekend, so do the team a favor and make sure that if we don't win that it isn't because of something we did wrong in prepping her, OK? Right, let's get it done."

Rather than add anything to what had been said, Battle turned to exit the garage and just then remembered that he needed to touch base with his house guest.

The evening before the big race would be filled with sponsor engagements for Scott and Michele. The least he could do was make sure that his house guest was going to be all right while they made the rounds.

Picking up his cell phone, he tried calling Brandon's number but there was no answer. He left him a brief message saying he would see him later tonight or first thing in the morning, prior to the race.

His friend never even heard the phone ringing. Parkes was entranced at that moment by the sound of 27 Porsches bouncing off the canyon-like buildings that surrounded the Monaco street circuit.

With the Porsche Cup race just beginning he found himself a spot to watch the goings on. Looking like a bunch of brightly colored Easter eggs the Porsche 911 GT-3's were nose to tail as they swept by his perch to complete the first lap. Indeed the Porsches he was watching were very much like the cars he had plied his trade in the Grand Am sports car series back in the states. In fact, he really wished that he could be out there with them now.

At 35 years old, Parkes had been racing cars for thirteen years. He had made his living in racing for the last 10 and hoped his trip to Europe would bring about an 11th. Growing up in an upper middle class family in Iowa had afforded him the opportunity to go to the University of Iowa and to do so with a degree of comfort. A two-year-old Mazda Miata was his high school graduation present along with a Visa card that he was told to use wisely.

His father, the owner of a small Des Moines bank, wanted him to pursue a business degree and come back to be groomed to take over the family enterprise. He went along with the idea, but wasn't really sure at that point what he wanted to do with his life. But for the red Miata roadster his parents gave him as a carrot, he might well have joined the military and then gone to school where he wanted and gotten a degree in what he was interested in.

Cars and motor racing were his first loves; it had been that way since an early age. He read all the books and magazines, especially the ones that pertained to European style road racing. The LeMans 24 Hours sports car race and Formula One were of more interest to him than the dirt track sprint cars, and late model stock cars that were popular in his native state of Iowa.

However, actually getting the chance to live his dream was about as likely as walking on water, so he went along with his father's wishes, and hoped that he might have a chance to race for fun someday. Given that half the drivers at LeMans were wealthy "gentlemen racers" who wrote out a large check for their seat, that was a goal that wasn't quite so impossible.

In the spring of his senior year at U of I he heard about a time trial, or autocross as they were called, that was being held in a large parking lot on campus. This was a chance to drive his own car at speed in a competition against others and he jumped at the opportunity.

While that first experience did not result in victory, he now had been bitten by the racing bug like never before. Attending a top-flight race driving school for a full one-week course at Laguna Seca in Monterey, California became his parents' reward for finishing college.

By the end of that week, there was only one guy in the class of ten that was faster than he was.

The young man who had so impressed the instructors had driven racing karts since he was 12 and now at 18 he was ready to step up to the single seat open wheel formula cars like those used at the school. The kid's name was Scott Battle.

The two became friends almost from the first day they met. Meeting girls and consuming Dewars by night and driving single seat racecars by day, Goose and Maverick from the movie Top Gun had nothing on these two during that magical week together. Both stayed in touch after racing school. Scott was soon competing with his Formula Ford at tracks like Sebring and the nearby Road Atlanta circuit.

Unlike Scott, whose father was one of the top cardio vascular surgeons in the world and a real car and racing enthusiast, Parkes father was not too interested in financing his son's dreams of going auto racing.

"I haven't worked this hard or sent you to college so that you can become a race driver," his father had told him in an angry tone. "We paid for that racing school with the hope that you would get this crazy dream out of your head."

Neither his mom nor his dad had any understanding of why he wanted to pursue a career as a professional racing driver. They simply didn't get it. That was all he wanted in life right now and he had to find a way to get his shot at it. He thought he might have enough raw talent to make it and was sure that all he needed was the money to cultivate it, and demonstrate the natural ability that he thought that he had been born with.

As fortune would have it, his Uncle Ron was something of a racing fan and had even raced stock cars a little in his younger days. While not in a position to fund his nephew's goals personally, he would be able to help him greatly.

Ron Parkes had gone to work in heavy construction right out of high school and had risen to become one of the top highway, airport and dam builders in the country; if not the world. He was like some John Wayne movie character in Brandon's eyes and the kind of guy you would want on your side in a bar fight in some exotic port of call. Having managed many large construction projects he was now in demand as a well paid independent consultant and in turn had a bit of clout when it came to what brand of construction equipment and other materials would be ordered for a major job.

Hence, Sumatu Heavy Industries signed a deal to sponsor B. P. Motorsports for the next two years. There was actually enough money to run the open wheel racer for two and half seasons, so Brandon was able to get started right away and do enough late summer races to qualify him for his national license.

Sumatu had already received an order for several million dollars worth of bulldozers, cranes and rollers to be shipped to a job site in Singapore that Ron Parkes was working on. The return on their sponsorship investment in the younger Parkes had already paid off handsomely for the company.

As important as that first deal was to getting started in racing, Parkes had also learned something many aspiring racers never did understand. Having leverage was the key to finding racing sponsorship. It was something that he never forgot and continued to use until this day. Some might think it unethical, but it was in reality how most of these "sponsorship" deals got done.

By the time the program with Sumatu had run its course he had established himself in the road racing arena and even managed to defeat his friend Scott in a Formula Ford race at Elkhart Lake, Wisconsin. Soon he was able to land a job as an instructor at a racing school based in Indianapolis, as well as picking up paid drives in long distance sportscar races like the Daytona 24 Hours and the Six Hours at Watkins Glen. Even if he never went on to be an Indy 500 winner or Formula One driver, he could in fact, call himself a paid professional racecar driver and much of the credit went to his uncle.

There was hardly a day that passed that he did not think of his Uncle Ron. He knew that he probably would still be working in his father's bank in Des Moines if it were not for the efforts that he had made on his behalf.

His racing career had taken a recent setback after the NASCAR drive that he thought he had lined up fell apart. Although NASCAR had never really been his goal, the road course events and superspeedway races were appealing to him as a driver. In addition, the money that even the average NASCAR racer could make was far greater than what the majority of sports car road racing drivers could ever hope for.

While losing the opportunity of competing full time in major league stock car races had left him feeling deeply depressed, the sights, sounds and smells of the racing here in Monaco seemed to renew his spirits and restore in him a sense of optimism about the future.

After a quiet Saturday night spent alone, he awoke on Sunday morning to another sunny day in paradise. Looking from the balcony toward the harbor Brandon could see the fleets of catering vans lining up to deliver all the fine food and drink that the yacht owners and their guests would enjoy on this amazing day. Each van was complete with its own fully uniformed wait staff to set up and serve the sumptuous menus that had planned for that day.

Making his way into the kitchen, he had sat down and poured himself another cup of coffee, when Scott walked in and joined him at the table. He had already done a light workout that morning in preparation for the race and was sucking on a drink bottle filled with the special concoction his trainer had created for him.

"Sleep well?" asked Battle.

"I did indeed, I got to bed early and feel great; the real question is how do you feel, Ace?"

"Ready to win, or at least manage to pick up a good finish and a few championship points" he said sternly before taking another swallow of the magic fluid.

"By the way, I have hospitality suite passes for both you and Michele. All you have to do is show up and you will find that your names will be on the list."

"Thanks" he said with a smile. Taking another sip of coffee, Parkes then asked if Scott felt ready. "You bet." he replied in a somewhat nervous manner.

Brandon leaned over and gave his friend a hug. He knew there was a fair amount pressure on his friend to do well today.

"Have a good run, I'll be rooting for you, pal".

After his friend left Parkes got cleaned up and escorted Michele to the Jamison Racing "hostility suite" as Scott sometimes called it. As he watched her easily mingle amongst the other guests he soon began to see what Battle saw in this woman.

The person he met two days ago was a complete contrast to the cordial, smiling young lady he was standing next to now. Maybe it was the champagne and orange juice she had just consumed, or perhaps it was the fact that she enjoyed the limelight just as much as Scott did.

Given that she was not only Scott Battle's girlfriend, but also an investment advisor to the wealthy and famous may have been the real reason for her sudden change in demeanor. This was a target rich environment for someone in her line of work. Whatever the case, Brandon was just glad that she seemed to be in a much better mood that she had previously displayed.

"Shall we go find a seat?" she asked him politely. "After you, Michele" he replied.

They quickly found a prime spot that was not yet taken. It was then that he began to take in the smells, sights and sounds of race day at the Grand Prix de Monaco. No matter how many times he attended a big racing event, or had participated in one, he was still enthralled with the bigger than life drama of major league motor sports. From the brightly colored pennants and posters that identified each Team; to the unmistakable smell of racing fuel permeating the air, this was truly a world-class event.

Billionaires, mere millionaires, movie stars and Grand Prix cars all made for an intoxicating mix. While even he knew that there might ultimately be more important things than the worldly trappings found in Monaco, Parkes had to admit to himself that being here was much more than just merely enjoyable. It was a happening.

He just hoped that his friend Scott would have as good a day in the cockpit as he was having right now as a spectator of the great event.

Monaco- Sunday afternoon

The transition from darkness to light was blinding as one exited the famous tunnel that was a part of the Monaco street circuit. Even on the warm up lap it had bothered Scott Battle and surely all the other drivers as well.

What made it all the worse was the sharp left hand turn that one encountered shortly after leaving the tunnel and heading straight down hill. It was far too easy to miss the first gear corner and go straight off the course into the run-off area, or bounce the car's tires over the curbing. If you misjudged his braking point by even a small degree it could mean a negative outcome. Every time that Battle made it through cleanly he was pleased and relieved at having done so.

After making a good start, Battle had simply tried to stay in place and not make any bold moves until later in the race. He hoped that by keeping his car out of the wall he could end up with a decent result, something that had eluded him so far this season.

Running in seventh place at the three quarter mark in the race, the Jamison Racing number twenty-one car had only moved up just one spot and that was due to attrition. The under steer condition that had plagued Battle in practice had returned as soon as his tires began to wear, and it made it hard to go as fast as he needed to, but he was on target to get in the points this time and with a front wing adjustment planned for his last pit stop he hoped that he could move up another position or two before the end of the race.

His teammate, Ricardo Sandoval, in the number 22 car was in second place according to what Ian had told him on the last radio update. While it put a bit more pressure on him to know that his younger teammate was in front of him, the news from Ian actually had a positive effect on his spirits. For the first time this season, the Jamison cars could both finish with championship points to their credit.

As he passed the start- finish line he heard the radio crackle and the voice of Ian telling him to pit at the end of this lap.

"OK, I will be there. Just make sure that we add a bit more downforce on the front wings....got that?"

"Right, I copy," Walters replied. Four tires and one turn of the front winglets. "

Heading up the long hill to the second turn, he noticed the red and white car of the race leader right in his mirrors. Eliseo Campari was coming up to lap him.

He called out once again to his team manager on his radio, "Ian… Campari is now driving right on my gearbox."

"Yes, do try to keep from going down a lap …and it sure wouldn't hurt my feelings, or those of your team mate in second place if you could help him to catch up to the leader in the process" exclaimed Ian in his crisp British accent.

Never one to balk another driver in a faster car when being lapped, Battle would try to hold the Italian driver off as long as could without appearing to block him. The Monaco street circuit offered few chances to pass so that wouldn't be too hard to do. That said, if the race leader got a good run on him coming out of the tunnel this lap he decided that he would have to let him through.

As he rounded the corner and onto the straight-away through the tunnel once again, Battle glanced in his right mirror and saw the Red Eagle Beer car of Campari, and one spot behind he had just caught a glimpse of a dark blue car. It had to be his teammate, Sandoval, who had managed to close right up on the man in first place and was now a real threat to win the biggest race on the F-1 calendar.

Now it was time for him to get out of the way and let both Campari and Sandoval by him cleanly he told himself.

Approaching the hard left corner that came after the tunnel straight, he stayed to the right so that Campari could out brake him and pass on the left. He would then allow his teammate to take him on the short straight that followed and the two could fight one another to the finish.

Battle braked early and Campari slid by him on his left hand side. Just as the Red Eagle car was about to make the tight left into the chicane, his brakes locked up and Campari was unable to turn in. He started to get sideways and that left Scott nowhere to go but into the left rear of the Italian's car.

The impact left both cars with immediate suspension damage and sliding across the chicane as though linked together with an invisible chain.

The worst part was yet to come.

Young Sandoval came screaming into this mess at the bottom of the hill and soon turned it into complete carnage. He t-boned Campari's car and carbon-fiber body parts lay everywhere. Only the relatively slow speed of the corner kept it from being even worse than it was.

The safety marshals quickly began to wave their yellow flags to warn other drivers of the incident. Since the track was blocked with wreckage the only choice was to have the remaining cars circumvent the accident by slowly driving around it.

As he stepped out of his racecar, Battle surveyed the damage to the left front of his racing car and then turned around to find that Campari was out of his own battered car and coming toward him in an obvious rage. With both fists raised in the air the little Italian looked like he was going to take revenge on him for what had been, at least in Scott's mind, something that had been Campari's own fault.

Just as Campari was about to grab him by the neck one of the larger track marshals stepped between the two men and broke things up before they got really ugly.

"It was your mistake and you're mad at ME?" screamed Battle. "I let you by and it was YOU who screwed the pooch- you stupid little jerk!

Seeing that the international TV cameras were focused on his tirade, Battle stood down and jumped into the back seat of the Mercedes course car for the long ride back to the pit area. To his surprise his young teammate was already sitting in back seat of the car. Sandoval was clearly not in a mood for words right now. His best finish in Formula One, which would have come at the year's most important event, had just fumbled right out of his hands.

"Sorry that you got involved with that deal, but I'm glad to see that you're doing OK", muttered Battle.

Sandoval didn't respond, he just stared out the car window as though no one else was there while he thought about what might have been.

The ride back to the Jamison pits was filled with anxiety. The two team mates hadn't uttered a further word to one another and you could cut the tension with a knife. The mood got even worse when Ian was spotted throwing his clipboard down on the ground as the course car rolled to a stop in front of him.

As they exited from the rear of the car, both men thought they were in for a verbal pounding from Ian Walters. The team manager's wrath was reserved completely for Battle.

"I asked you to hold Campari up a bit, not to end up crashing yourself AND your team mate out of the race!" exclaimed the irate Walters.

"Wait a minute, Ian? What did you just say? I mean were you actually watching the same motor race that I was just driving in?" replied the equally upset American.

Smashing his helmet against the garage wall the American stormed out vowing to never return to race again for Walters until he had- "bought himself a clue".

Race to Damascus

The media was acting like sharks in a feeding frenzy as Scott pushed his way through the throng of reporters in pit lane. "Does this cock-up at the chicane mean that you're finally done with Team Jamison?" asked one of the British scribes. Rather than punch him in his beak like nose it was better just to keep walking, thought Battle.

"Where in the hell are Michele and Brandon when you need them?" he asked himself as he searched his briefcase for the cell phone. He needed to get out of this place and to do it right now. Everyone was blaming him for the shunt and he thought it best to get out of there and back to his home as soon as he could.

Having finally contacted him with a text message it only took a few minutes more for Parkes to show up to rescue him.

"Thanks for getting here so soon. Man, I am really glad to see you!" said an exhausted Scott Battle as he got into Michele's silver Mini Cooper S. "Just get me home as quick as you can, Brandon. By the way, where's Michele?"

"She stayed behind for the party. I guess she figured you would want to cool down and be alone for a while".

"Sure" replied Battle with a slightly disgusted look on his face.

"What a day. Did you see what happened out there?"

Simply nodding in response to the question, Parkes was beginning to think that it was indeed best that Michele had stayed at the sponsor party, as Scott clearly did need a bit of time to decompress. He understood Battle's frustration though, to have someone wreck you was bad enough; to get blamed for causing it was doubly upsetting.

As they drove the narrow streets towards Scott's condo Parkes was wondering if this time alone in the car might be the right moment to talk to his friend about helping him out by teaming up to race a pair of AMG Mercedes in the International SuperSedan Challenge. Besides, with all that had happened in today's race it just might be a welcome diversion for him on his off weekends, assuming that his contract with Jamison would allow it.

His friend continued going on about what a moron he thought Ian Walters was and what an idiot the team manger must be to think the accident was his fault. Brandon just nodded his head, agreed with him, and drove on.

As the angry tirade continued, Parkes decided that this probably wasn't quite the time to ask for that favor after all. Perhaps letting him rant a little more was in order. He knew that he had to ask him about it fairly soon as he was headed back to Paris in the morning and needed to find out Scott's level of interest in his idea before his planned side trip to meet team owners attending the conference for this new international racing series. Right now was clearly not the most opportune time to discuss such things.

Chicago, Illinois - Midway Airport- Sunday evening

At 67 years young, and with a financial worth of several billion dollars, life had exceeded even Dan Mandel's expectations. Success in business had allowed for the better things in life and he now felt that he could begin to relax a little and start to enjoy those things fully.

As he boarded his Gulfstream jet he decided to poke his head into the aircraft cockpit and say hello to his long time pilot, Jack Rhodes. He then asked him how their new recently hired co-pilot was working out.

"So far, so good" he replied. "I think I'm even going to let him handle the take off tonight" said Rhodes while looking over at the young man in the right seat.

"Good evening, Mr. Mandel, all set for our trip to the old country?" asked co-pilot Pete Flynn. "Yes I am, Pete," replied Mandel. "How long until we are wheels up?"

"We should be in the air in about ten minutes, sir"

"Good, I just hope my brother gets here soon. He is always late these days." he said as he checked the time on his watch.

"By the way, how is that baby girl of yours, Pete? She's what, three weeks old now?"

"She is doing well. In fact, she just turned a month old yesterday. Thanks for asking."

As he turned to find his seat, Mandel felt good as he thought about how fortunate he was to be in the position at this time in his life. Pete Flynn had been hired just a week before his baby daughter had been born. To know that he could provide a good job to some young guy like Pete was a real joy to him. He had begun to view his people as an extended part of his own family and had a genuine concern for their well-being.

It had not always been like that though. There had been a time when he was thought of as being completely ruthless in his business dealings, and that he didn't give a damn about anything other than making money.

That was all changing; if fact it had been gradually changing for some time now.

Even he had started to realize that you couldn't take it with you and that you might actually be accountable for your actions at the end of the day.

His jet was the one thing he wished he could take with him when he died. He really loved it and it was by far his favorite possession. Looking at the cabin with its buttery soft leather seating and a wood paneled galley he was happy that he had gone ahead and indulged himself when he had spent the extra money to make it so comfortable.

As he sat down, his tardy brother Harry stepped into the aircraft and apologized for being late. "Thanks for not leaving without me" he added.

"Sure, get seated. The boys say we are about ready to go." said the younger Mandel sternly.

For some reason it was still hard for Dan Mandel to express the same kind of warmth or forgiveness to his brother that he now extended freely to others.

As the Chief Operating Officer of Mandel's Discount SuperStores Harry had helped build a good sized privately held empire from the five & dime stores that their father had started years ago in Chicago.

However, most people credited Dan Mandel with the success of the now 305 store chain. That die had probably been cast when their father, Eli had made Dan the president and CEO of the family firm some 40 years ago.

Eli Mandel had survived the Nazis in Holland and then the Arab conflict in the early days during the establishment of the State of Israel. He then decided to come to America with his wife and two young sons, armed with the dream of owning his own small business. His first small thrift store in Skokie, Illinois soon led to a second location. It was about this same time that his eldest son Harry was accepted to Stanford. Eli was living his version of the American dream.

Two years later when his younger son Daniel was graduating from high school and making plans to attend nearby Northwestern

University; those plans were to change suddenly when Eli suffered a massive stroke and was left virtually bedridden.

With no one to run the stores, then eighteen-year-old Dan had no choice but to step into the gap and take charge.

By the time that Harry came home with his finance degree from Stanford, Dan had not only run the stores well, he had actually expanded Mandel Stores to three locations and was starting to look at opening a fourth.

It was fair that his younger brother was made the head of their family business since it was Dan who had sacrificed his formal education to save them all from ruin. At least that is what Harry told everyone at the time.

It was the elder of the Mandel brothers that had come up with the idea of much bigger stores. This was the wave of the future in retail; large warehouses with big ticket items like TVs and lawnmowers, as well as the smaller merchandise they already carried, was the way forward in his mind.

In 1966, they opened the first of what were now known as Mandel's SuperStores. It was Harry who put together the financing that had allowed them to expedite the growth of the chain.

While it was Dan's task to expand profit margins by squeezing vendors for every penny and insisting on paying them on net 120-day terms, strategic thinking was Harry's area of expertise and his efforts had been a very large factor in the success of the enterprise.

The stores were fixtures in suburbs and medium sized towns all over the Midwestern United States by the late eighties. That the brothers had accomplished it all without outside investors made their story even better.

They had both prospered and their father died a happy man, knowing his sons had been given a solid foothold in life and that they were each making the most of it.

Owning a large retail chain had not only provided substantial wealth, but his suppliers had provided Dan with the ability to realize his goals as a team owner of a professional motorsports team.

It all started years ago when he had first driven down from Chicago with a friend to see the Indy 500. He was hooked from the moment he arrived. The color and drama were better than anything he had ever experienced.

The following year he asked a soft drink company to co-sponsor a team in the race in exchange for preferred shelf space in all of the Mandel's then fifty-one stores.

The sight of the jet black "Mandel Special" rolling out for qualifying at the Greatest Spectacle in Racing was one of the proudest moments of his life. Better yet, with stores in Indiana and Illinois, and a vendor paying for it all, the whole thing even made business sense.

That first sponsorship had led him to form his own Indycar team. Now that first involvement in racing had led him to what might become an even bigger motorsports venture on the native continent of his late father, Eli.

Mandel smiled to himself when he thought how far he had come in his life. Now a new chapter was beginning and he was starting to become excited about the prospects that this newest venture might hold for him.

The trip across the Atlantic was uneventful and ended when they touched down at a small private airstrip outside of Paris. The Mandel brothers, as usual, had not spoken more than a few words to each other for the duration of the flight.

Looking out the window of the airplane as they taxied in, Dan Mandel saw the man that he assumed he was here to see.

With a slim, but muscular build, and handsome features Silvio Marino looked more like the perfect stereotype of an international racing driver than he did a motorsports promoter, he thought.

Standing next to his British racing green Jaguar XF, Marino put on his sunglasses and looked out across the tarmac to watch the white and powder blue Gulfstream, with the distinctive Star of David on the tail, roll up to its assigned parking spot.

When the jet came to a halt, Marino walked toward the plane and Mandel eagerly stepped out to meet him.

"You must be Mr. Marino"

"Yes I am. Good to finally meet you." responded the Italian.

The two shook hands and began walking towards the Jaguar sedan. Mandel looked behind for a moment to see his brother and their co-pilot conversing by the wing of the aircraft.

He waved to them and they both men waved back. Harry would meet him at the hotel after renting a car to use during their stay. Right now he wanted to have a one-on-one with the head of the racing series he was about to become involved with.

"Let's go to my office, it's a bit more quiet than here at the airport" said Marino with a smile.

"OK, provided that they have some coffee there." he replied.

"We have that. Is there anything else you might desire?"

"Coffee would be wonderful, but I don't need anything else" said the American as he got into the car. "I really am looking forward to hearing more about the plans for your Euro stock car series, Silvio"

"I am just pleased you could make it here in time for us to talk prior to the conference." said Marino as he buckled his seat belt. "By the way, the official name we came up with is International SuperSedan Challenge"

Mandel didn't respond, he just concentrated on adjusting his watch to Paris time and asked if Marino would be offended if he took a quick nap on the drive over since it was now Monday morning and he hadn't gotten any sleep on the airplane. Without waiting for his host to approve, he adjusted his seat back and closed his eyes for their trip to the suburbs of Paris.

ISC headquarters – Monday afternoon

Sipping on a bottle of Coca Cola, an impatient Brandon Parkes sat in the lobby of the Organization Silvio Marino while waiting to see if his credentials for the International SuperSedan Challenge luncheon and press conference were ready. He knew that the meeting wasn't until tomorrow, but this was France and he didn't want any screw-ups in the morning to prevent him from attending.

He was feeling like a coward right now for not being able to ask his friend for help while he was there with him in Monaco. With all that had happened, he just couldn't bring himself to bother Scott, who clearly had his own issues to deal with right now.

Instead of talking to Battle that morning, he had simply gotten up early and taken the morning shuttle back to Paris. Before he left, he did take the time to leave a note that explained his early departure, as well as informing him of the opportunity that he was pursuing and asking if he might be interested in joining him on the Scimitar Mercedes team in the ISC.

Just as he began to rationalize in his mind that, given the situation, he had done the right thing, a very attractive, dark haired middle-aged woman approached him from behind.

"Mr. Parkes; I am Christine and I work for the series as Director of Public Relations."

He stood up and turned to shake hands with her. "Hello, Christine."

"I am afraid we have no record of you being registered for the conference, but don't worry, we can sign you up now. The cost for registration is one thousand Euros and we will accept a check or a major credit card," said the woman.

"Can we first find out if I am already signed up under one of the teams?" he asked.

"I am sorry, but I already have done that. There is no record whatsoever."

Just then, two men walked through the front door. Both men looked very familiar to Parkes.

Recognizing Marino from TV interviews and photos in racing magazines, he excused himself and walked over to meet him.

"Hi, I am Brandon Parkes." he announced as he extended his hand.

"Silvio Marino" said the Italian in a blunt tone.

"Let me introduce you to Mr. Daniel Mandel."

"I thought that was you, Mr. Mandel, it's nice to see a fellow American over here."

"So are you planning on competing in this new racing series that Marino is cooking up?" asked Mandel

"I am hoping to; right now I just would be happy just to get my credentials sorted out so that I can get into the meeting tomorrow."

He went on to explain that the team that he was to be meeting with had not put his name on the guest list and that he might have to register as a team owner in order to be able to attend. Upon hearing this Mr. Mandel offered to have him register as his guest so that he could use one of his team passes to the conference.

Mandel turned to Marino. "Is it OK to just add him to our list of attendees?"

"Yes, Christine will take care of it for you. Now if you will excuse us, I need to spend some time with Mr. Mandel. See you tomorrow then?"

"Indeed, you will." Before leaving Parkes thanked Mandel for assisting him and told him how much he looked forward to joining him at the conference.

As he walked toward the front desk to add his name the guest list, he became curious as to why Mandel was even there. The fact that an American Indycar team owner was interested in the ISC was something that Parkes had not expected. He always kept up with the latest motorsports rumors and he had not heard anything regarding any American team in the series.

Though he felt a bit slighted by the somewhat less than warm welcome from Marino and his not being included on the Scimitar team's list, his mood quickly improved as he thought about the prospect of Mr. Mandel fielding a team in the series. The fact that the owner of that potential entry had been kind enough to provide him access to what might be the most important meeting concerning

European road racing in many years made him feel much better about his having made the effort to be here.

Upon walking out the front door of Marino's offices he suddenly found himself thinking of the Mandel Stores advertising jingle that almost anyone in the Midwestern United States knew so well. "Watch your savings start to swell; whenever you buy from Dan Mandel" he sang softly to himself.

He laughed at his own foolishness, but singing that familiar tune had reminded him of Indianapolis. No matter what the outcome of his trip to France, at the very least he knew that he could return to the comfort and security that he felt when he was back home again in his adopted Indiana hometown.

Chapter Two

Paris, France-Tuesday morning

It was a sunny morning that greeted Parkes as he arose to make ready for the ISC conference. The hotel room mini-bar held an assortment of bottles of miniature juices and water; so he quickly selected two of the bottles of orange juice to wash down his handful of daily vitamins.

He had hardly gotten any rest the night before. Like a child on Christmas Eve he had tossed and turned in his bed and when he did finally fall asleep it was for only about three hours or so. Yet at seven fifteen in the morning he felt fully rested and ready for what he hoped would turn out to be an exciting day.

Turning on his cell phone he listened for any messages. There was just one, and it was from Scott.

"No doubt calling about the note I left for him," he said to himself.

Not wanting any bad news to ruin his day, he decided to listen to Scott's response to his proposal later on. He needed his attitude to be positive right now because he was about to enter an arena that was full of opportunity.

He smiled to himself as he thought about what awaited him that day. It could be a great day or a dismal one. But like race driving, part of the excitement was overcoming the odds.

After a long hot shower, he turned the water faucet to give him a blast of cold water, just to get fully awake. He then brushed his teeth and combed his hair. As he put on some moisturizer he laughed at the thought of his boyhood hero, AJ Foyt, putting expensive skin lotion on his face before going off to sign to drive the Ford GT at LeMans.

"Not bloody likely" he said aloud while smiling at himself in the bathroom mirror.

He quickly dressed himself in a fresh white dress shirt, black slacks and a gray blazer. After checking his look once more, he grabbed his black leather brief and headed out the door of his room.

When the elevator stopped on his floor and the door opened he was as stunned as if he seen a ghost.

"Scott, what in the hell are you doing here? I… I was just about to call you"

"Well, I just thought I would give you a big surprise by showing up this morning", said Battle. "Did you listen to my voicemail message?"

"Yeah,… uh I mean no, I just saw that you had called and was going call you back later on this morning… anyway, just what brings you to Paris?"

As the elevator began moving toward the ground floor Brandon watched as the numbers counted down. Scott said nothing until the door opened again as they had reached the main floor lobby.

"Let's go get some coffee, we need to talk" said Battle in a rather tense tone.

It appeared that Scott was upset. Why he would be upset enough that he would track him down in Paris for a face to face was beyond him at the moment.

He had gone from a feeling on top of the world to thinking that he was about to catch hell for something that he had done wrong. Perhaps it was what he had told the Scimitar team about how both he and his F-1 star buddy were interested in driving for them.

"If the Scimitar guys had called Scott and he said that he wasn't interested then they would have cancelled my pass to the meeting. That must be what this is about", he thought.

As the two men entered the hotel coffee shop Parkes was nervously mulling over what he could tell his friend that would cause him to settle down and decide not to carve him a new nose right there and then.

Battle removed his sport jacket and sat down at the first available table. As he draped the jacket over the open chair next to him, Brandon sat down and placed his leather brief on the floor and leaning against the chair next to him.

They were soon welcomed by their young waiter who, assuming they were French, asked them what they would like to order. Scott responded in French and asked for two black cups of coffee as well as a basket of croissants.

As the waiter left them Scott began to speak. "I got a call yesterday morning that I wasn't very happy to get, BP."

"I'm sorry to hear that, who called? "he asked with a tentative tone in his voice.

"It was Ian Walters."

At that moment it was as if Parkes had just removed a thousand pound weight from his chest. The call had to do with the Jamison Racing team manager and not anything concerning the opportunity with the Scimitar Mercedes team.

"What did he have to say, Scott?"

The waiter's reappearance with their coffee and croissants delayed Battle's response. As the waiter walked away he answered the question.

"Well, had you bothered to listen to the message that I left, you would already know that I've been sacked at Jamison."

"Wow... I... am really stunned," said Parkes in the most sympathetic tone he could muster.

He was just glad that he wasn't in trouble. Besides, now the idea he had in mind might be more interesting to his friend than it would have had he mentioned it a day or two before.

Scott took a sip of coffee and leaned back in his chair. "Of course it wasn't a complete surprise, but I didn't think it would come until silly season when all the deals for the following year were going on. Even then, I figured I would finish out the year with them and at least have a chance to find something for next season in the meantime."

Although he had expected the same scenario to unfold for his friend; seeing Scott tossed out before the annual mid to late year musical chairs session was not something that he would have ever predicted.

"The good part is that most of my driver contract must be paid for the balance of the year. On the other hand, none of my personal endorsement deals are valid if I can't find another seat within thirty days of my last Grand Prix race. They all need an active driver, not one is no longer racing." said a forlorn Battle who now stared into the air as though he might be looking to the heavens for an answer.

Picking up his coffee cup Parkes said nothing. He then began to drink from it, hoping all the while that Scott would mention the note that was left concerning the opportunity they might have with Scimitar.

"Will you pass me those, BP" Battle asked as he pointed to the croissants that rested on Parkes side of the table.

He did as asked and then returned to focusing on his cup of coffee.

As Battle began to spread butter on half of a warm flaky croissant, he asked his friend to tell him about the Saudi's and the deal with the Mercedes touring cars.

"Sure" said Parkes as he reached for his brief and the information he had collected, which now included a down loaded copy of the recent AutoWeek article about the series. "I don't know if this will be a fit for you or not, but I thought it was worth a look."

As he began to bring out the data concerning the International SuperSedan Challenge as well as that pertaining to the Scimitar team it occurred to him that he had to be careful not show too much enthusiasm for the idea that he was about to present. It was one thing to ask Scott to give up four of his off weekends from Formula One racing, but now he was asking his friend to go from being perceived by others as a Grand Prix star to a guy who was now just a full time touring car driver. The closest analogy he could think of was that of being a starting NFL quarterback who is cut from the team and told by his agent that his only option now is playing in the Canadian Football League. He didn't want to blow the unexpected opportunity to talk about the Scimitar Mercedes team by overselling the idea.

After calmly presenting his case for over an hour, Parkes realized that it was time for them to head to the ISC luncheon.

"There are no promises, BP." said Battle as he walked through the hotel lobby. "I will meet with the people and see what they have in mind, but don't get too excited yet."

He knew that his getting a chance with the Scimitar team would almost certainly hinge on getting his friend to sign up as well. While Parkes didn't like seeing Scott lose his F-1 seat, it did mean that had much more leverage over the situation than he had only a day or two ago.

Stepping from out of the hotel into the beautiful sunshine was made even better by the sight of dozen high performance racing cars parked right in front of them. It was like a picture postcard and it reminded him of why he got into the business.

"Wow, just look at that, Scott" he exclaimed with unusual glee.

The muscular race cars presented in front of the hotel made for a perfect picture postcard. These fantastic automobiles, in their many different colors, gave people a taste of what to expect when the series hit the track in a few weeks time. Parked side by side, the racing versions of these expensive sport sedans looked fast just sitting still

Two white Scimitar-AMG Mercedes C Class race cars had black Arabco Petroleum logos adorning the hood and sides of the cars and were parked up front and in the center of the display. Parkes pointed them out to Battle and the two drivers naturally decided to look them over first.

Just to the right of the two Arabco sponsored cars was the bright red Audi of the GT Italia team. Since they had all wheel drive, Parkes had a feeling that the Audi's would be tough to beat. Even more so if a race was run in the rain, which was likely to happen at least once this season.

There were several BMW M3's, another AMG C63 Mercedes, a Lexus IS-F as well as a pair of red Maserati Quattroportes that completed the list of cars on display.

All of them looked as good as he had imagined, but he wondered if he would end up driving one of these cars this season or not. Unlike Scott, his salary for the season was not being paid after he and the NASCAR team had ended their brief relationship. The thought of being broke and unemployed was overwhelming to him. However, he decided that he simply wasn't going to allow himself to worry about it right now. What he needed to do was to stay focused, confident, very calm and hope that no one would see him sweat.

As the two men walked toward the shuttle bus that would transport them to the luncheon, Parkes looked around and saw that many of the top team owners and managers from the international sports car and touring car scene were present. Many of them came up to say hello to Scott and asked him what he was doing here. It seemed no one had heard the news about his firing, as of yet.

Since it was mostly European teams entering the series, Parkes doubted if anyone here would even who he was, much less be familiar with his own history in the sport.

Once seated on the bus it occurred to him that the one team owner who did know him did not have a car on display. What plans Mr. Mandel had for the ISC, if any, were seemingly unknown to anyone outside of the team at this moment. Parkes had to keep his options open and he hoped that Mr. Mandel might just have a seat for him when the music stopped playing. For now he would stay locked on the task at hand, that of landing both himself and Scott with the Scimitar Mercedes outfit.

As the bus left for the restaurant, Scott asked him if he could ask him what might be a sensitive question.

"Since you know what happened with me, I think it is time you tell me your tragic story of success, followed by abject failure in NASCAR. That only seems fair," said Battle with a slightly devious smile.

After a deep breath Brandon replied "OK, but what you really need to know started about a year ago. I was testing a Porsche at Watkins Glen when I was approached by a NASCAR team owner about the idea of coaching his driver on his road racing technique. Well, one thing led to another and before you knew it, they asked me to run a second car at the Infineon road course event for them. You may remember the press release that I emailed you about that?

"Sure I do. You also sent me the article about how you lead the race, but fell down to what was it….thirty-first?"

He paused and considered saying something equally cutting to Scott, but decided not to.

"OK, anyway, that led to my being asked to replace their driver in the primary car at the Watkins Glen race in August and a fourth place finish." I guess that I had become an official NASCAR road course ringer. Since their sponsor liked me I was then asked to do an oval test at Daytona International Speedway with the idea that they would offer me a full season seat in the car if it all went well."

"So my question is how did you screw up and fall out of grace so quickly with these folks?"

The bus was coming to a stop in front of their destination. When it came to a halt Parkes stood up and told his friend "Let's get to our table and have a drink first, and later on I'll share with you the worst part of the story, alright?"

"Fine." said Battle as he stood and gave him a slap on the back, "I could use a drink too now that you mention it. "

The second story banquet room of the restaurant was like a set from a movie.

Round tables, with the names of each person attending on a placard at their appointed seat, filled the room.

It was after leaving the bar that Parkes remembered that Scott wasn't even registered for the luncheon. "Excuse me while I check out what table we are at," he blurted out as he headed to where Christine the PR lady with the ISC was standing.

"Mr. Parkes how are you today?" she asked him.

"Good, but I have a slight problem. My friend, Scott Battle, came along with me and I don't think he's registered for the conference."

"Actually he is on the list, and he is in fact already over by the Scimitar team's table right now, she said while pointing to the front of the room."

"Well, thank you for clearing that up for me" he replied who was already moving toward the full table where his friend was now seated and holding court.

"Hello" said an unsmiling and very large Sayid Mustafa, the team principal at the Scimitar racing team. Parkes just nodded back at the handsome dark skinned man and shook his hand.

"You see that Mr. Battle found his way to our table. We can only thank you for your help in getting him here to the meeting."

"Sure, it was my pleasure" he said with a forced smile.

"Sorry there wasn't enough room for you to join us at our table, we had some unexpected guest from home decide to join us." said Mustafa.

"No problem, I'll just be seated over at the table hosted by Mr. Mandel, maybe we can talk after the presentation?"

"Please do enjoy your lunch." replied the Arab with a dismissive tone.

Shooting a glance at his friend, Parkes asked "Will I see you later, Scott?"

"Yeah, we'll get together later on" he replied with a wink.

As he made his way to his seat Parkes was once again feeling a bit unsettled. It was something that he was growing all too familiar with as of late.

Just before the meal was served, Dan Mandel showed up at the table and greeted him with a hello and a firm handshake. He then told him that he was glad that he had been able to join him today.

As the billionaire took his place across the table from him, Parkes now had a warm feeling come over him as he thought about how really kind Mr. Mandel was being to him.

Having just been rejected and treated poorly by the Saudis, some good old American hospitality was exactly what he felt that he needed right now. Surprisingly, no one at the table said much about racing. Mr. Mandel was cordial, but never let on about any plans concerning the ISC. Instead, most of the discussion the others engaged in had to do with Mandel's chain of stores and talk about, SKU's, end caps and weekly circulars.

Thankfully, he knew what those terms meant, but he chose to focus on enjoying lunch rather than sticking his nose into something that wasn't his business.

No sooner had he finished his meal and emptied the glass of wine, than he heard a voice coming from the front of the room.

"The new International SuperSedan Challenge is the first step in creating a world-wide racing series for race cars based on the high performance sports sedans that are being produced by some of the world's finest automakers." explained Silvio Marino from the podium.

As the head of Organization Silvio Marino, he had become one of the more powerful figures in international motorsport. What was now about to kick-off could make him the biggest player of all and he was slightly nervous right now because he knew that this was likely one of the most important moments of his professional life.

After taking a deep breath the Italian continued his speech.

"The first season of the ISC will consist of four big events. Eurospeedway, Lausitz in Germany will host the inaugural event. Monza in Italy, Spa in Belgium and the circuit in Cairo, Egypt will hold the other three races. Our goal is to hold eight to ten events by year two of the series."

After taking a sip of water from the glass on the lectern he proceeded.

"The cars competing will be full race versions of V8 powered cars from Mercedes, Audi and BMW. There will also be two Maserati Quattroportes in the series and hopefully, a pair of Jaguars from the UK. Also, an unexpected, but very welcome presence in the ISC will be a team that we will introduce in a few minutes", said Marino with a smile.

As he glanced down at his notes on the lectern, he paused.

"In addition, there is also a very strong looking effort from a Lexus team as well. In fact, fields of twenty or more entries are expected at each event and some of the top professional teams and drivers will be racing with us in this, our first season of competition.

"The championship will be unique in many respects. One example is that the results from each team car will contribute to a team title. While the prize money for each race will be according to the number of points earned by individual drivers on the team, there will be a team bonus awarded at the end of the season."

Marino stopped to smile at the crowd before continuing.

"In fact, I should also mention the fact that the first place team in the series will be awarded a one million dollar purse courtesy of our new series' sponsor, Mandel's SuperStores."

The surprise announcement brought a standing ovation from all those assembled in the room.

Silvio Marino then stepped away from the podium and walked over to shake hands with Mr. Mandel who arose to meet him. As the applause dissipated, the crowd sat down to listen to the American billionaire share the how and why of his commitment to the new series.

Thinking about a million dollar pot for being the ISC champions, Parkes was excited. Prize money like that, for a mini-season of just four sprint races, was unheard of in this form of motorsport.

He looked back up to see Marino gesturing to Mr. Mandel to come before the microphone to speak to the audience. Everyone in the room seemed to eagerly await the words that would follow.

"Well, first off we are about to open 12 new stores in Europe. They should all be up and running by the end of this year. It is our hope that our series sponsorship and my decision to enter a team in the ISC will promote that fact to the public. "What Silvio has put together here has the potential to be as big as Formula 1 or perhaps more likely, something like an international version of NASCAR. As a racing fan and as a business man I just could not miss the opportunity to get involved with this series while it was still on the ground floor" said the American billionaire with a broad smile.

"Besides, the SuperSedan series sponsored by our SuperStores seemed to be a natural fit." he announced with a laugh.

The last comment brought another round of applause. Marino shook hands with Mandel and stood next to him as he signaled an assistant to open the two large doors to the left of the lectern. No more than two seconds passed before a young woman drove a shiny new black Cadillac CTS-V racing car into the large conference room.

Parkes was happy to see that Mandel would be racing in the series and that he'd be competing with a car from the U.S., but wasn't really too sure that the Cadillac could be competitive with the racing versions of cars from the German manufacturers. Still, he thought it was going be nice to watch these great looking sport sedans competing in the series, especially given the current state of the U.S. car industry.

International SuperSedan Challenge logos and those of Mandel's SuperStores graced the hood and sides of the Cadillac. As the car came to its final resting spot the driver blipped the supercharged V-8's throttle twice before switching the engine off.

The cheering and clapping continued as the driver stepped out of the car wearing a black Nomex suit with Mandel's SuperStores across the front and a black cap with the white letters that said ISC.

"This could turn out to be really great" a smiling Parkes said to the man standing next to him. Judging by the crowd's response, most of those looking to compete in this new racing series were probably thinking the same thing.

The crowd of motorsports reporters and well-wishers that surrounded Dan Mandel and Silvio Marino made it all but impossible for Parkes to get a chance to speak to either man before he was to depart. However, the attractive young lady who drove the Cadillac into the dining room was standing by herself in front of the ebony race car and so he decided to approach her.

"Hello, I 'm Brandon Parkes" he said to the woman.

"Sure, I know who you are Mr. Parkes, what can I do for you?"

"Well, first off it's nice to see yet another person from the states over here. So, will you be speaking to Mr. Mandel later on?"

"Probably, why do you ask?" said the woman with a trace of a grin.

"Could you give him my card and tell him thank you for getting me a seat at his table for the luncheon today?"

"Sure" she replied as she put the gray business card in her pocket.

"Thank you very much" "Oh, by the way, do you work for the team full time, or is this a one off modeling appearance?"

"I don't work for the team, but you could say I do work with Mr. Mandel on certain special projects," she said as she brushed her strawberry blond hair back away from her face.

"We have a very close personal relationship as well, so I wouldn't be surprised to see you at one of the races"

"Thanks again", he replied with a smile.

As she walked away Parkes thought he had just met an angel.

"It must be great to be worth a few billion and have lovely young women surrounding you." he said under his breath.

Just then he felt a hand on his shoulder.

As he turned he saw that it was Scott that was trying to get his attention.

"You know, flying on private jets, being the center of attention and having twenty something girls who work on your "special projects" must be demanding" Parkes blurted out to his friend.

"Hey now, that girl you were talking to is Mandel's daughter, Liz" replied Battle. "I met them at the Speedway when I visited qualifying for the 500."

Still surprised that the young woman knew who he was, Parkes was even more stunned to find out who she was. He found himself in a momentary daze as he thought about the young woman that he had just met.

"Wow, that's his daughter? My question now has to be-is she married and if not, does she like race car drivers?"

"I don't think that she is married BP; anyway, the thing I wanted to tell you is that the Scimitar people want to have dinner with us tonight and discuss the idea of you and me driving for them".

Suddenly Parkes was focused on his friend and he shook his hand. "Yes, that is fantastic news. I had been worried, but clearly things went pretty well." he said with a grin.

"Yeah, and it didn't hurt that the money being talked about was quite good. Also, they will allow me to keep my personal sponsors happy by putting their logos on both team cars. So this really is a deal worth pursuing. Anyway, they want to meet at 5 o'clock, so we need to get back to your hotel to get cleaned up and changed, Parkes"

"Roger that. The shuttle will take too long. I'll go hail us a cab"

As he passed through the doors of the restaurant, Parkes couldn't help but be excited. It was become quite clear to him that this really could turn out to be a much better year than he had originally thought it would.

After visiting his hotel to freshen up the two men took a cab the short distance to the restaurant they were to meet with the head of the Scimitar Mercedes racing team.

"Sorry if we are a little bit late, gentlemen" announced Sayid Mustafa as he and a twenty something Arab man approached their table.

The Americans both stood up and shook Mr. Mustafa's hand.

They were then introduced to Mansur Bin Salman.

The young Saudi driver had placed sixth in the Monaco Porsche SuperCup race, according to Mustafa.

"I thought I recognized that name", said Battle.

Parkes rolled his eyes and smiled. He had actually seen the Porsche Cup race and didn't recognize the name, so he seriously doubted that Scott had any idea of who this kid was.

"I hope you didn't mind me bringing our young protégé along to listen to you two experienced veterans of the sport" said Mustafa as he patted the unsmiling Bin Salman on the back.

"Not a problem. In fact it is my pleasure", said Battle.

Just then the waiter asked if the newcomers would like anything from the bar.

"Just bottled water for the two of us" said Mustafa while pointing to the younger Arab.

"Another round of scotch and soda over here for me and my friend" said Parkes.

Holding up his hand, Battle made it clear that he had enough and would also have water. "I need to stay in shape, and I might as well start right now" declared Battle.

"Me too, right after this one last drink" announced Parkes with a smile.

Mustafa didn't find it humorous. In fact he quite suddenly launched into a probe of Parkes career that was about as subtle as a tax audit.

"Do you have a copy of your CV with you, Mr. Parkes?"

"Yes, of course. Just let me reach in here and get it for you" said Brandon as he picked up his leather brief and found a copy of his resume.

As he handed the two page document to Mr. Mustafa, the Saudi man put on a pair glasses and began studying his career history with the same focus that one would expect of a man who held a law degree.

It seemed like a half an hour before Mustafa looked up from the table. As he completed reviewing the second page he removed his reading glasses and asked Parkes a question that was delivered with a laser like stare.

"Can you tell me about your experience in NASCAR racing?"

"Well, I did pretty well in my two starts there" he replied. "They were the road course events at Infineon Raceway and….."

Before he could continue the older Arab man stopped him and reminded Parkes that he had just read his resume.

"No, what I want to know is why you were let go prior to the start of this season?"

Just then the waiter arrived with the drinks and offered to take their dinner order.

"I'll explain that in a minute, Mr. Mustafa. Right after we have had a chance to order".

Mustafa picked up the menu and began to look it over in the same manner that he had studied Parkes' work history.

"The Gestapo had missed out by not hiring this guy", thought Parkes.

Just then he noticed his buddy Scott was smirking while reading his own menu.

"I think I'll be having the cooked goose" said Scott under his breath with a quick wink at him. "Are you having that as well, Brandon?

Parkes just gave him a stern look and asked the waiter to bring him a medium rare New York strip.

After ordering a green salad Mustafa repeated his question to Brandon about what brought his time in NASCAR to an end.

Taking a long draw on his Dewars and soda, Parkes then went on to explain what had been the most exciting, yet disastrous part of his career to date.

"After some success on the NASCAR road course events I got ready for the test of a NASCAR Cup car on the Daytona super speedway. They signed me to a contract that was contingent on a good test session at Daytona. The only issue for me was that the deal was for only 100 thousand in retainer and forty percent of the prize money for the entire season."

The option they gave me was to take no salary and receive half the prize money. The other part of that deal was that if I could land a five hundred thousand dollar associate sponsor I could keep two hundred and fifty of it" he explained.

Since he could sense that Mustafa was already growing bored, he decided to cut to the chase.

"Anyway, to make a long story short- I put together a secondary sponsorship program that would have helped round out the budget and also pay me a quarter of a million up front, but once it was done the manager told the sponsor I had found, as well as their primary sponsor, that I was just a sports car driver, and that what they needed on the oval tracks was this twenty three year old who was a real stock car racer."

"The fact that you wrote off one of their cars in your first test at Daytona and broke your leg in the process didn't help your cause either" said Battle.

Slightly embarrassed, Parkes stared down at the table for a moment and gathered his thoughts before looking up again at Mustafa.

"Anyway, I got the word just the day before New Year's eve that I was going to be out of the car." Parkes took another long pull from his scotch and soda and set the now empty glass down on the table. While he wanted to mention that his lawyer back in Indianapolis was suing the team for a fifteen percent commission on the sponsorship monies that he had brought to them, he thought better of it when he remembered that Mustafa, was a lawyer himself and didn't want him to think that the driver they were looking to hire was some sort of litigious jerk.

Battle stared at him but said nothing.

Finally the silence was broken when Mansur Bin Salman spoke for the first and only time that night. "It sounds like you have had some misfortune, Mr. Parkes. I do hope that your luck improves"

"You and me both" he replied with a smile.

Just as he finished his sentence the waiter came with the first course of their meal.

"Let us enjoy our dinner and speak of better times ahead, gentlemen" said Scott Battle.

"Indeed ..." replied Parkes "And please share with us about your plans for the Scimitar team, Mr. Mustafa. "

As Mustafa began to speak Parkes was just relieved to finally be off the hot seat. He just hoped that the negative things that happened to him in NASCAR would not negate what he could still do behind the wheel of a race car on the road race circuits like those that would be seen in the ISC series.

Paris - Wednesday 11:15 AM

Dan and Harry Mandel stepped out of the right side doors of the Jaguar sedan belonging to Marino, and walked with the Italian through the front door of his office building. As they entered they were greeted by his assistant, Christine.

"Hello, we have everything all set up for you in the conference room.

Your lunch will be brought in about an hour from now."

"Thank you, Christine" said the ever smiling Marino.

The three men sat down at the long conference room table. Marino sat on the same side as Harry Mandel.

"I just want to thank you for taking the time to meet and have lunch with me before you fly back to America" said Marino. "It only made sense" replied Dan.

Harry said nothing. He just stared at the wall.

"Now, let's discuss how Mandel SuperStores can use the International SuperSedan Challenge "to promote themselves here in Europe."

"Before we start on the details, can you share all that you told me yesterday with my brother?" asked the younger Mandel. "Also, you had mentioned that you were planning on having more races next year. Do you really expect to expand from the four events that we have now to a ten race slate of events next season?"

"At least ten races, but I would still like to see the biggest four events, the original four circuits from this year, make up a grand slam of touring car racing, excuse me- maybe I should say stock car racing- along with that million dollar prize" replied Marino with a smile at his benefactors. "Full international TV coverage and hopefully no conflicts with the Formula One schedule. We want all those F1 fans to be watching our events on the weekends when there isn't a Formula One Grand Prix taking place."

An expressionless Harry Mandel appeared to be taking notes as Marino filled him in on all the details of the series. Despite having heard most of it before, Dan was hanging on every word that the Italian said. This was a sign to anyone who that knew him that he was truly enthused, otherwise he would have bluntly asked Marino to tell him something new.

"Sports car and touring car racing has traditionally been all about endurance events, but we think that six, twelve or twenty four hour races featuring multiple classes of cars is considered boring to many people in this day and age.

I have nothing against the classic endurance events myself, but they are also very expensive to put on TV. That is why we have gone to the format of ninety minute sprint races; with just one class of high performance sedans." explained Marino.

Harry's eyes were about to glaze over by the time that Marino started talking in detail about demographics, television numbers and projected live gates for the series.

"Why don't we take a short break for some coffee and then finish up afterwards?" suggested Marino.

"Sounds like a good idea to me." Harry replied.

"After we are done with discussing business we will have some lunch and then get you to your plane for the flight back to the states. Does that sound OK?" asked Marino.

"That will be just fine" said Dan as he stood up from the table. "Hopefully my daughter Liz will be here for lunch, or at least arrive by the time we are ready to leave for the airport".

"We will make sure of it. I'll send my car and have her picked up at the hotel" said Marino as he left the room.

As he poured himself some coffee Harry looked over at his brother and shook his head.

"I just hope this makes you happy, because it looks to me like great expense with very little in return for our money. We can use the vendor co-op dollars for other promotions that surely would provide much more benefit; I mean I can shoot down all these numbers he is giving us with quantifiable results from marketing programs that we already know will work."

"Look, it makes me very happy."

The elder Mandel brother sighed and then responded, in a somewhat condescending manner "Well, then I guess that I am very happy for you, Dan."

New York; JFK Airport-Wednesday evening 6:45pm

While he sat in the John F. Kennedy Airport terminal waiting for the flight that would take him home to Indianapolis, Brandon Parkes was getting very tired and more than a little bored. Worse yet, was the fact that the more time he had to sit around and think, the more anxious he became about the future of his racing career.

His anxiety was mainly due to the fact that he had to figure out a way to make sure that he was part of the Scimitar Team's plans. If he didn't, the trip to France would have been for naught.

Finding some additional sponsorship would normally be the best way for a driver in his position to have a better shot than the others; but these oil rich Arabs had no real need for extra dollars. So he knew that the prospects for someone of his age, ability and perceived value of getting the opportunity to drive one of the Scimitar Mercedes were not very good.

His "ace in the hole" was still the fact that he had brought Scott Battle into the fold. So he had to get Scott to tell them that unless they took both of them, the deal was a non starter as far as Scott driving for them was concerned.

"I'll worry about everything tomorrow" he thought. He then closed his eyes and leaned back in his seat to rest a bit before boarding the plane.

No sooner than he had closed eyes, then he was startled to hear the loud voice of a woman over the loudspeaker. "Paging passenger Henry Lee Mond. Please come to the gate seventeen service desk"

He closed his eyes again. The woman at the desk repeated her page.

Opening his eyes once more, Parkes saw a middle aged man standing in front of the check in desk. The man looked familiar to him. At first he thought it was Jean Reno, the actor.

Then the man walked away from the counter with his ticket in his hand and positioned himself to be the first one in line to get on the aircraft.

The name announced on the public address system was not one that he knew from racing, yet the man looked so familiar. Had he met him in the states? Maybe he had seen him in France, or at the Grand Prix in Monaco? Whatever the case, the guy looked really familiar to him. It even crossed his mind that it was Reno and that he was traveling under an alias.

Responding to the call for first class passengers to board the aircraft Parkes entered the jet-way. Just as he did so his cell phone rang. The caller ID said it was Scott Battle, so he quickly answered it.

"Hey bud, where are you?" asked the familiar voice.

"I am at JFK and headed back to Indy. In fact, I am about to get on board. So what do you know, Mr. Battle?"

"Things are getting pretty serious with Scimitar. I should know more by tomorrow. Anyway, I just wanted to touch base with you and tell you thanks for hooking me up with these guys"

"I am glad to hear that things are going well and that you are indeed interested, Scott.

If it all comes together, when do they plan to have us get started with testing?"

There was no response to his question. The call had failed as he had entered the cabin of the plane.

He hit the redial button and waited for the call to go through. Once again the call was lost and now the phone was telling him that his battery was low so he switched it off and put it back in his brief case.

As he strapped himself into his seat he noticed that the man he thought he knew was seated just across the aisle from him. He was already looking intently at a copy of Time magazine.

He thought again about where he might have known this man from. It was driving him crazy that he couldn't place him; but remembering how he knew the man sitting across from him, wasn't nearly as disconcerting as his worry about securing a new job.

His father had always told him that one's biggest hopes and worst fears are seldom realized. The concern Parkes had right now was that not only would his current hopes be dashed, but that his greatest fears would indeed be realized if he couldn't turn things around soon.

Chapter Three

Indianapolis, Indiana-early Thursday morning

The cab ride from the Indianapolis airport to Parkes' townhouse in the upscale suburb of Carmel added about a half hour to his trip which made it was well past midnight before he got home. After the long flight from Paris, two hours sitting in New York and another couple hours getting to Indy, he was totally exhausted both mentally and physically. In fact, it was all he could do to get undressed and pull the sheets back.

His deep sleep was interrupted just a little after nine-thirty am when the cell phone rang. He almost didn't answer it, but didn't want to miss the hoped for call about the opportunity to drive the Scimitar Mercedes.

"This is Brandon" he said with his eyes still closed.

"BP, this is Scott. Did I wake you?" "Yeah, as matter of fact" replied Parkes. He was still a little upset with his friend about what he perceived to be an attempt to throw him under the bus when they met with the Saudis over dinner in Paris. "You had better be calling me with some really good news, pal."

"Turn on your television and tune it to Fox news channel" shouted Battle.

"Mr. Mandel is plane missing and it is believed that they may have crashed".

Parkes went into his living room and switched on the TV.

After finding Fox news he turned up the volume with the remote. Just then Dan Mandel's picture appeared in the background.

"Hey, thanks for calling and letting me know about this, I'll get back to you in a minute or three, OK?" He hung up before Battle could reply. He turned up the TV volume a bit more and sat down on the couch.

"French authorities have released information that American business man Daniel Mandel, his two company pilots and the Mandel private jet disappeared from radar sometime after 10:30 Paris time." said the woman newscaster.

He turned the volume even more as the newswoman continued with her report.

"Mandel is known as a strong supporter of right wing politicians in Israel, and there are suggestions from unidentified members at the U.S. State Department that this might have been politically motivated sabotage. However, no terrorist group has stepped forward to claim responsibility for the action. As of right now the aircraft is missing and its status is unknown. French aviation officials say that a search for wreckage in the area that the plane went missing in is now underway."

No sooner than the newscast went to a stock market update Parkes had grabbed the phone and hit the redial button. Scott Battle answered with "Can you believe that crap"?

"I can't believe it. What do you bet it was terrorists? Probably some Muslim radicals if I were to make a guess."

There was a pause before Battle responded. "Maybe you are right, but given the fact that I just signed with an Arab team I don't think I'll go there."

"Uh… wow. So you already have a deal with the Scimitar guys?" asked Parkes with a slight feeling of despair as he wondered if he would also be part of the package.

"Yeah, and I really thank you again for all your help. This is proving to be a good move for me on many levels." Battle paused again and sighed. "Listen, I am just sorry that it turns out that there isn't going to be a spot for you. In fact, I just heard confirmation that it will be me as number one and Bin Salman who will drive the second car.

Just as he learned his of fate Parkes land line began to ring.

"Well, thanks for calling Scott. Listen, I have a call on the other line so I'll catch you later, OK?"

Without even bothering to hang up he threw his cell phone across the living room. It crashed against the wall and shattered into pieces.

The land line continued to ring, but he didn't care who it was.

"Damn you Battle!" Parkes yelled out loud as he headed to the refrigerator.

Opening a cold can of Dr. Pepper he used it to down two sleeping pills followed by a couple of tablets of Ibuprofen. He shook his head as he thought about the news concerning Mr. Mandel. That was bad enough for one day, but then to find out that his old friend had signed with the Scimitar Mercedes team and left him high and dry was just too much to take. He looked at the nearly full bottle of prescription sleeping pills and thought how much easier it would be to just take them all and drift off forever.

Prior to his crash at Daytona he would have rarely taken an aspirin, much less sleeping pills or a tablet of his new favorite medication, Xanax.

As he drank down the last part of the can of soda he noticed the picture of his uncle Ron on the living room wall and suddenly he felt ashamed of himself.

"I know what you would tell me; winners never quit and quitters never win." said Parkes to the photograph. He smiled at the thought of his uncle and his positive attitude about life.

Still, he felt hurt, cheated and lost. His wreck at Daytona and the fact there were fewer opportunities due to the current decline of the world economy had put him in a difficult situation. Landing a seat in this new European road racing series had looked to be the answer to his dilemma. Now, even his back-up plan of approaching Dan Mandel about a ride in one of the Cadillac race cars had seemingly disappeared with the Mandel company jet.

He looked up toward the ceiling and silently asked for help. He wasn't even a believer, but thought it didn't hurt to try.

"Maybe a bit more sleep will help my outlook" he told himself as he grabbed a blanket and made his way to the living room and the big soft leather couch.

Paris, France - Thursday evening

Crying like she never had before, Liz Mandel sat in her hotel room sobbing uncontrollably, in a near state of shock at the news that her father's plane was presumed to have been taken by hijackers and was maybe even lying at the bottom of the Atlantic.

Her Uncle Harry was in the adjoining room trying to get information from the French authorities as to what might have happened to her father and the company aircraft.

The elder Mandel brother had decided to stay behind in Paris to check out potential store sites while Dan flew back to Chicago by himself. Liz had also originally planned on returning with her father, but had instead decided to remain in France to supervise the creation of the new racing shop which was to be located just outside Paris. The last time they had seen Dan Mandel was as he left Silvio Marino's office and drove off to the airport.

As her uncle walked back into Liz's room he hung up his cell phone and told her what he had learned.

"It seems that plane took off and headed out over the ocean. Radar tracking lost them shortly after that. The last radio contact was just prior to them going off the radar screen."

"If only we had gone back with him, maybe there is something we could have done to stop this." she screamed.

"I don't know what to say, Liz. Let's just hope we hear something soon."

Then Harry walked toward her and put his hand on her shoulder in an attempt to comfort her. "Get some rest. I'll be in my room calling the US Embassy to see if they can help us find out anything else."

She just nodded at him.

As her uncle left the room she began to think about what her dad would want her to do right now.

She soon decided to call the racing shop in Indianapolis and let them know what was going on.

The team was about to test one of their Cadillac CTS-V racing cars at the Indianapolis Motor Speedway road course that day and she wanted them to go ahead with it, despite her father's disappearance.

It was just past noon in Indiana as Liz picked up her international cell phone and called team manger Griffin Ashmore.

"Hi, this is Liz." She took a breath before she continued." I guess you have heard about what's happened to dad and the pilots?"

"Yeah, it's all over the news. I am really sorry, but don't give up hope; maybe they will find all three of them floating in the life raft… or something like that."

"Thank you, Griffin" she said as she wiped her nose with a tissue. "Listen, I want you to go ahead with our plans to go testing the new car, because I think my father would want us to move ahead, despite whatever he is going through right now."

She just couldn't bring herself to say that Dan Mandel might be dead. Thinking positive and seeing the glass as half full was always her way of handling her emotions.

"OK, if you think that is best. We are at the track now and were just about to have some lunch. The car ran good this morning and now we will see if we can tweak it for more speed." he replied.

"So tell me, did you get in touch with the driver we want to hire for the other car yet?"

"No, but I will try again. It would really be nice to have two guys here for the test and both of them giving their feedback." "Anyway, don't worry about the race team. Just take care of you right now."

"I will Griffin, thank you so much."

As the call ended she felt a little better just having talked to someone she knew and trusted.

She thought her father would be pleased that she didn't just fall apart, but rather was trying to keep it business as usual. Besides, she realized that it is all she could do right now. As she sat back down on the king-sized bed her Uncle Harry came back into the room.

"No new information from the embassy, except that they now do think that it may have been terrorists who took over the plane. It still isn't known if they brought the plane down or not. It could have been a bomb from within the aircraft, or maybe a missile launched from the ground. It might well have even been a Flight 93 situation. Anyway, they won't know that until they find the plane. To be honest, I am not too sure that anyone really knows anything at this point."

Liz held up her hand to get her uncle to stop telling her any more about the hijacking.

"I'm going to go get in contact with some other people I know. Like I told you before, you need to just lie down and get some rest."

"Fine, Harry just let me know if you do hear any confirmed news, OK?"

Once Harry left she laid her head down on the pillow and prayed that her father might have survived a probable terrorist attack and the possible crash of their company jet.

Then she prayed for the strength cope if Dan Mandel did not come home alive.

Indianapolis, Indiana – Thursday 7:57 PM

He was resting comfortably when he awoke to find his black and white cat, "Big Al" licking his face. Brandon Parkes was surprised when looked over at the clock by his bed and saw that it was almost eight in the evening.

"Alright, buddy. I am getting up." His trusty companion was more like a small dog in both size and personality. "Let's go eat" he said as he rubbed at his eyes.

Emptying a can of food onto the cat's plate he noticed that someone had called while he had been sleeping.

As he picked up the land line he saw that the same someone had tried calling three times. It was an Indianapolis number that Parkes did not recognize. Instead of listening to any message he hit the redial button and waited for an answer.

After the forth ring a male voice with a British sounding accent answered. "Hello mate"

"Hello, my name is Parkes and you…"

Before he could finish the man on the other end of the conversation blurted out "I have rung you up several times and was beginning to think you were avoiding me." Initially Parkes thought that the man had a British accent, but by the end of the sentence it sounded to him like it had to be Australian.

"I have just returned from Europe and was sleeping" he replied in a slightly terse manner.

"Well, I have been looking at a copy of your resume and was hoping that if you weren't too busy that perhaps you could come down and join us for the test session we are having at the Indianapolis Speedway road course. We are meeting tomorrow at our shop at eight AM. By the way, you should also know that it was Liz Mandel who asked me to call you."

"I thought that, uh, with Mr. Mandel's plane going missing that, well is...is this about me coming to test the Cadillac then?"

"Indeed it is. Despite what has happened to Mr. Mandel, his daughter says that we are going forward. We both think it's what he would have wanted. In fact, you should know that she also told me that her dad took an immediate fancy to you and that giving you a tryout with the team would be what he would have done had he.... well, you know ".

"Yes, I just saw him in Paris and he seemed very excited about the new car and the ISC program."

There was a brief moment of silence. For a couple of seconds neither man seemed to be able to speak after thinking about what had just been said in the previous exchange.

"Well, right then." The man sighed and cleared his throat. "Will we be seeing you at our shop at eight o'clock tomorrow morning then?"

"OK, I mean yes, I'll be there right at eight" he answered nervously.

Then Parkes paused for a moment to collect his thoughts.

"Uh, by the way, I know where the shop is, but I just realized that I didn't get your name"

"Griffin Ashmore. I am the team manager, crew chief and head honcho here. Anyway, we'll see you tomorrow then."

As he heard him hang up the phone Parkes wasn't sure if Ashmore was a man of few words or simply all choked up. Perhaps it was a bit of both he thought.

He took a moment to close his eyes and reflect on all that had transpired. Feelings of shame about his earlier thoughts and deeds now haunted him.

"Thank you, Dan Mandel, wherever you are right now" he said out loud.

He then bounded up the stairs to find his best driver's suit and racing helmet. The thought that he was driving a new road racing car down at the Indianapolis Motor Speedway in the morning began to sink in and it made him excited to be alive again.

While gathering his racing gear Parkes shook his head and wondered why he had to go Europe only to try out with a team located right here in his own backyard. Just as quickly he decided that it didn't matter and that he was just lucky to have another chance behind the wheel of a racing car.

Paris, France-Friday morning

The wake up alarm on Liz Mandel's watch had been set for 10am. As the chime went off she realized that she had already been up for over two hours. Aside from a brief phone call to a friend of her father's in Israel, most of that time had been spent in prayer. She had felt like that was all she could do right now and was very composed and at peace as a result.

After a quick shower she dressed and ordered tea and orange juice from room service.

Finishing her order she noticed a note that her uncle had left her saying that he would be at the US Embassy trying to learn more about her father's plight.

Flipping on the television to CNN there was news about an earthquake in Afghanistan.

That was followed by a story on a United Nations global climate meeting in Tokyo, but nothing about her father's missing plane.

There were apparently more interesting headlines than her dad's story she told herself as she hit the TV's mute button.

Just then she heard a knock at the door. She expected it was her breakfast order.

A handsome man in his early forties appeared as Liz opened her door.

"Good morning, I am Levi Bernstein. A mutual friend from Israel suggested that we meet concerning your father." said the man in almost American sounding English.

The man showed her his identification and she invited him in. "I didn't expect to hear from you yet, Mr. Bernstein. Please excuse me for one moment" She then picked up the phone and asked the kitchen to bring up another tea cup as well as an additional glass of juice for her guest.

"I have some information that may help you solve your father's case, Miss. Mandel."

"Please tell me of any news that you might have." she said before sitting down on the couch. She wondered to herself if she really wanted to know the details of what had happened.

"Daniel Mandel was…I should say… has been a good friend to Israel. That is why I am here so soon this morning. But as you know, being our friend is also quite likely part of the reason that your father's plane is missing." said Bernstein who had remained standing.

"You must know that it was confirmed today that one of the ground crew, who happens to be a Muslim from Morocco, has also disappeared. We think that he was the one who hijacked the plane."

"So where is the"... before Liz could speak another word, Bernstein told her what she really didn't want to hear.

"We think that it is probable that your father and the crew fought with the man and that the hijacker flew the plane into the ocean."

"I know, something similar to Flight 93 on September 11th she replied. " My uncle already told me that might be the case."

"We do not feel it was a matter of pilot error nor was it a mechanical problem. This was a hijacking for sure, Miss Mandel."

She was clearly upset and Bernstein tried to comfort her with his words.

"Just be assured that we will do all it can to capture and punish those behind this act." said Bernstein.

"Thank you, but that won't bring my father back if he is already dead." she cried.

The Mossad agent said nothing. He just stared down at the floor. There was really nothing for him to say.

Indianapolis, Indiana – Friday 7:50 AM

The Team Mandel race shop was located near the Indianapolis Motor Speedway in an area that had come to be known as Gasoline Alley. This had always been a bit confusing to Parkes as the garage area within the Speedway itself was also known as by the same name.

The shop had once been the place where Indycars were prepared, now it was where the Team Mandel Cadillac CTS-V's were being readied for competition.

As he drove his silver Porsche Boxter S into the parking area he saw that he team transporter had been backed up to receive its cargo of wheels, tires, and a brand new race car for that day's test session.

He entered the building and smiled at the woman at the front desk and asked if Griffin was in.

"Just a moment", said the woman with a Hoosier twang as she picked up the telephone sitting in front of her.

"Mr. Ashmore, there is a young man here to see you…. O.K., I'll send him back".

"Just go through the door over there to the left and that will take back to the shop area."

"Thanks for your help" replied Parkes.

"You bet hon." The woman had just spoken to him while barely looking up from her copy of that morning's Indianapolis Star.

As he passed through the twin swinging doors and entered the expansive garage area he was stunned by its clean room like environment. The white tile on the floor looked like you could eat off it. This was as impressive a racing shop as he had ever seen.

Walking toward the race car that was about to be loaded onto the transporter and saw a short, fifty plus looking guy with reddish hair approaching him.

"'Hello mate." The man then stuck out a freckled arm and shook his' hand. "I'm Griffin, team manager and the glue of this whole bloody operation."

"Pleased to meet you in person" he replied. He was now all but certain that Ashmore had to be Australian. Between now hearing him speak in person and his use the word of mate there was little doubt about it.

"Good to have you with us today, come on over here, there is someone else I want you to meet." said Ashmore speaking a mile a minute.

Out of the driver's seat of the black Cadillac CTS-V stepped a man wearing a t-shirt that said" Spa 24 Hours" across the front.

"Henri LeMond, this is Brandon Parkes."

The two drivers shook hands and it was then that Parkes realized that the man that he was meeting was the same familiar face he had seen at the gate at JFK and then sitting across from him on his flight from New York. While he had been wrong about the man's identity, he had at least gotten the nationality right.

'I'll let Henri show you the car and get you up to speed while I go and return a phone call.

We have about an hour before our track time starts so we need to get going in about thirty minutes." said Griffin as he began walking toward the office.

"Shall we get a coffee first?" asked LeMond in his heavy French accent.

"Sure, sounds good to me." Parkes fought off the impulse to make small talk and mention the fact they had been on the same flight a couple of nights before.

He did ask him something that he had wondered about since the previous evening's phone call from Ashmore. "How are things here at the team, you know, morale wise, Henri?

"Well, of course the situation with Mr. Mandel has us all bothered. Far too many drivers and racing people seem to die in private aircraft crashes, but the idea that he might have been hijacked seems to be even more upsetting to most of us."

Parkes nodded in agreement as they walked toward the kitchen area of the facility.

After pouring the coffee the Frenchman led him to the back of the shop where another Cadillac, this one painted white, was in the process of being turned into a race ready car.

"OK, as you may already know, the ISC rules call for production based V8 powered cars with stock appearing bodywork. However, the doors, trunk and hood can be made of light weight carbon fiber."

Pausing to take a drink from his cup LeMond then continued with his talk.

"Now, while the series is called the SuperSedan Challenge, four place sedan based coupe body styles can be used as well. Not a big deal in my opinion. In fact your old Trans American Sedans back in the late sixties and early seventies were actually all two doors like Mustangs and Camaros."

"OK, that explains the Audi RS5 coupes and two-door BMW M3's that I saw in Paris." Parkes interjected.

"Correct. Of course we could have run the new CTS-V coupe, but Griffin decided to stick with the four door version of the car. I thought that his background of racing Holden V8 sedans in Australia had made him decide that a proper touring car had to have four doors, but he said that it wasn't the case as it was coupes that raced at Bathurst back when he was there."

Then LeMond turned his attention back to the race car.

"Now, ISC cars must have a production based engine and the same drive set up that the road car has. You should know that all wheel drive is legal and obviously an advantage in wet conditions, but it also makes the car heavier which averages things out for those with rear wheel drive. Cadillac has it available as an option in the street cars, but we decided against it for now."

LeMond moved to the front of the car putting his hand on the carbon fiber wheel flare on the driver's side, as he began to speak again.

"The front valance, wheel flares, side skirts and the rear wing are the aero changes allowed to the car. Five hundred and fifty horsepower is the maximum; which should mean very few blown engines as that is about the same amount of power found in the road cars."

Taking another sip of his coffee he walked around to the driver's side door to show Parkes the cockpit of the car.

"OK, the rules do allow for a racing spec sequential gearbox which means there is no need to lift off the gas when you make an up shift, or to use the clutch pedal as you would with a standard manual transmission. There is a clutch pedal though, and you may want to use it on down shifts.

"How many race cars will the team have?" Parkes asked as he leaned in to take a look at the inside of the car.

"This one as well as the black one we will be testing today will be our primary cars. The car that is already at the shop over in France will be the backup." replied LeMond.

As Parkes thought about the Cadillac he saw at the kickoff luncheon in Paris he felt a sudden sadness as he remembered when Dan Mandel spoke that day. "Too bad that Mr. Mandel was going to miss all this," he thought to himself. As he replayed that moment in his head he suddenly realized that he had not seen LeMond in Paris at that time.

Before he could ask why he had seen LeMond on the plane, but not at the ISC meeting, Griffin called out to them from the front of the shop.

"The lads are loading up the race car, guys. Brandon, we'll meet you over at the Speedway, OK?"

"Yeah, I'll see you over there."

"So are you ready to give it a try? " LeMond asked him.

"You bet, Henri. I can't wait to get behind the wheel of a real race car again."

Indianapolis Motor Speedway - 9:25 AM

Driving onto the grounds of the Indianapolis Motor Speedway always gave Parkes a chill up his spine. This hallowed ground was a Mecca for almost anyone who had the racing bug.

The first Indy 500 had been held in 1911 and continued to be the world's "Greatest Spectacle in Racing". The latest edition had just been held on the very same weekend he was in Monaco for the F1 race.

In the last few years IMS had expanded from just the Indianapolis 500 to hosting NASCAR and their own Formula One Grand Prix. Motorcycle racing was the newest addition to the list of events held at the track and a long distance sports car contest was being discussed. The infield road course that the F-1 cars had utilized was the same circuit that they were using for today's test of the Cadillac CTS-V racing car.

As he drove to the garage area the knowledge that most of the great race drivers in the world had driven here at one point or another was exciting to him. This was his first time that he had ever actually been behind the wheel of a car on the circuit and he was giddy that the chance to do it had finally arrived.

Finding a parking spot close to the entrance to the garages, he got out of the car and was soon approached by an officious older guy in a yellow shirt who asked him what he was doing here. Before he answered, Parkes grabbed the leather bag that contained his gear from the car and then went on to explain to the man that he was here to test a race car. He headed toward the Mandel garage without bothering to look back at the track official for his approval.

Once he had found the team garage Griffin told him to go ahead and get suited up and ready for the test.

Excited and nervous about what he was about to go out and do, Parkes put on the Nomex underwear and slid into his silver gray driver's suit. With an American flag on the left sleeve and a silver full face helmet he looked a bit like an astronaut. The big difference was the fact that Parkes had just changed into this outfit in a men's room next to the Mandel team's temporary garage space at the Indianapolis Motor Speedway instead of being dressed by a team of technicians.

He placed the helmet back in its bag and proceeded to carry it to the garage, only to find that the car and crew had already gone to the pit area.

As he walked from the famous Gasoline Alley garage to the front straight pits he heard the engine of the car he was about to drive roar to life in the distance.

"Good. Henri is going out first" thought Parkes.

The black Cadillac was flying down the front straight when he arrived in the pits. Parkes thought that the exhaust note from the engine was a bit higher pitched than a NASCAR racer would be, but there was no mistaking that sound for anything but a powerful American V8. It made him smile.

After recording several more laps on the Indianapolis road course LeMond brought the car into the pits.

As the black car rolled to a halt Parkes could feel the heat coming off it. After the engine was turned off there was heard the metallic tinking sound of cooling metal. Exiting the car LeMond walked to the position that Parkes occupied in back of the pit wall. As he removed his distinctive Stand 21 touring car helmet, a crew member handed him a cold bottle of mineral water.

"How was it out there?" Parkes asked.

After a swallow of water LeMond began to wipe the sweat from his face with the white towel now hanging around his neck.

"The car is under steering on entry and over steering on exit, but it isn't too bad." The engine is fantastic, plenty of power down the straight." said LeMond as he took another drink of water. It was then that Parkes noticed that the one small sponsor patch on the French driver's white Nomex suit was the same logo as the one on the bottle of water he was consuming.

"Excuse me for just a moment, Brandon." LeMond walked toward Griffin who was still downloading data to his laptop from the dash of the car. The two men spoke for a couple of minutes on the driver's side of the car. Ashmore then called to a crewman to make a suspension adjustment before they sent the car out again.

"I told Griffin about the handling problem and he agrees that we should soften the rear a bit to provide more grip." he announced as he came back towards Parkes.

"Thanks. Do you have any last minute thoughts for a nervous rookie?"

"Yes, relax and have fun. It is a great car to drive." replied LeMond with a kind easy smile.

Fifteen minutes passed as the suspension changes were made. Parkes sat in the car with the door open and his helmet and gloves on the bare metal floor next to the sequential gearbox.

The roll cage in the car was painted a dark shade of gray primer. The interior didn't appear much different than the NASCAR racer that he had driven. He already liked it better due to the fact that you got into this car though the door instead of having to climb through the window as one did in a stock car.

The red driver's seat was quite comfortable to sit in as he waited for the work on the car to be completed, but he was beginning to get anxious about getting started. The sky was now overcast and he didn't want his first time in the car to be on a wet, slippery race track.

Just as he was looking up and surveying the weather, Griffin walked up to the driver's side of the car and said "Get your helmet on, mate. It's time to roll."

With a sigh of relief he put on his helmet and strapped it down tight. He slipped his gloves on and checked his belts, then plugged in his radio connection. "Radio check, radio check" said Parkes into the helmet mike.

"We read you fine" replied Griffin on his headset.

"Here we go then"

With the thumbs up from Griffin who was standing in front of the car, he pushed the red starter button on the dash.

As soon as the Cadillac fired to life, Parkes reached over to the sequential shifter and clicked it down once to place the car into first gear. Not unlike a motorcycle, there was no hunting for the proper gear like you had in a normal manual transmission. It was a simple matter of moving the shifter forward or back to effect a change of gear.

Starting down pit lane he moved the steering wheel back and forth to get a feel for the car's steering response and to help warm up the wide racing tires before entering the track. As he turned for the first corner of the road course he could already tell that the car had a solid feel and that the V8 engine could provide a ton of torque when needed.

Then he noticed the distinctive whistling of the supercharged engine on acceleration. That sound was soon overwhelmed by a typical loud American V8 thunder.

Slowly he began building up speed on the famous raceway. Each lap he completed was faster than the last. The car was indeed easy to drive and he was really starting to get into the groove when he heard Griffin tell him over the radio that he should pit in at the end of the lap.

Pushing the radio button on the steering wheel he responded to the order "OK, but I'm just getting going here." Just as quickly the radio crackled as Griffin shot back with" You are doing great, but we would like to check the tire temperatures, so bring it on in."

Nearing the pit entrance he braked and down shifted to slow the car to the pit lane speed limit. Then he pushed in the clutch pedal and allowed the car to roll the last few feet into the pit box and the waiting crew members.

"At least they are smiling" he said to himself as blipped the throttle one last time before shutting off the car.

Opening the driver's door was Henri who knelt down and said, "Take off your helmet so I can talk to you."

He did as he was asked and began to brush his sweaty, brown hair with his hand while glancing into the rearview mirror to be sure it looked alright.

"What do you think you were doing out there?" asked LeMond in a stern tone.

"What exactly do you mean?"

"What I mean is that the first time in the car you did a lap that was only two tenths off my best; are you trying to make me look badly?"

Knowing by his broad smile that LeMond was kidding him, Parkes responded.

"This Cadillac really is an easy car to drive."

"Good to hear you say that. Why don't you get out of the car and I'll buy you something to drink while you give me all the details "suggested LeMond.

"Henri, you don't happen to have any more of that spring water do you?"

"Yes, as a matter of fact I do. They are a personal sponsor of mine." he exclaimed as he pointed to the logo on the chest of his driving suit.

"I figured as much. I'll grab one right after I climb out of here."

As Parkes undid his seat belts and stepped out of the car, Griffin came to congratulate him on a good first run and to inform Henri that he had about ten minutes before he would go out on the track again.

"We still have a bunch of work to do today. Remember that we have no idea if the times we are setting are fast or not compared to what our rivals are doing" said Griffin to the two drivers.

"OK. See you in about ten minutes then" replied LeMond as the Aussie turned and headed back towards the garage.

"He is right of course", LeMond told his new acquaintance.

Then he added, "But don't let him ruin your enthusiasm with talk about not knowing if we are doing as well as we think we are. You and the car looked great out there, Brandon. I think that there is every reason to believe that they will make you an offer to join us."

He thanked him for the vote of confidence. The question now was whether anyone else thought that he should join their racing team. He really hoped that they would offer him the ride. Either way, it felt good just to be back in the saddle and praised by one of his peers.

Indianapolis, Indiana - 8:05 PM

Union Jack Pub was one of those places that anyone visiting Indianapolis, Indiana had to go to. Located down the road from the Indianapolis Motor Speedway, and close to many of the racing shops, it was as likely that you would find people from the racing community gathered there as not.

Since Henri had yet to experience the great food there, Griffin had suggested that they all meet there for dinner that night. Parkes drove into the restaurant parking lot and he couldn't have felt any better about life.

The rain that had been forecast never came during the remaining four hours that he and the Mandel team had been at the track. Much progress with the set up on the Cadillac had been made in that time and he knew that he had contributed with his input.

Entering the restaurant he saw that Henri was already seated in a booth and enjoying an iced tea.

"May I join you?" asked Parkes as he approached the table.

"Please do" replied Henri as he gestured toward the open seat across from him.

"I am glad to see that you had no problem finding the place." He said as he settled into his seat.

"Actually, I remember seeing it as I drove to the speedway for the first time, so I knew exactly what you guys were talking about" responded LeMond.

"So Henri, how do you think it went today?"

"It was about a nine out of ten. I really think that car is almost ready." He said it with an air of genuine confidence that made Parkes feel better about the job he had done today, as well as the team's chances in the championship.

As the Frenchman began elaborating on his thoughts about the racing team's current status; Parkes began to think that this team just might be the real deal. LeMond was as experienced a driver as one could find in this form of racing, so if he thought that they were ready, they probably were.

It turned out that LeMond did not begin racing cars until he was twenty four years old, but Parkes had learned that this would be his thirtieth year of competing in the sport. Prior to motor racing he had been a member of the French World Cup Ski Team. From eighteen until the age of twenty-three he had done fairly well, but never became a World Champion, nor did he manage to medal at the winter Olympic Games. A knee injury suffered just prior to his second Olympics had ended his dreams of ever becoming a true superstar in the sport.

Motor sports had only been of passing interest to LeMond as a younger man, but the chance to drive a car in a celebrity ice racing event in France started him on his way to a long career in sports car and touring car events that had taken him all over the world.

Still, while he had many race wins on his C.V., he had yet to score a championship in any of the categories he participated in. At this point in his life, time was running out on achieving that one last goal. It seemed likely that the opportunity with Mandel in the ISC might be his last chance to win anything of any real merit.

Perhaps this sense of urgency was the reason LeMond had worked so hard to make sure that the Cadillac race cars had been prepared as much as possible prior to their first race in Europe. This intense focus was visible, and it gave him a sense that all was being done to ensure that the team would have a real shot at success.

After over an hour of talking about the team, the car and their backgrounds, Parkes became curious as to why Griffin and the other crew members had not shown up.

He looked down at the chronograph on his wrist and decided that he would call the race shop to see if they were coming to meet them or not.

"Let me see if I can get a hold of someone and find out what's keeping them." he said as he looked for the shop number on his cell phone contact list.

Just as he found the number he was looking for, Griffin and one of the younger crewmen from the team walked in. The young man started toward the bar while the team manager came over to their table. "Sorry I'm late, but we have been busy diagnosing and fixing a problem with the sequential shifter. Anyway, we have more work to do so I can't stay. We are here just to pick up some Rueben sandwiches for the boys"

"Was it something that I did wrong?" inquired Parkes in a tentative tone.

"We aren't sure if it is a driver issue or simply a premature failure, but the car had lost second and third gear when we drove it back from the pits to the transporter. We need to get it resolved before we go to Germany, so we are looking at another late night at the shop." replied Griffin.

The Aussie stood up as the crewman returned from the bar with a pair of large bags filled with their evening repast.

"Before I go I should tell you that I spoke to Liz, and that she is doing pretty well given the circumstances. Oh, and lest I forget, she asked me to give you this, Brandon. Anyway, see you both in the morning" said Griffin as he handed him a white envelope. He then turned and with the crewman in tow headed for the door.

Quickly opening the packet he found that it contained a formal written offer from Liz Mandel as well as a legal contract to drive for Team Mandel in the upcoming International SuperSedan Challenge.

"Waitress, will you please bring us the best bottle of real Champagne that you have?" he shouted excitedly across the room, waiving the contract as he did so.

"Welcome aboard, my friend." LeMond said with a smile. "We can only have one of those bottles though; because we have to get to work testing the car you will be racing this season first thing tomorrow morning!"

Chapter Four

Dresden, Germany

An enthused Brandon Parkes was so happy about getting the opportunity to drive one of the Mandel Cadillacs that he had not complained to himself once about the sixteen hours it had taken to get to Dresden. He was just pleased that he was actually on the entry list for the race that was being held that weekend at the Eurospeedway Lausitz racing circuit. It had only been a couple of weeks since he had wondered if he would be racing at all this year.

Still, as he left the airport he was pleased that he was only about a half an hour away from his hotel. He was also glad that he was able to upgrade to a new Cadillac CTS for only a few Euros more than his per diem allowed. Equipped with a three point six liter V6 and an automatic transmission, the car had plenty of performance and decent handling. Given that they were racing Cadillacs he thought it only appropriate to be seen driving one, even if the Mandel team didn't have official backing from the beleaguered General Motors.

While making his way to his destination it suddenly occurred to him that this part of Germany had been under communist rule not all that long ago. The fact that he was driving an American car like this one in the former East Germany made him smile.

It was just after 9:45 in the morning when he spotted the inn where he and the team were staying. At this point he couldn't wait to check in and get into a bed. He had not been able to sleep on the second leg of his trip, from Chicago to Frankfurt, and was beginning to want to make up for it now.

"Guten morgen" said the pleasant middle aged woman behind the hotel front desk.

"Hello". You should have a room reserved for a Brandon Parkes." replied the American with a tired smile.

"We have you in room 121." the woman informed him in almost perfectly spoken English.

She then handed him his key and as he turned to go to his room he was surprised to see this attractive young strawberry blond haired woman standing behind him with a big smile on her face.

"Welcome, Herr Parkes."

"Good to see you" he replied.

He thought that it was Liz Mandel, but he wasn't completely sure. If it was, she looked even better than he had remembered. Certainly she appeared to be doing much better than he would have expected given all that had occurred since he first met her in Paris.

"We are just so happy that you were available to join us. Dad had suggested that we contact you to see if you might be interested. I guess he wanted an American on the team and he took a liking to you, so here you are." she explained.

A moment of silence followed. Parkes didn't really know what to say.

Race to Damascus

"I am really honored to be a part of this team, Miss Mandel" he told her in a somewhat reverent manner.

"Listen, you probably need to get some rest. I am having dinner at 7:00 and would like you to join me. I'll call you about an hour before that so you can get cleaned up and awake. Does that sound OK to you?" asked Liz.

"It sounds perfect. I'll talk to you later on then." replied Parkes.

"Rest well." She then turned and headed for the door to the parking lot.

"Wow, what a great young lady" he thought to himself while watching her walk out. She reminded him a little of a news anchor that one might see on Fox News; she was that attractive to him.

Liz stepped out the front door and got into the back seat of Mercedes S Class. A forty something man joined her in the back seat and the car drove off.

"It figures that she already has some wealthy guy. So much for us having a romantic dinner when we get together tonight" thought Parkes. He was a little jealous and slightly disappointed to think of her already being involved with someone else.

"Time to get some rest" he thought as he opened the door to his room. Inside was a beautiful king sized bed that beckoned to him with the promise of a few hours of much needed rest.

Before he knew it there was a loud knock on the door that woke him from a very deep sleep. It felt like he had just gotten into bed, but when he glanced at his watch he soon realized that it was already six thirty in the evening and that he had actually been out for some time.

Dressed only in his boxer shorts he threw on a pair of khaki pants and answered the door.

"Did I wake you up?" the young woman standing before him asked.

"No, I mean I was really just lying down on the bed; anyway, is it dinner time already?"

"Almost; I tried calling your cell number and your room phone, but didn't get an answer."

"I am sorry; I guess that I must have dozed off when you called".

"Yeah, I guess so. Well, I'll see you in the dining room as soon as you can get yourself dressed." said Liz Mandel in a tone that reminded Parkes that he was an employee and that he had better hurry up and get ready for dinner.

"I'll be there in a flash." he replied as he shut the door.

Dropping his pants and boxers, he was soon climbing into the shower and diving under the still cold water. As the water heated up he started washing his hair with the shampoo in the small bottle that the hotel had supplied.

As he rinsed the lather off his head, he thought about how he hated to be late and having to rush around like he was doing now.

After quickly brushing his teeth and combing back his newly trimmed short hair, he threw on a new pair of white boxer shorts and then the khaki pants he had just worn. Reaching for his wallet and watch on the dresser he quickly put them both into his pants pocket. He then grabbed a fresh black Team Mandel sport shirt from his luggage.

Still putting on the new shirt as he headed out the door; he quickly tucked it in to his pants while he walked down the hallway. Approaching the dining room he strapped on his Rolex, glancing at it he noticed that it was just six forty-seven, as he greeted the dining room hostess.

"Good evening, just one tonight?" asked the hostess in English.

"Actually, I am joining that young lady over in the corner" he said pointing to Liz Mandel's table.

Following the hostess through the cozy restaurant, Parkes saw that she was smiling; better yet, she was by herself. He took his seat across the table and smiled back at her.

"Wow, you were really quick" she exclaimed.

"That's why you hired me, right?" he replied as he placed his napkin on his lap.

She smiled, paused for a moment and then asked him to forgive her for acting like a demanding child when she went to his room and knocked on his door. She then went on to explain how she had been looking forward to meeting him and that she had moments when she became a little depressed about her father. As a result she felt that sometimes she was a bit more irritable and short with others.

"I guess that I was already feeling kind of sad about Dad not being with us at this first race when I arrived back here at the hotel" she explained. "Then I called you and there was no answer, I got a bit anxious and came to your room and started pounding on the door. When you answered I wasn't upset that you weren't ready, but mad because you had worried me. It was rude and I do ask you for your forgiveness."

"Actually I think it's really nice. Given the circumstances I certainly understand." replied Parkes in a sympathetic tone.

Her blue green eyes suddenly made contact with his and he thought that she now looked more like a pretty, but frightened, little girl instead of the difficult employer he had perceived her to be back at the door to his room.

"Besides, I was glad that you woke me up after I overslept."

Just then their waiter walked up and took their dinner order. Steaks, asparagus and a lovely bottle of red wine appeared at their table while they got to know more about one another.

He soon learned that Mandel SuperStores had already been in operation for many years when Liz joined the Mandel family as the second of two children. She clearly had never known anything but wealth and opportunity, but he thought she still had a down to earth quality about her. She shared with him that she had one brother six years older who had been something of a disappointment to their father.

Michael Mandel was intelligent and sensitive, but he had no interest in the family business. After having excelled in school he had gone on to join a Catholic order in Boston. Liz informed Parkes that this did however; please their Irish Catholic mother, whom the brother resembled both in looks and demeanor.

She went on to explain that her dad had no problems with his son choosing to be a Catholic Christian. Despite the fact that he himself was born and raised Jewish, he had no real faith anymore, except maybe in capitalism and simply did not care. What had bothered her father was that he would seemingly have no heir to take over the business. What he had not counted on was the fact that it would be his daughter who turned out to be most like him.

By age 12 she attended her first Indianapolis 500 and had absolutely loved everything about it. On summer breaks from high school she would go along with her father to both Indy car races and on trips to visit their family owned chain of stores. It was during this time she found she was just as driven for success as her father could be.

The question Liz had was whether she could ever be tough enough to run things. It was clear to Parkes that she felt that the short term success of the racing team under her guidance would be a big help in proving herself to the board members and gaining support within the family in order for them to vote her in as CEO some day.

"So, I have told you about myself. What about you, Brandon? What can you tell me about yourself that I don't already know about you?"

He looked down at his watch and saw that it was almost midnight.

"Listen, I think I had better get some more rest if I am to be my best tomorrow" he said with a smile. "Maybe we can pick up this conversation the next time we get together and I'll tell you everything you want to know, alright?"

"OK, I guess that you are probably right. Anyway, I think am going for a night cap in the bar" replied Liz.

"Sure. Thank you very much for a wonderful dinner and the great conversation. I will see you in the morning Miss Mandel."

He smiled and left the dining room. Stopping at the front desk to check for messages, he picked up a note from Griffin that told him to be at track registration at eight AM.

After putting the piece of paper in his pocket, he turned toward the direction of his room when he caught a glimpse of a silver Mercedes which pulled up and dropped someone off at the front door. It was the same S Class, and the same man he had seen meet Liz earlier in the day.

"I guess that's her night cap" thought Parkes cynically as he entered his hotel room. He really hoped that he was wrong. Liz Mandel was fascinating to him, but he was sure that he probably wasn't the only man to feel that way.

As he climbed into bed he thought of the fact that was getting paid good money to drive a five hundred and fifty horse power race car in the morning. He then reminded himself that he needed to email his Uncle Ron with an update right after he qualified tomorrow afternoon. The thought of his supportive uncle back in the states put him at ease and Parkes was soon fast asleep.

EuroSpeedway Lausitz

Like Indianapolis and Daytona, the EuroSpeedway Lausitz utilized parts of a long oval track combined with an infield road course to create a circuit used for sports car and touring car races. It was also similar to Daytona International Speedway in that it was a three cornered, or tri oval configuration. This layout suited Parkes and Team Mandel just fine, since their test sessions at Indianapolis had given them recent experience on the same style of track they would compete on here in Germany.

Having arrived early, he had a chance to get his credentials and then have a look around the facility. He thought it was a very modern, but somewhat sterile facility. The giant new age windmills near the circuit seemed to add to the industrial feeling of the place. The knowledge that Alex Zanardi, one of his favorite drivers, had lost both of his legs here on the oval course didn't improve the atmosphere for him, either.

His team was already set up in the garage area and Parkes soon found the crew applying sponsor decals to the Cadillac CTS-Vs. All three cars were now a shiny black with white Mandel SuperStores logos on the hood and sides. Associate sponsor logos filled the rest of the body work; most of these were the logos of companies who were suppliers of products found on the shelves of Mandels' stores.

One of the Team Mandel crewmen was applying a white decal strip across the top of the windscreen of the car he would drive this weekend. The car that LeMond would drive had a red one, while the backup car had been given a blue one. The different colors on the top portion of the windshields would help crew, race officials and fans alike with identifying the otherwise virtually identical racing cars. It would also serve as a sunshade, which was their original purpose.

American flag decals adorned all three of the black Cadillacs and it reminded him of a picture of the late Peter Revson and his black Shadow Formula One car; the very one that he had lost his life driving. Parkes couldn't help but feel a little proud at that moment that he was carrying on the tradition of an American driver competing in an American car on the international stage.

He began looking around for Griffin to tell him how impressed he was with the appearance of their cars but couldn't see him anywhere in the garage. With nothing else to do he decided to spend a few minutes checking out the competition.

Most of the racing teams were doing similar things to their cars as his team was doing right now. Waxing, wiping and other appearance enhancement tasks were taking place throughout the garage area.

Some of the other competitors were still doing work that probably should have been completed before they ever loaded the cars into a transporter; however The Scimitar Mercedes outfit was not one in this category. Scott Battle was in his pristine new driver's suit and standing in front of his AMG Mercedes C Class race car as Parkes walked by.

Battle put on a pair of wire rim sunglasses and then nodded at him. Parkes gave a quick wave back and kept on going. He had better things to do right now than to risk having Scott playing head games with him. Besides, he was still angry at his friend and the team that Battle was driving for.

Continuing his tour of the garage area he was very impressed at how professional and major league the cars, transporters and crews all looked.

Now he was becoming curious as to which of the many teams here might have factory backing, or at least technical advice and support. Every one of them could be getting help from the manufacturers for all he knew, despite the fact that this was supposedly a series for privateer entrants. The rules were meant to keep the costs of competing in the series to a minimum as well as preventing the ISC from being dominated by a single juggernaut team fielded by a car company who was simply willing to outspend everyone else to win.

One of the most noticeable outfits in the paddock was Total Control Racing and their well turned out BMW M3's. Parkes knew that Total Control Racing was a brand of radio controlled model cars produced by an Italian company that had decided that backing an Italian Touring Car Cup winner like Mario Barilla would be a great way of promoting their products.

As the TCR crewman rolled Barilla's silver M3 out of its garage stall and into the sunlight Parkes noticed the sparkle of the eighteen inch BBS made racing wheels and the red, white and green racing stripe that ran down the middle of the car.

Two more new BMW M3s sat in the TCR garage. One car was a reserve and the other would be driven by journeyman driver Hans Schneider, a former touring car champion in his own right who had clearly been hired as a number two on the team with the job of helping to make sure that young Barilla won the title.

As he made his way back to Team Mandel's garage he saw that the two British racing green Jaguars of the Conrad Investments Team were just being unloaded from their transporter. Wealthy gentleman driver, Conrad Templeton III had brought the funding which had allowed him and his hired gun, Simon Wilson, to race these cars. The program had been finalized only a week ago, so the team had been a last minute addition to the field and seemed to be behind everyone else in the field in terms of preparation.

Thankfully the Mandel operation seemed to be running on all eight cylinders, thought Parkes as he approached the team garage.

"First practice is in a few minutes lads" yelled Griffin to all who could hear him.

"Brandon, your new suit and helmet are in the transporter. Go get dressed" said Griffin with a sense of urgency.

"Roger, that" he replied.

He then walked into the transporter and opened the door to the small air conditioned driver's lounge. Henri was just getting his black driving suit on as Parkes walked in.

"Good morning" said LeMond. "How are you feeling?" asked the Frenchman as he opened up a bottle of his personal sponsor's spring water.

"I am great, my friend. Are you ready to go?"

"Almost; I think that I just need to hydrate a bit more before I go out on the track."

"Yeah, it is going to be pretty warm today, so that's a good idea." said Parkes as he looked for his new driver's suit.

"There is plenty of cold bottled water in the cooler in the pits and there's some more in the refrigerator."

The American didn't respond as he was focused on finding his gear.

Seeing his team mate in distress, LeMond reached into a closet that he was standing in front of and handed Parkes a black helmet bag and a brand new driver's suit that hung from a coat hanger.

"Also, there is a second driving suit for you in the closet." explained his team mate.

"Thanks, Henri. I'll see you in the pits." said Parkes. As LeMond stepped out the door of the transporter lounge he turned and gave Parkes a thumbs up and a wink.

"This is a great track, Brandon. I am sure that you will do fine"

"That guy has to be one of the best people that I ever have driven with" thought Parkes.

He couldn't help but be enthused as he went through the ritual of suiting up and was soon on his way to the pit area and the start of the morning practice session.

Standing at the pit wall Griffin was taking lap times with his stopwatch as Parkes strolled up, his new helmet in hand, to join him.

Team Mandel was busy executing last minute tasks on the two black Cadillacs while Henri LeMond paced between the two cars looking to see that all was in order.

An Audi RS5 was the first car that came around the final corner of the circuit. It quickly proceeded to accelerate down the straight in front of the pits and past the spot he was standing.

Familiar with their performances with the Audi R8 LMS, he knew that the GT Italia racing team had switched from Grand Touring class sports car racing to the ISC, but that they had decided to stay with the Audi brand.

The sound coming from the RS5 initially made Parkes think that it was a fairly similar exhaust note to that of his own Cadillac, but soon the song emitting from the four point two liter V8 motor reminded him more of a Formula One car as it reached maximum rpms and top speed at the end of the straight away.

A black AMG Mercedes, a white Lexus and one of the red Maserati Quattroportes went by next. The look of these cars and the wonderful noise that their V-8 engines made gave Parkes a giddy feeling as one after another they continued to fly by his perch, which was located midway down the pit wall.

With a nudge from behind him Griffin yelled in his ear to remind him that it was time to stop spectating and get in the car.

Once again Parkes was pleased that someone had the wisdom to make sure that ISC racers had real working front doors. There were roll cage bars running across the inside that you had to climb over to get into the racing seat, but it was not too difficult for those of average size or smaller.

At five foot and eleven inches, Parkes was about average height. For a human being, that is. Most racing drivers were on the small side, no matter what series they competed in or where they were from. In turn, the cockpits usually fit those of smaller proportions best.

After entering the car it was time to put on the HANS and his racing helmet that now sat on the floor by the shift lever.

The Head and Neck Safety device was now required equipment by all the major sanctioning bodies. This yoke-like apparatus was still not something Parkes liked wearing, but knew better than most that the HANS Device could keep a driver from breaking their neck and ending up paralyzed, or worse. Despite this knowledge he had felt slightly uncomfortable when he was wearing one. After several months away from being in a racing car the HANS was something that he would have to work to get used to having on.

As he tightened the chin strap on the Stand 21 touring car helmet he smiled as he knew it was Henri who had ordered this for him and was the one who had it painted silver with Parkes spelled in big black letters and a little American flag on each side.

Though it was a full face helmet, it didn't have a flip down face shield. Since they were driving enclosed cars this was not needed, nor wanted, as it would get very hot inside a closed car like the Cadillac. A new pair of Ray Ban Aviator sunglasses would protect his eyes.

Putting the racing belts over each of his shoulders and cinching them down, Parkes checked to make sure that he couldn't slide around in the seat. Despite the high bolsters on the seat it was still possible to slide around in a race car if one wasn't belted in properly.

The red Nomex flame proof gloves were next, followed by plugging his helmet connection into the radio.

"OK, I am ready to go." he announced as he keyed the microphone with the button on the steering wheel for all his crewmen wearing headsets to hear.

One of the young men on the team opened the driver side door and double checked the belts. After doing so, he patted him on his shoulder, wished him luck and was gone just as quickly as he appeared.

Pushing the starter button Parkes smiled as he listened to the supercharged V8 start up. He blipped the throttle a few times as he waited for the temperature of the engine fluids to come up to operating level.

His team mate's identical car sat in front of him in the pit lane. He had decided to let Henri go first and that he would follow him out and try to pick up the proper racing line on this track, since it was one that he had never seen before.

The radio crackled in his helmet as Griffin keyed his mike. "It's show time".

Then the two black Cadillac race cars proceeded down the pit lane, nose to tail, and soon joined the other cars on the circuit for their Lausitzring debut.

Near the end of his second of two warm up laps Henri had clearly pushed down hard on the gas pedal on the number eleven car and started down the pit straight away on his first tour of the track at speed.

Following LeMond's lead he accelerated quickly down the main straight away and found that he could keep right behind him through the left hand turn and then through the right turn that followed. It was almost a lap before the French driver began to use his previous experience at the circuit to gain a substantial lead over him.

The car was already feeling good to Parkes, but he needed to learn his way around before he could provide his team mate any sort of real challenge. He took some consolation in the fact that none of the other cars on the track were even catching up to him, much less passing him. Each lap got easier as he began to figure out the track and his lap times seemed to reflect that as his times dropped a little with every lap of the circuit that he made.

He had even managed to catch up to one of the fast Audis towards the end of the practice period and it had greatly helped his confidence to have done so.

The session had only about five minutes to go when Griffin called both Mandel team cars into the pits. Parkes complied with the order first, then LeMond came in as well.

As they climbed out of their new Cadillac race cars, both Mandel drivers were greeted by their team manager, who had a very large smile on his face. "Good job, you two. Let's go back to the transporter and talk about it"

Beaming as they stepped into the air conditioned refuge; Griffin seemed more enthused than usual. "You guys were first and tenth in practice, which is bloody fantastic! Now, you guys sit down and tell me what we need to do to make the cars even better."

Parkes looked over at his team mate for his response. LeMond then turned to Griffin and told him that the car seemed close to perfect to him.

"Yeah, I agree with Henri. I just need to get more track time" added Parkes.

After only few more minutes of debriefing the team manager's curiosity seemed satisfied.

"Alright, get yourselves a cold drink and stay hydrated. Also, be sure to eat all your pasta at lunch time lads. You'll be glad for it later on. Anyway, plan to be back here at a quarter after one for the second practice session." Griffin ordered.

"OK boss." said Parkes as he closed the door behind him.

"I want you to know that you did a good job out there, Brandon"

He turned to respond to his team mate just as the Frenchman was reaching into his pocket for a Gitanes. "You were the one with the best lap. In fact, maybe you could tell me about your braking point as you go into turn one. How late are you waiting to brake when you are on a qualifying run and have a clear track?"

"Keep up with me in the next practice and you will have a chance to find out for yourself" replied LeMond with a mischievous grin.

EuroSpeedway 2:50 PM

Arriving at the track some twenty minutes after race qualifying had started had left Liz feeling anxious.

The driver of her silver Mercedes dropped her off just outside the pit and then drove away. She showed her pass to the man watching the gate to the pit area and proceeded to make her way to the spot where Team Mandel was located.

Silvio Marino spotted Liz and flagged her down before she had even advanced a few feet.

"Miss Mandel, how are you doing?" asked Marino.

"I'm OK, but I am late for qualifying." she responded.

"Your cars have been running well. Number eleven was fastest in both practice sessions and the number twelve ended up eighth quick at the end of the second session."

"Thanks, I'll see you later then" she replied.

Liz didn't know if she trusted Marino. After all, he was the one who had dropped her father off at the airport the day his plane disappeared. Maybe she was being paranoid, but she wasn't sure of just whom to trust right now, with the exception perhaps of the men who made up the Mandel racing team. With them she felt safe and at home.

As she climbed up and seated herself next to Griffin on the scoring stand she saw that her drivers were currently second and sixth in qualifying. She put on a head set and asked how much time was left before the session ended. "We have a little over twenty minutes remaining" said Griffin.

Scott Battle had set the fast time in his AMG Mercedes and had then parked his car in the pits. Henri LeMond was still on the track trying to put in a faster lap than Battle and claim the pole position for himself.

Unlike a NASCAR oval track race, or the Indy 500, the ISC didn't have cars go out one at a time to qualify for the race. Instead, the organizers decided that an open qualifying session that allowed drivers to go out and make a faster run would be more exciting for the fans. The only negative was that with all the cars on the track at once it sometimes made it difficult for a driver to improve on his time.

It was clear that LeMond was going as hard as he could, but was being balked by a slightly slower car. The fact that it was the white Scimitar Mercedes of Bin Salman was not a surprise. The Arab was sacrificing his opportunity to set a faster time just to make sure that his team mate kept the pole.

LeMond keyed his mike and told Griffin that he couldn't get a clear lap and that his tires were now getting worn. He then asked if he could pit for new tires and try to set the fast lap.

"Yeah, bring it in, Henri." radioed Griffin in a frustrated tone.

Despite wanting to ask why Brandon's qualifying was not going better, as he was starting back in the order, Liz decided that it was best not to. She had learned from her father that you had to trust the people you hired. It might sound like she was being critical if she questioned what was happening. Besides, with Henri currently in second place, the team was doing well.

Bringing his car to a halt in his designated pit stall LeMond's crew went to work changing tires and cleaning the front windshield. As the service to the Cadillac was taking place he slipped one position as Bin Salman moved up from fifth place to the second spot on the grid.

"You are now in P3, Henri, the Scimitar boys have the front row to themselves" reported Griffin over the radio.

The French pilot responded by putting the car in gear and laying down some brand new Dunlop rubber on the pitlane. There were now only a few minutes left to improve his starting position for the race.

As LeMond left the pits, Parkes' Cadillac entered them and came to a stop in his pit box. He was now down in fourteenth position and had resigned himself to the fact that it wasn't going to get any better, so he parked the car and turned off the engine.

She wanted to go over and console Parkes, but Liz's attention soon reverted back to the track as her remaining driver attacked the circuit with the vigor of a man less than half his age.

With a nearly clear track and no Bin Salman and his Mercedes to hinder him, LeMond thundered down the main straight and into Euro Speedway's turn one.

He was just two tenths of a second behind Scott Battle and less than a tenth behind Bin Salman's best time. He knew where to find the tenths he needed, but it would require more than skill. He would need the courage to go flat out and a bit of good fortune as well.

Bouncing off the low curbing in every corner and braking as late as he dared after every straight away, LeMond was now in a zone and chipping away hundredths of a second at every turn.

When he crossed the start-finish line he was told on his radio that he was still in the third position, but that he only needed to pick up twenty-five one hundredths of a second to move back into the front row of the grid.

The black Cadillac seemed to respond to his every urging. The big eight cylinder under the hood provided massive torque that launched him forward coming off every corner. He kept his foot on the gas and as he entered the final turn he just hoped the car would stick and not under steer up into the outside wall.

As though he was in a state of slow motion, LeMond saw that big white wall getting closer and winced as he hit it with the side of the car. He kept his foot planted on the pedal anyway, despite his natural inclination to lift off the gas.

When he opened his eyes he realized that he had merely glanced off the wall and in fact had hardly lost any momentum. Speeding across the finish line and soon heard static in his headset as Griffin keyed his microphone. "Great job mate "

"Sorry about hitting the wall, did we get second place back?"

There was silence. Then a woman's voice came over the radio. "Henri, you are on pole, by almost two-tenths of a second." exclaimed Liz.

Then there was another pause.

"Thanks Liz, but the crew should get just as much credit for this."

"You are so right, Henri. After you return here to the pits be sure you that tell them that yourself."

"Yes, I will be sure to do that. I'll see you all back there in a minute or so."

Saturday afternoon- 4:05PM

A slightly sullen Brandon Parkes had already taken a brief shower and gotten dressed before Henri LeMond had even finished being interviewed by the media about his dramatic run to the pole position for tomorrow's race.

His own fourteenth qualifying spot wasn't all that bad, but the team's other entry had really shown everyone what the Mandel Cadillac's were capable of.

Driving his rental car away from the track, he felt a sudden pang of guilt as he realized that he had not even taken the time to congratulate LeMond on his excellent performance in qualifying. Instead of being happy for his team mate he had been focused on his own somewhat disappointing results.

"I'll be sure to tell him in the morning" he thought to himself.

Approaching the hotel he saw that same Mercedes closing on him in his rearview mirror. When Parkes turned into the hotel parking lot, the silver sedan did the same and followed him to a parking spot next to his own.

As he exited his car, he saw Liz get out of the back seat of the Mercedes. Hey mister, aren't you a famous racing driver?" she asked him with a friendly smile.

"Not today. That honor goes to my team mate who just took pole position over at the track this afternoon." replied Parkes in a stoic tone.

It was at that moment that it occurred to him that Henri's setting the fast time today was the first good news that Liz had received in weeks. It wasn't right to take away her moment of joy by acting down-trodden and feeling sorry for himself.

"Anyway, you should be pretty happy about the team taking the pole." said Parkes with a meek smile.

"Yes, it was a big lift to see Henri go out again and manage to go that quickly. You also should know that neither Griffin nor myself are as disappointed with your performance as you seem to be."

"Thanks. I appreciate you saying that."

By the way, you also need to know that Griffin is making some set up changes to your car tonight that will hopefully help you in the race tomorrow." she explained .

"Good, I hope they are the same things they tried on Henri's car." he replied.

"Listen, I have to go meet someone for dinner. You go and get yourself something to eat and then get some good rest. I'll see you in the morning, OK?" said Liz as she got back into her car.

Brandon waved as the Mercedes drove off. She was no doubt headed to see her friend that had accompanied her last night he thought glumly.

He then turned toward the front door of the inn and looked forward to a quiet night of solitude. Depressed, he hoped that he would feel better by the time of the race and that his performance would be more to his own standards.

Euro Speedway Lausitz – Sunday afternoon

Excited fans started to cheer as the crewmen of the various teams began to roll the colorful collection of cars onto the grid for the start of the first round of the International SuperSedan Challenge.

The warm sunshine felt good to Brandon Parkes as he looked up at the rapidly filling grandstands along the main straight of the track. Being the first event it was nice to see the very promising turn out.

Having taken Liz's advice about eating and getting some rest, he was feeling rather more positive today. Part of his optimism came from the gearing and suspension changes that Griffin had made, as had been promised the night before.

His race car felt quicker and quite a bit more stable in the morning warm-up. Despite starting back in fourteenth place he was hopeful about the race itself.

As he walked up to his car, he noticed a white decal with his last name in block letters on the rear door windows; and an American flag was next to his name. There was another identical decal at the top of the front windscreen.

He gazed at his car with pride. Then Parkes suddenly remembered that he needed to contact his Uncle Ron back in the States. With twenty minutes until the start he had just enough time to run back to the transporter and make a quick call on his new international cell phone.

When he arrived at the Mandel transporter he saw Henri heading toward the pit.

"Good luck, Henri. I'll see you out on the track" said Parkes as he galloped by him.

"Bon chance" replied the Frenchman with a slightly quizzical look on his face.

Finding his phone in the helmet bag he called his uncle's number. There was no answer, so he left a quick message and dashed back to the starting grid.

As he ran back it toward the track it occurred to him that it was probably only about five AM in Branson, Missouri and that Uncle Ron was probably still sound asleep. Even if he could only leave a message, he was glad he had taken the time to do it.

The German national anthem was starting to play on the public address system as Parkes neared his car. He decided to show respect and wait until it was finished to slide behind the wheel. He had always liked to hear the German anthem and as he listened he began to soak in the atmosphere of the moment. Bright sunshine, a good crowd, and a colorful grid of fantastic cars made him feel lucky to be there.

As the music ended he opened the door of the Cadillac and settled into the cockpit. It was then that he suddenly realized that he had not seen Liz Mandel yet today. "Was she watching this on TV with her boyfriend?" he wondered to himself as he put on his helmet and Nomex gloves.

All thought about anything else except the task at hand went away as he heard Griffin tell him over the radio that the order to fire up the engines was coming in one minute.

He looked over at the BMW M3 to his left and then at the red Maserati Quattroporte behind him in his rearview mirror. The car directly in front was another M3, the number seven driven by Mario Barilla. As Parkes weighed the opposition he decided he would stay right on Barilla's tail at the start. "He won't be any more content to stay back than I am" he told himself.

The warm-up lap saw one of the Jaguars pull into the pits as the field came around to take their positions on the grid. It was the number eighteen car of Conrad Templeton and it was smoking badly.

All of the remaining twenty-three starters had come to stop on the main straight and waited to view the first of three red lights to glow up on the starter's stand. Then the second red light came on. The drivers began to blip the throttles of their cars as they waited for the final red light. Once this happened it would be just a split second until a green light would signal the start of the race.

The moment he saw the green light Parkes pushed his right foot down and the gas pedal to the floor while concurrently lifting his left foot off the brake. He had just made the best standing start of his career and had gained two positions as the cars funneled into the track's left hand turn one.

Things had not gone as well at the start for LeMond in the other Mandel Cadillac.

Not only had Scott Battle's Mercedes jumped ahead of him and into the lead, but a BMW had bumped his car from behind. Both LeMond and the M3 driver spun off the track and into the dirt and grass of the infield.

Cruising by the pair of stalled cars meant that he was up to tenth and right on the bumper of Barilla's BMW.

The cars began to sort themselves out into a single file formation by the end of the first lap, but there were still many attempts being made by drivers to get past one another at each opportunity.

Barilla out braked an Audi into a corner on lap two and Parkes was able to get by as well.

Now only one place away from a points paying position he was beginning to feel like he was one with the car.

The torque of his car was allowing him to stay with Barilla off the corners, but the Italian driver seemed to be able to carry more speed entering the corner.

As soon as his Cadillac would catch up on the straight, the BMW would go even deeper before braking for a turn, negating the gain his car had just made.

Still, even though he couldn't quite get past Barilla's car, Parkes had made it up into sixth place by the one-third mark in the race by simply staying behind the quick Italian.

It was almost like having someone lead block for you on a football field, he thought.

The two cars had caught up to the lead pack, but couldn't get past them. Battle continued in the lead, followed by Heinz Bartels' BMW, the Audi of Johan Springer, Scott Chin's Mercedes and the Maserati driven by Max Sigala.

Suddenly the first three cars in the race peeled into the pit. Sigala became the leader of the race, with the Barilla BMW second. Parkes was now in third place with the Cadillac and was feeling pretty good about his prospects.

Keying the radio button, he asked. "Griffin, are we still looking at making our stop past half distance?"

There was no response. He pushed the mike button again and repeated his question.

"Hold on mate, we are running the numbers to figure how long we can keep you out there" replied Griffin.

"Yeah, we can go until roughly the one hour mark on the gas you have. The question is can the tires last that long?"

"The tires are good." replied Parkes. "But two-thirds of the way might be a little too much to ask, so I'll let you know if they start to go away."

"Right… Just keep up the good work"

Then he heard another voice in his ear. "You are doing great. Just let us know when you want to come in."

He was pretty sure that it was Liz that had just talking to him, but due to some static he wasn't positive.

"Thank you," he said with a tentative tone in his voice.

His Cadillac was just entering the next to last corner on the circuit and he had come in way too fast. In fact he almost collected Barilla's rear bumper. He quickly braked hard and as he finished gathering it all up he decided he needed to focus on the track instead of talking on the radio.

Barilla had begun challenging Sigala in the Maserati and had nearly gotten by him a couple of times. Sigala had shut the door on Barilla's BMW twice, but the third attempt was the charm.

Now the M3 was in first place. Within two more laps the Italian BMW driver was pulling away from his countryman's second place Maserati by half a second each lap.

Able to stay right behind the red Quattroporte, Parkes felt his tires were losing more grip each lap and knew that Barilla was building up a lead over both cars. He soon decided that it was about time to get new tires and enough gas to finish the race.

"I think that I am coming in at the end of this lap."

"OK, mate. We are ready for you." responded Griffin.

As he entered the pit lane he saw that Barilla's M3 was already coasting to a stop at his pit box. Sigala stayed out on the track and his Maserati now led with a little more than thirty minutes left in the ninety minute contest.

His crewmen leaped over the pit wall the moment that Parkes brought the Cadillac to a stop. One man plugged in the hose for the under car air jacks which allowed other crewmen to remove the wheels and tires and replace them with brand new ones. As soon as the tires were on, the same man who had inserted the air jack hose removed it while another crewman added fuel. He put the car into first gear and headed down the pit lane as soon as Griffin had yelled for him to go.

The crew had managed to get him out of the pit in only twelve and a half seconds.

As he rejoined the race he was now in tenth position, right behind the Jaguar of Simon Wilson. Parkes looked in his mirror and saw that his team mate's Cadillac was just behind him in eleventh place.

After taking about a lap to get the tires up to temperature he decided to make a run on Wilson and got by him on the straight that lead up to turn six. He began to pull away, but saw that his team-mate, LeMond, had not gotten past the Jaguar.

A crewman came on the radio to tell him that one car that had been in front of him had just pitted. Parkes would be in eighth after he passed the start finish line.

Just as he dove once again into the first turn he heard Griffin shout in his earphones "Shunt in turn three… wreck in three".

An Audi and one of the Lexus IS-F's had come together exiting turn three and the resulting carnage had been strewn across the track. The Audi was off the track resting against a barrier while the Lexus was sitting sideways and completely blocking traffic. He could tell from the damage that both cars were out of the race.

Just managing to get slowed down before he became part of the accident, Parkes was now carefully weaving around the shards of carbon fiber body work and other debris that covered the track. He then drove his car on the grass very slowly and around the damaged Lexus.

Race to Damascus

Then the officials threw a full course caution and the corner workers were all waving their bright yellow flags to alert the drivers not go back to racing speed once they had cleared the spot where the trouble had occurred.

Clear of the accident scene he took the time to thank Griffin for the heads up that probably saved his race -and perhaps his life. He was now in sixth position, but wondered about the condition of his tires after driving through the wreckage.

"My only question is if I should come in now for new tires. We might have a slow leak after driving through that garbage. Anyway, what do you think?" asked Parkes as he keyed the radio.

"Let's just see how long this caution period lasts."

Two more laps passed under the full course caution. The signal came for one more lap under yellow lap from the flag stand.

"Brandon, it's just one lap to restart. Where are you on the track right now?"

"I am going through turn eight as we speak." he replied.

'You need to come in at the end of the current lap, I repeat you must come to the pits on this lap if you want those new tires." Griffin keyed the mike again. "I suggest that you stay out there and roll the dice."

Given the short time remaining in the race, Parkes couldn't argue with his team manager's advice.

"We are in the points right now, if I stop we don't have enough time to get back to the front if I come in" said Parkes with a slightly anxious tone in his voice.

"That's my thinking, mate" replied Griffin. "OK, next time around you'll get the green and will only have a few more laps to go"

The remaining cars in the race followed the Mercedes pace car in a single file formation as the field completed the final lap under caution. As they approached the pit entry the silver and black Mercedes E63 pace car dove into the pits, as the field drove into the final turn before the start finish line.

Battle's white Mercedes was out in front as it made its way through the curve onto the main straight. Directly in front of Parkes was the Audi of Hans Springer. In his rear view mirror he saw that Wilson, in the green Jaguar, occupied the position right behind him. LeMond was currently in eighth, which would gain the team a championship point, providing that LeMond could keep the position until the finish.

Hoping to not just keep his current position in the points, Parkes would do everything possible to get one of the three places on the podium.

As his Cadillac headed down the straight his radio crackled with static "Go,Go,Go!" exclaimed Griffin.

The Audi in front of him had gone very wide as it under steered going into the first corner and Parkes stuck his car underneath his rival and gained a position at the start. Just two more spots he thought.

Driving like he thought himself invincible, he came off the circuit's last corner and used the super charged Cadillac's torque to his advantage once again. This time the big V8 allowed him to catch up with the black AMG Mercedes that was in fourth place. Two laps later he won a side by side drag race down the back straight to claim the fourth position. There were now only a few laps to go as he set his sights on the BMW of Mario Barilla. The Italian's car was more than three car lengths ahead as they thundered down the main straight and into turn one.

The Cadillac closed the margin on the BMW through turns five and six. Parkes downshifted and braked for turn seven and suddenly realized that he was right on Barilla's rear bumper.

As he up shifted into third gear and applied the gas the engine suddenly began to sound like it was running at higher revs. Soon the engine was screaming for mercy as the tachometer needle bounced off the rev limiter, yet the car was slowing down.

Moving the shifter up into fourth and then fifth gear Parkes finally found that only sixth gear worked. He pulled off to the side of the track as the cars that had been behind went past him.

The problem was apparent; it was the sequential gear box. Since he now only had second and sixth gear his day was over early.

"I am sorry…. but we are out of the race" he told his crew by radio.

There was a moment of silence.

"Was it a cut tire that went down?" Griffin asked.

"No, it seems that it was the gear box. I can get it to engage in second and sixth, but we have no third, fourth or fifth gear."

There was a long pause before Parkes spoke again.

"Anyway…, I guess I'll see you back there in a little while." he then unplugged the radio jack and took off his helmet, the HANS Device.

He would have to wait until the race was concluded before he could be towed back to the pits. Trying to drive back with only sixth gear would make his car into a rolling chicane, so he decided to get as comfortable as he could and wait for the tow truck. Perhaps it was for the best as he knew that he needed some time to blow off some steam. He was absolutely livid to have worked so hard and then have nothing to show for his efforts.

Viewing the last laps of the race from his stricken car Parkes cringed as he saw Battle and the Scimitar Mercedes team take the win. Making it even worse was the fact that Stephen Altenburg's Audi had spun out of second place on the last lap which meant that Barilla ended up in second with Scott Chin and his Black Tiger Mercedes moving up to third. If only his gear box hadn't broken he would have been on the podium for sure he thought.

The wrecker arrived to tow the black Cadillac just as Scott Battle was doing his victory lap of the track.

When the tow back to pit lane finally ended, he climbed out of the car and was greeted by Liz. She had brought him a Team Mandel cap to put on and told him he had run a good race.

"Yes, but we should have placed and been up on the podium" replied Parkes.

"Right now I really don't care at all about that." She paused for a moment and then continued. "All I know is that I just learned that my Dad's plane has been found."

He saw that she was smiling, but teary eyed.

Speechless, Parkes did the only thing that came to him. He reached out his arms and wrapped them around Liz, while she did the same.

Chapter Five

Paris, France-Monday morning

Bright rays of late morning sunshine were coming through the window of the hotel room that Brandon Parkes had checked into the previous night and they were now waking him up.

His watch told him it was almost eleven AM, but he was still having trouble getting out of the comfortable bed. Two days had passed since the race in Germany, but he still felt bruised, tired and a bit down after the disappointment of dropping out and gaining no championship points in the first event.

If it weren't for the post-race team meeting at the shop later that day, he might well have not bothered to do any more today other than order something from room service and watch television. "OK, it is time to get up. " Climbing into the shower, he let the warm water beat on the back of his legs; it felt so good that he stood there for nearly half an hour before getting out. As he dried himself off with one of the giant white towels he laughed to himself as it occurred to him that he could now tell people that he has slept in THE Paris Hilton.

After dressing he grabbed an orange juice from the mini bar, and sat down on the edge of the bed. He turned the television on and began to search the channels to see what the cable news people were saying about Mr. Mandel's Gulfstream now that they were aware that it had been located Saturday night.

As he waited for any new information concerning Mr. Mandel, he picked up his cell to call the shop and make sure the meeting was still on for that afternoon. However, before he could even find the number to the shop, his room phone began to ring.

He muted the television and answered "This is Parkes."

"Hello, this is Liz. Can you come up to my room for a few minutes? There is someone here that I want you meet"

"Sure, but I can't stay long because Griffin has a team meeting planned for two thirty."

"I know that. We will be finished in time to get to the shop for the meeting"

"OK, I'll see you up there in a just a little while then." He then wondered why she wanted him to come to see her in her hotel room, but decided he wouldn't worry about it as he would find out soon enough.

As he hung up the phone he saw a woman reporter on the television standing in front of a private jet. He turned up the volume on the controller and listened to the report.

"Mr. Mandel and the two pilots are said to be alive but the group responsible for the hijacking is demanding ten million dollars and the release of Palestinian prisoners jailed in Israel if the Americans are to be returned alive. There apparently has been no reply yet from either Mandel's family, or from the Israeli government to the hijackers' demands. This is Jill Kelly reporting from just outside Damascus, Syria."

He had mixed emotions about what he had just heard. While he was happy that Liz's father had not crashed into the ocean and perished, just as quickly he realized that it didn't necessarily mean that they would get Mr. Mandel back alive. .

As he turned off the television and headed to meet with Liz, he wondered what her reaction would be to what he just seen on the news.

When he arrived at her room he was surprised to see the man who had been with her in Germany answer the door.

"You must be Brandon, I am Levi Bernstein. Please come in and join us"

"Great, I finally get to meet Liz's boyfriend" he thought as he entered the room.

"Liz will be with us soon. Can I get you a coffee or perhaps something else?"

"No thank you, I'll just wait here on the couch."

Bernstein took a seat in the chair next to him.

Parkes looked around the suite and figured it was about two or maybe even three times the size of his own room. Bernstein must have read his mind, since he commented, "Nice, isn't it? It is always so much nicer to go first class, if one can readily afford it"

"Indeed it is" he replied with a slightly dour look on his face.

A few minutes later, Liz walked in and apologized for being detained on the telephone. She explained that she been giving Griffin an update about her father and letting him know that she would be also coming to the meeting at the shop.

"The reason I asked you here before we headed to the meeting was so that you could meet Mr. Bernstein and let him fill you in on the details of all that we know so far concerning Dad."

"I happened to just see on television that the plane has been found and that the terrorists have made a ransom demand." Do you know anything more than the press is reporting? asked Parkes.

Liz looked over at Bernstein and suggested that the Israeli address that and bring him up to date.

"Of course I will. But before I do that, I have a few questions for Brandon, if that is OK?"

Sitting down on the couch next to him, Liz explained that it was alright for him to speak because Bernstein was a Mossad agent who was investigating the case.

"So am I now a suspect in all of this?" asked Parkes in a defensive tone.

Before Bernstein could even respond, Liz stopped him with her outstretched hand. She turned her head back to look at Parkes. "They are just talking to everyone who was connected to Dad and hoping that it might lead to some further clues that would help them find him"

"Brandon, what I really need to know is, what is your impression of Scott Battle's girlfriend, Michele?" asked Bernstein as he started the questioning.

"Look, I really can't tell you that much. We watched the Monaco Grand Prix together and I haven't seen her since."

"Did you know that she is from Algeria…or the fact that we believe that she may be something of a Muslim radical?

Race to Damascus

"No, I guess I didn't know that. What do you think this has to do with Mr. Mandel's kidnapping?"

"Well, we believe that the kidnappers are actually Algerians or perhaps from Morocco. It seems to us that their goals are likely more financial than political. Despite their asking that the Palestinians in our prisons be released, we believe that money is all these people are really after. That of course is good news if it's true, as there is no way that Israel will let a single prisoner go, no matter how much Mr. Mandel has helped our country in the past." explained Bernstein.

"I still don't see why you might think that Michele is part of this. There are many decent Algerians who are living in France and other countries in Europe." said Parkes.

"Brandon, I know that you and Battle have been longtime friends, but the fact is that he owes several million dollars in back taxes to the IRS." He isn't broke, but combined with being dropped by his team in Formula One he has a financial motive to have done it."

"We want you to help us find out if there is anything to our theory, Brandon. So what do you say, will you?" pleaded Liz.

He sighed. "You should know that Scott and I are not exactly on cordial terms right now, and besides, despite all that, I can't believe that either he or Michele have anything to do with this."

"Well, all we are asking is for you to find out where Michele is so that we can speak to her. You should also know that she has been away from Monaco since the day after the Grand Prix and if Battle can produce her we might be able clear all this up…or, if we are correct in our assumptions we might find out where Mr. Mandel is being held."

"I'll do what I can" he replied with a frown. "Fine then, we will be in touch, Brandon" said Bernstein, as he said good bye and left the room.

"Maybe we should go get some lunch before we head to the shop" suggested Liz.

"Sure, that would be nice."

As the two headed for the hotel lobby, he found himself in something of a stupor.

Was it conceivable that Scott Battle could have changed so much that he might actually be involved with kidnapping Dan Mandel? He told himself that it couldn't possibly be true and decided he would do as this Bernstein guy asked; if for no other reason than to prove his friend's innocence.

Chicago, Illinois-Monday 10:30AM

Leaning back in the black leather chair that his brother Dan normally occupied, Harry Mandel took a drink from that morning's first cup of coffee. He was in a reflective mood wondering about how things might turn out in the weeks to come. Would they be able get his brother back? Even if they paid the ransom, he had begun to wonder if he would ever see Dan or their pilots again.

He then started asking himself if the board would vote him in as the CEO of Mandel SuperStores or might they decide that his niece should take over for her father in the event he not return home alive?

The dream of taking the company public for had lingered in his mind for some time. Not only would Harry's portion of ownership then become liquid with millions in shares that he

Race to Damascus

could sell on the open market if they went public, but the finances needed to expand from a regional to a national retailer would allow the growth of the company that he had envisioned. The idea still had great appeal to him and it might even be realized should his brother not return.

Because Dan Mandel liked being in control, he had kept the company privately held so that he could pursue projects like his racing team. The expansion into the European market with a handful of stores was only done to justify their involvement in the racing series over there.

The concept of finally taking charge was pleasing to Harry, but he also knew that he had to get his brother back. Despite their disagreements, Dan was still his brother and he did ultimately still care about him and his well being.

"But for us having to set up that stupid race team and those stores in Europe, none of this would have ever happened" he thought.

His daydreaming was rudely interrupted by the ringing of the office telephone. "Mr. Mandel, there is a call for you from a Mr. Andre on line two" announced his female assistant, Holly, on the intercom. Mandel picked up the phone. "Hello, this is Harry Mandel" He listened to the voice on the other end and began to grimace before he responded to the caller.

"Look, you know that you will get your money very soon, Andre. Just understand that I want this to be over just as much as you do." said Mandel. He then slammed the phone down and stormed out of the office and asked his assistant to get Liz on the line. As he looked at his watch he saw that it would be almost four in the afternoon in Paris. "Try her on her cell phone first."

A few seconds later his assistant buzzed his office again. "It's busy Mr. Mandel, should I try again and leave a message if she still doesn't answer?" "Just call her back again in a few minutes, Holly. If you don't get her, try contacting her at the hotel, OK?

"Yes, Mr. Mandel. I'll let you know as soon as I reach her" she replied.

Team Mandel European Shop; near Paris-Monday afternoon

Despite being anxious to wrap up the Mandel team meeting and let his crewmen have what was left of the day to themselves, Griffin decided to let Liz explain to all who were gathered what the status of her father was. She had been talking for a little over an hour now and he could tell by looking at his boys that they needed to go to the motel and rest up.

The crew had spent the last day diagnosing the shifter problems that had plagued the team in Germany and he felt they had found the culprit.

The data that Griffin had downloaded from the car told him that both drivers had been keeping their foot on the gas pedal when they shifted to a higher gear. He also knew that LeMond had been using the clutch and blipping the throttle on downshifts, just as one would do if racing a car with a conventional manual gearbox.

However, Parkes had banged down through the gears without using the clutch. It appeared that the result was a gearbox failure on the number 12 car.

The fact that his car had broken during the race in Germany was partially his own fault. Obviously he hadn't made it clear to Parkes that he should use the clutch pedal on downshifts instead of just shifting down the gears without pushing in the clutch pedal and left foot braking like you would in a Formula One car.

Race to Damascus

His driver may have been driving the car hard, but the veteran crew chief and team leader now realized the sequential gearboxes they had installed in these big V8 Cadillac's simply were not yet up to their task.

As he waited for Liz to finish her speech to the crew, Griffin decided to just keep the drivers there for the discussion about gearboxes and let his eleven crewmen go ahead and leave early. Besides, he realized that he had already covered everything that concerned the lads in the first few minutes of the meeting.

Liz's cell phone rang just as she was wrapping up her talk and she took it out of her pocket and answered. Then she paused and announced that she needed to take the call. She thanked them all for listening and headed for one of the adjacent private offices and shut the door behind her.

"I am sure that we are all glad to hear the promising news concerning Mr. Mandel" said Griffin as he stood up from his chair.

"Now lads, I want you to know that I appreciate all your hard work. You are all ordered to go back to the motel for some R&R. And don't any of you come back here until Thursday. Got it? "

The weary crewmen let out a brief cheer and began to disperse.

"Brandon and Henri, I need you two to stay for a couple of minutes more" he announced over the noise of the scraping chairs and banter of the crewmembers.

"I'll be brief" said Griffin as the two drivers took a seat. The problem we had with the number twelve car at Lausitzring was due my failure to advise you to use the clutch on downshifts" replied Griffin.

It was at that moment that Parkes remembered when Henri had suggested this method, but he had not followed that advice since the first lap he drove in testing back in Indy. "So what about up shifts, do you want us to lift for them as well?" he asked.

"Henri's car had no problems, so we can assume that it is just a case where we can't have you slamming down through the gears coming into a corner. We don't want a repeat of what happened in Germany so we'll have to be a bit more gentle until we get it sorted."

"Is that all you have for us?" asked Henri.

"Yes it is, but do be sure to remember that we are testing at Magny Cours on Friday" he said with a smile. "Now both of you get out of here and leave me to my work."

As he left the office Parkes saw that Liz was waiting for him.

"We need to get back into town, Brandon. That was my uncle on the phone and he says I should to go to our bank and make arrangements to withdraw the funds to make the ransom payment."

"I understand. Let's get going then."

The couple walked out to the waiting car and its taciturn driver.

"I suppose he is Mossad, too?"

"Of course, a girl can't be too careful these days" She was straight faced and serious as she said it.

Parkes opened the driver's side back door for Liz and then went around to the other side of the car and joined her in the back seat for the trip back to Paris.

Sinking into the leather seat in the rear of the Mercedes S class, Parkes decided that he actually liked being driven around in luxury.

As the car sped back to Paris he just sat back and relaxed while Liz called the bank and made an appointment to see the manager.

As she ended her phone call she informed him that their meeting with the bank manager was on for four-thirty.

"Once we are done at the bank we need to call Bernstein to find out what to do next." she added. "Are we going to pick up the cash?" he asked.

"No, we are actually just making sure that the funds have been transferred and that the bank will have enough money to cover the purchase of the bearer bonds for the payment. Bernstein will then set up the drop with the kidnappers."

"Speaking of Bernstein, I have to tell you something, Liz.

I had thought that you two were an item."

"How do you know that we aren't?" she replied with a mischievous grin.

Monza, Italy

Historic Monza was Italy's most famous racing circuit and Parkes had been infatuated by it since the time he first saw the movie "Grand Prix" with James Garner. The fact that he was actually about to go racing at a place that he had often dreamed about was just starting to sink in as he walked past the grandstands on his way to the Team Mandel garage.

It had been three weeks since the race in Germany. Things had gone well at the half-day test session in France earlier in the week. The question now was, would both cars be fast, as well be able last the distance here at the famed Italian circuit?

The crew was already working to get the Mandel Cadillacs ready for the morning practice session as Parkes slipped into the garage. Qualifying was scheduled for early that afternoon so they would be practicing with the cars in qualifying trim.

His team mate was suited up and in rare form as he approached Parkes to greet him." How is our secret agent man today?" asked LeMond with a broad smile on his face.

"I am hopefully done with that stuff for awhile" replied Parkes.

"Seriously Brandon, what can you tell me about what is going on with Mr. Mandel?"

He then took a sip of his espresso followed by a drag off his cigarette and waited for a response.

" Well…. you need to keep this to yourself, but this Israeli guy -who by the way, really is a secret agent helping the Mandels, and has been in contact with the kidnappers. He told them last Thursday that proof of life would be needed before their demands could be met. Anyway, that was over a week ago and there apparently hasn't been any contact from the kidnappers since."

He took another drag of his cigarette before putting it out on the ground.

"So do you think that the Israelis' are actually willing to let any Palestinians out of jail?"

"No, of course they aren't, but this Agent Bernstein guy seems to think that if Liz just gives them the ransom money they will let Mr. Mandel and the pilots go. He believes that this whole thing is really more about money than it is politics or jihad."

LeMond nodded. "I guess that I would probably have to agree with him on that, at least based on what I have seen so far. Give them the money and it seems like Mr. Mandel will be returned."

Parkes checked the time and realized that he needed to go back to the transporter to get dressed for practice.

"Let me get changed and I'll see you back here in a few minutes."

"OK, I'll see you soon" he replied.

Turning back, he looked LeMond right in the eye. "Remember, you have to keep all this stuff to yourself."

The Frenchman gave him a wink, a quick a thumbs up and then reached in his driver's suit pocket for another cigarette.

When emerging from the team transporter Parkes saw that a huge crowd had come for practice and qualifying and had now began to settle into the grandstand seating in preparation for the day's action.

The temperature was warm, but it was now overcast, as practice for the second round of the International SuperSedan Challenge commenced. Several cars were already out on the circuit while the two Team Mandel drivers were still being strapped into their mounts and making ready for their practice run.

Both of the Cadillacs had been backed into their garage stalls so that the drivers could easily pull onto pit lane. LeMond rolled out of the garage first and headed toward the pit exit. Parkes was still busy plugging in his radio and pulling on his flame resistant gloves.

"Radio check." he said into his microphone.

"We hear you just fine" replied Griffin.

Putting the shifter into first gear, he eased the car out of the garage. He then proceeded to merge his car into the traffic already on the circuit.

Slotting in between a BMW M3 in front of him and one of the Maserati Quattroportes behind him, he steered into the first chicane. After getting safely through it the red Maserati zipped by him while another BMW closed up and got past him as well.

He was happy to let cars get by as he needed about a lap to get the tires up to temperature. Approaching what was called the Parabolica, the final turn before the long start-finish straight away, the car felt ready for a lap at full speed.

The Cadillac dug in and blasted off the corner and was soon at maximum velocity as he raced down the start finish straight. The RPMs on his tachometer told him he was doing over one hundred and seventy as he flew past the grandstands in sixth gear.

Just before entering the chicane at the end of the high speed straight away Parkes lifted his right foot off the throttle and pushed in the clutch with his left foot. His right foot now straddled both the brake pedal and the throttle pedal as he began to apply the brakes with the left side of his racing boot and blip the gas pedal with the right side of his foot prior to each downshift. He did this until he reached second gear and the turn in point for the chicane. This technique of revving the engine before each downshift and having the engine RPMs match the gears allowed for smoother downshifting which in turn would help save the transmission and avoid problems later in the race.

Sometimes called heel and toe, because the toe of the boot is on the brake pedal while the heel revs the engine, this technique was hardly used anymore at the top levels of road racing due to semi automatic gearshifts replacing standard manual transmissions. Although Team Mandel's cars didn't require lifting the throttle or pushing in the clutch during upshifts, they still had clutch pedals for downshifts, as Parkes had learned the hard way.

By the end of the second lap he had caught up to and passed two cars. Quickly he powered by one of the cars on the straight before the second chicane. The other pass had been made under braking for the circuit's third chicane.

"Imagine how much faster this place would be without those damn chicanes" he thought as he crossed the finish line and began the third circuit of the track.

"You had a good trap speed on the front straight away that lap" reported Griffin on the radio. "Your lap times are about four tenths behind the top car right now."

"Roger, that."

Each lap that Parkes did he became more comfortable and much quicker as well.

By his tenth and final lap he was second quickest of the twenty-four cars entered.

Backing up that performance, Henri did a time that was third quickest.

Qualifying for the race was up next on the schedule and the Team Mandel cars were looking very good to claim two of the top spots.

After a light lunch of salad and iced tea the Mandel drivers made their way back to the pit garage to make final preparations for the qualifying runs that would determine the grid for the race on Sunday.

Henri had stopped to pick up a printout of the practice speeds from the timing and scoring stand and after looking at it handed it to Parkes.

"Battle in first and then me and you." remarked Parkes.

"Yes Brandon, he is going to be tough again. This track is one he knows pretty well."

Thinking about Battle had reminded Parkes of his promise to Bernstein to see if he could get any clues about his friend's possible involvement in Mr. Mandel's disappearance.

"Listen, I have something I need to do before we go out, Henri. I'll see you back here in a couple of minutes."

"Don't be late, unless you want to catch hell." replied LeMond.

"Don't worry; I won't be gone for too long."

As he made his way up pit lane to find the Scimitar Mercedes' garage the sounds and smells of motorsport filled his senses. The familiar sound of air wrenches tightening bolts of the wheels onto the cars while their racing motors were being warmed up was combined with the smell of high octane racing gas. Add to that the colors and the crowd in the grandstand and you had an environment that Parkes truly loved being a part of.

Battle's team was in the third and fourth garage stalls which put them close to the exit of pitlane. The Scimitar Mercedes' drivers were just climbing into their cars as Parkes approached. He would have to look Battle up after the qualifying session and talk with him then.

"Hey Parkes, are you going to qualify your car or stand here and just watch?" asked a voice behind him.

He spun around and saw a smiling Liz Mandel, and walked toward her.

"I was just doing what you and Bernstein asked me to do."

"Did you find anything out?"

"No, I have nothing to report yet."

"Well it's time now to go do your day job" she said as she took his hand and began leading him back to the Mandel garage.

Henri was just putting his helmet on and about to climb into his car as they arrived. Parkes quickly put on his own HANS, helmet and gloves.

He still found the HANS device to be somewhat uncomfortable, but once again reminded himself that it had probably already spared him when he had his wreck at Daytona.

As he got settled into his driving seat Griffin walked up to his window and told him that the car had new tires and a slight change to the front suspension set up. He gave him the order to start the motor and then took a step back from the car while putting on his radio head set.

The engine started and Parkes took in a deep cleansing breath and let it out.

As he drove past the pit exit and eased onto the track he noticed that his teammate's black Cadillac filled the rear view mirror as they both headed into the first chicane.

Making his first lap at only three quarter speed Parkes warmed the new tires and let the engine come up to temperature. LeMond went by him on the main straight, just before they entered the chicane for the second time.

Now a half a car length from LeMond's rear bumper, this was an opportunity for Parkes to learn from a veteran who had raced at Monza many times before.

Through the second and third chicanes he found that he could keep up with him. He also had no problem keeping pace on the straight away that lead to the final turn.

Braking and downshifting for the final turn, the sweeping Parabolica corner, he was right behind the number 11 Cadillac, but as they exited the corner he began to feel the front end washing out. Called under-steer in road racing or pushing in NASCAR parlance, the front of the car was losing grip and causing him to slide out and lose speed as he was forced to lift his foot slightly off the gas pedal so as to not run out of road and go off the track.

The car in front had tracked right through the corner and was now almost two car lengths ahead as they passed the start finish line.

He made up some ground by drafting, or slip streaming behind his team mate as they headed down the main straight. A bit more was gained by braking later than LeMond going into the last chicane. As a result, he was back to less than a car length behind as they approached the Parabolica.

Once again the car under steered in the corner. This time it was worse than on the last lap. . Because of the tires sliding across the track he also knew that the tires would wear faster than normal and quickly become less effective each lap.

He had good power down the straight away, and was still close enough to LeMond to get the benefit of the draft, but he was again almost two car lengths behind his team mate entering the first chicane. As he glanced into his rearview mirror he saw that a red Audi was catching him. It was time to come in to the pits.

As he approached the second chicane he slowed up and allowed the Audi behind him to pass on the inside. He continued at a reduced pace until reaching the pit entrance which was on the right side of the main straight away.

Pulling into his pit box he then shut the car off and stepped out. Since he had not radioed Griffin and alerted him that he was coming in he wasn't surprised that most of the crew was still at the pit wall watching the action instead of being ready to service his car.

Taking off his helmet Parkes walked toward the pit wall. He tapped Griffin on the shoulder and told him about the under steer condition.

"I don't know what to tell you. It's the same set up we have on Henri's car and he just set the quickest time of the session." said Griffin with a smile.

"Maybe it was just this set of tires then" he replied.

"Well it couldn't have been too bad for you. You are sixth fastest, right now."

He smiled at the news. "Yes, but with a little adjustment to the front end I might be ahead of LeMond"

"OK, laddie I will do as you ask. New tires and a quick reset of the front suspension to what you had yesterday"

Turning to one of the crewmen standing at the pit wall Griffin told him what he wanted him to do to the number 12 car. The young man shook his head in agreement and within moments there were three other black shirted Team Mandel crewmen pushing the Cadillac back into the garage.

Ashmore turned his attention back to the action on the track as Parkes headed for the cooler at the back of the garage. Inside the blue cooler he found several bottles of ice cold water waiting for him; he opened one, and downed it quickly, and then reached into the ice to grab another.

Sitting down in a plastic lawn chair at the back of the garage he watched as the crew made the adjustments he had requested. He just hoped that their efforts would pay off when he went back out and made an attempt to better his time.

As he opened his second bottle of water he noticed the live video feed on the television set mounted in the left front corner of the garage.

Scrolling across the top were the lap times of the drivers who had made qualifying attempts so far.

His team mate still led with a time of one minute and fifty-five point three. In second and only a tenth of a second behind LeMond was the BMW of Mario Barilla. Scott Battle had moved his Mercedes into third place with a time of one fifty-five point six.

He knew he would be very fortunate to get into one of the top half dozen starting positions, even if the changes now being made to the car made him quicker than he had been before.

The best time he had recorded thus far today had been one minute fifty-six point two seconds. While he had been sixth a few minutes ago he had now fallen down to ninth on the grid.

He began to visualize the circuit and think about where he might be able to improve when he went back out; he decided that if his team-mate could be fastest than there was no reason that he couldn't better his own time.

"We are all finished" yelled one of the crewmen. He took another long drink of water and looked down at his watch. There were just fifteen minutes left until the end of qualifying.

Parkes promptly put on his helmet and got in the car. With the help of a crewman he then fastened his seat belts. After starting the engine he checked the gauges and drove the black Cadillac out of the garage and down the pit lane. As he adjusted the rear view he saw that LeMond was pulling into his pit box. In fact, about half the cars had retired to the pits. The other half were still trying to post a qualifying time that would move them up the starting grid for tomorrow's race.

One of the cars doing laps was the Mercedes that Battle was driving. Though he was in second qualifying position, his old friend was unlikely to leave anything on the table. Battle still had time to snatch the pole position and would surely drive flat out to do so.

Just as he had finished his warm up lap the white Mercedes rocketed past him. He saw the number three on the side and knew for certain what driver the car belonged to. After checking his gauges he took a deep breath and began the pursuit to catch his rival. Confident that he could keep up with Scott he felt his times would surely improve, especially if the changes he had asked to be made to the car were indeed effective.

Through the right and left of the first chicane Battle began the trip down the long sweeping section of road known as Curva Grande that led to the left-right complex that comprised the second chicane.

The Cadillac managed to close up to the C63 as the two cars made the left, then right turns and onto to the short straight and into the corner known as Lesmos. It was actually two right hand corners that were separated by a short straight between them.

He observed that Battle was using every available inch of the track, and decided that he needed to do the same if he was to stay with the white car. He blasted down the long backstretch ultimately hitting sixth gear and about 160 miles per hour before braking and downshifting for Monza's third and final chicane, the left right left combination named Ascari.

The straight away prior to the Parabolica saw him gain on the Mercedes and narrow the gap to no more than a single car length. As he tapped the brake pedal and downshifted to fourth gear he wondered if the problem of under steer would continue to plague him.

To his relief the Cadillac stuck like glue through the Parabolica and he soon found himself in sixth gear on the main straight and right on Scott Battle's tailpipe.

"You are P3" he heard Griffin exclaim over the radio. He didn't bother to respond, he was too focused on getting past the Mercedes.

The black Cadillac seemed to have the advantage coming out of the corners. The torque of the powerful eight cylinders that he couldn't use before was now available to him since the car was no longer pushing as it went through the turns. The speed he carried into, through and out of the corners was translating into higher terminal velocity on Monza's long straight aways as well.

The fact that he was in the vacuum behind Battle's car on the straights was also a part of the equation. Drafting was clearly a factor with these cars on the high speed sections and Parkes was using it to his full advantage.

The two cars continued to circulate nose to tail for the next four laps. They occasionally went by other cars, but the track was all but empty as the qualifying session was drawing to a close.

"There is time for about two more laps" Griffin told him on the radio. Parkes knew that Battle's tires had to be fairly worn by this time and decided it was time to get by him. He figured the best place to pass was down the main straight.

Coming out of the Parabolica corner once again, he stayed on the bumper of the Mercedes and used the draft to make a sling shot move to get past him just after the start finish line.

Griffin had just informed him that he was now in second place and that Battle had moved up to the first qualifying position.

The Cadillac began pulling away from the white Mercedes after the second chicane. It was almost three car lengths ahead after the third chicane. Parkes wondered if Battle's tires were already gone. Perhaps it was a case of him backing off now that he had set the fast lap.

Either way, Parkes was going to finish the lap just as strongly as he begun it. Shifting down to fourth he went into the Parabolica for the final time that day. The car was hooked up like a slot car as it tracked through long sweeping corner. With the gas pedal on the floorboard he made the shift up to fifth, then sixth gear and thundered on across the finish line. Whether he had claimed pole position or not, Parkes knew that he had given it his all.

Liz Mandel and the entire crew were gathered inside the Team Mandel pit garage as Brandon Parkes brought his Cadillac to a halt and shut off the engine. He unplugged his radio, climbed out of the car and took off his gloves and helmet; Henri was the only one who walked up to meet him.

"Good job, Brandon. You beat Battle to the pole position by just over a tenth of a second."

"Thanks, he was really tough to beat. Anyway, what exactly is going on here?"

"There is a live web-cast from the kidnappers." replied LeMond.

The two drivers entered the garage and saw that everyone was gathered around a laptop computer. They were viewing the image of three masked men standing behind three blindfolded men who were on their knees. Once his drivers arrived Griffin brought the garage door down to keep out the press, who might be coming to interview Brandon but would end up instead seeing a grieving daughter.

Crying softly at the sight of her father and his pilots Liz was further burdened by the fact that the man who was speaking on the TV screen was doing so in French. As a result, only the occasional phrase was understandable to her. Fortunately one of the two French crewmen was writing down as much as he could on a note pad. The other Frenchman on the crew was standing next to Liz and giving her the main points of what was being said.

"Henri, can you hear what they are saying?" asked Parkes in a hushed tone.

"It is difficult. The sound quality is not so good. The balaclava over his mouth and the accent make it difficult as well." he whispered.

Both men leaned in towards the laptop and focused intently on what was being said.

LeMond then turned his head back towards Parkes. "The deadline is Monday night at eleven o'clock Paris time."

The web cast ended with shouts of "God is Great" in Arabic coming from all three of the hooded captors.

"Great timing guys" he thought. "I win the pole position and you Arab morons decide to have a web cast". He now had an idea of how the actors felt at Ford Theater the night President Lincoln was shot. You felt badly for the victim, but cheated after just having put on a great performance.

After a quick shower and a change into street clothes he re-emerged to find the motor sport press seemingly more interested in getting a reaction from him about the web cast, than they were in the qualifying session. He refused to respond to the questions, but did say that he wanted to dedicate his winning the pole position to Mr. Mandel and adding that the whole team was hopeful of the team owner being released soon.

Breaking away from the pack of photographers and journalists Parkes made his way to the Scimitar garage. Scott Battle was still there talking to his crew chief and still wearing his drivers suit.

When Battle noticed that Parkes was walking towards him he broke off his conversation and approached his friend with an extended hand.

"You and that Caddy sure were tough out there today." said Battle as he shook his hand.

"You kept me honest" he replied. "I think you'd say that the fans really got their money's worth today."

"Yeah, but tomorrow in the race is when we really earn our keep, BP."

"So you feel like you have two wins in a row in you?" asked Parkes.

"Yeah, but there is this other guy in this Cadillac that I have to beat before that happens"

He smiled and wished Battle a good night. His friends compliment had seemed genuine and he was glad they could speak cordially. Then he remembered the main reason he had wanted to talk to Scott.

"Be sure to say hello to Michele for me. Is she here this weekend?"

Battle averted his eyes for a moment before he responded. "Uh, no. She has gone to visit her family for a while. But the next time she calls I will be sure to say hi for you"

"Sure. Anyway, we'll see you here tomorrow."

"Looking forward to it, pal" replied Battle.

As he headed for his rental car Parkes thought he should try to find Liz and she how she was doing. The fact was that he really didn't want to deal with sadness right now; he only wanted to celebrate that day's success. Though he felt guilty for feeling this way he had needed an accomplishment to feel good about for a long time and wanted to relish the moment, even if nobody else did.

Driving towards his hotel he remembered that it was still just late morning back in Missouri. He knew of at least one person who would laud him for what he done, so he picked up his cell and called his uncle to tell him the good news.

Early Saturday evening

The Hotel De La Ville was only about two kilometers from the Monza circuit and Liz Mandel was thankful for that as she rushed into the lobby in search of Mr. Bernstein.

Once she spotted him she walked over to where he was sitting and asked him to come to her room so that they could discuss what to do next concerning the return of her father and the two company pilots. As she was leaving the lobby she saw Brandon walk in the front door. She gave him a quick wave and a faint smile and continued walking towards to her room with Mr. Bernstein along beside her.

Seeing Parkes reminded her to call him after her meeting with Bernstein to congratulate him on winning the pole position. She felt badly that all this had happened right as he had achieved his moment of glory, but the situation with her father was now a matter of life and death.

Opening the door to her room she was greeted by a dozen roses that had been sent by the staff. She wasn't sure if they were a gesture of sympathy or congratulations for the team qualifying first and third at the track. They were lovely, either way.

She offered Bernstein a drink and he asked if she had a soft drink. Opening the mini bar she found a cold Coke which she handed to him along with a glass. She then grabbed herself a small bottle of wine and poured the contents into a wine glass.

Bernstein sat down on the couch while Liz paced the floor and drank her zinfandel.

"So, what do we do now? We both know that if we don't deliver ten million in bearer bonds and an airliner filled with Palestinians, these people are going to execute my father and his pilots Monday night while the whole world has a ringside seat via the net".

"Since the Israeli government isn't about to negotiate a deal that involves trading out any prisoners what should we do to get my dad back alive?" she asked him in an agitated tone.

"Give them the money. Again, that is all they are really after. I really believe that all these demands for jailed Palestinians were nothing more than a bargaining chip that they will forget about if you simply get them the money before the deadline."

"Let's call Harry in Chicago and get his input." said Liz as she hit the call button on her cell phone.

As the phone rang she promised herself to never give another dime of family money to any Israeli causes if Bernstein was wrong in his assumptions. Losing her father and the pilots would be bad enough. The idea that they gave them ten million dollars based Bernstein's incorrect hunches would be like pouring a can of salt on a very deep wound.

Saturday 7:35 PM

It was after seven thirty and Brandon Parkes decided that he would head to the hotel dining room for some dinner. He had reflected on the day's activities and decided that his performance in qualifying was likely one of the high-water marks of his career.

The fact that the team was focused on Mr. Mandel's plight was to be understood, besides, it wasn't like he'd won the race, it was just a first place in qualifying.

He knew full well that the race tomorrow would be the real test, just as Scott had said earlier. After he showered again he dressed and was putting on his watch when the telephone rang.

"Hello"

"Hello, this is Liz. Can I buy you a drink later on to celebrate the magnificent job you did in qualifying?"

"Actually, I was just headed down to the dining room to get something to eat, but I would love to see you later for a drink."

"Nine o'clock down in the bar then?" asked Liz.

"That sounds great."

"See you then, Brandon"

As he left his room Parkes smiled at the thought that Liz had been considerate enough to remember him, despite all that she was going through right now.

Dressed in khaki slacks, a black Team Mandel sport shirt and Gucci loafers, he was feeling rested having taken an hour long nap. The idea of having a light dinner and then a drink before turning in

Race to Damascus

for the night suited him. With the morning warm up at ten AM and the race at one o'clock he didn't need to have a late night.

Pasta salad and a glass of red wine followed by an espresso made up his meal that night. It was quite good and much needed. Just as he was finishing his espresso Liz walked in to the dining room and sat in the seat across from him. She was fifteen minutes early.

"So, are you ready to move into the bar for that drink?" she asked.

"Let's just stay here" replied Parkes with a smile.

"I've gotten rather comfortable in this spot."

Sure, why not?" The waiter soon appeared and asked her if she would care for something.

"How about bringing us each a snifter of Courvoisier"

He smiled and nodded in agreement with Liz's choice.

"So, how are you doing, Liz?"

"Better now that we made a decision about paying the ransom. Bernstein just flew to Paris to make the drop"

He really didn't want to get involved by giving his opinion on the matter. If it was his father he would have used some of the ransom money to hire mercenaries to do a snatch and grab. Instead, they were going to pay out millions in the hope that it would placate these people and that they would in turn let Mr. Mandel and his pilots go free. But he felt he wasn't in a position to give his advice.

"Do you trust this Bernstein guy?" asked Parkes.

"If you are asking if I think a Mossad agent would steal our money, then the answer is that I trust him. What I am not so sure about is whether or not I trust his judgment. He thinks handing them the money alone will be enough"

Parkes literally bit his tongue. If these kidnappers were motivated by more than money it wouldn't matter to only meet half of their demands. If the Palestinians weren't released Mr. Mandel might be killed anyway. He knew that Liz was aware of this fact and saw no point in bringing it up now.

"Well, surely the Mossad know what they are doing. "

The waiter brought them two snifters of Courvoisier along with the bill. Parkes grabbed the silver Cross pen clipped to his shirt and signed for the meal. He then picked up the snifter of Courvoisier that the waiter had placed in front of him.

"To your father, his safe return and to Team Mandel" he said raising his snifter.

"Thank you." replied Liz as she raised her own glass and then took a sip.

"Thanks also for all the hard work you did on the track today." she added. "We have won two pole positions so far and I know that Griffin is very pleased with both you and Henri right now"

He thought for a moment and raised his glass again.

"Let's just hope that we have a good race tomorrow and some encouraging news on Monday night"

She reached for his left hand with her own right hand and grasped it tightly.

"Just know that I'll be praying as much for your safety on the track, as for the return of my dad." He squeezed her hand and then let go as he took another drink of Courvoisier.

"Tell me Liz, what of your mother? You never have talked about her."

"She and my father are…..shall we say…separated. She has set up a very large mission, and along with my brother they help poor Mexican children. It is located between Puebla and Mexico City."

"Understand, they don't ever fight with one another. I guess that they have just grown apart. Dad has set up a trust fund that allows them to operate the place. About the only time we see them is at Christmas time and even then it is usually only for a day or two."

"What has been her response to your dad's kidnapping?"

"She finds it ironic that dad would be kidnapped for ransom when he is always worrying about the same thing happening to her there in Mexico".

"I do believe that she still loves him, and I know that she is more worried than she lets on. She keeps telling me to be anxious for nothing and that she has put him in God's hands."

"Have you done that?" Parkes asked.

"What else can one do? In the end our faith is all we have."

Since Parkes didn't really have the energy to get into a religious discussion right now, he downed the rest of his snifter and was about to say goodnight when Liz told him that she thought it was too early to turn in for the evening. He just smiled and led her by the hand to the hotel bar.

Monza, Italy – Sunday Afternoon

The gray sky above the Monza circuit on race day looked as though it could deliver a shower at any moment. Crews were taking wheels to the tire truck and having them fitted with treaded rain tires, just in case they were needed later on.

Having stayed up later than he had planned the night before, Brandon Parkes was still a bit tired as he and Henri walked into the team Mandel pit garage.

Liz had conspired with the Mandel crew for them show up at the bar the night before to belatedly celebrate the pole position that Parkes had achieved. None of them had missed the party, and as a result, most of them were moving somewhat more slowly than usual due to the previous night's activities.

Although the team get together had not been an over-the-top affair in terms of excessive use of alcohol; the party had just gone on much later than anyone was used to staying up these days.

Cups of coffee, cold bottles of water and cans of energy drink were seen in abundance that morning as everyone at Team Mandel was trying to get up to full speed in preparation for the fifteen minute warm up session scheduled to start at ten o'clock. With the cars qualified first and third, no one wanted to see the advantage wasted by not having everything prepared as perfectly as possible.

While Griffin and the crew went through all the checklists prior to the morning practice the drivers went to the lounge in the transporter to suit up.

Henri got dressed first; while Parkes sat down to finish getting thoroughly hydrated with a bottle of LeMond's favorite sponsor's product. Before getting dressed he reached for some vitamins that were in his helmet bag and downed two of them with the last of his water.

After putting on his driver's suite Henri picked up his helmet and announced that he was going off to find an espresso and to have a cigarette.

The driver's lounge was tiny, so Brandon was happy that he now had more room with the departure of his team mate. The solitude also allowed him a few minutes to gather his thoughts concerning the day ahead. He would take it easy in practice, in fact he would likely just do a lap or two to make sure that all was right with the car and then park it before some bone-head crashed into him.

In the race itself he figured his best bet was to get ahead of Battle at the start and stay in front of him into the first chicane. The Cadillac probably had the ability to out drag the Mercedes, but the problem was that Battle would start to his right and had the inside line entering the right hand corner. Ironically, due to the track layout at Monza, it was actually of more benefit to qualify in second, than to be in the pole position.

It was typical that even though he had been fastest, Battle once again seemed to have the advantage, he thought to himself.

He felt that he had no choice but to power by the Mercedes at the start and keep him behind him for the whole race if he wanted to win. It may be quite a task, but it would be easier to do that than having to pass Battle later, should he let him take the lead at the start.

With his helmet and gloves in hand he headed to his race car. Raindrops had just started to fall as Parkes walked into the garage; he overheard Griffin tell the crew to change the tires just moments after the rain turned into a full downpour.

"Well, this will certainly make things more interesting" he said to Griffin.

"Don't worry lad, we are taking care of you even as we speak."

"Are you making any other changes, besides rain tires." asked Parkes.

"No, just rains for now. But let me know how it feels out there and if we need to soften up the suspension a little bit just give me the word."

The team manager then turned his attention to getting the tires changed on LeMond's car.

Walking to the back of the garage area Parkes put on his helmet, HANS device and Nomex gloves. The warm up session had now turned into a very short test of how the cars would perform in the wet.

At the end of his first lap the car felt pretty good to him. Though driven at just three quarter speed, the rain tires seemed to be doing their job. The second lap would tell him more as it would be run flat out.

With his headlights on and the big single arm windshield wiper moving back and forth at full speed the number twelve Cadillac CTS-V came down Monza's main straight away and its driver prepared to brake for the first chicane. Due to the wet conditions Parkes thought it better to brake earlier than he had done when the track was dry.

Despite being cautious, he found himself coming into the chicane faster than he should have. The wet track and damp brakes combined to create this situation and he narrowly made it through the chicane without going off course.

An Audi passed him on the straight just before the second chicane and left a wake of water behind as he went by. Despite the windshield wiper the mist that trailed another car made it very difficult to see.

He soon recovered his composure and closed in on the RS5. He managed to catch up to and stay with the red machine, despite the fact that his foe had the advantage of all-wheel drive on a very slick track.

It wasn't just the rain that made the circuit slippery, but the oil on the track that mixed with it. The rain tires were helping him to stay with the Audi in front of him, but Parkes felt that some changes would need to be made to the Cadillac if he wanted to be a real factor in the race.

He continued for another lap and a half behind the red Audi, but couldn't make a clean pass. The more he had followed the car in front, the more he became convinced that he had to take the lead at the start. Once he was leading it would be tough for Battle or any other challenger to get by him with the spray that he would be throwing up behind him.

Since time was running out in the warm up session Parkes decided to pit. He keyed the radio mike and told Griffin that he was coming in and wanted the crew to soften up all four corners and set the brake bias back.

Ashmore agreed that softening the suspension would give the car more grip and let Parkes know that they would be ready for him when he arrived back at the pit garage.

Braking and downshifting as he entered the pit lane, the only question he had was not concerning making changes to the car, but what degree of change would be appropriate. It might stop raining in the next two and a half hours prior to the race. Even if the same conditions existed when the race started, there wasn't enough time left in the practice session to make the changes to the car and then get back on the track to find out if they were right.

Pulling into his pit box he decided to let Griffin make the final call about how far to go with the adjustments. He had no choice right now but to trust the man's years of experience and hope for the best.

As Parkes stepped out of the car he saw his team mate pulling into the pits. Both machines were soon being rolled back-end first into the garage. The crewmen on the number eleven Cadillac raised the car on its internal air jacks and began to remove the wheels. His crew wiped the rainwater off their car with towels.

The sound of power wrenches soon filled the garage area as the all the teams worked to ready their cars for the rainy conditions that they all now faced.

Predictably the all wheel drive Audi's were atop the leader board for the just completed warm up session. The three fastest times all belonged to cars carrying the familiar four ring logo on them. The rear wheel drive cars were not as sure footed in the wet and their lap times reflected this fact.

Corralling his two drivers Griffin told them about the exact changes that were being made to their mounts.

"We are going softer with the rear springs and shocks at the rear. Hopefully the power over steer and fish tailing that you guys were experiencing coming out of the corners will be reduced as a result. The gearing is also being changed so we can minimize the wheel spin and get the tires to hook up with the wet track."

"How about the front end, did you make any changes there?" asked Parkes.

"We didn't want to go too soft and end up with too much body roll going into a corner, so we just took it down one notch from where we had been."

"Oh, and we will be setting the brake bias to the rear, just as you asked for, Brandon"

Race to Damascus

"Please, I would like the same done to mine and dial the wing and front splitter to max down force" requested LeMond.

"Alright, we will do it, Henri. Anyway, I think you will find that you'll have a pretty good rain set up by the time we are done. Now why don't you two guys go get yourselves a coffee and let us get on with our work?"

"OK, and thanks a lot." replied Parkes with a smile.

As the two Team Mandel drivers made their way to the hospitality tent the skies looked to continue dumping precipitation on the track. They both felt fortunate right now to have someone like Griffin Ashmore looking out for them.

The rain did not seem to be keeping the Italian racing fans away. In fact, the spectators that had come to see the race here at Monza had simply brought umbrellas and rain coats to protect themselves from the elements and were filling the grandstands as the cars they had come to see were being rolled out to take their place on the starting grid.

Sitting in the seat of his black Cadillac race car and in the first starting position on the grid, Brandon had opened the driver's side door to allow cool air to enter the cockpit. Despite the rain, the humidity was still fairly high and dressed in his driver's suit and helmet he had begun to feel slightly uncomfortable. Besides, he knew that a TV interview was going to take place soon and he wanted to be ready for it.

Adjusting his rearview mirrors he saw his team mate's car directly behind him. LeMond was putting his helmet on and just about to get in the number eleven car, when a female reporter with a microphone in hand suddenly began a live interview with Parkes.

"Brandon Parkes, you are starting from the pole position, but the conditions have changed some since your qualifying run, do you now think that the rain will change your strategy in the race?" asked the woman with an Italian accent.

He leaned his helmeted head toward the microphone.

"Well, first off I just want to say that the Mandel crew did a great job preparing the car for qualifying. As far as the weather is concerned it hasn't changed our plans for the race much at all."

"Who is your biggest competition here today?"

"My own team mate who is right behind me. Then I guess my fellow American who is starting next to me and after that just about anybody with an all wheel drive Audi!" said Parkes with a laugh that was muffled by his full face helmet.

The reporter turned to look right into the camera to wrap up the interview.

"While Parkes may have been fastest in qualifying, he will clearly have his hands full in the race, especially in these very slick conditions. Now, let's send it back to Simon, up in the booth."

The young woman flipped up the hood of her yellow rain coat and thanked Parkes for his time before moving on for an interview with Scott Battle.

Parkes plugged in his radio connection and made sure it was working.

"Radio check, radio check"

A second later Griffin responded.

"We hear you just fine, Brandon. Now go out and have a good run, mate"

"Roger that." he replied.

Suddenly he heard Liz Mandel's voice. "Be safe out there in that rain." she said.

He paused for a moment and then responded. "If I can't be safe, I'll try to be good"

"Brandon, before I forget, be sure to turn on your headlights and fog lamps" Ashmore reminded him.

"Don't you worry; I will do it just as soon we get started out on the warm up lap".

The order to start up the cars came and soon the entire field of twenty four cars was on their way for the one pace lap of the circuit prior to the standing start. Rain was still falling steadily as the drivers followed the Mercedes pace car in formation and made their way around the Monza circuit on their way back to their starting positions on the main straight away.

When his Cadillac CTS-V came to a stop at its starting spot there was a slight squealing sound that Parkes noticed. It was no doubt due to the brakes being wet.

Looked behind into his mirrors he could see that most of the field was in place for the beginning of the race. He knew that in just moments a red light would be seen on the starters stand on the start finish line. It would be followed by a yellow one and finally a green light that would signal the start of the race.

As the red light came on, he blipped the accelerator pedal twice with the right part of his brushed leather driver boot. The other part of the boot was holding down the brake pedal. Then the yellow light appeared and he pushed the clutch pedal in with his left foot and kept it there while he made sure the car was in first gear. In anticipation of the start Parkes continued to rev the engine and when the green light came on he let the clutch out and launched the car off the line.

With the throttle all the way to the firewall, he shifted into second gear, and into third, as he approached the first corner. He glanced over to his right and saw that he was slightly ahead of Battle going into the corner. Downshifting back to second while braking, he thought that he would be the leader as the pack snaked through the chicane.

Scott had backed off and looked like he was going to let him have the position and the lead going into the chicane. As he started to make the right turn Parkes felt the sting of a car crashing into his rear bumper. A split second later he was turned around and found a car crashing hard into the right front corner of his own.

Incredibly, LeMond had not been able to get slowed down enough and had punted his teammate's car into a spin and out of the race because of the resulting accident. His race from pole position was over almost before it had begun.

As he sat in his disabled racecar and reflected upon what had just happened, Parkes went from the shock of having just survived a big on track incident to feeling devastated about the opportunity that had slipped through his fingers. The realization that he had just been put out of the race by his own team mate, Henri LeMond, was simply beyond his comprehension.

Chapter Six

Chicago, Illinois-Midway Airport

The white and blue Gulfstream jet taxied to its parking spot as though it knew the way home, or so it seemed to Harry Mandel.

It was more than a little unsettling for him to see this ghost like plane reappear after having thought to be lost. When the pilots hired to pick the plane up in Syria stepped out of the aircraft everything that had occurred to the regular pilots and his brother suddenly hit home. "Make sure that it is completely checked out and then see that it's thoroughly cleaned and washed." Mandel told the new captain.

"Yes, sir" said the pilot. 'We'll get right on it"

He wasn't sure if the salute he received from the pilot was meant to be sarcastic, but right now he had more important things to worry about than whether or not a new employee was being a smart ass or not. Besides, by tonight these guys would end up being temporary hires if things went as Harry hoped they would.

The cell phone in his jacket pocket rang but when Harry saw that it was a number he didn't recognize he decided that he wouldn't answer it. He put the phone back in his pocket with his right hand, while with his left he found a roll of antacids in his side pocket. Once he had chewed a couple of them he felt a bit better, but his stomach never felt right anymore.

He got into his white Lincoln Town Car and decided that he would just go straight home to wait for the TV broadcast that was expected to come from his brother's captors.

There was nothing going on back at the office that couldn't wait until tomorrow, and besides he could really use a good strong drink right now. Just the mere thought of a gin and tonic with a slice of lime made him smile. This method of liquid escape had become something that he had grown too fond of lately, but he told himself that self medicating was justified right now given all that he was enduring. If he could just get through the next few days everything would be alright again. At least he hoped so.

Nearing his home he saw that there was a gray late model Chrysler sitting in his driveway. Harry turned in and went to the right side of the visitor's car and drove into the already open garage. He had no idea who it was, but soon found out, as the driver and a man in the passenger seat of the Chrysler got out and walked towards the garage to intercept him.

The driver was in his early thirties and looked like he worked out daily. The man that followed him was shorter, older and while solidly built, looked slightly overweight. Both men were wearing sport jackets with open collar shirts and given their well tanned skin neither looked like they worked in an office every day.

"Mr. Mandel, my associate and I are here on behalf of some friends who are concerned about a financial matter that you need to address" said the older man.

"My name is Nick and this here is Paul. We have been given the job of overseeing the repayment of the money you owe.

"I guess you could say that we are like a collection agency for very large delinquent accounts like yours and we need to find out what your plans are regarding this matter"

"You tell your friends that they will be getting their money any day now." replied Harry in a firm tone. He wasn't used to taking orders from anyone, not even a couple of Chicago wise guys.

"Well you know that our friends told us that you said that already. They still haven't seen any money. That's why Paul and I are here visiting you now".

"Your friends know that once my brother is returned safely that they will get their money"

"Alright, but we are obliged to start charging you interest on your loan. Ten percent a month until the debt is paid in full." The man who called himself Nick turned to his associate. "Come on Pauly, let's go and let Andre know that Mr. Mandel has been informed of the new terms of his loan."

"We'll be in touch, Mr. Mandel"

Harry said nothing in response. He just watched as the two men got into their car and drove away and hoped that the nightmare he was living through would soon be over. As he saw the Chrysler fade from his view, he was proud that he hadn't been all that nervous about the mob enforcers that had just been in his driveway.

He turned toward the front door and let out a sigh of relief as it occurred to him that in just a few hours the whole thing would be done. His brother would be back safely and his gambling debt paid soon afterward. The knowledge of that was the main reason he hadn't been as scared of the debt collectors as he might have been otherwise.

Walking into his spacious home he saw the note that his housekeeper had left him taped to the mirror in the foyer. He smiled as he read it and knew that Miss Shirley had taken good care of him as usual. The note let him know that dinner was being kept warm in the oven and that a new bottle of cold gin was waiting for him in the refrigerator.

Since his second wife had left him a year ago Harry had come to rely on Shirley to keep his life together. Miss Shirley had to be at least seventy, but with her high energy level and youthful looks she could have passed for fifty. She was the most attractive woman that Harry had ever known and were she not happily married he might have proposed to her. While that might have sounded crazy to some people, she certainly had cared more about him than either of his wives ever did.

As he headed up stairs to change clothes he thought how he needed to sell this house and get a condo. Almost six thousand square feet of living space and all he ever used was the kitchen and the family room.

The bedroom was just a place to change clothes, as he would always fall asleep on the couch while watching TV. Even the computer, with its connection to the internet, was now on a desk in the corner of the family room.

After changing into sweat pants, sport shirt, white athletic socks and slippers, he made himself a gin and tonic and sat down on the couch in front of the big screen television and used the remote to tune it to Fox News.

It was now just after three o'clock in Chicago and there should be some word fairly soon as to the fate of his brother and their company pilots.

Paris, France-Monday evening

The suite that Liz Mandel was occupying at the Hilton looked more like a "Monday Night" football party to Parkes than a vigil for her father. There was a buffet and a bar set up for those joining her to wait for the any news from the kidnappers. A big screen television hooked up to her laptop computer had been installed and would allow all in attendance to view the web cast.

Henri and Griffin were already there and watching the television when he came up from his room to join them.

Liz was sitting in the middle of the couch, holding a wine glass in her hand. She looked tired and not like herself. While she was trying to maintain a brave face, Parkes sensed that she might break into tears at any moment.

"Get yourself something to drink, Brandon. There are sandwiches and other things to eat if you are hungry." she said sweetly, but with a forced smile.

"Thanks. I think I will."

As Parkes poured himself a glass of scotch at the bar, Agent Bernstein entered the suite and after greeting everyone asked if he could be excused to meet with Liz in private.

After she excused herself she led Bernstein to her room. Parkes just hoped that Bernstein wasn't here to give her bad news.

He sat down on the couch that Liz had just vacated. Griffin was sitting in a chair to his right while Henri occupied the chair to his left. One of the French speaking crewmembers was present as well and standing off in the corner eating appetizers. As he was part of Henri's crew, not his own, he didn't even know the young man's name.

"So, you were able to salvage something for yourself at Monza, Henri. Good to hear, given that it's a team title that we are after."

"Yes, we managed to come back and finish eighth, Brandon. I'm just sorry that we both didn't have a much better day."

"Henri was punted from behind and into your back end by another car" added Griffin.

"I am sure that was the case; but that still doesn't make it any easier to accept. Sorry to be so upset, but I mean we both could have had a really good result yesterday" lamented Parkes.

The conversation about the previous day's race ended when Liz and Bernstein came back into the room. "The ransom has been delivered to a drop site here in Paris" announced Liz.

"All we can do now is hope for a response and pray that my father will be released soon."

Finishing his drink Parkes looked at his watch. It was now eleven thirty. It was one half hour past the deadline that the kidnappers had set.

Damascus, Syria

As he lay on an old mattress in a dimly lit room, Dan Mandel knew that something was going on as he heard his captors, just outside his door, talking in an agitated manner.

The men were laughing and were more animated than they had been in the whole time he had been held in this dirty hell hole. Perhaps a ransom had been paid and they would be freed. Maybe they had their money and they were waking us up to finish us off, thought Mandel.

His two pilots were being held in two other rooms. The only contact he had with them was when they were brought out to appear on camera. They had all been blindfolded during that time so Mandel had not actually seen the pilots since they were hijacked.

Suddenly the door to his room opened and the biggest of the captors, came in and told Mandel to get up because he was going to be on TV again. This baboon, had been on the ground crew at the airport in Paris, and was one of the ones who had hijacked them at gunpoint. Another of the captors waited outside the door armed with the mandatory AK-47 rifle. His face was covered with a black balaclava that Mandel thought made him look like a ninja.

As Mandel was walked out of his room he saw that both pilots had been brought out and were being guarded by a third man who had on an olive green balaclava and who also carried an AK-47.

He nodded at both of his men. "Are you guys OK?"

"I am fine, but the wine list in the dining room isn't the best." joked Jack Rhodes.

Pete Flynn was silent and just stared at the ground.

"You both have a good start on a beard going on there." noted Mandel.

"Shut up, Zionist" shouted the biggest kidnapper. "All of you get on your knees in front of the camera. The Zionist pig goes in middle" said the man in his broken English.

The three men did as they were ordered.

As Flynn went to his knees Mandel had noticed that he had a tear running down his left cheek. He seemed to be less afraid than he was sad. Jack, who was kneeling to his right, was just as stoic as one would expect from a man with U.S. Air Force fighter pilot survival training.

Mandel was more upset that he and his people were being treated like this than he was afraid of dying. In fact, the thought that he would be killed in this ordeal had never seriously entered his mind. He thought that he was too valuable to be killed and too mean to die at the hand of some third world animals.

"This is just show and tell, boys". They want to put us on TV again to let my family know that we are alive and well so that they'll pay a ransom."

Young Flynn was quietly sobbing now. "I think this is it. Either they didn't pay them….. or, or they did and we are expendable now that they have the money."

The newly hired pilot paused to wipe his eyes with the left sleeve of his shirt. "I am really sorry about all this Mr. Mandel, I really am."

"How is your fault?" replied Mandel.

Before he could say anything else Mandel felt the butt of a rifle hit the back of his head.

"I told you before to shut up, Jew" shouted their leader who was now equipped with a rifle of his own. "Hands behind your backs"

All three men did as they were told and the man in the black balaclava tied each man's wrists with rope and then did the same to their ankles. It was just the same routine as the last time they had been on camera, only they didn't bother to blindfold them this time.

While they were being tied up the man who had hijacked the plane went into a closet and brought back with him a dark gray balaclava and three long knives.

He handed each of his cohorts one of the knives and put on his mask.

"Son of a bitch" said Mandel under his breath.

Rhodes looked over at his boss and seemed to look for a sign of what to do next.

"This is not good, Dan."

"I hear you." whispered Mandel. His mouth was so dry that he could hardly get the words out. He knew that if someone like Jack was scared, then he probably should be too.

The biggest kidnapper wearing the gray mask glanced at his watch to check the time. He was wearing the Tag chronograph that he had taken from Mandel their first day in captivity.

He then said something in Arabic to the man in the green ski mask. The man responded and moved behind the digital camera located across from the three Americans and made it ready for use.

The big man in the gray mask gleefully laughed out loud and rubbed his hands together.

"OK. Now we make a movie for your friends at home."

Paris, France-1:30AM

Watching Henri LeMond sleeping in his chair had become Brandon Parkes' focus for at least the last hour and he knew that he had to get some fresh coffee soon, if he was to not drift off himself. The now muted TV was tuned to monitor the terrorists' web site, but as nothing was occurring no one was watching it now.

Griffin was stretched out on the couch and was also sound asleep.

Bernstein and Liz were sitting beside one another at a table and staring at the laptop computer. They had been scouring the internet for any kind of news. Except for their occasional whispers and Griffin's snoring; the room was very quiet.

He got up from his chair and was headed to see if there was some coffee or anything left to eat when Liz's cell phone rang. She picked it up and answered.

"Hello. No. We have heard nothing, Uncle Harry."

"Yes, I have Bernstein, Griffin, Henri and Brandon here in my room with me. Also Bertrand is here as he is fluent in Arabic as well as in French."

"OK, I will let you know the moment we have any word. Thank you for calling."

A weary Parkes took a sip of the coffee he had just poured and waited for Liz to say something.

"Harry hasn't heard anything either."

Taking another drink from his cup he asked if he could get her anything.

She just shook her head and began searching the internet news sites. Parkes could tell that Liz was starting to get really concerned. He was about to suggest that he, Henri and Griffin should go to their own rooms and wait for her call when he heard a voice from across the room.

"Hey, I think that you guys need to see this" announced LeMond. Henri, now standing, grabbed the television tuner to turn up the volume. He had found something on CNN International.

The image coming at them was of Dan Mandel, with his pilots to each side of him. They were kneeling as two men in ski masks stood behind them.

One of the kidnappers began speaking in broken English.

"We would like to thank the family of Mandel for doing as instructed and delivering the ransom of ten million U.S. However, since not all of our demands have been met we will not be letting anyone go free tonight"

Now standing with Bernstein at her side, Liz flashed a look of anger at the Israeli as she heard the terrorists' words, but she said nothing.

As the man on the screen began ranting about his Muslim brothers being held unjustly in prison Parkes quickly took a seat on the couch next to a now fully awake Griffin who had sat up to give him room.

The man in the dark gray mask ended his tirade by repeating that their prisoners were not to be let go because his comrades from Palestine had not been released.

That same man put his hand on the shoulder of the younger pilot. "We will now allow these men to speak and tell all of you in America how well they are doing."

Flynn, who had been staring at the floor looked up and began to speak in a quiet voice.

"Carol, just know that I am doing OK. We are being treated well. Take care of yourself and the baby. And know that I am really sorry about all this...."

Before he could say any more the man in the gray mask touched Flynn's shoulder again and told him that his time was done for talking and that it was now the next man's turn.

Dan Mandel began to speak. "I love and miss you all. Liz, be sure to tell your mom and your brother that, too. If you need anything just ask your uncle. You will be able to count on him if we….if we don't make it back home"

Parkes saw that Liz had tears running down her cheeks. She moved to sit beside him on the couch. He moved closer to the middle and she snuggled up next to him. He held out his hand and she placed hers in it.

As Jack Rhodes stared into the camera his eyes began to blink. He looked to be too choked up to say anything. He finally blurted out "I love you, Sara" and then returned his eyes to the floor.

A third man wearing a black mask now appeared on camera. He took his place behind Rhodes while the man who had done all the talking moved behind Mr. Mandel.

Suddenly the man in the green mask who was standing behind Flynn grabbed his hair and pulled his head back. He then drew a large knife and placed it at his throat.

Seeing this, Parkes' instinct told him to squeeze Liz's hand to distract her from what they were watching. She buried her head into his chest and began to cry.

The man in the gray mask then began to yell over the protests of Flynn.

"You must now be taught to understand how serious we are with our demands for the release of our Palestinian brothers!"

He then turned to the man holding the knife to Flynn's throat. "God is great" he yelled in English and with that his comrade's knife began cutting into the flesh of the young American's neck.

Yelling out the word no as the knife cut deeper, his assailant was now using a sawing motion on him. Flynn's final no's were accompanied by a gurgling sound as blood filled his throat.

Finally there was nothing more coming from the television, except the repeated yelling of God is great, in Arabic, by all three kidnappers. The man in the green mask had completely severed the pilots head and was now walking toward the camera holding it by the hair like a trophy.

Soon the man and his prize filled the screen. As the macabre web cast from hell concluded, Henri turned down the volume on the TV.

The muffled sound of Liz crying into the chest of a stunned Parkes filled the room for most of the next half hour as everyone tried to come to grips with the incredible horror that they had just witnessed.

What he thought almost worse was thinking about a fact that all gathered here knew all too well. The Israeli's weren't ever going to let a single Palestinian out of jail. They didn't do it at Munich and they wouldn't do it now.

Despite having paid the kidnappers ten million dollars in ransom money, Parkes knew that Liz might well see the terrible thing that just happened to Pete Flynn occur again.

Chapter Seven

Spa, Belgium

Moderate temperature and a clear sky welcomed the crews of the International SuperSedan Challenge as they made ready for the Saturday morning practice session at the historic Belgium circuit known as Spa Francorchamps.

Getting back to work less than a week after the last race was a real relief to Brandon Parkes and all those employed by Team Mandel. The stress of competition was nothing compared to what they had seen transpire earlier in the week. One pilot had been executed, and Liz and Bernstein were doing all they could to gain the release of her father and their senior pilot, Jack Rhodes.

More than happy that he was away from all the upset; Parkes couldn't help but feeling guilty for having to leave Liz back in Paris with only Bernstein to help her deal with things. He took consolation in the fact that her uncle was coming back over to Paris and would be with her soon and hopefully bringing the ordeal to a relatively positive conclusion.

Driving down the pit road in his Cadillac CTS-V, Parkes suddenly felt a sense of well-being and security. It was as though the cocoon of the cockpit, the bolstered seat and full face helmet had made him safe from anyone who might try to harm him.

Race to Damascus

He even felt good about wearing the HANS device as he had finally gotten used to it. His attitude was confident today, but he was still a little cautious after what occurred at the last race.

The ISC was using the newer Formula One pit garages here instead of the old ones that still remained and which were now used for endurance sports car events. Rolling out on to the track he started the downhill run to the Eau Rouge corner. With the old pits to his right, and grandstands to his left, he looked straight ahead and set up for the left right and then left combination of Eau Rouge, one of the most iconic corners in racing. Getting it right was the key to setting a quick lap in the minds of most drivers. Steering to the left, he then made the uphill right that followed it.

He was now on the long Kemmel straight that led to the right left combination corner named Les Combes.

The car would be doing close to one hundred and sixty five miles per hour in the race. Since this was just the warm up lap Parkes was only going about one hundred and forty before he started the downshifting and braking which would slow him down to a little less than sixty miles per hour as he made his way through the corners.

The short straight after Les Combes led to the third gear, Malmedy corner. After the downhill run to the Rivage hairpin he braked and went down into second gear. The tires were warming up already and the car felt like it was set up just about to his liking.

After getting through a group of the twisty third and fourth gear corners he stood on the gas coming out of what was called Stavelot corner for the almost flat out run to the chicane located just prior to the start finish line. This portion of the track could not be called a straight away as there were kinks to the left in the road, including the difficult and daunting sweeper named Blanchimont. Parkes lifted the throttle a bit as he made his way through the left hander before he re applied the gas for the short straight that led to the famous chicane known as the Bus Stop. The Cadillac was doing in excess of one hundred and sixty before braking hard and getting sufficiently slowed down to make it through the newly reconfigured right left chicane that led to the pit straight and the finish line.

He noticed a bit of power over steer when he exited the final corner, but got the fishtailing under control as he went past the pits. The slowest part of the track, the Le Source Hairpin, otherwise known as turn one, was coming up and Parkes decided it should be taken in first gear. When he heard the engine and transmission protest he decided to try it in second gear the next time, or maybe have the cars gear ratios changed before qualifying.

Accelerating downhill once again he set up for the ascending Eau Rouge complex and took it the second time at a much greater pace. This momentum carried him to a higher top speed on the straight away than he had reached on his last lap.

Shifting up through the gears on the long run to Les Combes Parkes couldn't help but smile at how well his car was performing.

Near the end of his first full lap Griffin reported on the radio that they had just done a two minute and twenty second lap. As he began lap three Parkes decided that he was content to keep about that same pace for another half dozen laps and just learn the circuit better, before trying to go much faster.

Heading to the Bus Stop chicane once again he turned right onto pit road, instead of continuing for another lap, and soon found himself welcomed by Griffin and three of the crew who were poised to take tire temperatures just as soon as the Cadillac came to a complete stop.

Just behind him he noticed that Henri was pitting his car as well. Both Team Mandel drivers climbed out of their cars and removed their helmets and gloves. They proceeded to walk toward one another as they did so.

Race to Damascus

"How was it for you?" asked Henri.

"Good. The car is very comfortable. You would never know it was the backup car."

How was your run?"

LeMond wiped his face with a towel before he responded.

"My car felt very good, too. Of course it may be a case of my really liking the track, but I do believe that it is a course that suits these cars of ours. With a couple of adjustments I think we could take the pole position here, too.

The sky was becoming overcast and Parkes now had a dull ache in his leg, the same one he had broken in the crash at Daytona. It had become his personal weather barometer in the last few months and he had found out that he could predict rain any time that he felt the pain. It was also a reminder to always take your foot off the brake pedal when you were about to hit the wall at a superspeedway.

"I sure wish that it wouldn't rain before we go out to qualify". Parkes said as he looked up at the sky.

"Brandon, this is Spa. That means we are in Belgium. Are you really surprised to see that it might rain?" asked LeMond with a smile.

"No, just hoping that we can qualify before it happens."

"I am going to the hospitality tent to get a coffee and have a cigarette. Do you want to join me?

"No thanks, Henri. I want to talk to the crew about set-ups in case it does rain."

"OK, but I don't think it will rain before we qualify. Anyway, I already told Griffin what changes I wanted to the car on the radio, so I am off to take a break. I'll see you later."

It was over three hours until the qualifying session. As cloudy as it was now Parkes knew that he should probably prepare himself for the likelihood that rain would be falling on the fast Spa circuit by the time they were ready to go back out on the track again.

The times from practice revealed that the Mandel cars had been sixth and eighth fastest; with LeMond having done a best of two minutes and eighteen seconds, and Parkes at two minutes nineteen and change.

The possibility of a damp track would almost certainly mean that the Cadillacs would qualify somewhat slower than their best practice speed.

The question was, if it did rain, would it slow the other teams by a similar margin, or would the grippy all-wheel-drive cars once again have an advantage?

Seeing some lightening in the distance Parkes went into the garage for some advice from Griffin and the lads on the changes being made to the car in anticipation of the impending rain, which was fast approaching.

Silvio Marino had scheduled a press conference for eleven forty-five to announce the plans for ISC's second season of competition. In addition to the media, most of the drivers and many of the team owners would also be in attendance.

A light rain had began to fall as everyone made their way to the large media tent to find out what Marino had in mind for next year.

It was strange that Liz wasn't going to be there. As he took his seat next to Henri and Griffin, Parkes wondered if Marino had found himself a new benefactor, since he, like the rest of them, was probably unsure whether Mandel SuperStores would be coming back as a sponsor next season.

"Too bad I didn't bet you about the rain, Henri."

"It is just a light shower, Brandon. I think that I am still going out with slick tires and a dry set up."

"Well, we shall see. I am playing it safe and going with rains and damp settings. I guess that I would rather be tenth or two slower than spin out in the wet and end up starting dead last."

Griffin interrupted his drivers." Whatever you guys want is fine by me. It may be wet out there, but I will trust your judgment; Henri. It may just pay off."

All three men then focused their attention on the front of the tent as Marino made his entrance. The press conference was about to begin. Christine, Marino's assistant, stepped up to the microphone and called the meeting to order. Soon all those in the tent grew quiet.

"We have some exciting news regarding the future of the series. So without further delay let me bring up the president of the ISC, Mr. Silvio Marino."

Marino stood up from his seat, and accompanied by the applause of the crowd, walked up to the microphone. As soon as the clapping stopped he began to speak.

"Thank you everyone. We have had a great first season so far. This has in turn led to interest from other circuits, sponsors and investors who we know want to be part of International SuperSedan Challenge next year and into the future."

"Our tentative schedule will see us expand from four events to ten races next year. New venues such as Moscow, Shanghi and a race in Japan will make the ISC a truly international series."

"There will be materials outlining our plans available for those of you reporters, or team owners who request them."

One of the members of the media raised his hand. "What is the status of Mandel Super Stores given the unfortunate kidnapping of the company's owner?"

Marino paused for a moment before answering.

"Of course we are hopeful that our friend, Mr. Dan Mandel, will come back to us safely and that it will happen very soon. While we do have many new series sponsors lined up, it is our desire to see Mandel Super Stores come back as the sponsor of the one million dollar grand-slam that consists of the four cornerstone events of Monza, Lausitzring, Cairo and the event here at Spa. In fact, Harry Mandel is flying here next week to discuss renewing this program for next year, as we agree that it is what his brother Dan would want." A round of polite applause followed Marino's words. Before the applause ended, Parkes leaned over and whispered to his team mate.

"Well, it seems that Mr. Marino has been busy assuring the future of the series, but now I need to go make sure of my future in the race. I'll see you back at the pits."

Leaving the media tent, Parkes noticed that the rain coming down was still a fairly light shower. He told himself he would stick with his idea of running a safe set-up for his qualifying run, even if the rain didn't get any worse than it was now.

With only a bit over an hour before the start of qualifying he decided he needed to get something to eat and some bottled water over at the team's hospitality tent.

Race to Damascus

En route to his repast he was greeted by an attractive young American couple who wanted him to autograph their program. He learned that the twenty something man was an F-16 pilot who was stationed there with NATO. The woman was his fiancée and was in Belgium visiting him for the week.

As he walked away from the couple it made him feel good to know that he had at least a couple of fans who were cheering for him. He just hoped that he wouldn't let them down. A good result was really needed this weekend and Parkes had resolved that he was going to get a good finish this time out.

No sooner that he got back to the garage did the crew hustle him into the car to make ready for qualifying.

The eight cylinder engine barked to life as Parkes gave Griffin a thumbs up with his gloved right hand. He put the sequential shifter into gear and slowly exited his garage. Then he steered right and drove down the pit lane to begin the warm up lap of his qualifying run.

Entering the track he noticed that while the rain had stopped falling, there was a bit of spray coming off the track from the Mercedes that had gone out just before him. With his windshield wiper set to intermittent, he proceeded up through the gears and soon found himself on the long straight away that led to Les Combes.

With rain tires and a fairly soft suspension set up, the Cadillac felt stable in the wet. The set up choices that he made might not win him the pole, but he was just happy right now that he wasn't sliding all over the still unfamiliar Spa Francorchamps circuit.

The same thing could probably not be said for the driver of the Mercedes in front of him. Parkes had decided to stay behind him during his warm up lap and watched as the driver fought with under steer going in to the corners and fishtailing over steer as he exited them.

The ill handling Mercedes soon veered to the right and entered pit road. "No doubt getting himself some rain tires" he thought with a touch of smugness. When he crossed the start finish line he was on the clock. This lap would count and with a clear track in front of him there wasn't any reason he couldn't put in a decent time.

He thundered downhill to the Eau Rouge corner and made it through perfectly. Driving on the limit down the long Kemmel straightaway he saw that one of the Audi RS5's was going slowly, no doubt doing his warm up lap, but the car stayed to the right as he blasted by it and then braked and shifted down for Les Combes.

The tricky Rivage hairpin corner gave him a bit of trouble on exit as he encountered a bit of power over-steer when he pushed down on the accelerator. He made a mental note to himself to squeeze the power on next time, lest he have another episode of the tail breaking loose on him.

On the back straight Parkes reported to his pit that the car felt good.

"Just take it nice and smooth, mate. The track is drying quickly so you will need to get your fast lap in soon since you are still on rains."

"Roger that." He then downshifted to second and turned in to the first corner of the Bus Stop chicane.

At the finish of his first full lap Griffin came back on the radio to inform him that he had just done a lap that was the second fastest time so far. After three more solid trips around the circuit he learned that he had improved his times, but that several others were now going even faster. Griffin told him to bring the car in to the pits.

"That's all we are going to get on rain tires with a drying track, mate" said Griffin on the radio.

"I agree. I'll bring it in."

By the time the black Cadillac made it back to its pit stall Parkes had dropped down the qualifying order to eleventh place.

His team mate had qualified ahead of him in fifth place with a last minute run on slick tires on a now dry track, but as he climbed out of his car he was just happy to have gotten through qualifying without incident.

Maybe he had been overly cautious in qualifying, but because the team had no backup car this weekend, due to the damage to chassis number 2 at Monza, playing it safe had been the prudent thing to do. The fact that he was pretty certain that he would have a good car for the race itself was some consolation for his less than stellar qualifying performance and an eleventh place starting spot.

Best of all, he was confident that he could be competitive if the track conditions were either wet or dry the next afternoon.

At least he hoped that would be the case.

Spa, Belgium-Saturday afternoon

The late afternoon had turned from cloudy to sunshine as Liz Mandel traveled from Paris north to Belgium and the city of Spa.

She slipped on her sun glasses as she leaned forward from the back seat of the Mercedes and reminded her driver that they were going to be staying at the Radisson Hotel and handed him the piece of paper with the directions that she had printed off the internet earlier that day.

The action at the track would be over by the time they arrived and since she was tired and hungry from the drive up, heading straight to the hotel only made good sense. She could get a snack, something to drink and cleaned up before the drivers and crew returned from qualifying.

Though tired from the journey, she actually felt better emotionally than she had for some time. Feeling helpless as she had watched the young pilot beheaded, she had begun to rely even more on her faith. She believed that her life was in the hands of God and that the test that she was going through was being allowed to happen so that she, and perhaps others, would grow spiritually.

She also began to realize that her main concern had not actually been as much about her dad losing his life, as much she was about her father losing his eternal soul. Her prayer had originally been that Dan Mandel would be delivered home safely. Now she asked that he would turn to God while he was enduring his captivity. Knowing her father as she did, Liz worried that this self reliant, agnostic man would never do anything of the sort.

As the big S Class neared the hotel she looked out the window and took in the sights of the charming city of Spa. There was no reason not to enjoy this opportunity to visit a place that she had never been before, even if her father was being held by a group of kidnappers somewhere in Syria.

The Radisson she was staying at was located right next to the thermal baths that gave Spa its name. She was hoping that she would have time to spend some time relaxing there during her stay.

When she tried to check in she was surprised that there was no reservation in her name. The woman at the desk informed her that due to a last minute cancellation there was a room available for her; however her Mossad driver would have to find other lodging as there was just one room vacant.

Bernstein wouldn't like it that his man would have be staying elsewhere, but this is where the team was staying and she decided to take the remaining room for herself and hope that her driver could find a place nearby. While registering she was pleasantly surprised when Brandon came walking up to her.

"Hello, Miss Mandel" he said with a smile.

"Brandon, I am so happy to see you here.

There was no reservation in my name and I was starting to wonder if I was at the right hotel".

Parkes laughed when he heard of her dilemma. "Well, the fact is that you aren't."

"Then what are you doing here?"

"I guess I made the same mistake you did, Liz. Believe it or not, there are actually two Radisson Hotels here in Spa. The crew guys are all staying at the other one, the Radisson Balmoral."

"So there should be a room for my driver, Mr. Roth, over at the other hotel then."

"Yeah, and there is a room in your name, as well. I had made my own reservation and just assumed that this Radisson was the one the team was at when I booked it, but there obviously should still be at least two vacancies over at the Radisson Balmoral."

"Well, since I am already checked in here, I will send Roth to the other hotel and have him cancel my reservation when he checks in." she said with a smile.

"Great; hey did you know that there was a tunnel from this hotel directly to the spa?"

"Why do you think I decided to stay here with you?" she asked him with a grin.

Ardennes Forest, Belgium-early Saturday evening

The sun was just beginning to set and thoughts about what had taken place here over sixty years ago began to flood Brandon Parkes mind. His own grandfather had been wounded here during the first days of fighting in what would come to be known as the Battle of the Bulge. He had felt a need to visit this historic place of honor and decided to take a quick tour of the area before picking up Liz for a late dinner.

While he had always been very proud of his grandfather and his service in World War II, he remembered that Albert Parkes had never seemed comfortable talking about his time here.

Severely injured when a German mortar shell landed next to him, it had actually been a blessing of sorts because it meant that he was taken from the front lines by jeep to a field hospital and then back to the states and an eventual medical discharge. As a result of his wounds, he had missed having to endure the extreme cold and intense fear that his fellow soldiers had experienced for many weeks. While a part of him was thankful for having been spared all that, it always seemed to Brandon that his grandfather had felt a little guilty about not having contributed more to the war than he had. Being a young officer who had been blown up by a mortar round before taking out a single German soldier wasn't how Al Parkes wanted to be remembered.

This sort of self deprecating thinking would plague his grandfather for his entire life.

Although he completely recovered physically, he always judged himself harshly after his return from the war. Not only had this negative thinking probably kept him from reaching his full potential as an entrepreneur, it also had robbed him of any joy when he did achieve a modicum of success.

Race to Damascus

Being your own biggest critic and never being satisfied with any result was the best way to realize your highest aspirations; his grandfather had often told him.

It now seemed to Parkes that this malady had skipped a generation as it was something that he was now dealing with as well. The need to be somebody, or whatever that nebulous desire to make a mark on the world was called, was something that he had.

More of a curse than a blessing to him, Brandon had become aware of these demons at an early age.

His father had never thought like this and had quietly managed to become a big fish in the medium sized pond that was Des Moines, Iowa. He was happy with his accomplishments and didn't have any guilt about enjoying his life just as it was. Maybe that was the reason his dad didn't understand why he had this need to lead the risky life of a professional racing driver when the security of the family bank was there for the taking.

A common thought he often had was the difference between a baseball player who came to the plate always trying to hit a homerun and one who was just satisfied with a base hit.

Grandfather had been a perfectionist who had dreams of knocking the ball out of the park, being a hero and a successful business man, while his father was more than satisfied with his less lofty goals and just getting a hit. The irony was that his dad's mind set had actually provided much more financial success, personal satisfaction and peace of mind than his grandfather's driven approach ever had.

As he walked the area near Malmedy, where the American soldiers taken prisoner had been executed by the SS Panzer troops, he thought about all the young men who never had the chance to live beyond twenty or twenty two and wondered why his grandfather hadn't looked upon his surviving the war as a bonus and just enjoyed the extra years he had been given?

Brandon already knew the answer. His own need for success and his fear of failure had driven him to where he didn't find much joy anymore, either. As he had grown older he had begun to feel that life was a disappointing place. People would let you down, double cross you or, as in the case of Dan Mandel, even kidnap you for ransom if you did manage to achieve real financial success.

But what other choice was there but to keep your guard up and continue to play the game? Even if he was growing tired of living this way, he didn't have a set of emotions other than the ones he seemed to have inherited from his grandfather. Simply put, he felt that one had to become a winner and then everything else would fall in to place. He was sure that he would be fine if he could just reach that hard to quantify goal of becoming more successful than he was now.

Of course his grandfather had professed the same thing right up until the time that stress induced heart failure claimed him at the age of sixty-eight. Knowing that was beginning to cause Brandon to question his similar philosophy of life.

It occurred to him as he drove back to the hotel that maybe the young men who died here as heroes might have been the lucky ones after all. He had little doubt that Al Parkes would have preferred that option, as long as it had come with the Silver Star or the Medal of Honor.

Spa, Belgium - Saturday evening-8:45PM

One would never have known that Liz Mandel was under the amount of stress that she was right now thought Parkes. Initially he thought it was because of having spent a couple of relaxing hours at the spa, but soon realized that her tranquility was due to more than just that.

As the couple walked through the quaint city of Spa, she had begun to share with him the revelation that she had been experiencing.

It was the knowledge that she really couldn't control anything that happened to her and that the only choice that she did have was to completely surrender her life and soul to God.

Normally Parkes would have avoided talking about religion, philosophy or politics, but tonight he was willing to discuss the subject that Liz had brought up repeatedly. Perhaps it was because he really cared for her, but maybe it was the due to the fact that he had become confused about life himself.

He was trying to take charge of his emotions as well as his career, and she was talking about the concept that there was no such thing as control. He felt he had such a loose grasp on things right now that the idea of turning his life over to a God he wasn't even sure existed had very little appeal to him.

"Look, I guess that I think that there must be a higher power. But I need to get my life in order before I start thinking about what I believe in. I mean, don't take this wrong, but you are the daughter of a billionaire and have the luxury of contemplating such things. I just don't have the time to sit and pray and philosophize about the big universal questions right now. My focus has to be on making your racecar and myself into winners, not sitting around hoping that God will do it for me."

"I think that you may have a little learning ahead of you." she replied with a smile. "Let me ask you something. If you put your all of your focus on racing and become the winningest, highest paid driver ever and then went out and had a tire blow out while testing…" She then paused for a moment while deciding what her next words would be. "Well, let's say that you were killed as a result of a racing accident. If that happened, don't you think that it would be too late to find out all about God?"

He really didn't know what to say because he had never thought about it before. Surely if he died he would go to heaven, if there was a heaven. He had not been perfect, but he certainly had never murdered anyone and he always had tried to be kind to others. No one had ever questioned him like this before, nor had he ever questioned himself about such things, either.

"I really don't know what to say, Liz."

"It talks in the Bible about what good does it do if you inherit the whole world but lose your soul. It is the same thing I have reminded my dad about, but he doesn't listen. My worry is that now it may be too late for him." she told him. "If I thought he had become a true believer then I wouldn't be nearly as upset by his kidnapping because I would know that even if the worst were to happen that I would see him again very soon."

Now Parkes was becoming an uncomfortable and decided that he didn't want to talk about these topics anymore. He certainly didn't want to talk about his dying in a race car. He felt that if you dwelled on what could happen you would never do anything, or at least not be competitive at racing. Others actually thought that the guys who think they are going to get it in a race car might actually be willing it upon themselves.

It was a good time to take the conversation in a different direction, he thought.

"Speaking of your father, if you aren't happy with Bernstein and the Mossad, why not get the FBI or CIA to help?"

"It would have been the FBI, since it was considered an act against an American citizen, but it was Uncle Harry who preferred to use the Israelis. Now I am not so certain about that choice. I suppose he thought that it would have been what my father would have wanted since he has many friends in the Israeli Likud Party."

It was Liz who now seemed to feel uncomfortable. She appeared to Parkes to be uncertain of what to do next when it came to her father's circumstances.

"Listen, we had better get you back to your room if you are going to be ready for tomorrow.

"I suppose so." he replied. He felt like a kid who was being ordered to go off to bed because he had school in the morning, but knew that he would feel better tomorrow if he called it a day right now.

As they headed back to the hotel, she asked him if he had ever read "The Lion, The Witch and the Wardrobe". When he said that he had when he was in the sixth grade, she told him that she had a copy of another CS Lewis book back at her room that she would give him to read.

"Sure. Is it another book for children?" he asked with a sarcastic smile.

"No, it's not just for children. It is a good book for everyone to read. In fact, it is my favorite of all his books."

"Alright, I will take a look at it if you say so."

"I do say so" replied Liz. "Just remember as you read it that this work is a best seller."

"Sure, but then you have to promise to have dinner with me again when I finish it."

"It's a deal."

While they walked through the Radisson to their rooms, Parkes had noticed that Scott Battle was there in the lobby huddled in conversation with two of his Arab friends. One of the men was Mustafa, but he didn't recognize the younger man that was with them.

He still didn't think that Battle had anything to do with Mr. Mandel's kidnapping, but Bernstein continued to ask for any info regarding Scott's actions. He made a mental note to mention what he had seen the next time he saw Bernstein and proceeded to escort Liz to her room.

As they got to her door he had hoped in the back of his mind that she was using this story about this book that she wanted to loan him as an excuse to invite him into her room so that they could turn in early together.

Taking out her room key she opened the door. "I'll be right back" she said with a smile.

She returned just a moment later with a soft cover copy of the book she had mentioned and kissed him goodnight on the cheek. "I hope you enjoy reading it" she whispered.

Then she shut her door, leaving him standing by himself and wondering what had just happened. Was he misreading her? He wondered if she looked at him more as a brother than as someone she was interested in romantically?

As he headed to his own room he looked at the book and saw that Liz had given him a copy of a book entitled "Mere Christianity". He smiled as he realized that he probably had not been a victim of rejection, but of Ms. Mandel's seemingly complete commitment to her faith.

In the hallway he saw Silvio Marino with Christine and stopped to say hello.

"How are you doing?" asked Marino.

"Not bad at all"

"What have you heard about Mr. Mandel's situation?

"Not much as of late. Liz mentioned that the man from the Mossad who has been helping them with the investigation is driving up tomorrow morning from Paris to meet her here and will give her an update on what they know. She told me that this Agent Bernstein had some leads he's been following up on, that might help find her dad; so hopefully she will know more when she gets to the track tomorrow for the race."

"Let's hope so" replied Marino. "Anyway, have a good run tomorrow".

"Thanks, we'll see both of you in the morning." Parkes went a little way further down the hall and opened the door of his own room.

It occurred to him as he was flipping on the TV set that Marino surely did want to see that Mandel was rescued. Without his return there might not be an ISC, no matter what Marino had told everyone about new sponsors and investors at the press conference earlier that day.

Spa Francorchamps – Sunday

The sunshine that had come to grace Spa for race day was a welcome change from the weather the afternoon before. Without a cloud in the sky it appeared that these conditions would last at least until late into the day.

Since the track would be dry the Team Mandel crewmen had been hard at work this morning changing the suspension set ups, rear wing settings and replacing rain tires with racing slicks.

The warm-up session was scheduled for eleven thirty am and Parkes had been glad for that, as he had been up late thinking about what Liz had said to him the night before. Despite not getting out of bed until 9:30, he had only gotten about five hours of sleep.

Nevertheless he felt good today. He actually seemed as rested as he would after the eight hours or so that he would have normally slept the night before a race.

After a quick shower he jumped into a pair of black sweats and a gray T-shirt, threw on a black Team Mandel cap and set off for the short trip to the track.

As he was getting in to his rental car Parkes saw a black Mercedes drive by his parking spot. It was a brand new AMG Mercedes C Class and it was being driven by Scott Battle. Seated next to him was Sayid Mustafa. The young Arab man that he had seen him with last night in the lobby wasn't with them.

His watch told him that he had plenty of time to get to the track prior to practice and so he decided to make his drive a leisurely one. He would take in the sights and sounds of race day at historic Spa while enjoying both the sunshine and the moment.

Although he was only qualified in eleventh place, he was still excited that he was about to drive on one of the world's best race courses on a nearly perfect day.

He put on his sunglasses and smiled to himself as he realized that it was times like this that he had dreamed of as a kid back in Iowa. As he drove toward the circuit he vowed to start enjoying what he had, instead of worrying so much about the future.

Entering the gate of the track he showed his credential to the attendant and drove slowly toward the parking area. Like him, most of the crowd was arriving now so that they would be there in time for the pre race warm up.

The bright sunshine was already making the temperature rise and it served to remind Parkes that he needed to start drinking water as soon as he got to the transporter so that he wouldn't get dehydrated and possibly end up suffering muscle cramps in the race.

Walking into the transporter lounge he found Henri sitting in his driver's suit consuming   a bottle of his sponsor's spring water.

"I was just thinking about needing to do that" he said as he pointed to the bottle in Henri's hand. The race would last an hour and a half, which worked out to be about 38 laps of racing and staying fresh would be one of the keys to victory.

After finishing the last of his water LeMond announced that he was going out to have a quick cigarette before practice began.

"What a surprise!" Parkes said with a smile.

"See you soon, Brandon." replied LeMond with a somewhat sheepish grin.

While getting dressed Parkes decided that he was going to have fun out there today and drive his car in a slightly less aggressive manner than usual, at least at the start. His plan was to be smooth, save the car, the gearbox and himself for the last laps of the race. This approach would hopefully lead to his getting a good finish for the first time this season.

Spa, Belgium-Sunday afternoon

The ringing of her room phone woke Liz Mandel. She reached over to the night stand to answer it. It was her driver and body guard, Ephraim Roth calling to ask what time he should come over to get her. She looked at the clock next to the phone and realized that she had slept past noon, but was happy that she had done so as she was more rested than she had been in weeks.

"Come over in an hour, I should be ready by then. Oh, and thanks for getting me up, Ephraim. Mr. Bernstein should be here soon and if it weren't for your call I might have slept the day away. Anyway, I'll see you in about an hour".

As she hung up she thought about ordering something to eat from room service. Since it would be here by the time she had finished bathing and getting dressed, she picked up the receiver and asked them to send hot tea, orange juice and English muffins for two.

After a quick soak in the bath tub she got dressed in khaki slacks and a black Team Mandel sport shirt. She was combing her hair when there was a knock at the door.

Opening the door, she found Agent Bernstein standing there.

"Good morning, Liz."

"Please come in. You arrived earlier than I had expected."

"Sorry." replied Bernstein."Uh, before I forget, you do know that your Uncle Harry will be flying to Paris tomorrow, right?

"Yes, he is coming to help us resolve this whole mess and to get my dad back safely"

"But did you know that your uncle is also planning on meeting with Silvio Marino while he is in Paris?"

She had a quizzical look on her face. "What's your point? He is seeing Marino to talk about continuing our sponsorship of the ISC. Harry knows that it is almost certainly what dad would want."

"Maybe, but. What I mean to say is that.... "

Before Bernstein could say any more there was another knock at the door. "Hold that thought, it is probably our order from room service" said Liz holding up her left index finger. "Is tea alright with you?"

"Yes, that sounds fine" replied Bernstein politely.

A dark haired young man with a white waiter's coat was standing behind a white draped service cart.

"Hello. You can just place it over there on the coffee table" she said with a smile.

The young man did as asked and then presented her the bill for her to sign.

"Do you have a pen?" she asked.

He reached slowly into his left inside pocket with his right hand and pulled out a long knife. With a demonic look on his face he turned and lunged at Bernstein.

The knife went into the unsuspecting Israeli's midsection, but instinct took over and he managed to knock his attacker away with a right forearm to the face.

Liz started to make for the door but the man tackled her and knocked her down before she could get there. As he drove the ten inch blade into her back she let out a loud scream; the attacker then got up and turned his attention back to the Mossad agent.

Bleeding profusely Bernstein held his left hand over the wound and prepared to defend himself with his balled up right fist.

The man started coming at him with the knife in his right hand when two gun shots rang out. The attacker dropped to the floor right in front of him.

He then looked up toward the door to see who his savior was. "Oh Roth, thank God...please call for an ambulance.

Bernstein was still grasping the wound to his stomach as he staggered toward where Liz Mandel lay motionless. He knelt by her and felt for a pulse before he passed out himself.

Spa Francorchamps - Sunday 2:00pm

The sound of twenty-four V8 powered supercars slowly making their way around the Spa circuit on the pace lap was but a sample of the aural delights that awaited the large crowd of spectators that had come to the Belgian track to witness the third round of the International SuperSedan Challenge.

As his black Cadillac came to a stop in his starting spot on the grid Parkes pulled down hard on his seatbelt straps and then checked his rear view mirrors. The fact that Liz had not been there before the start had bothered him, but he told himself that surely she was caught in traffic and would be here in time for the race.

His only real concern right now was to make sure that he avoided any trouble at the start. Going into La Source and then the Eau Rouge corners were the two bottlenecks on the track that concerned him most. If he could get through these two cleanly he felt he would be fine as the tight pack of cars would likely string themselves out into a single file, nose to tail, freight train as they headed down the long straight away that followed.

Suddenly the red starters light came on. Ten seconds to the green.

Yellow signaled five seconds to go. Parkes brought up the revs and prepared to launch.

The green light came on and the Cadillac shot down the straight away headed for the tight right turn La Source hairpin.

There was some banging of bumpers and sheet metal going on in front of him, but nothing too serious had occurred as a result and his own car wasn't harmed at all.

Coming down the front straight Parkes girded himself for the treacherous uphill Eau Rouge corners. The left right and then left again series of corners that were a challenge every time he had to negotiate them.

Once again there was some contact going on in front of him, but still no one had spun out or crashed as had happened at the start of the previous two races.

He tucked up behind a BMW and drafted with him on the Kemmel straight until just before Les Combes corner. Seeing the opportunity for a clean pass he pulled out from behind and sling-shotted past the M3, taking him on the inside of the track. Parkes was already up to ninth position and he felt that he wasn't even trying all that hard.

Staying ninth place for several laps was in keeping with the plan he had committed to of conserving the car and keeping out of a race ending on track incident.

Crossing the start finish line to begin lap ten of thirty-eight Parkes decided it was time to check in with his crew.

He pushed the button on his steering wheel between the shift from second to third gear and called for Griffin on the radio.

Ashmore didn't respond until Parkes was driving through Eau Rouge.

"Sorry, I was a little busy when you called back, Griffin."

Parkes shifted into fifth gear with his right hand before continuing.

"When do you think I should plan on stopping?"

There was a pause as Griffin thought about what to tell his driver.

"We had planned on halfway, but just like in Germany, if your tires are still good I figure that we could put it off until a bit later."

He took a moment to compute what stopping earlier might mean to him in the final laps while he simultaneously downshifted and braked for the right and then left combination at Les Combes.

After getting through the Malmedy and Virage corners he informed Griffin that he was fine with that idea before taking the left hand turn and on to the straight section of track that followed.

"We'll plan on seeing you just after half distance, mate"

"Roger that" he replied.

The car really liked the Spa circuit and Parkes was pleased that he had been able to stay with the lead pack while still keeping to his plan of running at a conservative pace.

By lap fourteen he had moved up to eighth, as all but one of the cars ahead of him stopped in the pits. Lap eighteen saw all but one car in front of him peel off into pit lane. His crew reported that he was now in P2, three seconds behind the new leader, Mansur Bin Salman in the Scimitar Mercedes.

The gap between first and second place remained at about three seconds or so, until the end of the nineteenth lap. Parkes flashed by the start finish line in the lead as the Arab driver came in to make his stop for gas and new tires. As he steered through the first corner and headed down the straight he couldn't help but feel happy. He had a broad smile behind his full face helmet because he knew that he was in a great position to garner a good finish and his first championship points.

One of his crew called him on the radio and informed him that Bin Salman was in second place, ten and a half seconds back and that Henri was in P5.

Race to Damascus

Now at full tilt in sixth gear on the long run to the final chicane, Parkes was feeling even better about his prospects of finishing well. The car was running strong and the tires were still OK. Still, he was glad to be coming in for some fresh rubber.

Entering pit lane he saw his team manager standing in his pit box with the neon green board with his name on it. He was signaling him where to pit, just in case he had forgotten where he was to stop.

The rest of the crew launched over the wall and commenced to change all four tires and add just enough gas to make it to the end. It only took about eleven seconds and the service was complete.

"Go, Go, Go" It was Griffin's now familiar voice coming across the radio in a most excited manner.

He was still taking a drink from his water tube when he steered the wheel to the left and stabbed the gas pedal. The speed limit on pit lane meant that he would leave the car in first gear until he re-entered the circuit.

A six car train had created a small gap between themselves and the rest of the field while he had stopped in the pits.

The leaders pulled away while the Cadillacs new tires came up to temperature, but after a few laps Parkes was right on the bumper of the Audi that was running in sixth.

With an estimated eight laps remaining in the race he started to think about when he should try to make his move past the cars in front of him. So far he had let the contest come to him and decided to continue his conservative approach for the next couple of laps. For now he would stay in contact with the lead pack, but wait a while to commence an attack to the front.

Just a lap later he noticed that the Audi in front of him had started emitting white smoke every time the driver shifted gears. He also saw that both the Audi and his own car were falling back from the rest of the lead group. It was time to get past and the opportunity presented itself as they came down the back straight side by side. At something of a disadvantage because he was on the outside lane going into the Bus Stop chicane, the Cadillac won the drag race and was able to get in front of the Audi before they entered the corner.

Ashmore called on the radio to inform him that he was now in fifth place as he went past the pits to complete his thirty- second circuit of the course.

He keyed his mike as he headed once more down the roller coaster like downhill straight that led to the Eau Rouge corner.

"Position five?" Parkes asked.

"Yes. You should know that Stephan Altenburg's BMW has just retired from the race."

Having simply outlasted Nino Bertolo's Audi and Altenburg's M3 had just moved him up two places.

The fact that he was now in a good position after thirty plus laps of the four mile course and still driving a healthy car encouraged him to believe that his plan for this race was working. The only question was if there were enough laps left for him to continue with this approach and still end up standing on the podium. Fifth was good, but he really wanted a top three and thought that he had enough car left under him to make it happen.

Slowing for the Virage hairpin he saw that one of the Jaguars had gotten lose and almost spun out in front of him. Parkes knew from the Union Jack decals on the car windows and the white racing stripe that it was Simon Wilson who was driving. A young F3 driver who had decided to quit banging his head on the door of Formula One and get a touring car drive that paid him a salary, he had done an excellent job to keep his car up front most of the day. Clearly the tires on the

Jaguar were going away. Seeing this Parkes was transformed into a hunter who knew that his prey was wounded and that he was about to make an easy kill.

The Cadillac out braked the British car down the inside just before turn fifteen, otherwise known as Stavelo corner. Turns fifteen and sixteen reminded Parkes of Monza and the Lesmos corners, especially since they led to a straight portion of road that produced high speeds.

Blasting along the long back section of the circuit, the big Jaguar sedan stayed right behind him, but only until they entered the braking zone for the Bus Stop's right then left combination. Parkes got through quickly and cleanly while the Jaguar pilot did not.

On the thirty-sixth lap he found out from that although he was up to fourth place, the top three were nearly four seconds ahead of him. Henri was now leading the race, Battle was in second and Mansur Bin Salman was now running in third place.

He cursed himself for not starting his run at the leaders a lap or two earlier. With four seconds separating him from the third place car, and only two and a half laps left to go in the race, finishing on the podium wasn't looking too promising to him right now.

With a healthy lead over Wilson's fifth place Jaguar he would just keep driving the same way he had all race long, instead of making a bonsai run to catch the leaders that might well end up with him throwing away a good finish.

"First and third place would have just been that much better" he then blurted out to himself.

Even if someone had been in the car with him they wouldn't have heard him say a thing. The Cadillac was at full song on the long run back to the finish line and he was going nearly one hundred and sixty five miles an hour. With two laps remaining he was content with his position and was now more concerned about his French team mate holding off the second and third place Scimitar Mercedes of Battle and Bin Salman.

"So how is Henri doing?" he asked on his radio.

"Battle has been right on his bumper for several laps now. He is bump drafting him on the straights and Henri is worried that your buddy might just decide to tap him hard going into a corner pretty soon." replied the team leader.

"You be sure to tell him not to fall for the cross over move. La Source is where he'll likely try it."

There was a pause before Griffin replied.

"Uh, I'll pass that on to him. Listen mate, you should know that you were only three and a quarter second behind Mansur Bin Salman as of the last lap, so you are catching him."

Since he hadn't driven any harder, he guessed that Battle and LeMond must really be going at it and that Bin Salman was happy to fall back, take third and let the team's number one driver go for the win.

There was a now chance that he could catch Bin Salman napping and get on the podium after all. He had to start getting focused on the objective at hand. Beating the Arab in a head to head fight would be rewarding, but first he had to catch him. Since he and Bin Salman had stopped for tires only a lap apart he thought that both should have about the same amount of tire wear at this stage of the race.

He started to think that the white Mercedes was getting a little closer to the nose of his own car and Griffin confirmed it via the radio at the start of lap thirty seven. The margin between the third place Mercedes and his ebony Cadillac was now just one point five seconds.

Accelerating down the straight toward Eau Rouge he noticed that most of the crowd in the grandstands to his left was on their feet. He soon saw the reason just in front of him. Battle and LeMond had gotten together attempting to go side by side into the corner.

Far enough behind to avoid the melee, Bin Salman swept by and into the lead. Parkes followed him up the hill and got right up behind him as they headed down the straight, nose to tail.

He shifted into sixth gear and radioed to see how LeMond was doing after his run in with Battle.

"They both got going again. They just touched each other and went straight off, but they didn't hit anything else. Anyway, LeMond got going just after you went past him and says his car is fine." replied Griffin.

Relieved that his team mate was able to continue, he started measuring up Bin Salman to figure out where he would pass him. He could see that the Mercedes was pushing a little going into the corners and was over steering on the exit of corners.

"I think that the Scimitar car may have already worn out his tires"

"Well don't wear yours out trying to catch him. Just keep your head about you, mate." replied the veteran team manager.

He knew that Ashmore was right. There was a chance they could win this thing if he kept his cool and waited for the right time to make his move. In the mean time he would try to rattle his opponent and get him to make a mistake.

To his credit Bin Salman had driven a great race. Parkes almost felt guilty that he was trying to spoil the young Saudi driver's day by taking a win from him, but it was his job to do just that. As they began what Griffin told him was the last lap of the race he started to push his rival even harder.

The attack started at the LaSource hairpin. He feinted like he was going to make a move to the inside of the approach to the corner, but quickly crossed back to the outside when Bin Salman tried to move inside to block. He knew that move would likely force the Mercedes driver to exit the corner wide -and it did just that. The Cadillac now crossed back over to the inside lane and a drag race ensued down the front straight.

Bin Salman had the advantage going into Eau Rouge and Parkes decided not to play a game of chicken as both of their team mates had done a lap earlier. He braked slightly and let the Mercedes go through the corner first. As he accelerated, he quickly made up any distance to the white car on the Kemmel straight away that followed.

His chance to take the lead was now just a little way down the road. A Lexus that was about to be lapped was running in the left lane at a speed only slightly less than he and Bin Salman were traveling. Parkes slipped out of the draft and moved to the inside lane before the Mercedes driver could respond. With the slower Lexus acting like a pick in a basketball game, he was able to get past and take the lead just as they entered the right hand corner.

The Cadillac then pulled out to a healthy advantage during the remainder of the last lap. Jubilant as he continued to push his car hard toward the finish, Parkes noticed that the white Mercedes had now become just a small white spot in his rearview mirror. Soon there was a black spot that was growing in his mirror as Henri had managed to catch, and then pass Bin Salman as well.

The Mandel crew were lining the pit wall and cheering for Parkes as he went by to take the checkered flag and the win. This was probably the happiest day of his life and he was going to enjoy it fully.

As he and Henri slowly drove their black Cadillacs around on the victory lap he couldn't help but remembering that it wasn't very far from here that his grandfather and many others had fought very hard and had won a great victory.

Now he and the Mandel team had managed to take on finest of the world's automobiles and beat them with a Cadillac sports sedan that was engineered and built right in America. They had done it on the same track that Dan Gurney had driven his own Grand Prix car to victory more forty years before. It occurred to him to make sure to carry on the tradition Mr. Gurney started around that same time by spraying champagne while he was up on the winner's podium.

Griffin's voice came into his radio ear phones once again.

"That was a fantastic performance out there, Parkes."

When he entered pit lane his car was mobbed by his crew. They picked him up and carried him off to the winner's podium.

After the accepting the first place trophy he had to choke back a tear as they played his National Anthem. Soon after it was time to spray the crowd, gathered at the base of the podium, with a magnum of Moet champagne.

LeMond drank some of his, before shaking the bottle up and showering two attractive blonde haired women who were both dressed in matching white sport shirts. He grinned at them and proceeded to drink down the rest of the bottle.

Mansur Bin Salman was probably already upset at himself because he had fallen back to third place, but now the Muslim driver was clearly mad at Parkes because of the Moet that had been sprayed on him.

"Hey pal, I was just showing you what to do with this when you win!" said Parkes in response to the young Mercedes pilots intense scowl and the raising of his right fist.

The Saudi driver had not even picked up the bottle of Moet that was placed in front of his spot on the podium. But now his Nomex suit was soaked in champagne after receiving a second dousing that came from Henri's magnum. Soon he left the celebration to the two Mandel drivers and their crew members that had just joined them up on the podium.

Looking out into the crowd Parkes realized that Liz wasn't anywhere to be found. This was his and Team Mandel's big moment and he didn't think it was right that she didn't even bother to show up. He told himself that he wouldn't let it bother him, but in fact he was slightly hurt that she wasn't there.

Ashmore soon came walking to the podium and shook both drivers' hands.

He then turned to the crew. "Well done lads, all of you on guys deserve it. You also deserve a drink or three on my tab at the hotel bar. Get everything into the garage and lock it up. We will worry about putting it all back in the hauler tomorrow morning"

The Mandel team's drivers headed back to take a shower and get changed before they joined the post race celebration over at the hotel the crewmen were staying at.

Henri showered first while Parkes sat guarding the Gold and Silver trophies they had just collected.

Enjoying some of LeMond's cold spring water he had just started to unwind when he heard a knock on the door.

As he opened it he saw that it was Griffin. He also recognized Liz's driver, Agent Roth. There was another man he did not know standing behind them in the spot that one of the racecars would normally occupy.

"Can we speak to you, Brandon?" asked his team leader in a stoic manner that seemed out of place given the circumstances.

"There is barely room for the two of us here in the drivers lounge. Can we do it outside?"

He shook his head in the affirmative. "Sure." replied Griffin.

"Mr. Roth here will tell you what he just told me. Then Griffin pointed to the other man. "This gentleman is with Interpol".

The celebration was clearly about to end given the demeanor of all three of the men who had come to see him. He told himself that it was probably bad news about Dan Mandel that he was about to receive. Having wondered why Liz had been absent from the race he assumed that it had to do with some kind of unfortunate information concerning her father.

"Brandon, Ms. Mandel has been attacked in her hotel room by an assailant dressed as a room service waiter" said Agent Roth with his strong Israeli accent. "Bernstein was attacked as well".

Parkes was just as stunned as he had been happy a short time ago.

"Is she…going to make it?" he asked him.

Roth paused and rubbed his chin. "Let's just say that both of them are in serious condition from deep knife wounds. If you are a praying man I suggest that you do so now."

Chapter Eight

Chicago, Illinois-Sunday evening

It was a damp and very dark night at Chicago's Midway Airport and Harry Mandel was not happy to be back here this night. He sighed and made his displeasure known when the new flight crew hired to fly the Mandel family's Gulfstream to Belgium had finally entered the cockpit of the multimillion dollar aircraft. They were only a few minutes late, but he was not in a mood to be delayed by subordinates.

A driving rain was pelting the roof of the plane by the time that the sleek jet taxied out for takeoff. Harry sat ensconced in his normal seat on the plane and was enjoying a gin and tonic. It was his second one since he had boarded and he had already decided that the lime flavored gin that was in the galley was now his new favorite.

He had already known that he would be flying to Europe, but he didn't plan on going until the next day. The report that he had just received about his niece having been attacked in her hotel room in Spa meant that he was leaving just as soon as humanly possible.

Between the situation that his brother was in and a large gambling debt that was hanging over him, Harry was just about at the end of his ability to cope.

Now he had to deal with Liz lying in a hospital on the other side of the ocean and that was the last straw. It truly was more than he could take.

The gin was starting to help him relax and once the Gulfstream was at cruising altitude he went to the back of the cabin and fixed himself another one.

As he sat down in his seat he put his drink down and pulled a pack of Marlboro Lights out of his pocket and lit one up. Harry had stopped smoking cigarettes over six years ago, but had bought a carton of them on his way to the airport.

He took a large swallow of his drink followed by a drag off his cigarette and wondered how all this could be happening to him. His stress level had never been higher and he promised himself that if he got through all that he was dealing with right now that he would never complain about his life being tedious or boring ever again.

As the trip would take several hours, Harry had plenty of time to think about a variety of things. He wondered if what Dan was experiencing had changed him. Would he finally allow him to be a full partner and accomplish what he knew he was capable of?

The first time he come to Europe to explore the idea of opening stores there, he had felt like an errand boy being sent to do the leg work for something that Dan wanted to see happen.

Harry had opposed the idea of stores overseas, mostly on the grounds that Mandel SuperStores had so much room for growth in America, but still he had been tasked with the implementation of Dan's program for expansion.

He had also been asked to meet with Silvio Marino on that first visit to discuss the possibility of becoming involved as a sponsor for the fledgling International SuperSedan Challenge. The elder Mandel had no interest in motor racing and saw little value in using it as a promotional tool. But he had enjoyed getting the royal treatment from Marino when he taken him to a friend's casino and being introduced to important Euro types who were impressed with the fact that he was the billionaire co owner of a large US retail chain.

In the suburbs of Chicago he had a very comfortable, if somewhat sedate life.

In Europe he got the respect he felt he never got at home. The excitement level was several notches higher as well. After his second failed marriage he had not been involved with any woman for over three years and rarely did anything outside of his day to day duties as Chief Operating Officer of Mandel SuperStores. On his first excursion to Europe, he suddenly found himself playing Baccarat for large stakes in a fancy Monaco casino with lovely women sitting by his side who were seemingly interested in him.

It had been great fun, at first. He had won nearly twenty thousand Euro's his first night he was at the tables. The second night he had instead lost that much plus a couple thousand more, but had still enjoyed the experience and decided that he wanted to come back to the casino the next time he was there on business.

About a month later he returned to check out more European store locations and Marino once again took him to the casino. Harry decided that this time he wanted to play Black Jack, instead of Baccarat. The nervous excitement of playing five thousand Euros a hand while consuming bottles of champagne had snared him like an insect in a spider's web.

His first night back he had run up losses of over one hundred thousand US dollars. After a two day trip to Belgium he returned to the casino with the idea that he had to win his money back. Instead, after ten hours of play he had managed to lose even more, bringing the total losses to almost two hundred thousand dollars.

Race to Damascus

The concept that he had now lost so much money was upsetting to Harry. Sure, he was technically half owner of Mandel's Inc. and was in turn entitled to half of the estimated four billion that the company was valued at, but Dan only paid him a half a million dollar yearly salary as COO. Living in Chicago and after taxes, alimony and child support he was just getting by, so 200K was a lot of money to him. In fact, his time at the tables had cleaned out most of his personal savings.

While Harry could absorb the gambling losses with only a modest amount of pain, it was the idea that his frugal father would have been so ashamed of him that bothered him the most. As he sat at the casino bar drinking a gin and tonic he had told himself that it had been exciting to play high roller, but that he would never do something that foolish again.

Besides, he wouldn't have the money to play at such a level of stakes for some time to come; or so he had thought at the time.

On his third trip to Paris he had vowed not even to travel to Monaco much less to the casino. The idea that had lost so much money still haunted him greatly. Perhaps his desire to get back his losses was as much to appease his late father as it was to actually replenish his own bank account. He fought the urge to try his luck again with what cash he still had available to him and threw himself into the tasks at hand.

He had managed to get all of the work for the new stores completed in the five days he had allotted and felt good about what he had accomplished. His third European tour was drawing to a close and he only had a dinner meeting with Marino in Paris left on his schedule before he would board a commercial flight back to Chicago the next day.

After their meal and business discussion Marino had suggested that Harry extend his stay a couple days and come with him to

Monaco for some rest and relaxation with a couple of women he knew.

He thought about it and decided it sounded like fun. Besides, he felt he had earned it.

"OK, but no gambling this time, Silvio. I can't afford it."

"Fine, but just know that Mr. Andre has extended you a line of credit should you decide to go to his casino. He knows you are good for it. Besides, your luck has to change sometime" said a smiling Marino.

Harry thought back to the moment that Marino said those words he began to feel slightly sick to his stomach. His luck did not change and his losses approached one a half million for those two days and nights in Monaco.

Although Dan probably would have paid the gambling debt for him, Harry had been too afraid to ask him. The verbal assault and lasting guilt that Dan would lay on him were worse than what any underworld type might threaten him with. A guy like Andre really just wanted his money. Dan would have exacted what little honor he still possessed as the older brother who was perceived as a junior partner at Mandel Inc.

The view out the window of the Gulfstream was of the complete blackness of the cold Atlantic Ocean below. As he looked out into the void he told himself that there had to be a way out of all this. He had to get his brother Dan back, pay Mr. Andre and end this nightmare.

His watch told him that there were now roughly five hours of flying time left. He wondered how his niece was fairing and who could have done such a terrible thing to her. She was just one more thing he now had to worry about.

He decided to down one more gin and tonic before trying to get some sleep. As he made his way to the rear he lit another cigarette and took a long drag off it. While pouring the gin he noticed tightness in his chest that he had never experienced before. He quickly downed his drink and put the cigarette that he had just started smoking into the now empty glass to extinguish it. His head hurt and he felt dizzy. His vision was becoming blurred as made his way back to the front of the aircraft and the comfort of his seat.

The numbness and severe headache that he had just experienced began to subside by the time he sat down and strapped himself in. While he wasn't certain of what had just happened to him, he did know that he needed to quit dwelling on his problems or he might end up making himself sick.

Dying wasn't what scared him at this point in his life. Death would be a blessed escape from the way his life was going right now. Surviving a stroke and becoming disabled and confined to a bed like his father had been was a much more terrifying thought to him.

Switching off the overhead lights Harry put his seat back. The darkness of the cabin, the sound of the jet turbines and a fair amount of gin had combined to have a lulling effect on him. Thankfully a deep merciful sleep swept over him in matter of only a few minutes.

Spa, Belgium - late Sunday evening

The smell of a hospital was something that had bothered Brandon Parkes from the time he had been a small boy in Iowa. At age three he had split his forehead open on a coffee table after falling off the living room couch that he had been jumping up and down on. His mother had rushed him to the emergency room to have the wound stitched up and the antiseptic smell he first encountered there had come to remind him of trauma ever since. Given the nature of hospitals he was sure that he wasn't the only one who felt this way, but going to hospitals seemed to bother him more than anyone else he knew.

As Agent Roth escorted him into the surgical ward waiting area Parkes was feeling nervous about what the physicians might tell him about Liz's prognosis.

After an hour of sitting in the waiting room he started to become even more anxious because no one had informed them of what was going on. He started to wonder if anyone even knew that he and Agent Roth were there waiting.

As Parkes paced back and forth, he was careful to not step on the cracks between the large white tiles of the floor. He stopped and smiled briefly at this ritual that he had learned as a kid. A moment later he returned to his march and he continued to make sure he didn't step on a crack. It would be bad luck if he did and there was no way he would do anything to jinx Liz Mandel's emergency surgery.

As the minutes dragged on, he had almost worked himself into a complete frenzy.

He couldn't ever remember being this anxious. Parkes was a control freak who was now coming to understand the point Liz had tried to make that there really was no such thing as control.

The emergency Xanax tablet that he usually kept in a pocket of his wallet wasn't there. He hadn't remembered to replace it and cursed himself for forgetting to do so.

His mind was racing with thoughts about the young Arab man he had seen at the hotel with Scott and how Bernstein had thought that Battle might be involved with the kidnapping of Mr. Mandel. Parkes thought about finding Battle and confronting him with his suspicions.

Agent Roth was still sitting quietly looking at some magazines. Parkes didn't see how the man could act like he was waiting for the oil in his car to be changed when Liz and Agent Bernstein were both lying on an operating table.

Suddenly a short man dressed in green surgical scrubs burst through the doors that lead to the operating rooms.

"Are either of you here waiting for Mr. Bernstein?" asked the man in English with what sounded to Parkes like a British accent.

Roth stood up and said, "I am his colleague. What can you tell me, Doctor?"

The man explained to Roth that he was the surgeon who had operated on Bernstein and that all the internal damage caused by the knife had been repaired.

A moment later a nurse, dressed in light blue surgical wear came out and told the doctor that he was needed to assist with the procedure going on in operating room one.

The surgeon and the nurse disappeared behind the large swinging doors before Parkes could ask them about how Liz was doing. The fact that Bernstein's surgeon was being asked to assist had to be a bad sign he thought.

Collapsing into one of the waiting room chairs he looked over to find Agent Roth once again reading a magazine. It was then that he was reminded of what Roth had told him back at the race track. Maybe it was time to try praying as worrying didn't seem to be helping, nor was it doing a thing for his peace of mind.

Over three and a half hours had passed since he had arrived at the hospital. Finally a nurse from the operating room came to the waiting area.

"Sir, Miss Mandel is in recovery and she will be moved to her room shortly."

"Is she OK?"

The nurse smiled and assured him that Liz would be fine. "She did well during the procedure, but I'll let the surgeon give you all the details"

"Thank you so much." replied Parkes. "Oh, and can you tell me her room number?"

"She will be in room 201"

As he began to comprehend what the nurse had just told him, he looked around the room for Roth, but he was no longer there. Parkes figured that he was probably checking on how Bernstein was doing, if not getting a statement from him.

There was a Coca Cola machine in the waiting room and Parkes decided that he finally had to have one if he was to keep going. He was thirsty, but it was the shot of caffeine that he wanted most. After he drank down a big swallow of the cold liquid, he smiled at the knowledge that Liz was indeed going to be alright. That thought seemed to trigger a sudden wave of relief from the stress he had endured for many hours.

He was genuinely thankful for the first time in his whole life. He had actually prayed for her and now he could see that maybe his prayers had indeed been answered.

As he approached suite 201 he saw Roth step from a room just down the hall from.

Parkes waved to him. "Mr. Roth. She is going to be OK!"

"I know. That is wonderful news"

"How is Bernstein doing?"

"Good, he is resting now. If you will excuse me, I must drive to the airport to pick up Ms. Mandel's uncle."

He sensed that there was something that Roth wasn't telling him. While normally taciturn, Roth's reaction to both successful surgeries seemed especially low key. Perhaps he was just tired and didn't have much to say, but something told him that the Mossad agent had a new concern on his mind.

"Before you go, I think you should know that I saw a guy with Scott Battle at the hotel who I think may be the one who carried out the attack."

"I will remember what you've told me, but I think we have a better idea now of who is behind all this and it isn't Scott Battle, nor is it the Arabs from his racing team."

"OK, well anyway, have a safe trip. We'll see you back here I assume? asked Parkes.

"Yes, I plan on bringing Mr. Mandel directly from the airport."

"Good. Oh, and before I forget, thanks for showing up when you did. Liz would likely be dead but for your intervention."

"I was simply doing my job, Mr. Parkes".

Roth then turned and began walking toward the exit.

Parkes stepped into Liz's room to find that she was sleeping, as he had expected. She was laying on her right side and was completely still. He watched her breathing for a couple of minutes, just to be sure that she really was alright.

The peace and joy that he felt right now far exceeded the thrill he had experienced in winning the race that day.

Near Damascus, Syria

The heat and a lack of fresh air had made the dingy room that Dan Mandel was being held in even more of a hell hole than it had been. It had become almost impossible for him to get to sleep that night and he felt that he couldn't be much more miserable.

Jack Rhodes had been able to drift off to sleep. Lying on the thin mattress just a few feet away from his own, Mandel could at least be thankful that their captors had let Rhodes move him into this room with him, after they had murdered Pete.

The thought of that young pilot's headless body in the room next to them didn't help him in his effort to get some rest. The decomposing flesh had seemed to have saturated everything with the pungent smell of death.

As he turned and tossed on his uncomfortable bed he began to get more and more frustrated. He knew right then that he had to get out of this place, or die trying.

Mandel decided he had waited long enough to be freed and was beginning to doubt that his fate would be any different than that of Flynn's, unless he took action to get himself and Rhodes out of this place.

Mandel went through scenarios in his mind about escaping. It was now two unarmed men against three with guns and knives, but he still thought the odds of breaking out were better than the odds that they would be released unharmed. If paying the first ransom demands had not freed them, he felt that giving these people millions more wouldn't set them free, either.

Race to Damascus

Since Jack had training in matters like escaping from captivity, Mandel wanted to wake him to discuss a plan, but decided to let him rest and wait until morning to get his input on the matter.

Simply having decided to become pro-active had made Mandel feel better. They would not be victims any longer. If he was to die, it would be as a man, not on his knees with some scummy Arab drawing a knife across his throat.

He closed his eyes and went still as visions of overpowering his captors and getting free from the prison he had been in for so many weeks filled his head. A restful sleep finally came to him when he began to imagine coming home and climbing into bed, between the cool silk sheets in his air conditioned room.

The wonderful dream ended when he awoke to being kicked in the ribs and screamed at by the man that Rhodes had named "Shorty". When he saw his pilot on his knees and being hit on the head with the butt of an AK, a groggy Mandel knew that he was still in this hell, and not back in Chicago.

"Didn't I ask to not be disturbed?" he asked the kidnappers sarcastically.

"I mean, here I was having a lovely thoughts about escaping and you jerks just ruined it"

Despite having just been stuck once again with a rifle butt, Jack Rhodes began to laugh when he heard his employer's remarks. "I think that I was having the same dream" he said, still laughing.

Having the last laugh cost Rhodes, as he was struck again with the AK, but this time the man his pilot called "Dopey", hit him with a blow to his face.

The former fighter pilot stood up as though he had never been touched and glared at his tormentor who had motioned for Mandel to rise from his mattress.

"Go, you will eat now." said the other kidnapper. Neither man had on a mask. Mandel wondered if that meant they weren't worried about being identified by him or his pilot anymore. For all he knew they weren't having breakfast at all, but were being taken out to be slaughtered.

The two Americans were ordered into the main room of the house and found two plates and a couple of small plastic cups waiting on the table.

When water was poured into the cups and pieces of bread were tossed on the plates Mandel felt slightly relieved that they weren't going to be executed, at least not yet.

The third kidnapper, the big one who Mandel thought must be the leader, wasn't there.

It seemed that the smallest of their captors was now the one in charge, at least while the big one was away.

"Eat now" he yelled when neither man had touched the meager repast set before them.

After glaring at his captors with a defiant look Rhodes smiled and then reached down to pick up the bread that was set before him. He then looked over at his boss and mouthed the words "just two".

He quickly nodded back and then stared down at his plate.

As he contemplated taking a bite of bread, the smell emanating out of the room that contained Flynn's decomposing body apparently caused Rhodes to lose his appetite and he threw the bread back on the plate.

"You eat the food now!" screamed the diminutive man.

He was soon joined by the other remaining kidnapper who tried to coerce Rhodes to eat by poking him in the back with the muzzle of his AK-47 rifle.

Looking across the table, Jack signaled him by winking. Mandel sensed that Rhodes was about to make a move. Suddenly Rhodes picked up his plate, turned and struck the man holding the AK in the face. As the ceramic plate shattered against his jaw the man fell to the ground. Mandel saw that Jack was quickly on top of him and grasping for the gun.

"Shorty" had no weapon so Mandel leapt from his seat and tackled him as he tried to reach the rifle leaning against the wall. The two men wrestled one another for control for over a minute, until they heard the muffled sound of a shot from a rifle.

Mandel and the little Arab looked up to see Rhodes standing over the other kidnapper with blood spattered on his face and on the collar of his white long-sleeved shirt. With the rifle in his right hand he staggered toward, he motioned to Mandel's opponent with his left hand to get up and move. With the gun pointing right at his chest the man got up and did as instructed and went into the room that they had slept in the night before. Rhodes closed the door behind him and then took a drink from one of the cups on the table. After one swallow he spit out the rest and wiped his mouth and face with his right shirt sleeve.

He was panting as he sat down on one of the chairs.

"Are you OK, Dan?" he asked breathlessly.

"Yeah, I am OK. Is that one dead?" asked Mandel, who still breathing hard himself.

Rhodes looked down from where he was seated and saw that the round had entered under the man's chin and exited through the top of his head.

"Yeah, he's a definite KIA"

"Good job."

"I thought we both did pretty well for a couple of older guys" he replied with a faint smile.

"It was like you were reading my mind, Jack. You know something; I almost woke you to talk about an escape plan last night."

Taking in a deep breath Rhodes slowly let it out and then took in another. "I am glad you didn't, 'cause I needed all the energy I had to subdue "Dopey" over here. In fact I'm feeling pretty beat right now, so give me a minute more to catch my breath."

It was obvious that his pilot was having a hard time recovering and was soon clutching his chest with his left hand while his right was still holding the rifle. "We'll talk about what to do next in just a sec, OK?" he said between breaths.

Mandel knew how Rhodes felt as he was still short of breath himself. But he also knew that the big man Rhodes had labeled "Jughead" would likely be back soon.

"OK, I'll go and guard the door" said Mandel as he grabbed the other AK-47. "You get a second wind and then we'll get the hell out of here."

"You bet, boss."

"Oh, and if it makes you feel any better you should know that your yearly salary just doubled as of a few minutes ago"

Nodding after flashing a brief smile, he then set down the AK, folded his arms and put his head back over the top rail of the wooden chair. He took one more deep cleansing breath and let it out as he closed his eyes.

Still worked up after experiencing the most combative moment of his life, Mandel looked back from the small window next to the door and saw that his friend and longtime employee was no longer breathing hard and already seemed to be doing much better.

"That's it, Jack. Just relax for a bit, and know that thanks to you we'll both be home soon, my friend."

Spa, Belgium – Wednesday-8:30 AM

It was a cloudy, rainy day that Liz Mandel saw out her hospital window as she was awakened by her nurse who had brought in the prescribed morning medications.

After she took the three pills the nurse left the room. She still felt sore today, but knew that one of the pills that she had just taken would take care of any discomfort she was feeling in just a matter of minutes.

Brandon and her uncle Harry had both come to visit with her the day before and they had left the flowers and the large plant that now brightened her room. She couldn't remember which one had brought the flowers and which had brought the plant because she was not very clear headed as a result of being as medicated as she was.

As a warm and relaxed feeling began to come over her again, she was now understood how people could get hooked on pain killers. Both physical and emotional pain were swept away after taking pills like these and she liked how good it made her feel.

She looked at her watch and squinted her eyes to find out that it was just after eight o'clock. Remembering that Brandon had told her that he would be back at noon, she decided to get some more sleep before he returned.

Just as she got into a more comfortable position the nurse walked in and informed her that she needed to get up and walk down the hall to get some exercise.

"I don't want to get up and walk, I just want to lie here."

"Well, the doctor has ordered that you do so" replied the nurse.

She sighed and resigned herself to the fact that she was going to have to get out of bed.

"Alright, I will do it, but I don't want to go very far."

The nurse, a woman who looked to her to be at least her mother's age, said nothing in response.

As she turned her hips and began to swing her legs out of the bed she was hit with a jolt of pain from the wound in her back. She wanted to lie back down but the nurse instead helped her to her feet.

Despite being medicated, the pain Liz felt was worse than she had ever experienced in her life.

"I don't see how you can expect me to walk when I can barely even stand up" she complained.

"You are doing fine" replied the nurse. "Now let's walk out into the hallway".

Each step she made caused Liz to grimace. By the time she had made it out of her room and half way to the next doorway she had tears in her eyes and decided she could go no further.

"I want to go back and rest now" she said. "Fine, Ms. Mandel. But you will have to walk back."

Liz gritted her teeth and turned towards her room. By the time she made back into bed she was exhausted from the ordeal.

"Is there anything I can do for you before I leave?" asked the nurse as she tucked her back into bed.

"Yes. Promise that you won't come back to torture me anymore today"

The nurse just smiled and left the room.

She liked to think that it was unusual for her to cry over something like her own suffering and she was more than a little embarrassed at her behavior. She thought that if she could just be allowed to lie there in bed for a little while longer she would be much better prepared for the next round of exercise therapy.

After just a couple of minutes of reflection she closed her eyes and soon got the blessed rest that she had craved.

Spa, Belgium – Wednesday-2:50 PM

As Brandon Parkes entered the hospital he turned to hold the door open for Harry Mandel and noticed that the sun was just breaking through the gray clouds.

"We seem to have brought some good weather with us."

Harry didn't respond. He had remained in a foul mood since he had emerged from his meeting with Silvio Marino and the weather was the last thing on his mind.

When he finally did speak, Harry commanded Parkes to go and get his niece and bring her to Bernstein's hospital room.

"We'll meet with Bernstein and then head back to Paris tonight, assuming that Liz is ready to be discharged." snapped Mandel.

"Yes sir. I understand." replied Parkes.

"I'll see you in a few minutes then, Mr. Mandel"

Parkes thought that Harry Mandel was an ass. Sure, he knew that he was under a lot of stress, but he doubted that the man was a very fun guy even in the best of situations.

As he approached Liz's room he saw a doctor and a nurse speaking to her. She was sitting up in her bed and the smile on her face told him that she was feeling better.

"So are you getting kicked out of here?" asked Parkes upon entering the room.

"Tomorrow afternoon, actually" she replied with a smile.

"We would like to keep her around for a couple more physical therapy sessions, but you can plan on collecting her no later than this time tomorrow." said the doctor.

"Is it alright with you if we go down the hall to visit Mr. Bernstein's room?"

Her nurse responded to the question "If she is up to it after all of her activity today, then it is OK with me."

"Well, I am about worn out after the physical therapy, but if I can get someone who will push me in that wheelchair I think I can manage a short visit" she replied while pointing to the wheelchair parked in the corner of her room.

"Good" replied Parkes. "Uncle Harry and Bernstein are waiting to see us."

The doctor turned to the door while the nurse went to retrieve the wheelchair.

"You should be proud of your girlfriend. She had a difficult time this morning, but by this afternoon she was doing much better with her exercise."

Liz looked over at Brandon when the nurse had called her his girlfriend. He just smiled back at her and then thanked the nurse for all her help.

After gently lowering her into the wheel chair, Parkes began to push her into the hallway and towards Bernstein's room. The nurse followed them out of the door and reminded them to be back in a half an hour because dinner would be served then.

"Thanks. We'll be back in time" replied Parkes as he continued pushing the wheelchair down the hall.

"Can we sneak out and have dinner somewhere else tonight?" pleaded Liz.

"If you are good, we'll do just that. But it will have to be tomorrow night, young lady"

The door to Bernstein's room was open so Parkes wheeled right in.

It was the first time she or Bernstein had seen one another since the attack and their meeting was somewhat emotional.

When Ephraim Roth entered the room, Liz thanked him for all that he had done for her.

"I only wish I had gotten there a little sooner" responded Roth.

Starting to look impatient, Harry stood up and said "OK, we have some things we need to discuss, so let's get down to business." He then walked over and closed the door to the room.

Near Damascus, Syria

As the heat of the day began to die down Dan Mandel took a drink of the rancid water his captors had supplied and started to wonder when the head kidnapper would return.

While the idea of simply leaving had crossed his mind, Jack was in no condition to take a walk in the arid desert. As a result, Mandel decided that they would need to get the kidnappers' car if they were to affect a successful escape.

"Dan.... can you give me some of that?"

Sorry, I didn't even realize that you were awake."

Mandel walked over to his pilot with the jug of water and helped him to take a drink of the lukewarm liquid.

"Thanks, Dan."

"How are you feeling?"

"Not so good. I wonder if I maybe had…maybe just a minor heart attack, b…but the pain… in my chest…it has all but disappeared." said Rhodes.

"You need to lie down. I'll open up the guest room for you."

Mandel opened the door to the room where the kidnapper was being kept.

He then took a step back, pointed the AK-47 at the man lying on the floor and ordered him to get up. The man rose and then just as quickly he fell to his knees and clasped his hands together. In his broken English he began begging Mandel not to kill him.

"Hey, this guy seems to think that I woke him up just to take him out and execute him." Jack seemed to be drifting in and out of consciousness and likely hadn't even heard what he had just said.

The sight of his stricken pilot and the idea that there wasn't much that could be done to help him frustrated Mandel. He was used to getting things done his way, but right here and now he was all but helpless.

"OK, you help my friend and I won't kill you" said Mandel as he motioned for the man to come out of the room.

After a bit of gesturing as to what he wanted him to do, Mandel soon had the man helping Rhodes from his chair and into the bedroom to one of the dirty cots that lay on the floor.

Once Rhodes was lying down, Mandel motioned for the kidnapper to come out of the room and to shut the door.

"Now sit down in the corner" he ordered.

The man understood and did as he was told while Mandel used his left hand to move one of the chairs from the table to a position in the room that would allow him to see both the door at the side of the house while keeping an eye on "Shorty".

Before he sat down in the chair Mandel took a drink of water and began to contemplate his next move. With Jack incapacitated, it was becoming clear that he would have to do something with the man sitting in the corner before the other kidnapper returned.

He was debating whether he should shoot the man or just tie him up and place him in other room, the one that contained Pete Flynn's rapidly decaying body.

The idea of shooting someone, even one these lowlife kidnappers was something that Mandel did not relish. He wasn't sure if he could just put a bullet in the back of another man's head, but knew that he might have to do just that if he wanted to escape with his own life.

He sat for several minutes trying to make up his mind as to what to do.

"Alright, let's go tie you up" said Mandel as he stood from his chair.

The normally tough minded billionaire had let his values lead him into the decision not to execute Shorty. However before he would tie and gag him, he would first make him drag the body of the dead kidnapper out of the main room of the house, and place it in the bedroom that held Flynn's torso and severed head.

Once he understood what Mandel wanted him to do, Shorty grabbed the ankles of his dead cohort and pulled the body towards the room.

A blood trail followed the body as it was dragged across the dusty concrete floor. Halfway to the room Shorty stopped, let go of the body and began speaking in his native language. The Arab was looking past Mandel and towards the entrance of the house.

He figured that it was just a trick that would cause him to turn his back.

"Get going, I'm not falling for your BS."

Shorty then put his hands behind his head and began speaking rapidly as he continued to look towards the doorway.

"Put the gun down, Zionist" shouted a voice from behind him.

Setting the rifle on the floor Mandel turned to see that Jughead had returned and that he had a pistol aimed right at him.

The big man then yelled out something in Arabic and Mandel suddenly felt a stinging pain in the back of his head. He realized instantly that Shorty had hit from behind with the butt of the rifle that he had just been holding. Now on the dirty floor and in a daze, he crawled on his hands and knees toward the door, but was kicked hard in his side for the effort.

Lying on his back, he was still conscious but kept his eyes shut, hoping that the kidnappers would leave him alone if they thought he had passed out.

His captors began shouting back and forth at one another. It sounded like they might be arguing. The next sound he heard was a sudden burst of machine gun fire. Instinctively he opened his eyes and began to sit up but was met by the butt of a rifle in his forehead. Mandel fell back to the floor as the blackness of being knocked out swept over him.

Chapter Nine

Paris, France

After his win at Spa, Brandon Parkes had gotten messages of congratulations from many in the racing business back in America. One of them had been from a former crew chief who was asking him to drive in the Grand Am sports car race at Watkins Glen in upstate New York. Since there were almost two weeks until the ISC finale in Cairo he got the OK from Griffin to go compete and then booked a ticket on a plane to JFK airport.

With a couple hours until the departure of his flight to New York, Brandon Parkes thought it best to go up and visit Liz Mandel in her suite at the Hilton.

As he began to knock on the door it occurred to him that perhaps he should have called first and made sure that she was up to seeing anyone.

The door to the suite opened and a dour Harry Mandel stood before him.

"Hello. I just stopped by to find out how Liz was doing before I left for the airport."

"She is resting right now, but I will find out if she wants to see you."

Harry turned and headed toward Liz's bedroom and left Parkes holding open the front door.

The rude behavior of Harry Mandel was soon replaced by a warm welcome from his niece.

"What a nice surprise" she said with a broad smile.

Dressed in a white terry cloth robe and pink slippers Liz led him by the hand to sit with her on the couch.

"I can't stay too long, I have to catch my plane to New York, but I wanted to see how you were getting along." said Parkes as he sat down.

Harry came back into the room and eased himself into a chair, careful to not spill the cup of coffee he was holding.

Turning to look at Harry, Parkes said the only thing that came to mind.

"I was really glad to hear you say in the meeting at the hospital that you didn't think that Mr. Marino is involved with the kidnapping of your brother."

Mandel said nothing in response.

"I know that Bernstein had suspected Marino was behind all this, but as you said, why would he kidnap his own series' sponsor?"

"He wouldn't." replied Harry. "He knows that if I had sole control of the stores, that I would have ended this relationship at the end of the season. Instead, when Dan gets back, Marino will be getting almost twice as much in sponsorship from us next year. In fact, I just OK'd the deal, pending Dan's return and his signing off on it".

After Harry took a sip of his coffee he added "I think Bernstein has seen too many Mafia movies and assumes that because Marino if from Sicily that he must be connected to the mob."

"Oh, by the way, Bernstein doesn't think it was Scott or his Arab friends anymore either." added Liz.

"I know that now, but when I heard about this man with dark hair who attacked you, I thought of the young man that I had seen with Battle the night before at the hotel and thought that they might be one and the same. I was pleased to learn that it was not the case and that he wasn't involved and that Scott and was no longer a suspect. "

Then he paused for a moment before he asked Harry a question. "So, who do you think is behind it, Mr. Mandel?"

Looking up at the ceiling before answering he shook his head; "I don't know what to think anymore. My guess is similar to Bernstein's. The people we are dealing with are probably some independent Muslim terrorists who think they can strike a blow for Allah while getting wealthy."

"So where are things at in the negotiations with the kidnappers, if I may ask?"

Liz responded before her uncle could speak. "Uncle Harry and I agree that we won't give them another cent, unless they agree to free dad at the same time we give them the money"

"I have told these people that I will pay the second ten million that they have demanded, but only if it is on our terms. My brother will be handed over, only then will they get an addition ten million in bearer bonds."

"So, how soon do you think we can get your brother back?" asked Parkes.

Looking down at the floor, sighed and then looked up. "Actually, there has been no response to the conditions that we have set, at least not yet."

After a brief moment of silence Parkes stood up.

"Well let's hope that this will all be over soon. In the meantime I am off to try and win a sports car race at Watkins Glen and then maybe a championship for Team Mandel in Cairo."

"Just do your best and stay safe. We don't want you to get hurt driving someone else's race car." pleaded Liz.

Her stern look as she said it turned soft again just as quickly.

"Anyway, are very proud of you and the team, no matter what happens in Cairo I know that dad would be pleased with the effort you have made."

"Thanks. I'll call you soon."

"Mr. Mandel, it was good seeing you, sir."

Harry didn't answer. He just looked up, nodded and gave a quick wave of his hand.

Watkins Glen, New York

The sight of the bright red Chevrolet powered Dallara sports car rolling down the Watkins Glen pit lane signaled the Mathis Sport crew that Jim Mathis was about to arrive in their pit stall and that they should be ready to service the car and make a change of drivers. It was now Brandon Parkes turn at the wheel of the Daytona Prototype car.

The hour long practice session would be his first time driving a DP car and the job at hand was to first get a feel for it and then make suggestions as to how it might be made to go faster. He hoped that his experience at this track in GT-3 Porsche's and the NASCAR race would be of benefit to him and the team.

In addition to his ability behind the wheel, part of why Parkes had been hired to co-drive with the wealthy team owner was the fact that he and Jim Mathis were about the same height and weight. No time consuming seat adjustments would be needed when they changed drivers during pit stops.

For a "gentleman" driver, Mathis had developed into a pretty good racer. A co-drive with two hired pros had netted him a second place finish at the grueling Daytona 24 Hour race earlier that season and he had several other good results since then, but no wins. Still, it already had been his best season in the sport to date.

The thirty eight year old had taken his family's beef jerky business to more than double its size in less than ten years since being made president and had sold it a year ago for more than six hundred million dollars. He rewarded himself by setting aside enough funds to get serious about Grand Am sports car racing.

The Dallara chassis was the same one that the team had used over the previous two seasons, but had been sent to over to Dallara in Italy for all the latest updates. When it arrived back in the states he had sportscar guru Kevin Doran and his crew in Cincinnati fit a new V8 built by Indy's Menard Engine Group in the back and did numerous test sessions prior to the season opening Daytona race. The Mathis Sport team's good results had proven the value of both the time and money that had been invested.

The only component Mathis was missing right now was his regular co-driver. The young Brazilian professional had been hurt in a testing accident and would be laid up for at least two more weeks. That unfortunate incident was the reason Parkes was about to climb into the low slung mid engined sports car for his first laps around the Watkins Glen circuit.

"The tail is a bit loose, but the car is fast" yelled Mathis through his full face helmet as he stepped out the car.

He then patted Parkes on the back and motioned for him to get in the cockpit.

Parkes gave him a thumbs up and slid behind the wheel. Already wearing his helmet, HANS and gloves all he had to do now was plug in his radio and cinch down the racing harness.

"Test, test" were the first words he heard in his helmet.

"I hear you fine" he replied.

"Any time you are ready" said his friend and Mathis Sport crew chief, K.P. Mason.

He hit the starter button and blipped the throttle with his right foot. The V8 engine that rested in back of his shoulder responded with a sound that was almost as exotic as any he had heard coming from a Lamborghini or Ferrari.

Checking his mirrors to make sure there was no traffic coming he eased the car out the pit box into the pit lane that was to his left. After a warm up lap he was soon at full speed and going uphill through the esses and onto the straight away that led to a chicane. He found that the sequential gearbox in the car easy to use and was similar to the one he had been using in Europe. The braking was completely different. After slowing for the chicane he was passed by a blue Riley-Ford Daytona Prototype just prior to the right turn into the chicane. Parkes cursed himself and vowed not to make the mistake of braking too soon again.

A Daytona Prototype sports car weighed much less than his Cadillac CTS-V and so it was possible to brake much later than he would have in his regular mount or than in a NASCAR stock car like the one he driven here just a year before. He reminded himself that he was in a sports racing car, not a heavy sedan.

Heading down the straight away he hit sixth gear and then girded himself for the left hand corner that he knew was coming. While he wanted to brake for the next corner as late as possible, his fear of out-braking himself and going straight off into the guard rail told him to not try to overcompensate for his earlier miscue.

As he neared the braking zone he remembered the point on the track that he used when he last raced a sports car here and gently began to apply the brake pedal and down shifted through the gears. It appeared that he had gotten through cleanly only to have the tail slide out on exit. Parkes saved it quickly and made a mental note to tell Mathis thanks for warning him that the car was loose.

Driving cleanly through the final corner and on to the pit straight the Dallara felt fairly fast to Parkes. After another eight laps of the circuit he thought he had a handle on the car and what changes he would suggest to make it work even better.

Pulling the car into the pit box he saw the team owner and his co-driver for the weekend, jump over the pit wall and walk around to the driver's side of the low slung sports car to greet him.

As he climbed out of the cockpit an enthusiastic Mathis shook his hand.

"That was awesome man!"

"Thanks, Jim. You know, it was a little squirrelly out there, like you said it might be, but the engine is great."

"We hit over190 miles an hour at Daytona on the banking at the 24 hour race with this baby. It was the fastest of anybody there."

Removing his helmet Parkes shook his head in agreement. "I'm not surprised to hear that, it really goes."

"You get together with K.P. and let him how you want the car set up for the qualifying run, alright?"

"Yeah, we'll do it over the lunch break."

Mathis said nothing as he began to walk away; he simply gave him a big smile and a thumbs up.

While it felt good to have the approval of the car owner, he just hoped he could back up the first laps of practice with a decent qualifying time and good result in the race.

The fact that the NASCAR teams were here gave him extra resolve to put in a good showing. He especially wanted to do well in front of the team he had driven for here a year ago that had subsequently let him go. If the young stock car ace that had replaced him didn't make the NASCAR race because of road course drivers like Boris Said and Andy Lally it would make Parkes visit to upstate New York all the better.

As he headed to the Mathis team's motor coach he saw his former employer rushing through the garage area on a small scooter. As the man drove by he didn't even acknowledge him. It only made Parkes resolve to win the sports car race here was now stronger than ever.

The changes the team made to the race car had made it more stable than it had been and he was easily able to qualify the Dallara in sixth place. The fact that the time he had set was with the car set up for the race, not in qualifying trim, was encouraging to him.

Jim Mathis would drive the car at the start of tomorrow's contest, as was his custom.

After the first stint he would bring the car to the pits and hand it over to Parkes who would do the remainder of the event.

As the "hired gun" Parkes was expected to bring the car home in first, no matter how the owner did during his time behind the wheel. He was fairly hopeful that the capable amateur would keep the car within striking distance of the leader and that when he climbed into the cockpit he would have a fighting chance of doing what he had been hired to do.

The first portion of the race would be out of his hands and being a control person, he hated that part of endurance sports car racing. Even if he was teamed with another pro driver it was hard for him to let go and trust the other guy to do the same kind of job that he would do. It was twice as bad for him when paired with someone who was just doing it for sport of it.

Watkins Glen, New York – Saturday afternoon

Sunny, warm and very humid was the forecast for Saturday's afternoon Rolex Grand Am sports car race at the Glen.

The weatherman had been correct and Parkes was happy that there wasn't a cloud to be seen when he arrived at the Mathis Sport custom Newell motor coach.

Mathis opened the door of the expensive palace on wheels and invited him in. The Oklahoma native was already suited up and was holding his white racing helmet in his left hand.

"Like it?" he asked as he surveyed the cream leather appointments of the Newell coach.

Before he could answer, Mathis started giving him the vehicle's history.

"I bought it from a movie star who used it a few times on location. The guy ran into some financial difficulties due to drug problems and when he went into rehab I picked it up for a song."

This went on for several minutes. After telling him about all the amenities available the proud team owner concluded the tour when he pointed to the rear of the coach. Parkes didn't have the heart to remind him that K.P. had already shown him all this the day before, so he just played along like it was his first time.

"Back bedroom is all yours. You can get changed into your driver's suit there, OK? See you in the pits"

"Alright, see you there, Jim" he said with a smile.

By the time Parkes made his way to the pit lane the race was about to get going and he trotted over to the open door of the Dallara just in time to kneel down and wish his patron and co driver good luck.

Mathis winked at him and began tugging on his seat belts as a crewman stepped in front of Parkes to shut the door. It was time to roll out for the start of the race.

The waving of the green flag saw Mathis lose two positions right at the beginning of the first lap. Two other cars made it past the Dallara during the second lap. By lap three the millionaire racer seemed to find his rhythm and by the start of the fourth tour of the circuit had managed to settle the car into a steady tenth place in the running order.

After a few laps, rather than get in the way of the crew, Parkes decided to leave the pit and go back to the motor coach to watch the race on big screen TV and get a little rest before he was required to get in the car.

"I'm going to the Newell. Come get me when it's my turn, K.P." The crew chief nodded and then turned his attention back to the race.

As he got settled into the big leather couch in front of the television he began to think about what his strategy would be once he got behind the wheel. If Mathis could keep the car in about the same position that it was in now and hand it over in good shape they might have a shot at doing well today. No sooner did that thought filter through his mind that the TV showed a black Riley Daytona Prototype out brake his co-driver going into the last corner and getting past to take over tenth position from him.

"That's just swell." said Parkes out loud. He took a drink from his can of Dr. Pepper, and pulled the red plaid comforter off the back of the couch. Closing his eyes he would try to get a short nap instead of worrying about something that he couldn't do anything about.

Not quite an hour later a loud knock on the door awoke him from his slumber. It was followed by an anxious plea from a twenty something Mathis Sport crewman who now stood before him. "K.P. wants you to come to the pits right now; Jim is bringing her in at the end of this lap."

"OK, so... where are we running?"

"We're in seventh place at the moment. Mr. Mathis got by one car and then there was a full course caution because of an accident. It took out the three lead cars and now we have a chance to pit under yellow." the young crewman told him breathlessly.

"Alright, let's go then" Parkes took a last swallow of his drink and set off with the young man for the pits.

The crew chief had his Stand 21 helmet, HANS and Nomex gloves ready for him. After settling into the seat and plugging in his radio, the crew chief gave him the news that they had stopped two laps sooner than expected, but thought that the laps under yellow would allow them to go the distance with only one more stop for fuel. As he listened to K.P.'s update the team owner cinched the safety belts down tight for him and then patted him on the shoulder prior to shutting the door and leaving him to the solitude of the cockpit.

With new tires and all the gas the tank could hold, Parkes headed down pit lane and rejoined the field in sixth. During the remaining three laps of cruising around under the yellow flag the car holding third position pitted which meant he would be in fifth place as the race resumed.

With pieces of three of the best prototype class cars being swept off the track, the odds of the Mathis Sport team having a good finish today had just improved exponentially.

"Green flag, Green flag" were the words he heard over his radio as the Dallara approached the Watkins Glen start finish line.

Squeezing the gas pedal to the floor and shifting up through the gears was the response to his crew chief's alert. It was a good restart for him and Parkes picked up a position going into the tight right hand first corner.

Just ahead was the race leader, it was the car of another wealthy amateur, Tracey Kane.

As he followed the Ford powered Riley up the hill to the straight away leading to the chicane Parkes keyed his mike button and asked if it was the car owner driving or the hired gun, Sam Cramer.

After a pause of several seconds the answer came. "It's Kane who's still in the car. You should be able to get by him with no problem, Ace."

While racing with a gentleman driver should indeed have been an easier task than getting by a former Indy Car pilot, like Kane's professional co- driver , it soon became clear that the fifty something billionaire driving the car ahead of him was not going to be dispatched with anything approaching ease.

Lap after lap the Riley managed to stay ahead of the Dallara. Multiple times it looked as though Parkes might make a pass for the lead only to have Kane close the door on him and then pull out to a several car length gap.

The most positive thing that was happening for Parkes was the fact that the pace Kane was running now meant that the two of them were slowly pulling away from the rest of the pack.

With only a little over an hour to go in the contest it was coming up to the time that all the cars would have to come to the pits for fuel and tires. Parkes felt he an obligation to get by the car in front of him before they pitted. It wasn't as much a matter of it being imperative to do so to secure the win at the checkered flag, but much more it was now a matter of professional pride.

Going flat out down the back straight that led into the left hand corner he closed up behind the Riley and committed himself to pulling out of the draft and taking Kane on the left hand side before they got to the corner. He would just put off his breaking a fraction of a second and finally get past.

Just as he began his move, Parkes saw a burst of flame emanate from the backend of Kane's car, as it headed straight off the circuit; and rolled into the sand trap that followed. The Riley had lost an engine and it was only his good fortune that he had initiated the pass at the moment he did or he might have slid off the track in the oil the Ford engine left in the wake.

As he entered the last corner, a right hander, he was told by the crew chief to bring the car into the pits.

"This is perfect! We get by the leader, there is a yellow because of his blown motor and we happen to be right by the pit lane when we need to make a stop." yelled an enthusiastic Parkes over the radio as he drove down the pit lane to his designated pit stall.

"Yeah, and we are going to be making a driver change, Brandon."

He was stunned to see a helmeted Jim Mathis waiting behind the pit wall as he rolled to a stop. He pressed the seat belt release, got out of the race car and removed his Nomex gloves. After Mathis got in he helped him cinch up the belts and closed the door behind him. The plan was to let the car owner drive to the finish. It seemed that his day at Watkins Glen was done and Parkes wasn't quite sure how he was supposed to feel about it.

Somewhere over the Atlantic-Saturday night

The flight from JFK airport to Egypt was only a third of the way to their final destination and Brandon Parkes was restless. The fact that he continued to obsess over his being pulled out of the car at Watkins Glen and replaced by the car owner did not help. Sure, Mathis had done a fine job and held on to win the race, but he couldn't help but feel the team had snubbed him when they didn't let him be the one to take the car to the end of the race. Was it the fact that he was unable to get past Kane's car until just before it blew an engine, or was it a case of Jim Mathis just wanting to drive his own car into victory lane for the first time?

Whatever it was, Parkes wasn't nearly as happy as he should have been after claiming another race win. In fact, he was embarrassed at his performance at Watkins Glen and in turn was starting to again to have nagging doubts about his future.

Trying to divert his attention away from what had been on his mind for hours, he opened his new copy of AutoSport magazine. He went right for the latest racing news portion of the magazine and smiled when he saw the article about the young Indycar racer who was announcing his move to Sprint Cup. That was the second open-wheel racer in as many weeks to have announced a move to NASCAR. The first was a British F-1 driver that had committed to go to the secondary level, Nationwide Series with the plan of moving up to the Cup cars after a year of seasoning at the triple A level.

Parkes decided right at that moment that he and his team had to do whatever it might take in the last race to win the ISC championship. Maybe if he could have that a success of that caliber on his CV he might join these other guys with a road racing background who found a spot in what was still Americas biggest and most lucrative racing series.

Chapter Ten

Cairo, Egypt

The first thought that Brandon Parkes had as he stepped from the taxi onto the sidewalk in front of his hotel was of how the smell of Cairo reminded him a little of Mexico City. Some called Cairo the "Paris of the Desert", but the combination of diesel bus fumes, exhaust from all the many cars and the extreme heat made him think more of the three visits he had made south of the border .

As he paid the cab driver it occurred to him that this was one of the oldest cities in the world and that he was should be glad to have the chance to come here for the first time, no matter what it smelled like to him.

The bellman took his luggage; one bag and his leather brief, into the hotel and Parkes followed him in. The cool air of the lobby was a relief from the hot sun and high humidity outside.

As he waited in the short line to check in, he felt a tap on his shoulder and turned to find Scott Battle and his girlfriend Michele.

"Hey, are you guys staying here, too?"

"Yeah, in fact we have been here for two days already." replied Battle.

While they spoke, Parkes remembered that just a few days ago he actually thought that his friend might be involved in Dan Mandel's kidnapping and nearly believed that he could have commissioned the attack on Liz and Agent Bernstein in Spa.

"Sir, would you like to check in now?"

He swung around to see that the man at the front desk was talking to him.

"Just one moment, please." Parkes replied.

He turned back to find Scott extending his hand to bid him farewell.

"Listen; let's plan on getting together for a drink or two tonight, OK?"

"You bet, Scott. Call me and maybe I'll see you later on" replied Parkes with a smile.

Having a confirmed reservation it only took a few minutes until he was in his room and tipping the bellman.

Parched from his trip, he checked out the mini bar and was pleased to find cold bottles of Coca Cola inside and quickly opened one and drank it down. He grabbed a second bottle, took off his shoes and was soon laying on his king size bed.

He was tired, but felt giddy at the thought that all he had to do tonight was sit in his air conditioned room, enjoy refreshing cold drinks and maybe have a nice dinner brought up from room service. The soft purring of the air conditioning fan and the cool temperature of the room combined to soon lull Parkes to sleep.

When he woke up to the ringing of his cell phone it was almost ten PM, the caller ID told him that it was Scott Battle.

He reluctantly answered. "Hello, this is Brandon."

The voice on the other end said hello and it wasn't Scott, but his girlfriend Michele who was calling.

"Hey, Scott wants to know if you can meet us downstairs for a drink like we talked about before."

"Yeah, I was just sitting here in my room doing nothing, so that sounds fine."

"See you down here in a few minutes then." she said in a cheery tone.

"Give me about fifteen minutes or so, OK?"

"Alright, see you soon."

With his shirt and pants wrinkled from napping in them, he decided to take a quick shower and change into some fresh clothes before he headed downstairs to the bar.

As he began to step into the shower his cell phone began to ring. Instead of answering it he let it ring. "If it is that important they will leave a message" he told himself out loud.

After his shower he put on a crisp blue oxford cloth shirt, black slacks and a pair of black Gucci loafers that he had just bought himself while in Paris. Now that he was cleaned up and dressed Parkes was glad to be going out for a while.

He arrived in the hotel bar and found Michele and Scott sitting in a booth. They were each drinking what looked to him like a gin martini.

"Martinis? With three olives no less." commented Parkes as he pointed to the drinks on the table.

"Glad you could make it, BP" said Battle with a warm smile.

"Me too, my friend" he replied. As he joined them in the booth he looked over toward the bar "Garcon', two of what they are having and a refill for my friends, please."

With a recent win in the bag and a chance of taking the championship this weekend, Parkes was feeling good tonight. A half a dozen gin martinis later, he was feeling invincible.

"Are you sure you need one more?" asked Michele.

"I am doing fine, one more won't hurt." replied Parkes as he looked around to find their waitress.

Scott and Michele had stopped after having consumed three martinis and were now drinking club soda, but Parkes decided he needed just one more. Besides, seven was a lucky number.

"I don't see our waitress, so I am going to step up to the bar." said Parkes as he chewed the last olive from his now empty glass.

"I'll get you guys another club soda while I'm there"

As he approached the bar he saw a stunning dark haired woman sitting there by herself.

"Gin martini and two club sodas with a twist." said Parkes to the bartender.

Upon his ordering of the drinks the woman turned and smiled at him.

"Hello, how are you tonight?" he asked her.

"I am doing well" the woman replied.

"Are you in town for the race?"

"No, my friend and I are here on holiday. Just seeing the sights"

"Well, if you get bored looking at old buildings I would be glad to get you some passes to come see me drive in the race on Sunday." said Parkes with a smile.

"No thank you" she replied with a politely.

"Are you sure? You should know that I won the last race and that you might get to see me win again if you decide to come."

"Thank you, but we do have a full schedule planned"

"So where are you from?" he asked.

"She is from Spain" answered a male voice from behind him.

He turned to see a man of average size, with dark skin standing behind him. He looked to Parkes like a very athletic, well built individual.

"I am from Spain, too; and I would like you to go back now to wherever you came from so that I can sit down with my girlfriend." the man told him in a terse tone.

Parkes took a drink from the martini that had been put in front of him. A moment later he decided that he really didn't like the man's attitude.

"Look, sport, I was just waiting for some drinks and struck up a conversation with your friend. You don't have to act like a hard ass."

"I thought I asked you to leave" replied the man.

After setting his drink down, Parkes started to say something in reply, when suddenly the Spaniard's balled up right fist hit him in his nose.

Stunned by the blow, he stumbled back a couple of steps and tried to regain his composure. He stepped forward to throw a left jab, but his opponent blocked it and retaliated with a kick to his sternum.

Falling backward again he winced from the pain he felt in his chest. It was the same spot he had bruised when he crashed at Daytona. With the man coming at him he took a quick breath of air and launched himself forward in an attempt to tackle his foe and knock him down to the ground.

The man's right knee crashed into his left cheek and he fell to the floor. His opponent stood over him and looked to him like he was going to continue the attack when a bouncer stepped in to stop the altercation.

As he got up he noticed that he had blood on the front of his shirt and decided that wiping the blood from his nose on his sleeve wouldn't matter. His oxford cloth shirt was probably ruined anyway.

"I guess that wasn't a fist fight as much as kick boxing" Parkes declared to all those in earshot. Then he felt someone pat him on his back. Looking behind him he saw that it was Scott.

"Come on buddy, let's get you up to your room" said his friend.

Cairo Motorsports Park - Saturday morning

The track that would host the final round of the ISC had been built to host the Grand Prix of Egypt Formula One race, but a number of other series had also competed on the circuit in the short time that the facility had been operational. The International SuperSedan

Challenge hoped that their event would be as least as big a draw for Egyptian racing fans that other events had been.

Those who had driven the course thought it to be one of the best circuits in the world. Highly difficult and very technical, it was probably the toughest stop on the ISC calendar.

Wanting to be treated as a modern city, instead of being viewed as a purely Muslim, Middle East enclave, Cairo's building of a world class race track had done much toward changing the perceptions of the country with auto racing fans from all over the globe.

The morning sun beating down on the circuit was bringing the temperature of the track surface to levels that had not been seen this season by the teams of the International SuperSedan Challenge.

The cars would likely be difficult for the drivers to control because of the slippery track surface that came as a result of the high temperatures that would be seen on this day.

Despite the air conditioning in Scott Battle's Mercedes it still felt warm to Parkes as they entered the gate of the circuit that they would both soon be racing on. Wiping the sweat off his face with a Kleenex, he then put his sun glasses on again and took a long drink off his bottle of mineral water.

"You did the Formula One race here, was it this hot then?"

"I think it is always this hot here, BP. But I would imagine that the real reason that you are sweating so much this morning is mostly because of last night's activities." replied Battle with a grin.

"Just keep drinking fluids. You should be fine in no time at all. In fact, the sooner that you get all that gin out of you the better you'll feel, so drink all the water you can and be glad that you are sweating all those toxins out."

"What is the deal with martinis and me? My head hurts and I pretty much feel like crap.

The thing is that, I mean I never get drunk or feel hung over when I drink scotch."

"It's probably those damned olives" exclaimed Battle with a straight face.

"Yeah, that's probably it. I just need to stay away from olives in the future and I will be just fine." responded Parkes with a faint smile.

Battle brought the car to a stop in front of the Scimitar team's motor coach and exited the Mercedes. Parkes rolled out of the front passenger seat and shut his door behind him.

"Are you going to be, OK?" asked Battle.

"Yeah, I'll be OK. Thanks for the ride. Anyway, I'll see you later on."

The sound of racing engines made his headache even worse that it had been. While his face was sore and slightly bruised from the blows he had sustained the night before, his pounding headache was physically what hurt him the most. He lamented the fact that he hadn't been able to take some Drinkin' Mate before he had gone down to the hotel bar the previous night.

The mental anguish and embarrassment he felt about getting into a bar fight, and then losing was much worse than any hangover pain he could imagine. He hadn't been hurt badly by the blows he had suffered and hoped that his foolish behavior didn't lead to a poor performance on track this weekend.

Team Mandel still had a chance to win the championship, but it would require smart driving and more than a little luck if it was to happen. He knew that feeling hung over and down on one's self was not the way to start things off.

"If I was Scott I would be feeling pretty good about his team's chances right now, given the shape I am in today." mumbled Parkes to himself.

He dismissed the idea that Battle had plotted all of what had occurred the previous evening as quickly as the thought had come to him.

Approaching a refreshment stand he decided that he could do with some strong Turkish coffee this morning. He finished his water and threw the bottle into a garbage can and ordered himself two cups of espresso.

After adding some sugar Parkes downed both cups of the hot fluid in what was probably record time. He now felt more awake as a result of drinking so much caffeine, even if he didn't feel much better.

Looking at his watch he realized that it was almost time to report for duty. He would have preferred to be doing almost anything else right now than driving a loud, raucous eight cylinder racing car. He thought about praying, but he knew that he had already recited the "God I don't know if you are up there, but I promise to stop drinking to excess if I could just feel better" prayer far too many times before.

It had gotten even hotter in the short time he been at the track. Sweat rolled down his face and he wiped it off with the napkin that came with his coffee. He looked up at the sun and wished that it would disappear and give him some relief from the oppressive heat.

If it was 91 degrees at ten o'clock in the morning, Parkes knew that by qualifying time it would be close to 100 degrees, or more.

How hot it would feel in the race car was something that he didn't even want to think about.

Paris, France

"Fox News says that the body of an American man was found in a back alley in Damascus" Liz Mandel shouted into her cell phone from her suite at the Hilton.

The person she had just called was her uncle who calmly told her that he would put her on hold while he contacted the Mossad in Israel to see if they had found out the identity of the slain American.

Anxious to know if it was her dad, but at the same time afraid to learn the truth if it was. She closed her eyes and said a silent prayer asking that she remain calm, whatever the report from Damascus might be.

Suddenly Harry was back on the phone. "Liz, let me call you back, OK?"

"Sure. I'll be waiting"

Hitting the flash button she sighed. As she placed the phone down, she remembered that she hadn't heard back from Brandon.

Having left two messages she decided she wouldn't try to call again. It was beginning to bother her that he hadn't called back. Given the circumstances right now she really wanted to talk to him and hoped he would call her soon.

You can't make things any better by worrying." she told herself.

Sitting down in front of the television she poured herself some coffee and turned up the TV volume with the remote. The news was one depressing story after another. That fact was oddly a comfort to her as it made her remember that she was not the only one with major problems in their lives.

After sipping about half of her coffee she put the cup down on the table and went to the mini bar to get a can of Seven-Up. Caffeine was probably the last thing she needed right now and besides, she desired something cold to drink much more than she wanted something hot.

No sooner had she opened the can than her phone rang. It was Brandon's special ring and when she heard it she told herself to act calm and not let on that he had upset her by not calling her sooner.

"Hello." she said in a manner of fact way. "Well hello, Mr. Parkes. It's nice to finally hear back from you. I had just wanted to make sure that you had gotten to Cairo safely. Anyway, is everything going alright?"

Taking a brief moment before he responded, Brandon began to confess some of his indiscretions from the night before. By the time he was finished he had told her almost everything and while not happy about it, she was just so relieved to hear from him. Then she suggested to him that he might want to take time to ask the Lord for his forgiveness and then try to let it go.

He said nothing in response to her suggestion.

Uncle Harry's ring tone blurted out of her phone and it startled Liz when it did.

"Listen, I have another call coming in; I'll call you after you've finished qualifying, OK?"

Before Brandon could respond, Liz hit the flash button and answered the call.

"Hello, Harry?"

"It isn't your dad that they found in that alley"

"Oh, that is the best news I have heard all day. Thank you."

Harry interrupted her. "It's Jack Rhodes that they found. He had half a dozen bullet wounds from an AK in his chest and a letter in his pocket that says your dad is alive, but that they still want another ten million to free him, supposedly because we have not had Israel deliver the Palestinian prisoners that they had demanded be released."

She was stunned and saddened to learn that it was Jack was who was found dead. She had known him, his wife and his family for many years.

Bursting into tears she thought of how they would not be getting Jack back and the fact that she would never see his confident smiling face again.

"Harry… when is this going to end?" she asked as she let out a sob.

"I think that it will be over very soon." replied her uncle in a stern tone. In fact, I am calling Bernstein right after I hang up with you to talk about how we can end this nightmare. You just go and get yourself some rest, sweetheart"

"Good bye Harry."

After she hung up the phone it occurred to her that Uncle Harry had never called her "sweetheart". Not even when she was little could she remember a time that he had spoken to her with such kindness.

Wiping her tears with a tissue she thought for a moment that Brandon should know what was happening, but quickly realized that he didn't need to be distracted before he went out on the track. She would wait until after qualifying to get in touch, just as she told him she would.

The pain from the wound in her back told her that she needed to try to relax, but with all that was going on it was so very hard to do.

Cairo Motorsports Park – Saturday afternoon

The heat rising from the racetrack was visible as Parkes' race car rolled down the Cairo circuit's pit lane and entered the track for his first lap of qualifying. Already sweating profusely, he blinked as he felt the familiar stinging sensation of perspiration in his eyes.

Practice, which had been held that morning, had been more about trying to put together a clean lap on this unfamiliar circuit than setting a fast time. It was the same for most of the other drivers, as few of them had ever been here before. The lap times Henri had recorded earlier that day were much better than his own, but Parkes wasn't worried, as his team mate was one of the competitors that did know the track well, having run a long distance sports car race there about a year ago.

A red Audi was right on his tail going into turn five and soon by him as they exited turn six. Parkes told himself that he didn't care where he qualified, he would be glad just to get this over so that he could get back to the air conditioned comfort of his hotel room and some much needed rest.

"Damn it, I really hate being hung over!" he shouted to himself out loud.

Heading down the main straight a white Mercedes blew by him. The driver waved to thank him for allowing a clean pass.

Once he saw who it was, Parkes held his gloved hand up with the middle finger extended.

"You are welcome, Scott." He said with a sardonic smile from behind his full face helmet.

As he did more laps it became even hotter inside the car. Each circuit of the track that he completed was a struggle for him and his best qualifying time reflected that fact. Parkes was only eighteenth fastest when he brought the car back to the Mandel pit.

While he wasn't at all pleased with his performance, he was very glad that the ordeal of qualifying was over.

Unstrapping himself from the seat, he started to climb out of the car when he was greeted by a stern faced Griffin Ashmore.

"Go get yourself something cold to drink while we put on some new tires, Parkes"

"Why are you putting on a new set of tires?" he asked with a quizzical look on his face.

"Because this car is better than where you qualified it, mate. You and I both know that you can go faster, even if you do have a case of the bottle flu."

Turning away from the Australian he headed toward the drink cooler without saying a word. He was too embarrassed to say anything at all.

Picking up a copy of the timing results Parkes saw that Henri LeMond had qualified in second place. Scott Battle was on the pole, but just barely, having beaten his Mandel team mate by less than a tenth of a second.

Looking at his watch he saw that fifteen minutes remained in the qualifying session. There was time to put in a faster lap, even if he didn't feel like going out and doing it, he knew that he had to at least be seen trying to do so.

Downing his bottle of water in short order he decided not to have another as it might cause him to get stomach cramps. He knew that if this were to happen out on the track at the wrong time it could prove disastrous.

Grabbing a small white towel from his helmet bag, he wiped away the sweat from his face and soon had his helmet back on for his attempt to gain a better starting spot for the next day's race.

"Now go out there and give it a good run, mate" said Griffin as he finished belting his charge into his seat.

Most of the other competitors were off the track and in the pits when Parkes ventured out on the circuit. The track would probably be devoid of traffic for the remainder of the qualifying session and even if he didn't improve his starting position, he hoped he could at least redeem himself in Griffin's eyes.

The new tires felt better than the last set he had, and he radioed his pleasure with the car to the pits.

"Are you sure that all you did was change out the tires" Parkes asked.

"Everything's the same, except the tires, but I am glad you like the way it's driving."

"Yeah, it feels good….. anyway…. at the end of this lap I am going to stand on it and see if I can get some real speed out her this time".

"Roger that." Griffin replied.

Exiting turn eight, the final corner before the front straight away, Parkes felt the Cadillac respond to the input of his right foot on the accelerator. As the car rocketed past the start- finish line; he held his breath knowing that he would be negotiating the sharp left hand turn one in just moments.

Exhaling on the exit of the first corner he soon felt he was in synch with the car and wasn't surprised to hear at the end of his first flying lap that he had indeed managed a time that was faster than his previous best.

"You are faster by almost a second and you are now in P11" Griffin informed him.

"Let me see if I can get a little more from her." he replied.

The new tires on his car had come up to temperature quickly on the hot track and the second lap at speed was even better than the first.

"You are now P6, repeat you are now in P6, Brandon"

A smile came to his face as Parkes headed into turn one for the final time. He was quick through the next three corners and charged toward turn five confident of his and the car's ability to cut an even faster lap time.

Approaching his usual braking point he decided to try to carry more speed into the corner this time as he attempted to shave another tenth of a second from the previous lap.

When he did finally apply the brakes for the left hand turn he got on them hard with his right foot which was also simultaneously blipping the throttle pedal to bring up the revs. His left foot was pushing in on the clutch pedal as his right hand shifted down through the gears until he reached second. His left hand was turning the steering wheel left and his eyes were focused on the apex of the corner.

It soon became apparent that he was having a problem. He had come in with too much speed, locked up the brakes and proceeded to plow straight off the circuit across the tarmac runoff area and into the gravel trap.

Nothing had been damaged on the car, but his qualifying attempt was over. He would be starting the Istanbul Park race from the sixth position on the grid.

Making his way back on the track for the slow drive to the pits he heard the sound of sand and small rocks coming off his tires and pinging off the bottom of the car.

The next sound he heard was Griffin's voice.

"I guess we pushed a little too hard there mate. But don't worry, sixth is obviously a much better starting spot that eighteenth and I would rather see a driver going for it and giving it their all than just see them going through the motions"

"Yeah, I want you to know that the car seems fine. I just came in a little bit hot and couldn't get her slowed up in time" Parkes replied.

"Thank you, Brandon. That was a really great effort."

"No, Griffin, it is you who deserve the thanks. Anyway, I'll see you back in the pits in a while." Before he got to his pit stall Parkes needed to get rid of the lump in his throat so he took his time.

Paris, France

An exhausted Harry Mandel climbed into his hotel bed after finishing off his last brandy of the night. He closed his eyes and had started to drift off when someone started pounding loudly on the front door of his suite.

Flipping on the light to his bedroom, he located the robe he had draped over a chair and started toward the door. "Who is it?" he asked through the door.

"It's Andre, Harry. We need to talk"

He thought about whether he should open the door or not. As the pounding began again Harry decided that he no choice but to allow the man in.

"Going to bed so soon?" asked Andre as he entered the room.

One of the hulking hired thugs from the club followed him in.

"You do remember my associate, Mr. Rochelle, don't you Harry"?

Mandel didn't respond.

"You don't look very happy to see us, Harry. Here we make this special trip to Paris and you look like you wish we hadn't."

"Who told you that I was here in Paris, at this hotel?"

The name of Silvio Marino came to Harry's mind the moment he asked the question.

"Oh, it was a mutual friend who also said that you would be offended if we did not drop by." Andre cleared his throat. Now, tell me Harry, where in the hell is the money you owe me?"

"You will get your money, plus interest as soon as the kidnappers return my brother. I have told you that repeatedly, but you don't seem to listen."

"I do listen, Harry. I just think that you could get the money if you wanted, but you have the excuse of your brother to keep from paying me. I heard that you paid ten million in cash to the kidnappers. So how come you can't take care of your gambling debt?"

"I don't have it right now. Why would I want to rack up interest with you? Don't you think I would pay you right now if I could?"

Mandel was emphatic and Andre now seemed to believe that he was telling him the truth.

"So what happens if your brother is found dead? Just what happens then?"

Harry paused for a second as he contemplated that thought.

"I will have to ask the board for it. We are…that is the company is privately held but we do have a board made up of family members as well as a couple of trusted advisors. I become Chairman and CEO, so don't worry Andre, you will get paid."

"Let us hope that I get paid soon. My patience is wearing very thin."

"Look, I am trying to get this thing resolved, that is why I am over here. Now let me get some rest so I can do what I have to."

Opening the door to the suite Mandel waited until his two late night guests walked out.

As he passed by Andre gave him a sadistic smile before exiting the room.

"We'll be in touch."

"Be sure to say hello to Silvio, Andre. Thank him for thinking of me." replied Mandel sarcastically.

He slammed the door and crawled back in bed, but could not sleep.

The image of his brother suffering in squalor and then being executed was something that he couldn't get out of his mind.

Getting Dan back to his family was something that Harry had to make happen. It no longer mattered what it might end up costing him.

Cairo, Egypt - Saturday evening

He had just left a message on Liz Mandel's cell phone telling her about the day's qualifying effort and Parkes decided that since it was earlier in Paris than Cairo and he was pretty sure that she was still awake. The reason she had not answered because she was already on the line with someone else, he told himself.

Sitting down on his king size bed he turned on the TV with the remote. After a moment of trying to find CNN International he finally located it and turned the volume up once he had.

After ten minutes of hearing about the latest news there wasn't much interesting happening thought Parkes. He began flipping through the channels in an attempt to find something more enjoyable to watch, when his cell phone rang.

Sprawling across the bed to grab his phone he wondered who it might be.

"Hello"

He was taken aback when he heard the voice on the other end of the call.

"Hello, this is Roth"

"Is Liz OK?" asked a concerned Parkes.

"Oh, yes. She asked me to call you to let you know that she got your message and that she will talk to you in the morning, before the race."

"Alright, but can I ask why she didn't just call me herself?"

"She is being interviewed on Fox News on her reaction to the Prime Minister of Israel saying today that Mr. Mandel should be released or that Syria and Hezbollah would be made to pay."

"Holy crap, I had no idea. In fact, I was just watching the news but didn't see anything about that".

"The US State Department has issued a similar statement that came out just a short time ago."

Parkes picked up the remote and found Fox News. The interview with Liz was just ending as he tuned in.

"Damn it, I just caught the end of the piece." he exclaimed.

"I am sure they will repeat it." replied Roth in his usual calm tone.

"Yeah, I suppose they will. Anyway, just let her know that I'll look forward to hearing from her tomorrow."

"You can be certain that you will. Have a good evening."

"Thanks, Roth. You have a good night as well."

As he ended the call Parkes sighed and began looking for something to do. A copy of the Hilton biography was on the end table next to his bed and started to read it. After skimming through it he decided to order dinner. As he waited for it to arrive, he reached into his suitcase and started to look at the book Liz had given him in Belgium.

He ended up reading it completely and pondered the words Mr. Lewis had written before he reached over to turn off the bedside lamp. Parkes was as calm he could ever remember and fell to sleep with ease.

Cairo, Egypt – 8:05 AM

Rain was the last thing that anyone had expected to see on race morning in Cairo. Looking out of his hotel room Brandon Parkes thought of the coming day and felt confident about his prospects for the race and the team's chances in the championship. He wasn't worried about the potential of slick conditions on the track; in fact he preferred to see wet weather instead of the oppressive heat that he had experienced the day before.

He had already done a light work-out of thirty minutes on the hotel tread mill and a few repetitions on the bench press before coming back to his room for a shower and a shave.

Dressed in one of his black Team Mandel shirts and a pair of khaki slacks he was waiting to hear from Henri who had rented a car and was going to give him a lift to the circuit.

With nothing else to do he stood in front of the bathroom mirror and brushed his short brown hair back again and noticed that he looked one hundred percent better than he had the previous morning.

After applying some moisturizer with sunscreen to his face and arms he was ready to take on the world.

He still had fifteen minutes to go until the time that Henri was to collect him for the drive to the track. Turning on the TV he sat down on the end of his bed and tuned to Fox News to see if he might catch Liz's interview from the night before.

The screen filled with the sight of Israeli Defense Force Merkava tanks and M113 armored personnel carriers, as the reporter spoke of military units gearing up for a possible assault on Syria from the Golan Heights should Dan Mandel not be released by his captors.

The whole situation had become surreal. A clip from Liz's interview finally came on. She said how she was pleased that Israel was pressuring Syria to make sure that her father was freed.

Following that was a live phone interview with Harry Mandel who said that he thought that his brother would soon be released. He went on to say that he was negotiating with the kidnappers and felt that they were close to resolution of the matter. His plea to all involved was to remain calm. He finished by saying that starting another Middle East conflict over the issue would be foolish and uncalled for.

There was a knock on the door. Parkes looked at his watch again as he headed over to answer it.

"Good morning, Henri. You are punctual as always. Please come in for a minute."

"I see you are following what is going on with Mr. Mandel?" commented LeMond as he pointed toward the TV.

"Yeah, I just can't believe it has come to this."

If he didn't have to go to the racetrack Parkes would have stayed glued to the television to watch the story unfold. The fact was that he had a job to do and the best thing he could do right now was to go and help Team Mandel win the International SuperSedan Challenge title.

"Are you ready to go today?" Parkes asked LeMond as he turned off the TV with the remote.

"Yes; in fact, I think that I have been ready for a moment like this all of my life."

Parkes smiled at his team mate's comment. "As have I my friend, as have I."

What Henri had just said had given him a brief shiver up his spine. While the chances of winning the team championship were somewhat slim, he knew that they still had a shot at it. Equally important was the fact that he was beginning to have faith that the goal could be reached.

"Let's go give it our best and see what happens, Henri"

The two men exited the hotel and LeMond tipped the valet who had been guarding the car for him.

As they drove to the track they discussed strategy and who they needed to finish in front of if they were to win the title today.

It was no longer raining by the time they reached the Cairo Motorsports Park. LeMond found a parking spot that was near the Team Mandel transporter. The crew members were carrying items from the team transporter to the garage as they got everything in place that would be needed during the day.

"Good morning lads" exclaimed Griffin Ashmore as the two drivers entered the air conditioned lounge at the front part of the transporter.

"So, what does the weatherman in you say will happen this afternoon; will it rain again, or will it be sunny and hot?" asked LeMond.

Race to Damascus

Lifting his black Team Mandel cap with his left hand Griffin ran his fingers through his hair with his right as he thought about his answer. "I think it will be clear and sunny, but not too hot. I should think it will be about perfect come race time."

"That sounds good to me" replied Parkes. "Now give us a minute or two to get dressed, OK?"

"I'll give you ladies some privacy, but don't take all day."

As Ashmore closed the door to the lounge behind him, Parkes and LeMond began the process of getting ready for the race to come.

It occurred to Parkes as he suited up, that this time was not just about putting on flame resistant clothing, but it was as much about putting on your mental and spiritual armor as well.

As usual, LeMond had finished dressing first and stepped out to have a Gitanes while Parkes finished getting ready. "See you in the garage." he said.

"OK, Henri. I'll be there soon"

After he zipped up his black Nomex driver's suit he decided to take a moment for a silent prayer. He didn't ask for victory in the race, nor did he ask that his team would win the championship today. Instead, he asked for forgiveness for wrongdoing and put his life and soul in God's hands. He had been thinking about this ever since Liz had started talking about her faith and he sensed a release of tension in his body as he prayed.

He then asked that if it were to be his final day of life he would have courage that could only come from knowing that he was now saved by His grace.

Lifting his head Parkes took a deep cleansing breath, picked up his helmet bag and exited the transporter. The sun was now shining brightly and the morning warm-up was about to begin. He felt that he was fortunate just to be here, getting paid to drive a racecar, but also realized that it didn't really matter what the outcome of this afternoon's race might be.

"Would anyone care who had won in ten years from now, much less a hundred years?" he asked himself. What did matter to him were the overwhelming feelings of peace and confidence that he was experiencing. It was a sense that everything would be fine from now on, no matter what the result was out on the race track.

Cairo, Egypt-2:15pm

The flight from Paris to Cairo had gone by quickly and Liz couldn't wait to get to the racetrack so she could surprise Brandon and the rest of the guys. The idea that she might miss her team take the title bothered her, so she and Roth were now on their way to the Cairo Motorsports Park for the big season finale.

They had rented a red Mercedes convertible and Liz decided to drive while Roth rode shotgun and acted as navigator. It was the first time she had driven a car since before the attack in Spa and she was enjoying it.

Despite Cairo being ninety percent Muslim, being here today didn't bother her, even though she was half Jewish.

Perhaps the fact that it had not always been that way is was what made it acceptable to her. She knew that most Egyptians were not extremists and many desired their country to be thought of as a modern, civilized nation. To her it was just that; unlike Syria, the country that her father was being held captive in.

As they drove up to the gates of the race track Liz remembered that she would need to present her plastic ISC all season pass.

"Can you grab my purse from the back seat and get out my hard card?"

Roth did as he was asked and when they pulled up to the man at the gate he got out his own credential and flashed it at the guard who waved them through and into the area where the competitors parked.

She got out of the car and picked up her purse from the back seat.

"Come on Roth; let's get to the pits before practice is over. Just leave the top down for now"

Taking off in the direction of the pits, her body guard was running behind her trying to catch up.

As they reached the team garage most of the crewmen were out on the pit wall watching the cars that were already out on the circuit.

Roth found a chair at the back of the garage while Liz walked across pit road to the team's timing stand. When Griffin saw her he smiled and made room for her to sit next to him. With the powerful cars blasting by it was impossible to talk, so she simply smiled back as she settled into her seat to watch the remainder of the pre-race warm up.

Both Mandel drivers flashed their headlights as they drove past the pit wall as they began their final practice lap. Liz couldn't help but feel a sense of pride when she saw them go by and thought that if only they ran just as well as they looked that the team would have a successful day.

When the cars rolled to a stop in their pit boxes she was there to greet them. Stopping at Henri's car first she said hello to the

Frenchman. As Henri sat in his car he removed his helmet and spoke to her through the now open door.

"How did it feel to you, Henri?"

"The car is very good. The lads have done a fantastic job."

Liz turned to see if Brandon was out of his car. He was, and he was headed towards her.

"What in the world are you doing here young lady?"

"I told you I would talk to you before the race, so here I am" she replied with a smile.

She motioned at Parkes' car and the mechanics that were looking under the hood "So what are they doing to your car?"

"We had an occasional misfire and I asked them to see what might be causing it. It should be something that can be easily fixed."

"I hope you are right because we will almost certainly need for you both to finish in the points if we are to have a chance to win the title." said Liz with a look of concern on her face.

"Don't worry. I think we'll be fine. Anyway, it is a really nice surprise to see you and to know that you were feeling well enough to be here."

"Nothing could have kept me away from this."

"So, can I buy you a cup of coffee, Miss Mandel?"

"Yes, you may. That would not only be lovely but also very much appreciated right now."

As they started to leave the garage Griffin approached them and told them the initial results of the check-up of his car.

"We are going to change out the plug wires and the spark plugs and see if that takes care of your misfire."

"Thanks, Griffin. We are going off to find a cup of coffee. Can we bring you anything?"

"No, I think am fine right now. Go and relax for a bit, but don't drink too much coffee."

"I promise to only have one, and then I'll switch to water; OK?"

Griffin looked Liz in the eye. "You make sure that he sticks to his promise."

She smiled back at him. "I will. Listen; we will let you get back to your work now. We don't want Brandon here to have any excuses if he doesn't perform well out there today" she said with a wink.

Climbing onto one of the black Team Mandel golf carts they drove off in search of a coffee vendor and a chance to catch up with one another.

Paris, France-Sunday afternoon

Lighting a cigarette, Harry Mandel once again started to pace the floor of his hotel room. He had not been able to sleep at all the night before, but hoped that he might get some rest once he had heard some concrete news from the Mossad.

All that the TV news channels had talked about that morning was the mounting tension on the Israeli-Syrian border. Tension that was rooted in decades, if not centuries, of conflict had been brought to life again as a result of his own brother having been kidnapped and held captive in Syria.

Snuffing out the half finished Marlboro Light, he reached into the mini bar for the last bottle of both vodka and orange juice. After pouring them together into a tall glass he then sat down in front of the television.

The Syrian ambassador to the UN was telling a news conference that his country knew nothing about the kidnapping, nor of Mr. Mandel's whereabouts.

"We notified the Mandel family via the United States ambassador to the UN that we had found their aircraft and told them that we would do anything else we could to assist in helping to locate Mr. Mandel and return him to his family. Other than that, we have no knowledge of the situation"

"You son of bitches collected a six figure fee for finding and guarding our plane. Tell them that part." Harry yelled at the screen.

The Syrian continued his speech. "We feel that Israel is simply using the missing American Jew as an excuse to attack our country and will attempt to wipe us out.

I call on all of our Muslim brothers to support us in the hour of our trials."

Harry reached for the remote and turned the TV off, and then picked up his cell phone. He scrolled down to Bernstein's cell number and pressed the call button.

It rang four times before Bernstein answered.

"Did you get hold of your people yet?" Harry barked.

"I am on the line with them now."

Race to Damascus

Pushing the drink bottle button, located on the opposite side of the steering wheel from the radio control, he got a mouthful of lukewarm water. The race wasn't even half of the way over and the water in the car was already getting warm.

It was a mental; if not a physical lift to know that the race once again seemed to be coming to him, just as it had at the previous event at Spa-Francorchamps.

Hurtling down the front straight for the tenth time, Parkes was almost in a position to challenge for fifth place when he encountered a lapped car heading into the first corner. The Lexus balked him from passing until they reached the straight away after turn three when his ebony Cadillac was finally able to muscle its way by.

He keyed the radio mike as he made his way down the long straight away between turn six and seven "Sorry, Griffin. I lost contact with the pack because of the lapped car that got in the way."

"No worries mate. There's a lot of race left."

Ahead of Parkes right now was another car that had just gone a lap down to the leaders. Unlike the Lexus that he had just managed to get by, the Jaguar of Conrad Templeton moved over to the right and let him go as soon as he caught up to him coming down the start finish straight.

He held up his hand to acknowledge his appreciation of the courtesy shown by the wealthy sportsman and then downshifted and braked the CTS-V once again for the first turn.

"You are now in P5, Brandon." Griffin informed him excitedly.

He responded with a hint of surprise in his voice.

"How can that be?"

"Battle came in to the pits and the car is going behind the wall with motor problems.

If the race ended right now we would be the champions, mate!"

The title had been Scimitar's to lose and Parkes knew that with his friend retired from the race there was now a very real chance of the Mandel team winning the championship. However, he was also aware that if Bin Salman finished in the points, or if he or LeMond were to drop out, that the Scimitar Mercedes team would still prevail.

"That's unbelievable news! Keep me posted on Bin Salman's position and where I need to finish, OK?"

"Yeah, it is obviously a fluid situation, mate, but I'll try to let you know what's happening."

His Cadillac was still running well, but Parkes was beginning to sense that his tires might not last until the end of lap 25. He felt the car under steering a bit on entry to the corners and was subject to some power over steer on exit. If his lap times grew substantially as a result of his tires going away then he would have no choice but to come in much sooner than had originally been planned.

Coming up to the halfway point of the race, the first four cars were still running strong. When his car crossed the finish line at mid race, Griffin informed him that he was still running about four seconds adrift of the last car in the lead pack.

"What do you think of the idea of coming in for the pit stop a bit earlier?"

There was no response.

Parkes pushed the radio button again.

"Griffin, Can I move up our stop up by a lap?"

After another moment of silence he heard the radio crackle to life once again.

"Stopping at the end of lap 24 would be just fine with me."

The thought that he would soon be getting new rubber on all four corners and better car control than he currently had was a relief as the car was getting loose coming out of the corners due to his cars rapidly eroding tires.

"OK, I'll go until the end of lap 24" he replied.

"Good. Henri is making his pit stop at the end of this lap and it will be much easier on the crew if you come in a lap later."

With a gaggle of cars in front of him as he approached turn five, Parkes was too busy to talk any further. He drove the car over to the left hand side of the track and passed a BMW, but quickly realized that he would have to wait until the long back straight to get by the next two competitors, a silver AMG Mercedes which was following closely behind the other white Lexus.

Quickly closing up on the Mercedes' bumper, he decided to try drafting past both cars as they approached turn seven.

Pulling out of the three car train he started toward the left side of the track to make the pass. The Mercedes' driver did the same thing at the very same moment and Parkes' Cadillac followed the silver car as it swept past the Lexus before braking for the left hand seventh turn.

Staying on the Mercedes' tail through turn eight and onto the front straight, he got by him just as the two cars went past the start finish line.

"The leader is on pit road .You are now in P1" announced Griffin.

"Too bad you don't get five bonus points for being the race leader like you do in NASCAR" replied Parkes.

There was no response from Griffin who was no doubt busy talking to LeMond and directing the crewmen who were servicing the other team car.

When his team mate drove into the pits for fuel and tires the next three cars behind him followed his lead and did the same. That was how Parkes had become the leader. He knew that it wouldn't be a long tenure as he would have to surrender first place the moment he headed into the pits himself.

As he looked out his front windscreen he could see that the track ahead was currently devoid of traffic. Unimpeded by slower cars he hoped that this would be an opportunity to make up a bit of time to the leaders.

By picking up a couple of seconds on the track, combined with a quick pit stop he just might be able to find himself right on the tail end of the lead pack when he came out of the pits and re-entered the race circuit.

The long run from turn six to turn seven provided a chance to get another swallow from the drink bottle. Despite the water having gotten warm, Parkes was glad to have it on board. He tried to suck out a couple of more mouthfuls but soon realized that the tank was empty.

The heat of the day, as well as the extreme heat coming from the racecar was starting to take their toll on him. He knew that he had to get something more to drink while the car took on gas and new rubber.

Downshifting and braking for turn seven the Cadillac was still running well.

Coming out of turn eight he pushed the gas pedal down and made his way back up through the gears as he crossed the start finish line to complete lap sixteen.

The radio crackled with Griffin's voice reminding him to head for the pits at the end of the lap.

The knowledge that it was past the halfway point of the race and that they still had a shot at the championship gave Parkes a sense that they just might be able to end up making it happen.

Squeezing the brake pedal with his right foot to slow down as he entered pit lane had triggered a cramp in his leg.

After bringing the car to a complete stop, the crew started to change tires while he reached down to rub the calf muscle of his right leg. Thankfully the pain subsided quickly. He then opened the driver's side door to let in some cooler air.

"Griffin, can someone get me some more water?" he yelled into the radio.

The passenger side door opened just seconds later. Griffin handed him a clear plastic bottle with a built in straw that would allow him drink with his helmet on.

As he swallowed the cold water he knew that it would not only be refreshing to him, but he hoped that it would also help him avoid any more cramping in his legs that might be a result of dehydration.

After downing about a third of the contents Parkes threw the bottle out the driver's side door and over the pit wall just as the Cadillac was about to come down off the jacks.

"Thanks" he yelled from behind the full face helmet.

Griffin nodded and closed the door behind him.

With tires changed and the gas tank refilled Griffin patted on the roof of the car with his right hand and keyed his radio mike button with his left. "Go, go" he exclaimed in his Aussie accent.

Parkes was ready to get back into the fight. As he merged back into traffic he was thrilled to see that he was only a car length behind his team mate.

"Fantastic job by all you guys… Man, I can't believe we are in second place, right in back of LeMond." said Parkes excitedly on the radio.

"You are actually still in fifth, mate. We had an air gun hang up and jam on LeMond's stop and he fell back to fourth."

The news surprised him, but he tried not to show it to Griffin when he called him back on the radio.

"Yeah, copy that. I already thought it might be too good to be true."

"Sorry to disappoint you mate. Anyway, give me a minute to do the math and I'll give you the championship picture as of right now, OK?"

"Roger that. I'll stand by"

He was now glued to LeMond's bumper, as the two black Team Mandel cars headed down the front straight away. Ahead of them the leaders were just crossing the start finish line to begin lap 25 of the race. The BMW of Mario Barilla continued to lead the field. His team mate Hans Schneider, who was about two car lengths behind, held second place and Stephan Altenburg's Audi was following closely in third.

While downshifting for turn three the radio crackled to life.

"Brandon, Bin Salman has moved up into seventh place on the last lap. So, if the race were to end now the Scimitar guys would have thirty-one points to our thirty."

Griffin had not bothered to tell him about Bin Salman's moving back into a points paying position until that moment. He wished his team manager had passed that bit of information on to him.

"Well then we obviously need one of us to pick up a couple more points, right?" Parkes replied with a slightly terse tone.

"Yeah, but you should know that the eighteen points those BMW's would get from finishing first and second is a bigger worry mate. That will give them thirty-two and the title."

While Team Mandel had focused on Scott Battle and the Scimitar team, they hadn't given the TCR BMW's much thought. Though Parkes knew that the silver BMW were running one-two on the track right now, he couldn't believe that they could end up beating his team in the championship.

"I thought you said that they needed a one-two finish and for us to have problems?"

He paused for a moment and then added "We are still in fourth and fifth place, aren't we?"

With no response coming from the radio, Parkes decided that it was time to become proactive and make an attempt to go get enough points to top their rivals.

Coming out of the turn five- six complex he started his run down the back straight away and was doing in excess of one hundred and fifty miles per hour as he approached the kink in the middle of the straight. He was going to try drafting his team mate and hoped to slingshot by him just before they arrived at the braking point for turn seven.

The back end of LeMond's Cadillac was starting to fill Parkes windscreen as he softly bumped the nose of his racecar up against the bumper of his team mate's identical car while at top speed on the fastest part of the circuit.

Through the back window he saw LeMond raise his right hand. It was the signal that there was a wreck ahead and that he should slow down.

His team mate then began to tap his brakes and Parkes knew then that he had better back off quickly. Tapping his own brake pedal to put some space between their cars, he soon knew why LeMond wanted him to get off his bumper before they got to the corner.

One of the Mercedes and a BMW had just gotten together and crashed out of the race. There were good sized pieces of the race cars scattered across the racing surface and it was Henri's actions, combined with a track marshal's waving yellow flag that had kept them from becoming involved in the wreck.

While driving around the debris on the shoulder of the track Parkes quickly realized that the cars in the shunt were lapped cars and that their dropping out wasn't going to have any effect on the championship. After he was by the accident scene he was back on the gas and once again in pursuit of the other black Cadillac.

Approaching the start finish line he saw the full course yellow caution flag come out and as he slowed the car down again it suddenly occurred to him that one of the drivers might have been hurt in the accident. All he had been thinking about is whether or not any of the cars that had been eliminated were ones that were ahead of his own in the race. He felt a tinge of guilt that his only concern had been for himself. It was not at all like him to think that way, since in the past he would have seen these situations as merely tightening the competition.

After he finished he decided to call to the pits to talk to Griffin. Before pushing the radio mike button he thought about what he would say.

"So what's the plan?"

A moment later Griffin answered him.

"Stay behind Henri after the restart. I don't need you two knocking each other off the track trying to move to the front, mate."

"I understand. Thanks, Griffin"

"Just take a deep breath and try to be cool." he told himself.

Be anxious for nothing is what Liz kept saying; but not agonizing over everything was a hard concept for someone taught to be their own worst critic, and believed that one could control their own life if they just tried hard enough.

A feminine voice interrupted his thoughts "Hey Parkes, are you ready to go after these guys?"

"I guess you were reading my mind. I was just thinking about you."

Listen, I know that you are about to get the green flag and I just wanted to tell you to have fun and just let things play out, OK?

"Alright, I will be seeing you soon, Liz" he replied.

With only 12 laps to go the field had bunched up behind the Mercedes pace car for the final lap under the yellow caution flag. The restart would give the Team Mandel cars a great opportunity to get past the third place Audi and then take on the BMW's that currently occupied the first two positions in the race.

Driving around the circuit at minimal speeds was causing the engine temperature to rise above its normal level and the extra heat in the car was becoming noticeable to him.

Parkes took a moment to wipe his forehead and cheeks with his gloved right hand to get rid of the sweat that had accumulated on his face.

He hoped that when the race restarted and he got back up to full speed the engine temperature would go down and that by driving fast again it would provide some air flow into the cockpit and make conditions a bit more bearable.

"Hey Griffin; be sure to remind me to have Marino allow cool suits when he looks at the rules for next year. There isn't much cost savings if you get heat stroke and crash."

"Don't be such a wimp, Henri isn't complaining about being hot." replied Griffin in a mischievous tone.

"Sure he isn't" said Parkes with a laugh.

As the field of cars rounded the final turn he readied himself for the restart. With four cars in front and six more behind him that had not been lapped he knew it was going to be a shootout over the last seven laps to find out who would win the race and the championship.

"OK, this is it, Brandon. Get ready .... Green, green, green" shouted Griffin over the radio.

LeMond had made an outstanding start and had managed to get past the Audi in third place. Parkes own car had pulled up on the rear bumper of the RS5 as the cars made the left hand turn and entered turn one.

The sensation of the rear tires sliding told him that he was starting to spin out.

One of the cars that had been in back of him slipped past as he struggled to regain control.

Just as he had gathered it all up and regained control, another car went past him.

Not remembering that he was on cold tires had cost him two positions. He was mad at himself for not being more aware, but was thankful that he hadn't ended up sideways and having another competitor center punch him and end his day.

The rear tires continued to feel slippery to him for the better part of two laps, but Parkes still maintained the seventh position. There wasn't much time left to go in the race and Bin Salman's Scimitar Mercedes was now right behind him in eighth The Arab was pushing him hard in an effort to take away the seventh position and the two points that went with it.

Flat out on the fast, back straight with someone right behind you was a bit tricky, he thought. The kink in the middle of the straight was hard enough to get through by yourself, never mind with a competitor's car following you. Driving with the throttle pedal pushed down to the floorboard Parkes tried to ignore the flashing headlights of the Mercedes and focused on taking the correct racing line through each of the corners of the circuit.

As his black Cadillac and the white Mercedes began braking for the turn seven and eight complex of turns, Griffin suddenly came on the radio with news that LeMond had moved up into second place. "Now you just manage to keep Bin Salman behind you" exclaimed Griffin.

"You got it" was Parkes' reply. He didn't have time to say anything more as the young Arab was now trying to get past him on the front straight.

Before he entered turn one Parkes saw in his mirror that Bin Salman had thought better of trying to pass and had slid his car back into place behind him.

Just behind Bin Salman was Sigala's Maserati, followed by a BMW and the other Maserati. These three were currently in ninth, tenth and eleventh place and were the last of the cars still running on the lead lap, according to Griffin's last radio update.

He continued to hold off the white Mercedes through the twisty portion of the track and down the straight away that led to turns five and six. In the process of keeping Bin Salman at bay, he had also closed up to within only one car length of the BMW that was in front of him.

Exiting turn six of the 44th lap the Cadillac's engine stumbled as he pushed down on the accelerator. It had only been momentary, but it had allowed Bin Salman to pull up beside him on his left side as they headed down the long back straight.

As the two cars raced one another toward the kink at the midpoint of the straight Parkes wondered if both could get through running side by side at over one hundred and fifty miles per hour.

Unable to get over to the left hand side of the track to set up the optimum line for the kink, Parkes opted to back off the gas to let Bin Salman by, only to discover that one of the Maseratis, the one driven by Theocopolos, and a BMW were following right behind the Saudi driver. It left his Cadillac with nowhere to go but to fall to the back of the line for the left hand turn seven.

As he applied the brakes for the turn Parkes slid into the space between the white BMW and the red Maserati Quattroporte. He had just gone from seventh to tenth place in the blink of an eye and was reeling from the shock of it as he drove toward the start finish line. As he went past the pits he felt ashamed about what had just occurred, despite it not really being his fault. Even worse was the realization that there were now only four laps left in the race and little time for him to make things right.

"The misfire came back as I was coming out of six and it gave Bin Salman a run on me. Then I just got hung out to dry by a couple of the others, too" exclaimed Parkes into his mike.

A moment later Griffin came back with a downcast response "Right. OK, Brandon, we understand".

With Sigala in the second of the Maserati entries still hounding him, Parkes had it cross his mind to just let the Italian driver by, especially when his car stumbled once again as he came out of turn four and onto the short straight that followed it.

Despite the Cadillac's momentary loss of power he found out that he could still keep the Maserati behind him on the straight away. Then, as he approached the braking zone for turn five he saw that a car had spun off the course and that the other cars had slowed to avoid it.

When he went by the Audi that had spun out he knew that he was up to ninth place and that only a half a car length behind the eight place BMW of Gunnar Andersen.

His car's engine was running fine as he powered down the straight. As Parkes downshifted into second gear for turns seven and eight the thought occurred to him that his efforts might prove to be too little and too late, but that he still had to give it his best.

Blasting past the pits to begin lap 48 he decided that he had to shut out any thoughts of points or championships, as he couldn't control that. All he could do was take things one step at a time and try to get past the white BMW that was right in front of him.

Going into turn two he planted the nose of his Cadillac just behind the rear bumper of the M3 in an effort to set himself up to get around Andersen on the run up to turn three.

Feinting to the left and then crossing over to the right of the track, Parkes got his car underneath the BMW going into the right hand corner and managed to out brake the Swede to take over eighth place.

The radio crackled with static and the voice in his helmet was that of Griffin Ashmore. "Good job, mate. You are now in P8. LeMond is still P2"

Three car lengths ahead Parkes saw that a battle for the sixth position was shaping up between the Maserati of Theocopolos and the AMG Mercedes of Mansur Bin Salman. The red Maserati seemed to be better in the turns, but the Scimitar Mercedes could keep ahead by going a bit faster on the straight.

Trying to drive as smoothly as he could, Parke found that as he did so, he was pulling ever closer to the sixth and seventh place cars. He was sure that their struggle with one another was allowing him to catch up, but wondered if he would be able to get past them once he had caught them.

With just over 2 laps left, he knew that there were not many opportunities remaining in the race to move up, but he thought that his best bet was going into turn five, or in turn seven. As he chased the big Maserati down the back straight into the braking zone he realized that he was not close enough to get him this time, but hoped that he might be able to pull it off on the lap to come.

"Brandon, you have to get by that white Mercedes." admonished Griffin. "LeMond is falling behind the leader and will be lucky to hold on for second place. "

"Yeah, I am in here trying, Griffin."

"We know you are, mate. Just keep giving it all you can. There is only one more lap to go after this one."

The fact that he just had recorded the fastest laps of the race was hopefully proof that he was indeed trying hard to catch his rivals.

Ahead of him he saw Theocopolos make an attempt to pass Bin Salman as they headed down the straight toward turn five. Just as quickly he fell back behind the Mercedes when the Greek driver realized that he wasn't going to be able to pull it off. Then Theocopolos tried once again to get past the Mercedes and Parkes hoped that if the Maserati driver got by that he might be able to slip his car by Bin Salman as well.

Instead, he had found himself having to brake hard to avoid the big Italian car when Theocopolos aborted the pass and got back on the proper line as he entered the corner.

The speed and the momentum that the Maserati and Cadillac drivers had just scrubbed off allowed Bin Salman to gain at least a car length on the straight away that followed the turn five and six complex.

That advantage disappeared when the Mercedes braked too late in the slightly downhill section that led to the left-hand seventh turn. He locked the brakes up when he tried to get slowed down and was now fighting to get the car to turn to the left. Theocopolos pounced on the opportunity that had just presented itself and placed his car on the left hand side of the track, late braked and was able to force his way past the struggling Arab and his Mercedes on the inside of the corner.

When Parkes saw what was occurring before him his instinct was to back off before he became part of a three car pileup. As the tire smoke cleared he could see that the Maserati driver had gotten past the Mercedes, but that Bin Salman had managed to steer his car to the left and get back on line just behind the Italian car.

Exiting turn eight and onto the main straightaway the Theocopolos driven car now led Mansur Bin Salman's Mercedes by about a yard. Parkes own car was now roughly the same margin behind the white C 63.

The first five positions in the race were looking to be all but settled as the BMW of first place Mario Barilla crossed the line to start the final lap of the contest.

Sixth through eighth place was a different matter. Running nose to tail as they entered turn one Parkes knew that the series championship would be decided in about two minutes time. Success for himself and the team was so very close, but still just out of his grasp.

Careful to avoid wheel spin as he accelerated out of turn four and down the straight, the American saw that he was close enough to have an opportunity to try to make his move past Bin Salman.

Going through the gears with his right foot planted on the gas, Parkes steered his black race car over to the left hand side of the circuit and pulled up beside the Mercedes as they entered the braking zone for turn five. The nose of the Cadillac was about even with the rear wheel of the Mercedes when he realized that he wasn't going to get past him on this attempt. Braking hard and downshifting into second gear, he then turned into the corner and unintentionally tapped Bin Salman's bumper. The contact unsettled the rear end of the Mercedes going into turn six, but the Arab caught it before it caused him to spin out. When the car in front of him checked up, Parkes saw a gap and found himself side by side with the Mercedes as they started the run down the back straight away.

Race to Damascus

Shifting from third to fourth Parkes felt the engine cough and stumble again. The Scimitar Mercedes shot by and got ahead of him just before going into the kink.

"You can't be serious!" he yelled to himself as he shifted the car into fifth.

The car's engine began to miss again and did the same after he shifted back down into fourth gear. He knew then that he wasn't going to catch his rival and that there was nothing he could do about.

Bin Salman had pulled ahead of his Cadillac by two car lengths as they approached the braking zone for turn seven.

Theocopolos had moved over to the right side of the track and was about to make his turn in for the left hand turn seven when Parkes saw Bin Salman's car dive to the left and then to the inside of the red car.

The Maserati pilot never saw what hit him as the right front of the Mercedes struck the left rear door of the red car.

Both automobiles slid off the track in a small cloud of tire smoke. Parkes braked and downshifted into second gear. He was a bit tentative as entered the corner, not quite sure of what he would find on the other side of the smokescreen.

As he got through turn seven he was stunned to see that Bin Salman and Theocopolos were off the track. He also realized that he was not on the perfect line for turn eight, so he slowed down, shifted down into first gear and soon found himself on the pit straight and headed toward the start finish line. As he up shifted into second he noticed a car was beginning to fill his rearview mirror.

It was Sigala, in the other red Maserati, that was catching up to him. Seeing this, Parkes held down the throttle flat to the floor and shifted up through the gears to third and then fourth.

This time the Cadillac's powerful eight cylinder engine responded to his input without hesitation.

The gap between the Maserati grew to more than a car length as the black Team Mandel entry surged ahead. Parkes glanced into his mirror and saw that Sigala was now resigned to having to follow him past the starter's stand and the waving checkered flag.

Driving on the cool off lap he listened to the cheers of his crew over the radio. He had just become co-champion of the first International SuperSedan Challenge. It was beyond surreal to him right now how this had all just come to pass.

Cairo Motorsports Park-Victory Lane

As she made her way to the podium ceremony a tiny tear of joy ran down Liz Mandel's cheek. The team had worked hard and she was so very proud of all of them.

With the Mandel Cadillac's second and sixth place finishes in this final event of the season they had secured the ISC team championship. Even more important to Liz was the fact that she and the members of the team had not given up, or become distracted because of her father's disappearance, but instead had endured and persevered which lead them to the success that they were enjoying now.

The Italian national anthem was just concluding as she arrived to take a spot in front of the rostrum next to Griffin Ashmore. The race winner, Barilla now held both fists high above his head while LeMond and Hans Schneider sprayed the Italian with their magnums of shaken Mumms champagne.

Liz put her left hand on the shoulder of her loyal team manager and he turned his head to see who it was.

"Congratulations, Griffin"

"Same to you." he replied with a smile and a fatherly hug.

Griffin then stared straight ahead as the trophies were being handed out to the race's top three finishers and didn't, or simply couldn't, make eye contact with her.

She knew then that this was an emotional moment for him, too. It was really touching for her to see this normally stoic man so overcome with emotion. No matter what the outcome for her father, capturing the ISC title was a fitting tribute to him and she was thankful for it.

The end of the ceremonies saw Sigala down on his knees spraying his own bottle of champagne at his pit crew who were standing directly in front of the podium. After he gave them a good dousing, he took a long drink from the bottle, before handing the remainder of the magnum down to one of his crew.

As he stood up Henri LeMond greeted him with a hand shake and leaned forward to say something into Sigala's ear. A moment later the two drivers were motioning for Brandon to come up from the crowd and join them on the dais.

"Come on up here, Brandon. You are the co-champion!" LeMond yelled out to him over the public address microphone.

Parkes, with his driver's suit unzipped to his waist and a black Team Mandel Racing hat on his head walked toward the stairs of the podium. With the additional prompting from the crowd he had no choice but to do so and was soon greeted by a large volume of applause as he met his team-mate at center stage.

Watching the proceedings Liz thought that it was curious to see how low key and humble Parkes was acting. She had expected him to be almost manic, as he usually was when things went well for him. Right now he seemed almost as though he was in shock about the bit of good fortune that he had just experienced.

LeMond then spoke to the crowd and thanked the Mandel team, the race organizers as well as the fans. "I also want you to know that this will be my final race as I have decided that it is time for me to retire from the sport."

The collective no that rose from the assembled crowd reminded Liz of a political candidate telling his supporters that he was conceding an election. The big difference was that LeMond was part of a team that had just won.

"Thank you, but I think this is the right time" replied a smiling LeMond to the audience.

A surprised Griffin turned his head to look at Liz.

"That is news to me." he said.

"I am just glad he was able to go out on a high note." she replied.

The announcement wasn't quite as much of surprise for Liz as Henri had already told her that he might quit driving at the end of the season, but she didn't know that he was going to announce it here and now.

A warm feeling of joy came over her as she thought about how he had realized his goal of winning the championship and the knowledge that his portion of the prize money would mean that he would be retiring with more than a few dollars in his pocket.

As soon as LeMond finished his remarks he grabbed Parkes' hand and held it in the air. "Lastly I want to thank my team-mate and friend, Brandon Parkes"

The crowd applauded as the American stepped to the microphone.

"This is a wonderful result for everyone at Team Mandel." he paused for a brief moment and continued. "When this year began I could not have guessed that I would be competing in this series and with this team, much less standing here celebrating winning the team title. I hadn't planned for any of this, so I guess I just have to thank the man upstairs for all of it."

As Brandon and Henri left the stage together; waving to the crowd, Liz Mandel was beaming. It seemed to her that Brandon was indeed a changed man. Given the way she cared about Parkes she couldn't have been any more pleased for him.

Chapter Eleven

Cairo, Egypt - Monday morning

Some of the Team Mandel crewmen were already seated for breakfast when Brandon arrived in the hotel dining room. Griffin was among them and he sat at the end of the table.

"I almost didn't recognize you guys without your uniforms. You all clean up pretty good." said Parkes with a smile to the group.

"Yeah, well a couple of the lads stayed out too late celebrating and are sleeping it off. But these gentlemen were able to join us. Anyway, have you seen our host this morning? Griffin asked.

"No, but she should be here pretty soon."

"Yes, she will be here any time now. She got tied up on a phone call out in the lobby." said a familiar voice from behind Parkes.

Turning to see who it was Parkes saw a smiling Henri LeMond.

"She said to go ahead and order."

"I think that I'll have the buffet." replied Parkes.

"Yes, me too." said LeMond as he headed to join the anxious crewmen who had already gotten in line.

Scrambled eggs with sausage and bowls of fresh fruit were brought back to the table.

Most were half way through their first plate of food when Liz entered the room.

"Good morning, Miss Mandel" said one of the crewmen.

"Yes, good morning." added Griffin.

"Hello, everyone." she replied.

The waiter approached and asked if she wanted to order from the menu or if she would prefer the buffet.

"Just coffee for right now" she said with a smile as she took a seat at the end of the table.

"Sorry I am late." she announced "But my Uncle Harry just called to let me know that he is on his way to meet us here in Cairo."

The waiter returned with a silver pot of coffee and poured her a cup.

"Henri, you should know that we won't be leaving for Paris any time soon."

"Should Brandon and I wait for you, or would it be better to just book a commercial flight?"

Liz took a sip of coffee before she answered.

"If you really need to go then you might want to catch a plane later today as I may be here another day or two."

"Actually, I do have a meeting late this afternoon, so I will see if we can book a flight out."

Parkes thought to himself for a minute. "You go ahead, Henri. I have nothing better to do and might as well stay here. Besides, a last minute ticket will cost a small fortune."

"I think I can afford it, assuming the team sends me my championship bonus." said LeMond as he looked over at Liz and gave her a wink.

"I'll make sure that it is sent out by Fed Ex before the end of business today." she told him.

"Henri, speaking of airplane trips, do you remember the flight you took from New York to Indy just before we met? Parkes asked.

He sat back in his seat and pondered the question. "Um, no I don't."

"Well, I never mentioned it, but I was on that same flight and sat right across from you."

"I am sorry Brandon, but I don't remember a flight from New York at that time, nor do I remember ever seeing you before we were introduced at the Indianapolis shop."

"Wow, I was certain it was you. But then again, maybe it was Jean Reno. You two look so much alike."

LeMond laughed at the suggestion that he looked like the famous French actor.

"Who knows, maybe it really was Reno sitting by you?"

Surprised at Henri's answer, Parkes decided to just let it go and change the subject.

"Anyway, Henri, I just want to say thanks for being such a good friend and team mate."

LeMond cleared his throat after he finished the last of his glass of orange juice.

"Well thank you, Brandon. You are very kind."

He stood up from the table, wiped his mouth with his napkin and held out his hand to Parkes. "You too have been a good friend and I thought that you did a fantastic job this year."

The Frenchman then looked to the others at the table.

"I must go now and attempt to get back to Paris. Thank you for your efforts to win this championship. Bon chance to you all"

He then took time to shake everyone's hand before leaving. Liz was the last he bid goodbye. He told her not to worry about her father, and that he was sure it would all turn out fine.

As LeMond walked away and left the room it made Parkes slightly sad. He had hoped that the team would remain intact for the next season and knew that things just wouldn't be the same without the amiable man there on the driving strength.

"I guess that all good things must come to an end." he mumbled to himself.

Liz heard his comment and replied. "Yes, and thankfully the same applies to bad things as well."

He knew that she was referring to her dad's situation and that she'd already begun focusing again on getting Dan Mandel home, safe and sound.

"Sorry, here I am thinking about what will happen to the race team without Henri when you have a much bigger concern on your mind."

She reached out her hands and gently wrapped them around his own as she leaned over the corner of the table and then looked Parkes in the eye. "One way or another I believe that this nightmare will be over very soon. Harry is bringing Bernstein with him and I don't think they are flying down just to give us their congratulations for winning the title yesterday."

Releasing her grasp, she took another drink of coffee before she continued in a near whisper. "We are sitting just a short distance from where dad is being held. He didn't tell me this, but I have to assume that they are stopping here before they head to Damascus."

As she spoke, Parkes found himself wondering if Mr. Mandel was even still alive, but just as quickly put the thought out of his mind.

"I am happy that I am staying behind with you, Liz."

"Thanks, I am too."

After taking a deep breath she took a final drink of coffee and then looked at her watch. It was obvious that the stress and anticipation was beginning to wear on her.

"My uncle should be here in about two hours or so."

At the other end of the table some of the crew had just returned from a second trip to the breakfast buffet.

When Griffin sat back down he looked up to see her smiling at him and he smiled back like a kid caught with his hand in the candy jar.

Parkes thought that Liz seemed pleased that her team manager and the "lads", as the team manager often called them, were enjoying their meal. He thought it a pleasant diversion that took her mind off her father's situation, at least for a moment or two.

"Since the crew guys are having a bit more to eat, would you stay behind and sign for breakfast?" she asked him.

"Sure, but where are you going off to?"

"I would like to go back upstairs until Harry arrives.'

Rising from her chair she picked up her purse and waved to Griffin and the crewmen. "I'll call you later on." she said.

Before he could respond she was already headed to her room.

Although he was feeling a little bothered that she would just get up and leave, he didn't have long to think about it as Scott Battle entered the dining room just after Liz had departed.

He rose from his seat to say hello to him. "Good Morning, Scott."

Battle extended his hand and greeted his old friend. "Hello and congratulations on your winning the championship, BP."

"Glad to see that you don't appear to be too upset. Will you join us?" asked Parkes as he gestured towards the table that he and the crew occupied.

"Actually, Michele is supposed to be meeting me, but I guess I could sit with you until she shows up from her morning shopping excursion."

As Battle took the seat that Liz had just occupied the waiter came over to clear the used cups, plates and glasses. "Can I bring you anything, sir?" he asked Battle.

"Yes, some hot tea would be great."

"Very well sir".

When the waiter walked away; Battle began to speak excitedly. "So, let me tell you what's been going on. I think it may explain why I wasn't that disappointed yesterday."

Just as his friend began tell him his news, Parkes noticed that Griffin and the remaining crewmen got up and started to leave the table.

"We have to get the transporter on the road, Brandon. Tell Miss Mandel thanks for breakfast."

"I will, Griffin. Take care of yourself."

Ashmore nodded and then led the three younger men out with him.

When they were out of earshot; Battle began to speak again.

"Anyhow, what I am about to say to you isn't official yet, but…. Well, I am going to be back in Formula One again next year!" he exclaimed.

The waiter brought a pot of hot water, tea bags and a fresh cup and saucer.

"So when did you find this out?"

"About two weeks ago. I signed a letter of intent with the Jamison team just before coming here."

Sitting back in his chair, Parkes reflected on what he had just heard his friend tell him.

"Jamison? How on earth did you ever make that happen?"

Taking a sip of his tea Battle then set the cup down and leaned forward and began to speak in a near whisper.

"Arabco will be the new sponsors. In fact, they will be the new owners of the team. The Arabco Jamison F-1 Team has a nice ring to it, don't you think?"

With a broad grin on his face Battle settled back into his chair and took another sip of tea. "Knowing that I will personally get to fire Ian when I return meant that there was no way I was going to be sad when we lost the title yesterday!" added Battle with obvious glee.

"Besides, I am happy that if we couldn't win; it would be you and the Mandel guys."

He just shook his head and smiled. His friend Scott was still truly bigger than life, and he was sure that he would never cease to amaze him.

Even though he might once have had thoughts about how unfair it was that he introduced Scott to the Saudi's, only to be left on the sidelines, he no longer harbored any such feelings. He now reasoned that things had worked out as they should have in the end and was proud that he had been able to help his friend.

"So what do you have planned for next year?" asked Battle.

"I guess that I'd have to say that my future is a little cloudy at the moment, but I think it will probably become much clearer very soon. I am hoping to continue in the expanded ISC with Team Mandel, but I am also trying to put together a deal to contest the Daytona 500 as well as the NASCAR road course races.

"With guys like Juan Pablo Montoya racing in NASCAR I had thought about putting out some feelers to see if there might be an opportunity there for me. The fact is that Formula One is where I want to be. Besides, I think I'm giving up my US citizenship and becoming a Saudi.

"Why would you do that?" asked Parkes in an incredulous tone.

"Taxes. Of course I will still have to settle things with the IRS if I want to race in a US Grand Prix or visit my family in Atlanta; but at least they can't touch my future income.

I mean, if have to pay a ton in tax on my current income, how would I be able to also pay off the back taxes, the penalties and the damned interest on top of it?"

The more his friend talked, the more Parkes saw the logic in what he was doing.

"You are hardly ever back there anyway, so I guess I do understand your thinking."

"Good, I am glad you understand. I'm not Anti-American, but I am very against risking my life to pay confiscatory taxes to a country that I only visit a couple times a year."

Battle took another sip of tea before continuing.

"Michele likes the idea of moving there and the fact that I will be converting to Islam."

"Really? You are really going to become a Muslim?"

"Converting is not that big of deal to me, since I like to think that we all believe in the same God. Besides, it will make the Arabs love me even more."

Then Battle looked down at his watch.

"Anyway, I better go find Michele before she spends my all of my next year's tax savings." Then he stood up and shook Parkes' hand.

"Thank you for everything, Brandon."

He smiled and told him that he was welcome.

As his friend walked away he suddenly realized that Scott had never really thanked him for anything before. It also came to him that but for his help Battle might well have been on the outside looking in rather than about to be driving in Formula One again.

But the more he thought about all that had happened, the more he began to admit to himself that he hadn't really done anything for Battle. Sure, getting him involved with the Arabs had meant much to Scott, but Parkes knew that his original concern had actually been finding a job for himself, not in helping his more famous friend.

A tinge of shame suddenly came over him with the thought that he no more right to expect thanks from Battle than he could take credit for landing with Team Mandel or the miracle that occurred when he won the championship.

When the waiter came and presented him the tab for breakfast he was startled out of his day dream.

After looking at the total he wrote in a tip of about twenty percent. He then signed it, put Liz's room number on it and handed it back to the man.

"Thank you sir, but you needn't have added gratuity. Fifteen percent was already included in the total."

Slightly taken aback by what he was just told Parkes thought about what to do next.

"Well don't thank me" replied Parkes with a smile. That extra tip was obviously meant to happen for you, and it is someone else who should actually get the credit for it" he said pointing up to the sky.

The waiter smiled gratefully while Parkes turned and made his way toward the lobby.

Cairo, Egypt - Monday afternoon

"Is the traffic always like this?" Harry Mandel asked his taxi driver with a frown.

"Yes sir, and some days it is even worse." replied the Arab man behind the wheel.

Mandel turned and asked Bernstein if he would mind if he smoked.

Before the Israeli could answer, Mandel was reaching into his jacket pocket for his fresh pack of Marlboro Lights.

He took a long drag off the just lit cigarette and blew it out the open rear window of the cab.

"Alright, as long as we have some time to kill, tell me your thoughts again about how you see this deal in Damascus going down?"

Bernstein hesitated as he noticed that their driver looked up and checked his rearview mirror when he heard Mandel use the word Damascus.

"I think that you should let me explain the whole thing when we get to the hotel and have every one assembled" replied Bernstein.

Mandel took another long drag off his cigarette and proceeded to toss it out the window and onto the street.

As he exhaled the smoke he responded "Sure, I guess if you think that would make more sense."

"Thank you, Harry. It will save my voice to not have to say the same things twice. Besides, I can see now that the hotel is only two or three blocks up the street."

Sitting back in his seat, Bernstein was feeling relieved that he didn't have to placate Harry by going over the plan he had devised for Dan Mandel's rescue. They had already discussed everything prior to their departure from Paris and he didn't feel that he needed to go over it again here in the cab, especially with their Arab Muslim driver listening intently to their conversation.

The afternoon heat, lack of sleep and an overabundance of stress was clearly affecting Harry. He soon became agitated with plodding along in traffic and told the driver to pull over and let them out of the cab, despite the fact that they were just a block or so from their destination.

"I guess that we'll be walking the rest of the way" explained Bernstein as he paid the driver.

With no luggage to carry the two men arrived at the front door of the hotel in a matter of minutes and were soon inside the air conditioned lobby.

Bernstein found a spot for Harry to sit down and wait while he simultaneously scanned the area for a house phone that he could use to contact the room of Agent Roth as well as that of Harry's niece.

"You just have a seat and cool down. I'll go and let Liz know that we are here."

Mandel nodded, quickly removed his sport jacket and settled himself into a large comfortable looking chair.

Once he had gotten Harry planted in a place where he could keep an eye on him, Bernstein walked toward the telephone at the end of the hotel front desk and sighed a very deep sigh. A feeling of relief came over him at the mere thought of getting a hold of Liz and no longer having to baby-sit her uncle all by himself.

There was no answer when he called Liz's suite, but Agent Roth answered his phone after the first ring.

"Hello, Ephraim. We're here and waiting in the lobby. Do you know where Liz Mandel might be right now?"

Roth hesitated for a second before answering in a somewhat defensive tone.

"Yes, of course I do. She is in her room which is just across the hall from mine."

"OK, I guess she must have been resting when I phoned her."

"Don't worry Agent Bernstein, I will locate her as well as our other agents and let them know that you and Mr. Mandel have arrived."

"Good." Bernstein glanced at his watch. "Have them meet us here in the lobby in an hour."

As she stepped out of her bathroom and began to towel dry her hair, Liz noticed the blinking message light on her room telephone.

The phone began to ring before she even had a chance to find out who had called earlier while she had been in the shower.

"Miss Mandel, this is Ephraim Roth and I am calling to let you know that Mr. Bernstein and your uncle are here and would like to meet in the lobby in about an hour from now."

"I see. Listen, that sounds fine, except let's meet here in my suite instead. I'll call room service and have them bring up some refreshments if you will let the others know that I think it better to meet here in the privacy of my room.."

"Fine. I will tell them to be at your room in one hour" replied Roth.

"Thanks see you then" she replied before she hung up the phone.

After checking her messages to find out that it had been Bernstein calling she quickly erased the message and dialed the number for room service. As she waited for someone to answer, she thought about her near fatal experience with room service in Belgium and it made her decide to have the coffee, Cokes and sandwiches delivered well after the time that the others were scheduled to arrive.

Just as she was finishing dressing there was a loud knock at the door. She picked up her watch and saw that it was still nearly twenty minutes until anyone should have arrived for the meeting.

Liz walked out of her bedroom and decided to stop at the spot where her purse was sitting. She quickly grabbed the can of mace that Roth had provided her before she moved any closer to the door.

"Who's there?"

"It is me, Brandon." said the now familiar voice on the other side of the door.

Relieved, she let him in.

"Is that for me?" he asked her pointing at the small cylinder he saw in her right hand.

Blushing with a little embarrassment she placed the mace back in her purse. "No, I guess that I wasn't expecting company quite so soon and wanted to be safe instead of sorry."

"I really do apologize for not calling up here first, but you haven't been answering either your cell or room phone; so I began to wonder if everything was alright."

"Yes, everything is fine. I took a nap and then I took a long shower. I was just finishing getting ready to see my uncle and have a talk with the men from the Mossad."

"Well, I was going to ask you to join me for dinner, but don't let me keep you from your plans. I'll be in my room down the hall if you should need me. " said Parkes as he moved toward the door.

"This is important, but I'll call you later, OK?"

"Sure Liz, I really do understand."

Before he reached for the doorknob there was a knock.

She looked at the watch that she had just placed on her wrist.

"It is probably my uncle. Go ahead and open the door."

Seeing that it was indeed Harry at the door Parkes greeted him and the other four men that followed him into the room.

"Gentlemen, I was just leaving. Enjoy your evening" he said with a nod.

Harry spun around and looked Parkes right in the eye with a stern look on his face.

"You do still work for us, don't you?"

"Yes sir, my contract with you is through the end of this year. Why do you ask, Mr. Mandel?"

"Well, you should know that we are headed down to Damascus tonight to get my brother back and we sure could use your help."

Without waiting for him to respond, Harry told him to find a seat and listen to what Bernstein and the other men have to say.

Looking over at Liz for a sign of her approval, Parkes was glad when she smiled back at him. He knew that he should stay for the meeting and find out what he could do to aid in the rescue.

"I'm willing to do anything I can to help, sir."

"Thank you, Parkes."

Mandel then turned his attention to Bernstein and asked him to start his briefing.

Once everyone was seated Bernstein stood up and began to speak.

As the plan was revealed to the group Parkes tried to follow along and understand what was being said. It wasn't that Bernstein didn't speak clearly, but instead it was a case that the terms being used were all so unfamiliar to him.

Despite this, he attempted to grasp the crux of what was supposed to happen later that night.

Bernstein explained to Harry that he would approach the building that Dan Mandel was being held in via a Land Rover.

"Parkes will be your driver and will wait outside for you while you go into the building to make the exchange of the bearer bonds for your brother."

Harry shot a look over at Parkes. "So, are you OK with that idea?"

Though he wondered what he was getting himself into he felt at this point felt that he had no real choice in the matter. He had committed to doing this and there was no turning back.

"I have no problem with that if you don't, Mr. Mandel."

"Your skill behind the wheel is exactly the reason that I asked you to come along."

Mandel looked back at Bernstein and gestured for him to continue with his talk.

As the briefing went into the second hour the younger Mossad operatives, introduced as Goldman and Rosen, began to ask questions and offer suggestions as to how the mission should be carried out.

Saul Goldman had been a Captain in the Israeli Defense Force; while Joel Rosen, an American from Pittsburgh, was a former US Army Ranger. Both men had athletic builds and a confident air that suggested that if called upon, they could most likely get the job done.

"Why can't Goldman or I go into the building to make the exchange?" asked Rosen. "Why put a civilian at risk when we could handle it?"

Bernstein paused for a second as he thought about the question.

Before he could respond, Harry began speak.

"They won't trust anyone else. Besides, I want to do it and furthermore, I've told them that if I was to give them any more of our family's money that they would need to hand over my brother to me at the same time. My feeling is that this is the only way we will be able to get in and out without any loss of life. Anyway, I just don't see how at this point we can change what I have already agreed to. "

Goldman began shaking his head and leaned forward to set the cup and saucer that he was holding back on the coffee table in front of him.

"With all due respect, I'm not so sure about that, Mr. Mandel. I mean, what's to keep them from killing you, your brother and maybe even your driver?"

"Nothing, I guess. Harry replied. "But won't you Mossad guys be covering our back side should things get ugly?"

Both Harry and Brandon looked at one another and then searched the faces of the Mossad agents looking for a response, but none came until several seconds had gone past.

"Well, all of us of course will be there, out of sight, but in close proximity to you." said Bernstein."

"You will both be wired for sound and will be wearing Kevlar flak jackets as well." added Goldman.

The last comment did little to make Parkes feel at ease about what he was about to embark on in a few hours. In fact, the need for bullet proof vests was a reminder that he and Harry were not just taking a run up to the corner store to pick up a loaf of bread, but driving right into the hideout of known killers.

As Bernstein brought the meeting to a close Parkes began to wonder what this night time excursion to Syria would be like.

Oddly, the idea of doing what he was about to do for the Mandel family was actually a little less nerve racking to him than sitting in a race car and waiting for a race that was about to start. At least that's how he felt right now. After all, he couldn't really see any way he could possibly screw this up. As he thought more about it, the only thing he had to worry about was that if instead of the Mandel brothers walking out to climb in the Land Rover, there might be some bad guys speaking Arabic would come out to meet him instead.

Just as he had finished thinking out what he committed himself to, Liz approached him and asked if she could get him something to eat or to drink.

"A couple of those tuna salad sandwiches that I saw over there would be nice."

"Would you like a Coke or a cup of coffee to drink?" she asked.

"Both, I think. This is clearly going to be a very long night."

Chapter Twelve

Levi Bernstein walked from the cockpit of the Gulfstream jet and sat down in the seat adjacent to the one Liz Mandel occupied. She had been looking out the window at the darkness below them and was surprised when she turned to see him suddenly sitting next her and buckling the safety belt.

"You need to know that I wasn't exactly thrilled when you insisted on coming with us."

"I am already aware of that, but you should know that I am not suggesting that I need to come along when you make the drive out to where my dad is. My plan all along was to stay with the airplane and wait for all of you to return."

"Fine, Liz. But I still think it would have been better for you to travel back to Paris and wait for us there, especially if this operation doesn't have the hoped for conclusion. "

The idea that things could go wrong hadn't even entered Liz's mind. The fact that Bernstein would talk in anything but a positive manner bothered her.

"Don't worry about me." she replied sternly. "I'm a big girl and I promise not to go to pieces should there be any sort of problem. Just try to remember that this is supposed to be an exchange of the ransom for my father, not some cowboy commando raid to bring these Arab guys down."

Bernstein sighed.

"Yes, in theory it should be a simple swap. We give them the ransom and we get Mr. Mandel. But let's not forget that we have already given them one black bag with ten million in bearer bonds and yet this evening we find ourselves flying to Damascus to do it once again. Anything could happen tonight, but I can assure you that we will do all that we can to make sure your father comes back to you safe and sound."

"I understand." she replied. "And I am sorry if I was rude just now."

"No apology needed. This is pretty stressful situation for all of us."

Bernstein closed his eyes and got settled in for the rest of the flight, while Liz returned to looking out the cabin window. Since she still couldn't see any lights below she turned her gaze upward and found a very bright star located in the south west sky.

It somehow gave her comfort to see this shining light in the night time sky.

"How are you holding up?"

She turned her head to see her uncle standing in the aisle holding what looked to her like a gin and tonic with a wedge of lime in his right hand. He had braced himself for any turbulence with his right hand on Bernstein's seat back.

"I am OK. But maybe you should pass on drinking any more until after we get dad back."

"This is just my first one, dear."

She looked at him with a frown and shook her head "Just be sure that it's the only one, alright?"

"Don't worry, I'll just have one to take the edge off, that's all I'll need."

Harry then made his way back to his seat at the front of the plane. Liz noticed how careful he was to make sure that he didn't spill his drink. The sight of him would have made her laugh if it hadn't already made her feel so sad.

Bernstein opened his eyes and turned his head toward her.

"You don't know this, but I saw your uncle down at least two drinks in the bar before we left the hotel."

"If the drink in his hand is only his third he should still be fine. It probably does help to calm his nerves. Liz sighed deeply. "Listen; let's just make sure he doesn't have any more to drink before we land."

"I'll make sure of it." replied the Israeli. He then unbuckled his seat belt and made his way forward to the seat across the aisle from Harry's.

Not long after Bernstein had moved to sit by her uncle, Brandon came back from the front of the aircraft and took the seat across from Liz.

"The pilots say that we should be on the ground in about half an hour or so." he informed her.

"Well, I guess this is it, Brandon. So, I doubt that when you signed on to drive with us that you ever thought you would wind up the season with a driving job like this."

A big smile came across Parkes face. "No, but I'd guess that this has to be the most important drive that I've ever landed."

She smiled back and looked into his eyes.

"Thanks for doing this for us. Knowing that you will be there with my uncle makes me feel much better. Please though, no heroics. Just give the kidnappers the money, put my dad into the Land Rover and get the hell out of there, OK?"

"That's the idea, Liz. Just pray that the kidnappers are willing to take the money and let us go on our way. If all goes to plan we should be back to the plane with your dad in no time at all. "

"Let's hope so." she said with a brave smile.

Near Damascus, Syria

The ants that he had watched crawling up the wall of his dusty room that morning had been the only visitors that Dan Mandel had seen in over two days. Although his captors had left him a clay pitcher of nasty tasting water to drink, he had not had anything to eat since they had brought him three small pieces of bread two days earlier.

Now as he lay on his dirty cot in the darkness of night he thought about the friend he had been to high school with who had been held in a Vietnamese prison for nearly four years.

What he had been through in the past few weeks was almost nothing compared to what his friend had endured, yet he was already close to giving up hope. The sense of being invincible that he had for so long was fading rapidly and he was finding out that in reality he wasn't anything close to invincible. Mandel felt tired, weak and he just wanted to go home. If he wasn't going to be released he wished that these damned animals would just shoot him dead and put him out of his misery.

The temperature was so low this night that he wrapped himself in a thin blanket and pulled it over his head like a mummy. The fact that it smelled like a wet dog didn't matter to him anymore. He was far too cold to worry about that.

Finally able to fall asleep, Mandel began to dream about his comfortable home in suburban Chicago. He imagined that he was back there and sitting in his Jacuzzi relaxing .While enjoying the warm water as it circulated around him, his masked captors suddenly burst in to his house and took him naked and blind folded back to their dingy hideout to hold him once again for a large ransom.

He would get released and then the kidnappers would once again find out where he was and they would kidnap him again. This nightmare happened over and over until Mandel finally awoke.

The vulnerable feeling he now had was something that he had never experienced before.

Wealth had always represented security and happiness in Dan Mandel's mind. His father had taught him that the more money you had the better off you and your loved ones would be.

Now he realized that it was the very financial success that he had striven for all these years that had made him a target for kidnapping and that no one was totally secure or completely in control of their lives.

It also occurred to him that the happiness that was supposed to come with great wealth had pretty much eluded him as well. While his life style was beyond comfortable and he still found enjoyment in achieving his goals; the facts were that he was separated from his wife of almost thirty five years, didn't get along with his brother and had never been able to connect with his son.

As he sat imprisoned in his room he had begun to think that the things that he always thought were important had been the very reason his life was as it was now.

While he had already started to be less of a task master and to find simple joy from the knowledge that he was providing jobs for thousands of people, he still had this insatiable need for excitement in his life.

The racing team and the on track competition had filled that need, but he knew that it shouldn't have replaced his family as his focus the way it had these last few years.

His daughter was the one bright spot in his life. But for his relationship with Liz he knew that he wouldn't have anyone that he could say he was close to. She was quite a bit like him, but she seemed to have managed to find more balance in her life and was a much happier person as a result.

Feeling convicted as he thought about how he had lived his life, Mandel made a pledge to himself that he would make more time for his family if he ever managed to get out of this horrid place alive.

Pulling the blanket back up over his head he tried to get some more rest. Just as he began to fall asleep the door to the room where he was being held opened wide and the light streaming from the other room made it hard for him to see.

"Get up Jew" yelled Jughead. "Your time here with us is almost at an end."

Damascus, Syria - 9:25 PM

The road that the rescue party was traveling on to their destination was dark, dusty and not very wide. Driving the lead Land Rover was

Ephraim Roth, with Brandon Parkes at the wheel of the second Land Rover which was following close behind.

Harry Mandel sat in the front passenger seat of the vehicle that Parkes was piloting and had chained smoked several Marlboro Lights since leaving the airport in Damascus.

When he wasn't busy lighting another cigarette Mandel was talking nonstop. Rambling from one topic to another, Parkes figured that he could forgive him for his behavior given the fact that Harry was the one who would be walking into the kidnapper's hideout and delivering the briefcase containing the ten million dollar ransom.

Sitting in the back seat was Levi Bernstein who had just put his window down half way in a vain attempt to dissipate the smoke that was filling the Land Rover's passenger compartment.

After taking one last drag off his most recent Marlboro Light, Harry opened his own window and threw the remainder of the cigarette out, even though he had only smoked it to about half way. It appeared to Parkes that Harry might be finished with smoking for tonight after having lit up so many in such a brief period of time. "Are you doing alright, Mr. Mandel?" he asked.

"Yeah, I'm getting a little tired right now, but I'll be fine."

Suddenly Bernstein began speaking into the miniature microphone headset that he was now wearing. "Alright Ephraim, I'll let him know.

"Brandon, Roth just called me and says that we will be stopping about a half a mile up the road to get you guys into your Kevlar vests and set you up so that you can communicate with us."

"OK, but how much further until we get to the target, or whatever you are calling it?" he asked.

"The GPS says that you won't have far to go after we make our stop. It will probably be less than another half mile further to the location where the exchange is supposed to take place. But since we don't have the exact address of the house, that estimate may be off by a few hundred yards."

As they got closer to their target Parkes started to tense up and feel uneasy about the plan they were attempting to carry out this night.

"So Bernstein, you do plan on giving Mr. Mandel and yours truly some weapons, right?"

Since there was no response from the backseat of the Land Rover, Parkes adjusted the rear view mirror so that he could see Bernstein's face.

What he saw was Bernstein pointing a finger toward the windshield and the glowing brake lights in front of them.

Taking his cue from what Roth was doing in front of him, Parkes steered the Land Rover off the road and came to a stop.

After getting out of the vehicle Bernstein walked over and told him in a whisper that he had just placed a loaded Beretta pistol under the driver's seat, but that he didn't want Harry to know because then he too would insist on being armed.

"Thanks, but since Harry is the one going in to make the exchange shouldn't he be able to defend himself as well?"

"No; I fear that he might start something that he couldn't finish, so it's better that he go in without a gun."

"Well, I guess that does make more sense, but it makes me feel better to know that I have a weapon, just in case I need it."

"Good, now let's get you and Harry wired up and outfitted with your vests."

Roth and Rosen were standing behind the tan Land Rover with the tailgate open removing all the needed equipment.

The Kevlar vests were a dark gray in color. Everyone gathered would be wearing one tonight. Bernstein instructed that only Harry would need to put his underneath his shirt. The Mossad agents and Parkes could wear theirs on the outside of their clothes.

Bernstein handed Harry the vest that he was to use.

"We don't want these guys to think you are there to make trouble for them Harry. Seeing a bullet proof vest might not give the right impression."

He gave no response. Instead Mandel removed the sport jacket he was wearing and took off his white, short sleeved, Polo sport shirt. After Rosen attached the microphone to his chest, he helped him put on the Kevlar vest. It just barely fit his ample body.

Somewhat embarrassed at having all these younger and much fitter men see him with his shirt off he quickly got dressed.

"I suppose that I probably need to start a diet and exercise program as soon as I get back home." Then he patted his stomach. "This is too many rich French meals; I always seem gain a ton of weight whenever I go there." he said nervously.

The vest under his shirt and sport coat made Harry look even more overweight than he was. Feeling badly for him Parkes decided to change the subject.

"So, can I see those Secret Service communicator things now?" he asked.

Rosen held a box containing the devices under his arm like a football. "Sure" he said handing one to Parkes. He went on to explain how it worked and then helped Parkes put it on. "We didn't want Mr. Mandel to have one as it might be noticed by the kidnappers and tip them off to the fact that he was not alone. But the wire that I just put on him will still allow us to hear what is happening inside the house, even if he can't hear anything that we are saying."

Suddenly Bernstein's demeanor became very serious. "All right, now that we have you two ready, let's go over the plan once more."

"First, Mr. Mandel and Mr. Parkes will depart in about twenty minutes." He checked his illuminated watch to confirm that he was right about the time before he continued.

"Now, when they arrive at the house the kidnappers have instructed them to park on the south side of the building and honk the horn three times."

"OK, and where will you be once we have arrived at the house" asked Parkes with a look of consternation.

Roth, who had been standing behind him, placed his right hand on Parkes' shoulder.

"Don't worry; the four of us will be in position to be of assistance." His tone was completely professional as he spoke.

"Besides, you should know that Rosen here will have a sniper rifle with a night scope."

Then Roth patted the back of the American born Mossad with his left hand. "He is as good a shot as anyone I've known."

"OK, if you say so, Mr. Roth; but what is supposed to happen once we get there?"

Race to Damascus

"Harry will get out of the SUV with the brief case containing the ransom and is to wait outside the front door of the house. One of the kidnappers will escort him in and he will hand over the bonds and walk out with his brother. We will then all meet back here at the rally point and make our way to the airport for the flight to Paris."

Bernstein paused and then added, "Remember if at any time either of you think that something feels wrong, say the word "X ray" twice and we will know to take action to help you. Also, Harry Mandel will have the radio designation of M1 and Dan Mandel is M2. Mr. Parkes will simply be called Driver."

Goldman, who was now carrying an Uzi machine gun, walked up and joined the group to inform them that he had completed installing a GPS tracking device in the Land Rover that Parkes would be driving to the ransom drop.

"We did that just in case they decide to kidnap you and take your vehicle we will be able to follow them", explained Goldman.

"Well, just knowing that makes me feel so much better." replied Parkes sarcastically.

Bernstein didn't respond to the remark. Instead he looked at his watch again before addressing the group for a final time.

"Gentlemen, if there are no questions, let's go get Dan Mandel and bring him back to freedom."

After climbing behind the wheel of the white Land Rover, Parkes sat and thought for a moment about the contrasts of motor sports and military or police operations. Both were dangerous activities, but the way that those in racing overcame fear was to laugh at the situation with a bit of gallows' humor.

These Mossad agents were so serious about every little detail. Perhaps the difference was because in racing it was normally just the driver who was at risk. With a situation like this, everyone involved here tonight could end up becoming a casualty even if they did everything one hundred percent right. Add to that the thought that Israel could be at war and wiped off the map should things go wrong and it soon became clear to Parkes why the Mossad took everything so seriously.

Soon Mandel got in and buckled his seat belt for the short trip to the house that held his younger brother. He then moved the bag with the ransom from his lap to the floor of the vehicle and leaned it against the transmission tunnel.

Rosen was doing a check of the communicators. Once everyone had responded that theirs was working Bernstein came on and gave the order to commence the operation.

"This is it. Are you ready?"

"Yes, I believe that I am, Parkes."

The Land Rover's engine came to life with a turn of the key and the two men were soon back on the narrow road and on their way to where Dan Mandel had been kept for all these many weeks.

Harry reached in his coat pocket and brought out a silver flask and opened it.

"Would you like a shot of gin?

He shook his head and watched as Harry took a long drink.

Mandel had already started to take another pull from the flask. "I think that is enough for tonight, sir."

"Yeah, I guess you're right." replied Mandel who put the top back on the silver container before he proceeded to toss it into the back seat.

Slowing down when they entered the small village Parkes looked on both sides of the road for their destination.

Then he found it. "The house is just ahead on the left side of the road; there is a small station wagon parked on the north side of the building, just like you said, Agent Bernstein."

"The kidnappers said that a dark blue Renault wagon would be parked outside. Make sure that it is a Renault and then park the Land Rover on the other side."

"Yes, this definitely is the place." said Parkes with quite a bit more excitement in his voice that he would have liked.

"Good. We are now in position, Driver."

After rolling a few more feet, Parkes brought the SUV to a halt and turned off the engine.

Before turning the headlights off, he hit the bright switch twice while tapping the brakes so that the Mossad men would be sure locate them in the dark.

"This is Rosen. We see you and have you in our sights, Driver. You are go for insertion of M1"

"OK, here we go then."

He took a deep breath and proceeded to honk his horn three times as he had been instructed.

Stepping out of the vehicle without a word, Harry headed for the front door of the building.

As he looked out the back window of the Land Rover and saw him turn the corner, Parkes noticed the silver flask in the back seat and retrieved it. He shook it and realized that Mandel had managed to drink up all the contents.

He didn't have much time to ponder what effects the alcohol might have on Mandel as the sound of someone speaking filled his earphone. "This is Rosen; M1 is now in the building." Harry was inside and Rosen's words had just confirmed it.

The sickening smell of death, sweat and filth overwhelmed Harry Mandel as he entered the main room of the kidnapper's house. Immediately he had the barrel of an AK 47 aimed at him by a short man who was wearing a mask and shouting at him excitedly in Arabic.

Suddenly one of the doors which went to the two side rooms to his left opened and a much larger man emerged. He wasn't wearing a mask and he smiled broadly when he saw Harry standing in front of him.

"Good to see you, Harry." said the man as he closed the door behind him. "I assume that you came alone, as instructed?"

The elder Mandel winced at the greeting, knowing that Bernstein was monitoring the conversation. He didn't need to come under the suspicion of the Mossad because of this man talking like they were old friends.

"Yes and I have the additional ten million here in this bag. Now bring out my brother."

"Be patient, Mr. Mandel. First I would like to see the money and count it."

Harry stepped forward and handed the black bag to the man. "It's all there, twenty bearer bonds, just like the first time. Go ahead and see for yourself."

Setting the bag on the large wooden table the kidnapper opened it and checked its contents. Satisfied that the bonds were both real and all there, he turned to the shorter man and said something to him in Arabic.

The man then looked at Harry and said "Now you will get to see your brother."

A moment later an emaciated Dan Mandel stepped out of the side room that he had been kept in and walked the short distance to where Harry was standing and looked into his eyes. His face was unshaven and his clothing was dirty.

"I knew that you'd come." were the only words that came from his parched lips.

So stunned at his brother's condition and appearance, Harry didn't know what to say to him.

Instead he turned to the bigger of the two kidnappers and began to display his anger at how Dan had been treated.

"I was assured that he would be treated humanely, but just look at him. He is unkempt, there are cuts and bruises on his face and he clearly hasn't been fed enough."

"We never promised to put your brother up at the Ritz."

"No, but I didn't expect this." said Harry while pointing his finger towards where Dan was sitting.

"Now tell me this, just how do you explain the murder of the pilots?"

"We had to show that we were serious. Besides, the first man was a risk. We thought he might talk if questioned and decided that we had no interest in paying someone half a million worth of the ransom when we could just as easily eliminate him and be done with it."

Harry shook his head in disbelief. "How about Jack Rhodes; why kill him?"

"He was already dead. I just made sure that he was by putting a few rounds in him and then dumped him in an alley and made it appear that we had executed him so that you had a little more incentive to pay the additional ransom." said the man with a devious looking smile on his face.

"The original demand had been ten million, for the return of all three men." yelled Harry.

"Yes, but the jailed Palestinians were not freed, so we asked you to compensate for that by paying us another ten million. Besides, since we had doubled the ransom we decided to double your take. Didn't our friend in Paris inform you of that?"

Stunned that the man had said this in front of his brother, Harry remembered that the Mossad agents were also listening in. It meant that his dark terrible secret was out and that everyone would soon know of his involvement in the hijacking of the plane, and the kidnapping of his brother and the two pilots.

Still reeling he turned to look at Dan who was lucid and had clearly understood all that had just been said.

"What makes you think that I won't implicate you and give your names to the authorities you stupid son of a camel jockey?" Harry asked in a rage.

He then quickly pulled a small silver pistol from his jacket pocket before the kidnapper could respond to his question.

"I have decided that you are going to give me back all the bonds, after what you just said right in front of my brother."

Looking over to where Dan sat Harry saw that the other kidnapper had the tip of his gun barrel right against the side of his younger brother's head.

"You tell your friend to put his AK down or you will no longer have use for what's in that black bag because I'll have ended your miserable life."

The man that Harry knew as Mohamed spoke to his diminutive accomplice and the rifle was raised away from Dan's head and now pointed to the ceiling.

"Now hand me those bearer bonds and tell me where the rest are hidden." Harry ordered.

"Our associate in Paris still has the first ones you gave us. You will have to ask him where they are."

"I'll do that just as soon as I get back there."

Mohamed walked over to the table, picked up the bag containing the ransom and threw it at Harry's feet.

As he glanced down at the bag before him he felt a painful sensation in his chest. Two more hammer like blows to his torso followed. Falling to his knees he faintly mumbled "X ray" before collapsing unconscious and landing face first on the floor.

"Shots fired, X-ray, X-ray." yelled Parkes as he simultaneously jumped out of the SUV.

"We are on our way. Stay where you are until we get there." responded Bernstein.

After hearing the sound of the other Land Rover as it approached, Parkes looked around the corner of the building. He saw that Goldman and Rosen had already taken positions on each side of the front door.

With his pistol in hand he slipped around the corner to join the two Mossad agents who looked to be making ready for an assault.

"Come in behind us." was all Rosen said as Parkes slid up next to him with his back against the wall.

Roth and Bernstein drove up in their Land Rover with the lights out and stopped near the front of the building. Then they took positions behind the front doors of the vehicle for protection.

No sooner had Bernstein given the order to go, than Rosen had the front door of the dingy house open and his partner was tossing in what looked to Parkes to be a grenade of some kind.

A bright flash of light accompanied by a loud explosion was the signal for Goldman to rush into the building. Rosen was right behind him.

His heart was now beating rapidly and Parkes was more afraid now than he had ever been in an entire career of driving race cars. He took a deep breath and entered the house where the Mossad operatives were already were engaged in a fire fight with the kidnappers.

Goldman was already wounded and lying on the ground as Parkes walked through the doorway while Rosen had his Uzi trained on a kidnapper wearing a balaclava. The man was yelling something in Arabic and pointing his weapon at Dan Mandel who sat bent over in a chair with his hands over the back of his head.

Harry was lying face down, and the second kidnapper, who was also wounded, lay near him on his back and clutching his chest in pain.

"You stay behind me, Parkes. Keep your eye on the guy on the ground and make sure he doesn't get back in the game." commanded Rosen.

"O.K." was all he could say in response. He then aimed his weapon at the wounded kidnapper who he now noticed still held a small caliber pistol in his right hand.

The situation was rapidly becoming a standoff. Harry needed to get medical care, as did Goldman, but the man in the mask wasn't about to give up.

"M1 is down. The remaining kidnapper says he wants the money and a car." Rosen reported over the radio. "What do you want me to do?"

A long silence followed. Finally Bernstein responded.

"Rosen, I now have your rifle and am in position to take out the target. You need to move a bit to your left and then get down when I tell you so that I have a clear shot."

"If Parkes could move back slowly and open the door a bit wider that would help me, too. Then I want him down on the ground when I give the signal."

"I copy" replied Rosen.

"Yeah, I understand. I'll back up a few steps and take care of the door" said Parkes who was starting to feel a bit more confident now that Bernstein was fully engaged in the operation.

As he took his first step back toward the door he told Rosen to "Keep him distracted, keep him talking so he doesn't notice me."

Keeping one hand behind him Parkes slowly stepped back and hoped that his fingers would reach the door and give Bernstein the extra margin he needed for a clear shot at the kidnapper.

"Ok, I am there. I now have two fingers on the door and will start to open it."

"Alright, that's good enough, Parkes. OK, I will count down from three and when you hear one I want you both to be on the floor." Bernstein instructed.

"Roger that" replied Parkes. He felt a little self conscious after using that response, even though he often used the same words while talking to Griffin over the radio in his race car.

Rosen, who was still talking to the kidnapper, responded a few seconds later. "Ready when you are, sir."

Thankful that the man he was aiming at through the scope had stopped acting as animated as he had been just moments ago, Agent Bernstein was ready. "Three, two, one" he called out before holding his breath and squeezing the trigger.

Just as he kneeled down, Parkes saw the front of the kidnapper's head explode. The man's blood and brain matter rained down on the back of a still crouching Dan Mandel as his captor's lifeless body collapsed behind the billionaire like a rag doll.

"Tango two is down" shouted Rosen as he stood up again. He then checked the two side rooms for any other threat. "The building is clear. The building is clear." Rosen took a deep breath. "O.K., now we need to attend to these wounded people and get out of this rat hole."

Rosen set his Uzi down and to began to assess Harry Mandel's wounds. A few seconds later, Roth brought in a large first aid kit and started attending to Goldman.

Bernstein was the last to enter the house and he walked directly to where Dan Mandel was sitting. Parkes was already down on a knee and talking to him.

"These guys are Mossad." Parkes explained.

Mandel gave no response. He was still bent over with his head down so that you couldn't see his face.

Bernstein's furrowed brow and squinting eyes gave him a look of deep concern.

"How is he doing?"

"I'm no Dr., but he seems…."

Before he could finish, Mr. Mandel raised his head answered the question himself.

"I am fine." he responded in an angry tone. "Damn it, don't worry about me. Harry is the one that got shot".

"Yes, and Rosen here has medic training and is looking after him."

Bernstein looked over to see that Harry's head was now being bandaged.

"Shorty shot him in the chest with his AK Then that son of a bitch we called Jughead shot him in the head with Harry's own damned pistol." Mandel screamed in a frightening rage.

"Well, they are dead now and Harry is still alive." said Parkes as he tried to console Mandel and calm him down.

"Actually, this one is still alive." said Roth as he took the pulse of the kidnapper lying closest to where Harry fell.

"Ephraim, do you think he will he make it?" asked Bernstein.

"It's hard to say. He has at least two rounds in his chest"

The man was then checked by Rosen.

"Unless you happen to have a field hospital set up at the airport I doubt that he can be saved, sir."

"How do you think Harry and Goldman are doing?"

Roth, who had seen to Goldman's wounds, responded first. "Goldman took hits in both legs. I managed to stop the bleeding, but he needs to be in a hospital soon".

Taking a deep breath, Rosen gave his assessment of the elder Mandel's condition. "Well, the head wound is the serious thing. It needs immediate attention. It is a small caliper wound, but he obviously should be in the care of a neurosurgeon immediately."

A worried look came over Bernstein's face as he thought about what to do next.

"The good news is that despite three rounds hitting his chest, he has no entrance wounds. Rosen added with a slightly more upbeat tone. "He's just badly bruised there. The Kevlar vest clearly did its job."

"That's good to hear." replied Bernstein. "OK. We are going to go to the contingency escape plan. Once we get back to the airport we won't go to Paris as planned. These men are too wounded, so we will fly directly to Israel instead."

He knew that it would be much closer than flying to Paris, but with tensions along the border of Syria and Israel Parkes wondered if it might also be riskier for all of them.

"I will contact the IDF and let them know of the change in plans so that we don't get taken out by our own anti-aircraft fire." Bernstein told the group.

"That's great" replied Parkes. "Here I was worrying about getting shot down by the Syrians and now you tell me that we could just as likely get it from your Israeli guys."

"We must take that chance, if we are to save Harry and the wounded kidnapper." replied Bernstein.

Suddenly Dan Mandel stood up. "Leave that Jughead son of a bitch to me...I want to see him dead." he said angrily. He walked over and picked up the Uzi that Rosen had left sitting the floor and stood over his wounded captor with the gun pointed at his head.

Everyone in the room was perfectly still as they waited for Mandel to pull the trigger and get his revenge.

Several seconds went by as Mandel contemplated finishing off the man who had caused him so much pain, suffering and humiliation.

"He isn't worth the bullets." said Mandel as turned and handed the weapon to Rosen.

"Leave him here and just let the son of a bitch bleed to death."

Then he stepped away from the dying man and sat back in the chair that he had occupied before and suddenly seemed to regain his normal firm, but measured demeanor.

"Now get my brother and that injured young man over in the corner out of here and let's fly them to Israel."

Although Bernstein had hoped to save the lead kidnapper's life and question him, he said nothing more about it.

As he looked over at the bleeding man that Dan Mandel called Jughead he knew that the odds were long that he would survive, even if they got him to a hospital soon.

Besides, Dan Mandel was once again in charge and Bernstein saw no reason to argue with him.

"Alright, Roth will you help Goldman to the Land Rover? Rosen and I will carry Harry out."

"I'll assist Mr. Mandel. That is if he needs any help." said Parkes.

"No. I can go it alone." he replied. "But wait. You can do me a favor, get my watch off Jughead's wrist and give it back to me. Oh, and don't forget to pick that bag up off the floor while you are at it."

"Yes, sir" he responded.

As he retrieved Mandel's watch from the dying mans wrist and then the bearer bonds he felt relieved and thankful that these many weeks of abuse and trauma had not snuffed out the great man's spirit.

All that had just transpired would have been in vain, otherwise thought Parkes.

He once again got behind the wheel of the Land Rover and it occurred to him that the mission was only partially completed and that it all might still be for naught if they didn't manage to get back home safely and without incident.

The trip back to the airstrip seemed to take forever, but Parkes was relieved when they finally arrived and realized that the plane had not yet been discovered by the Syrian authorities.

The tan vehicle that Roth was in backed up slowly to within just a few yards of the waiting Gulfstream so that the two wounded men he was transporting could more easily be loaded into the aircraft. The co-pilot who was guiding Roth gave him the hand sign for him to halt, and then opened the rear doors of the SUV to find Harry Mandel and Agent Goldman, both with eyes closed quietly laying in the back.

The white Land Rover that Parkes was driving carried Rosen, Bernstein and Dan Mandel. It was now parked nearby with the nose pointed towards a fence. No sooner had the vehicle come to a stop than Liz ran up and opened the right rear door and embraced her father.

Bernstein told Rosen to gather up the equipment and weapons. He then instructed Parkes to move the tan Land Rover and park it next to the white one.

"Just leave the keys in the glove box and lock them up. We'll contact the rental company later and let them know where we left them."

"OK" replied Parkes who then headed over to the other vehicle. As he did so he noticed for the first time that the tail of the plane no longer had the Star of David on it. Remembering that he was in Syria he was glad someone had thought of temporarily removing it.

The pilots had already started the twin jet engines and the identification lights were flashing. Parkes usually treasured the sounds, sights and smells of an aircraft as much as he did those found at the race track, but tonight he felt more than a little fearful about the flight that they were about to embark on.

He told himself to let these thoughts go and look at as this as an adventure. Then he climbed into the tan SUV, moving it to where Bernstein had told him to.

Given the fact that they were rented in his name and with his credit card, it made him a little uncomfortable about leaving a pair of expensive vehicles like this, but just as quickly he realized it was petty of him to mention his concern given the circumstances.

When Rosen had completed checking through both vehicles Parkes placed the keys in the glove box of the tan Land Rover and locked it.

He was about to do the same thing with the white one but Dan Mandel was still sitting in the back seat and continued to hold his daughter who was still leaning in the open rear door.

Parkes walked up and tapped Liz on the shoulder. "Sorry to interrupt, but it's time to go."

She let go of her father and put her arms around Parkes. "Thank you." she said softly.

"Come on, we really need to get on our way. Let's get your dad on board the jet and your uncle to a good Israeli surgeon." he said with a warm smile.

After climbing into the confines of the aircraft and taking their seats, it was only a matter of minutes until the white Gulfstream was climbing into the night sky and winging its way to the safety of Israel.

The plane's cabin was kept dark for those who wanted to try to rest. The only sounds to be heard were the muted voices coming from up front in the cockpit. The door was propped open so that Bernstein could stand in the doorway to listen to the radio communications from the Israeli Defense Force and respond in Hebrew if needed.

Sitting in the first row of seats, Parkes had heard Bernstein say that the IDF wanted them to gradually drop down to the low altitude of only three thousand, five hundred feet. They had also instructed their pilots to fly around the positions where Syrian troops were located, near the Golan Heights and the Israeli border.

While he knew that it would take longer to head over Lebanon, it would probably be safer since they would hopefully avoid the Syrian anti aircraft or SAM missile batteries that they might encounter if they continued on their direct flight path into Israeli airspace.

Unbuckling his seatbelt, Parkes stood up to stretch and look back at the rear of the cabin to see that Roth and Rosen were attending to Harry whose bandaged head was resting on a pillow. While he lay on the floor of the galley, he was covered by a yellow blanket.

Just in front of where Harry was located, a heavily sedated Goldman seemed to be sleeping comfortably in one of the two seats in the back row. He was also under a blanket and had the seat back as far as it would go. Parkes was jealous. Goldman would get to sleep through it all and if a SAM missile did hit them he probably wouldn't even know about it.

Sitting down again he decided to try to let it go from his mind since there was nothing he could do about anything that was happening right now. He reminded himself that the Israelis were tracking them on radar and guiding the pilots in the cockpit on the best way to get safely back on the ground, and to do so in friendly territory.

Liz and her father sat quietly side by side in the rearward facing seats across from his own. It was at that moment that Parkes remembered why he was here.

When she looked over at him he responded with a nod and then gave her a thumbs up.

"I think that we are gonna be O.K." he whispered.

Nodding back at him she smiled, but said nothing.

Adjusting his seat back Parkes closed his eyes. He knew that he couldn't sleep, but hoped that he could at least rid himself of the remaining anxiety that he still felt. Soon he was focusing on all the positive things that had happened to him in the past few months and realized that his worrying had not helped to bring one of them to fruition. He had been worried and upset when he failed to land a drive with Scimitar, but all that consternation was not what had gotten him the seat with Team Mandel. He knew that he had been delivered before and decided that he needed to believe that he would be delivered again.

With his eyes still closed he sensed that the aircraft was banking to the right. Once the plane leveled out he felt the rate of decent increase and opened his eyes to find Bernstein taking the seat next to his and strapping himself in while explaining what was happening.

"Ground radar is picking up two bogeys that are closing in on us rapidly. The IDF told the pilots to head for the deck as they are all but sure that there are Syrian fighters coming after us." the Mossad agent stated calmly.

Bernstein turned around in his seat and looked behind him to find Roth and Rosen still sitting on the floor next to Harry. "Get yourselves and Harry seated and buckled up, there are two Mig fighters following us and it could get rough."

The pilot now had the nose of the plane at a steeper angle of attack and the engines sounded to Parkes like they were at higher RPM's.

"We are trading off altitude for airspeed, but even with the engines at full power we obviously can't out run them. " Bernstein said. "On top of that they have the angle on us because of the turn west that we made to avoid their anti aircraft batteries."

A worried looking Dan Mandel leaned over to put his hand out to his daughter so that he could comfort her. "If Jack Rhodes was flying right now he'd manage to fly us out of this."

She didn't respond to her father's outburst about their late pilot. Her eyes were closed tight and her hands clasped together. Parkes hoped that she was praying and that her faith was overriding any fear that she might have right now.

As the plane continued its dive toward the ground it occurred to him that if the pilots didn't level out soon they wouldn't have to worry about being shot down by the Syrian Migs.

He knew if the Syrians did get close enough to fire on them the impact of an air to air heat seeking missile would at the very least take out one of the Gulfstream's engines and probably knock out the flight controls making the airplane impossible to fly properly. The result would be that they would fall from the sky and die upon impact.

More likely, a secondary explosion would cause the whole aircraft to erupt in a fire ball which would kill them all in a matter of seconds. He just prayed that none of those aboard would survive an explosion and be blown into the cold darkness of space.

Neither scenario gave Parkes hope that his passing would be an easy one. Falling from a great height or burning to death had long been his two greatest fears and now they were both looming in front of him.

Suddenly he thought he sensed that the nose of the airplane was lifting and soon after he heard the sound of the flaps extending as the pilots had finally leveled out.

Looking out the window he was pretty sure that they were at less than thirty five hundred feet. Twelve hundred feet seemed more like it, but it was still dark and with only a few lights on the ground it was difficult to be certain.

Parkes was just happy that they had pulled up at all; but the Syrian Migs were surely still following and he searched the sky out the small right side cabin window in an attempt to see if he could spot them.

The plane began banking to the left and it was then that Parkes caught a glimpse of another airplane.

"Did you see that?" he yelled out.

The pilots had finished their banking maneuver and the plane seemed to have begun gaining altitude. Soon the first officer's voice was being heard over the Gulfstream's PA system.

"We thought you should know that we have just entered Israeli airspace and that the Israeli Air Force sent us a couple of their F-16's to escort us the rest of the way to our destination."

When Bernstein heard that news he told Parkes that it would be only a few more minutes until they would touchdown at the small Jerusalem Airport and that once they were on the ground it would just be a short trip on to Hadassah Hospital.

As he listened, he realized that he could never remember having seen the man really smile, until now.

Chapter Thirteen

Jerusalem, Israel

As he struggled to wake up, Parkes remembered the King David Hotel as the place that his own father and mother had stayed when they vacationed in the Holy Land, some twenty years before. The fact that he was here seemed like a dream to him. He knew that last night really had happened, but it was hard to believe that it was true.

While he had once been bored hearing about his parents' trip and seeing the pictures they had taken, he was glad to have the unexpected chance to be there now. However before he could see the sights he needed to get to the hospital to check on Dan Mandel, and his brother Harry as well as look in on Agent Goldman.

Despite the clock telling him that it was almost noon, he really would have preferred sleeping much longer, but knew that he should get up, take a shower and get on his way to the hospital.

It was when he got out of bed that he remembered that he had no clean clothes, just what he had on the night before. His bag was still on the plane and he had been too tired to go back to the airport for it when he checked in, but now he wished that he had.

He decided to get a shower, put his dirty clothes back on, and then take a cab back to the airport to retrieve his bags.

After turning on the shower he came back out of the bathroom to see if there was any juice to drink in the mini bar when he heard a knock at the door.

Grabbing his pants he quickly put them on and went to open the door. A bellman had brought his luggage. "Miss Mandel asked me to bring these to you." said the young man with a smile.

"Great, just set them over there by the bed." said Parkes as he searched his pockets for some money to give him. "Listen, I'll have to catch you later to give you your tip."

"No problem, sir. My name is David, just like this hotel." he said with a grin. "Please let me know if there is anything else that I can do for you." He closed the door behind him and Parkes picked up his cell phone to call Liz and say thank you for her kindness.

The phone rang three times before she answered.

"Good afternoon, sir. Did you sleep well?"

"I suppose you have been up since eight or nine, right?"

"Actually I got up at seven thirty and was back at the hospital by eight to be there for Uncle Harry. He just got out of surgery."

"How did it go?"

"The procedure went well, but it's too early to know his long term prognosis."

"OK, just know that I am about to get cleaned up and will be there soon.

And thank you for getting my clothes to me."

"Well be sure to thank the pilots, they are the ones who picked them up for you."

"Yeah, well I'll be sure to do that"

"Anyway, speaking of Bernstein, he is coming here to the hospital at about one o'clock or so to give dad a briefing on what he thinks happened and who might be behind his abduction. If you hurry you might be able to come over here with him."

"Alright, I'll hustle up and see you there soon." he replied.

Knowing that he didn't have much time to get ready, if he planned on meeting Bernstein before he left, Parkes showered quickly and was waiting at the front door before his watch said it was ten minutes to one.

When one o'clock rolled around there was still no Bernstein. Parkes was about to hail a cab and head over to the hospital by himself when he felt a tap on his shoulder.

"Good morning, Mr. Parkes." the smiling Mossad operative said as he held out his right hand. "How are you feeling today?" he asked.

"Well, I am a bit tired, but everything considered I'm pretty darn good. I just was about to get a taxi, but if you are still planning on going over to see Mr. Mandel maybe we should ride together?"

"Yes, of course. Besides, we really have no choice. Remember who we are going to visit. As wealthy as he is, he would surely throw a fit if he knew that we took separate cabs when we could have shared one." Bernstein replied with a smile.

The doorman open the rear door of the taxi and Bernstein tipped him for his efforts.

Their driver told them that he knew where the Hadassah Hospital was located and that he could have them there quickly.

"Good, because we don't need you taking us on a tour of the city today." he warned the driver.

Having grown up here, Bernstein was proud of his home town. The family had come here after the Six Day War and despite the difficulties with the Palestinians he felt that Israeli rule of this most holy city was vital to his people. He explained to Parkes that it was rather commercial anymore, but it was still the Holy Land to people of three religious faiths.

As the cab approached the hospital Bernstein explained that this is where they had brought former Prime Minister Sharon and that it was considered one of the best medical facilities in the world.

While he spoke, it was almost as though the Israeli felt that he needed to reassure Parkes that the care that the Mandels were receiving was the best available and as good as anything that could be had in the states.

"Yes, I am familiar with it and I'm sure that it is a very good facility." Parkes said politely. "I just think that we have to stop having meetings like this in hospitals." he added in an attempt to lighten things up.

Taking out his wallet Parkes asked the driver if he could pay the fare in American dollars. As they pulled up to the curb he was told that it was not a problem.

"Don't forget to get the receipt." Bernstein said with a laugh as he left the cab.

"Yes, and I'll be sure to let them know that what I paid covered both of us, Mr. Bernstein." he replied with a smile.

By the time the two men made it to Dan Mandel's hospital room everyone but Ephraim Roth had arrived for the debriefing that Bernstein had scheduled.

Entering the room Parkes saw that Liz was sitting in a chair next to her father's bed. Dan Mandel was sitting up and drinking a can of Coke though a straw.

A female doctor was on the other side of the bed and studying the chart that contained all the information that had been gathered in the battery of tests that had been conducted that morning.

"We are going to leave the IV drip in for the rest of today because you are still in need of re-hydration, Mr. Mandel."

The retail magnate shook his head in agreement. "I understand."

"I'll be back here later this afternoon to see you and check on your progress."

"Thank you, Doctor. I'll see you later then." replied Mandel.

As his doctor left the room, Mr. Mandel welcomed his new visitors and instructed them to find themselves a seat."Let's get this meeting underway, Bernstein." he said in his usual commanding manner.

"We are just waiting for Roth to join us. He had stopped in the Intensive Care Unit to get an update on Harry."

"Fine, we'll wait for him a bit longer then."

He took another drink from his straw and then turned his head towards Parkes.

"My daughter has been telling me some good things about you."

"What has she been saying about me, sir?"

"That while I was gone you, Henri LeMond and the team won the championship."

"Yes sir, we did indeed." he replied humbly.

"Well done. I also have to thank you for coming along to Syria to help get me out of there."

"I didn't do all that much, but I did want to be there and when asked I was only too happy to volunteer. I must admit to you that these Mossad operatives are actually the ones who get credit for getting you out, Mr. Mandel"

As if on cue Agent Roth knocked on the door and came into the room. He had brought Goldman with him in a wheel chair that was being pushed by an attractive, dark haired young nurse.

"What a nice surprise to see you here, Saul" Liz remarked.

As he looked at the nurse Dan Mandel smiled. "I think I can see why he is up already and feeling better."

The nurse, slightly embarrassed, smiled back at him as she walked back out the doorway. She closed the door behind her and just a moment later Bernstein stood up and began to speak.

"Alright; are all here now?"

Reaching into the right side pocket of his sport jacket Bernstein brought out the folded piece of paper that contained his notes for the meeting. After a quick look at the talking points he folded the paper up again and placed it back his pocket.

"We are here to debrief Mr. Mandel as well as inform him of what we know and also what we think we know. Before we get started, Ephraim Roth has been to visit the ICU and spoke to the neurosurgeon caring for Harry Mandel and would like to give us all a report on his condition."

Roth stood up and as usual was taciturn in his delivery.

"I am glad to report that Harry Mandel came through the surgery to remove the bullet lodged in his brain. However, he is in serious, but stable condition at this time and will be kept in an induced coma until the swelling of his brain has subsided. His long term outlook won't be known for at least a week or more from now. For the record, that information came from the head of neurology just a few minutes ago."

"Thank you for that, Ephraim." said Bernstein. He then turned his eyes toward Dan Mandel.

"Please tell us what you remember about the hijacking Mr. Mandel."

After drinking the last of his Coke, the Mandel set the can down on the nightstand next to him and cleared his throat. "All I recall of that day is that Marino drove me to the airport and dropped me off. There was nothing that looked out of the ordinary as I got on the plane. It was right after we took off that a man came out of the back of the cabin. I guess he had been hiding there. He was one of ground crew, or at least he had on blue coveralls. He was armed with a pistol and he held it to my head and began yelling that he wanted to go to Damascus and that I would be dead if we didn't do as told." Mandel paused for a moment then added "That was the guy you say was Mohamed Benbitour. We called him Jughead".

Bernstein took out his notes again and scanned down the page before he asked his next question.

"Did you have any sign at that point that Pete Flynn was a part of the hijacking?"

"No, but I wasn't in the cockpit, I had been bound in my seat with duct tape."

"How about Jack Rhodes, did he say anything about Flynn to you?"

"We were separated at first, but even after we were together he never mentioned that he had been suspicious of Pete being in on the hijacking."

"I see. Well, we now know from the brief conversation that Harry had with Benbitour that Pete Flynn was indeed involved. My guess is that if Jack Rhodes didn't cooperate with him Benbitour knew he would need someone to fly the plane. Would you agree, Mr. Mandel?"

"Yes, I am afraid that you are right, Mr. Bernstein."

Most of what Mandel went on to tell about his experience at the hands of the kidnappers was already known. However, the amount of brutality and neglect wasn't something that those assembled could have imagined.

"We were fed very little and were often hit, usually in the head with the butt of their AK's.

The lack of water was the worst part for me; days would go by before they would give me anything to drink and when they did it was just awful."

Mandel smiled faintly as he remembered the day Rhodes had overpowered their captors.

"Jughead had left the house and with only two of them there Jack and I decided to try to escape. Rhodes killed one of them and we placed the other one in the room we had been kept in. But then he seemed to be having problems breathing. I thought he was just exhausted after having wrestled his guy to the ground, but he told me later that he was afraid that he might have suffered a mild heart attack."

No longer smiling, Mandel seemed to be choking up as he recounted what had occurred. Bernstein asked him if he wanted to take a short break.

"No." he said shaking his head. "What I want to say is that it was because of me and my lack of guts and…. clear thinking… that Jack died."

"No, that's just not true." Liz told him.

"Yes it is, Liz. We had a chance to get away and I know now that if I had just done things differently Jack might well be with us now. Instead, he was shot and killed and I was knocked out and remained a prisoner. I just can't stop thinking about what I should have done that day."

"Mr. Mandel, you need to know that Jack succumbed to the heart attack he had. In fact, the doctor who did the autopsy said that without medical care to remove the blockage he may have actually had a second heart attack and that was what did him in. The bullets were just put into his body for effect. Maybe you could have handled things better, but I don't know with any degree of certainty if that's true. Either way, you need to know that your pilot had already gone to his rest by the time his body was shot at." said Bernstein emphatically.

"Yes, but…. if I had it to do over I would have had the guts to have executed the one we called Shorty, and then we would have just had Jughead to worry about. I could have killed him when he came back, taken his car and gotten Jack to a doctor. Even if I couldn't have saved Jack's life, I could have gotten away myself and Harry wouldn't be in a coma now"

Mandel paused to take a deep breath and to quickly wipe his eyes with a tissue.

"And this young man wouldn't be sitting wounded in a wheelchair, either" he added as he pointed over at Goldman.

"Dad, you have to let it go and quit second guessing yourself. You seemed to have a little survivor's guilt, but I don't want you blame yourself anymore." Liz told him as she patted his hand.

"Thank you for sharing with us what happened to you, Mr. Mandel. I know that it has been somewhat difficult for you to relive it" said Bernstein. "Now allow me take a bit more of your time and let you know you what we have learned so far."

"Some of what I am about to say may be hurtful to you, but it will hopefully allow you to understand what we believe transpired. It seems to have started with Harry going to a casino in Monaco with Silvio Marino. The place is owned by a mob connected man named Andre who was a long time acquaintance of Marino. Your brother lost money there, and then came back again and lost even more. We aren't sure of the exact amount, but can assume that it was seven figures, in U.S. dollars. It seems that the casino had supplied him a line of credit because of who he was, but they weren't aware that he didn't actually have access to that kind of cash. In fact, his bank records tell us that he only had about five thousand in a checking account after his first visit and so he clearly hoped that he could recoup what he'd lost the first time by coming back and playing on credit from the house. "

"So my brother had me kidnapped for a ransom to pay off his gambling debts?"

"Yes, but we now think it was all Marino's idea."

Incredulous at what he was hearing Mandel asked "Why? Why wouldn't Harry just ask me for the money and why would Marino do this to me?"

Bernstein took a deep breath and exhaled very slowly before giving an answer to Mandel's questions.

"My theory is that Harry was afraid to tell you about what he had done. Marino told him that they could get someone to kidnap you for the ten million that your insurance policy would cover and figured that no one would be any wiser, nor would anyone be hurt. But then Marino and his friends got greedy and decided that they wanted more money and they changed the deal."

Raising his hand Parkes asked Bernstein what his theory was on why Liz had been attacked.

Before he could respond Dan Mandel looked at Bernstein and interrupted. "When did this happen?" Then he looked over at his daughter. "How come you didn't tell me about this?"

"Sorry, I thought you knew already." said Parkes sheepishly.

"I'm not mad at you Parkes, but I would like to be let in on the secret."

"I am sorry daddy. I didn't want you to get upset and I was planning to tell you about it later."

"Well I am upset. So tell me what happened?"

Roth spoke up and told Mandel what had occurred and how he had shot and killed the young man who had attacked Liz and Agent Bernstein that day in Belgium.

"The man in question was from Rome, just like Silvio Marino. I think that Marino thought that we were getting a little too close to finding him out and decided to do something about it."

Mandel looked at his daughter. "Have you recovered, sweetheart?

"Yes, I am OK."

He then turned his attention back to Bernstein.

"What about you? How are you fairing?"

" We are both doing fine. In fact that was part of the reason we saw no reason to tell you right away." said Liz.

She looked over at Bernstein hoping to gain his support. "Isn't that right?"

"Yes, we are doing very well, Mr. Mandel. Thankfully there were no permanent injuries for either of us."

"Anyway, "Bernstein paused to take another deep breath and exhaled. "Harry told the kidnappers that he would not drop the second ransom payment off in Paris, as he had done before, but insisted that he be allowed to bring the bearer bonds directly to Damascus so that he could be certain that you would be returned safely."

Bernstein looked around the room at the others assembled before returning his focus to Mr. Mandel.

"The reason we think they let him do it his way was because they figured that he would come alone, since he was in on the plot, and assumed that he just wanted to make sure he got his share since this Andre character had not been paid out of the first ten million as was originally promised.

"I fear that if Harry had trusted them that you would both be dead, as there would have been no reason not to simply kill you and make off with the rest of the ransom." added Roth.

Wagging his index finger in the air like an attorney making his summation, Bernstein was smiling with satisfaction, as he finished his presentation. "What the kidnappers didn't count on, Mr. Mandel was that your brother Harry had decided that it had all gone too far and that he'd brought along a gun, Brandon Parkes as well as the Mossad to help him rescue you."

King David Hotel - 6:45PM

The King David Hotel boasted some of the most comfortable beds available, and if the night before had not convinced him, the catnap Parkes had just taken confirmed it for him.

It was nearing seven PM and he was looking forward to his dinner date with Liz. He realized that it would be the first time they had been out together that she didn't have the weight of her father's abduction hanging over her, or that he wouldn't be pre-occupied with thinking about auto racing.

As he neared the dining room of the King David he looked for her but did not see her.

He smiled at the thought that he had actually arrived first, for a change, and decided that he would get a table instead of standing around waiting for her to appear.

Following the hostess to his seat he saw that Levi Bernstein was dining alone at a table on other side of the room. Parkes waved casually and continued toward his table.

After taking his seat he reminded himself to turn his cell phone on and check for any messages. He had two; one was from his Uncle Ron and the other from Henri.

He figured that it would be a good time to make a call to Branson, Missouri and catch up with his uncle whom he felt guilty about for not calling sooner. In fact he hadn't spoken to him since the night before the race in Cairo and when he reached him the first thing he did was apologize for failing to get in touch with him right after the race. Uncle Ron seemed to understand and quickly forgave him. It was nice to hear both his uncle and aunt say how pleased they were for him, having seen on the internet, that he and Henri had taken the championship. He decided he didn't need to tell them about his excursion to Syria.

"Listen, my date has just arrived, but I promise to call you when I get back to Indy. And thanks again for everything, Uncle Ron. Love you, both. Goodbye."

As he folded his cell phone he rose to greet Liz.

He thought that she had never looked better.

"Good evening, Miss Mandel.

"Hello there, Mr. Parkes" she replied with a demure smile as he helped her to push in her chair.

"You can bring out the champagne when you have a chance." he told the waiter.

"Of course, sir"

As he looked at her across the table he thought how glad he was that he had remembered to have his sport jacket cleaned and pressed this morning. He would have felt even more unworthy than he did now if he had not. She looked that good tonight.

Race to Damascus

Once the bottle of Moet had been opened and both of their glasses filled, Brandon held up his glass for a toast. "To a lovely night together"

She smiled and took a sip. "That tastes wonderful"

"Excuse me, but I thought I should stop by before I turned in."

Parkes turned to find Bernstein standing before them.

"Hello. Would you like to join us for a drink of champagne?"

"I would love to, but I must get up early tomorrow. Besides, I wouldn't want to intrude."

"You aren't intruding." said Liz. "Brandon and I would both enjoy your company."

"No, I just came to say good bye and to let you know that Interpol picked up Silvio and Christine for questioning late this afternoon."

"I still can't believe it. It makes no sense to me that he would do something like this." said Parkes as he shook his head in wonder.

"Well, I know you liked Marino, but they found them in Zurich and I honestly don't think that they were there buying chocolates."

Liz took another taste of her champagne and then looked up at Bernstein. "When you add up all the evidence it looks like they might well behind all this."

"We will hopefully know more soon. Of course we feel our best bet in solving this, is still your Uncle Harry. We may never know the full story until he recovers and comes out of his coma."

When the waiter walked up a few seconds later Bernstein moved away from the table to allow the waiter to serve them. Their server had brought a tray with the shrimp cocktail that Parkes had ordered earlier.

"I won't keep you from your appetizers." He then politely nodded and said "Good bye to you both and do enjoy your evening together."

Reaching over to grasp Bernstein's hand she said "Good night, Levi, and thank you so much for everything you've done for us."

As the Israeli left, Parkes couldn't help but think about how he had once assumed that Liz and Bernstein were romantically involved. While he was glad to find out that they weren't, he was also happy to have gotten a chance to know the man and decided that he really admired and liked him a lot. "I think I'm going to miss having that guy around."

"You may have a chance to see him again, Brandon. No one else knows this, but my dad has asked him to come to work for us as our new Director of Security. I don't have any idea if he will accept the position, but based on his response at the time he seemed to be interested in pursuing it."

"Good for him. He is clearly a good man. But there is still something I don't understand - why did you use the Mossad instead of having US authorities help you?"

She paused for a moment. "Like I told you, it was Harry's idea. He said that he trusted them more as he thought them to be more capable. Knowing what I do now, I think he figured that if his role in all of this was found out that the Israelis wouldn't pursue the matter, unlike the FBI."

Finishing the last of his shrimp, Parkes wiped his mouth and took another swallow of Moet. It was going through his mind that the best way to make sure that the whole episode was forgotten was to give the Mossad operative in charge a job with a nice raise in pay.

"So what does your father think should be done with Harry? I mean, assuming that he recovers."

"With Bernstein's talk that made Harry out to be the hero who led the raid, I think it unlikely that he is unlikely to do anything. In fact, he said that he would rather not have it known that Pete Flynn was involved, either. Of course it might be considered to be insurance fraud to make a claim for the ransom that was paid, or to allow Flynn's wife to make a claim on his life policy. So, we'll have to eat the lost money and pay Flynn's family an amount equal to what the policy was valued at, but that's what dad wants to do."

It was hard for Parkes to get his head around Mr. Mandel's thinking. He wondered how anyone could just forget about something like this. Knowing his reputation as a tough business man made it all the more surprising to him.

"You are probably thinking it's crazy, but I think dad feels guilty about how he's treated my uncle over the years and feels he is making up for it by forgiving him and wanting to forget that it ever happened."

"Maybe, but it would be hard for me to do something like that."

"I believe that my father has just had a small taste of what hell is like and he has been broken of his need of getting revenge because of it."

"Yeah, I guess you may be right. Do you think he'll have the same attitude when it comes to Silvio Marino, assuming that he turns out to be the criminal mastermind that Bernstein thinks he is?"

"I don't really know. It may be one thing for someone to forgive a brother who you feel that you've treated badly, especially given the fact that Harry did do the right thing in the end.

But Marino may be a slightly different story."

"I just can't see how people who were so kind to me could turn out to be the ones who did these things. Kidnapping your father for ransom? OK, maybe, but killing the pilot and taking a contract out on you seems beyond what Silvio Marino or Christine are capable of."

"Well, I am not as taken aback as you are, Brandon. I liked them well enough, but wondered from the beginning if they might be involved. Think about it, it may all be circumstantial evidence, but there are too many things that point to it being them. The fact that they were picked up in Zurich today should tell you that it is likely them, and that they were there to deposit ten million in bearer bonds that they stole from my family."

"No, don't get me wrong." said Parkes shaking his head. "My point was this- how could people who seem to be so decent turn out to be so bad?"

"Those with no moral compass or faith have no one to answer to. They seem to think that they are only bad people if they happen to get caught doing it."

"Yeah, I can buy that being the case. But if it is them, they sure had me fooled."

He took another drink from his champagne glass and then set it down again.

"So tell me this, why didn't the hijackers just sell the multi-million dollar airplane rather than leaving it to be found and returned to you?"

"Too hard to unload, I suppose. It's not like fencing diamonds or some other concealable item. Besides, Uncle Harry probably asked them not to."

He shook his head in the positive.

"Sure, that makes sense... Anyway, let's talk about something else. How about we discuss the idea of Mandel SuperStores entering a car for me in next year's Daytona 500?" Parkes suggested with a smile.

"How about talking about what we are going to order, instead?" Liz said with a grin as she picked up her menu.

"Fine, but before I decide what I am going have I have to ask you something."

"Yes?"

"Are you going to have time to take me on a grand tour of the Holy Land tomorrow?"

She set her menu back on the table and looked Parkes in the eye.

"Is that really what you want to do, or are you just saying that because you think it will please me?"

"No, I would truly love to have you take me to visit the very places that are talked about in the Bible. In fact, it's really weird; I never before had any desire to come here, but the idea of walking where these events actually happened suddenly sounds really exciting to me, especially if I get to see those places with you, Liz."

She smiled at him sweetly.

"You know, it just came to me today; that Saint Paul had his conversion on the road to Damascus. It seems that you clearly did, too."

"Yes, and like Paul, I didn't have any interest in hearing what you or God had to say."

He paused a moment to gather his thoughts; then continued "You know when you first mentioned your mom and brother being missionaries I had images of them welcoming Hugo Chavez to their mission in Mexico. Do you know what I mean? I thought they might be some of those kinds of people that think Jesus must be a socialist."

"Nothing could be further from the truth. They are both part of the Catholic Renewal and more conservative politically than I am.

" Well that's good to hear. But aren't some of those conservative Christians who go to church every week nothing more than self righteous hypocrites?"

"Well, I can assure you that my Mom and brother are the real deal."

"Oh, I am sure that they are." he replied.

"Anyhow, I was really down on God until I met you."

Liz smiled at his comment. "Just know that at one point I was not so interested either. It wasn't until I went to a Billy Graham Crusade my junior year of college that I truly became a Believer."

After taking a swallow of champagne she set down her glass on the table before continuing.

"You say that you were down on God, Brandon, but it seems to me that you were actually down on some of the people who claim to worship the Lord. It seems to me that you were allowing the failings of others to keep you from getting right with God."

He took a deep breath and let it out slowly as he contemplated the words he had just heard; "I guess you're probably right and just know that I am very thankful to have met you and that I can call you my good friend."

Leaning across the table Liz took his face in her hands. "Good friend?"

He blushed and smiled uncomfortably.

"You know what? The fact is that while you have truly become my good friend....

I, well, the fact is that I am truly in love with you, Brandon Parkes."

The kiss that followed was even more incredible than he had ever dreamed it could be. Although he still did not think of himself as her equal, nonetheless, he was thrilled that she felt the same about him as he did about her.

Somewhere in Morocco

The muted sound of the cell phone ringing from inside his brown leather valise brought Henri LeMond out of his focus on the television and off his living room couch. He walked across the living room to answer it, hoping that he didn't wake his mother who was sleeping in a lounge chair in front of the television. The caller ID told him that it was his former team mate.

"Hello!"

"Good evening Henri. I meant to return your call earlier, but I was out to dinner with Liz and the time just got away from us. So anyway, how are you doing my friend?"

"Actually, I am quite good. I was just resting in front of the TV, like any other old retired man would do." replied LeMond with a warm laugh.

"So where are you right now?"

"I am here at my mother's home. She moved here from Paris recently. In fact, you know the time that you said you saw me sitting by you on the airplane? I remember now that I was returning from my trip to help her to pick out a new house here in the town where she grew up. I guess what confused me the other day was the fact that I didn't remember seeing you on the flight, but I do now remember the trip."

"Well, I was pretty sure that it was you that I had seen on the plane. When we met that day at the Mandel's shop I was certain that you sat across the aisle from me just two nights before."

"No, you did not imagine it. I believe that it was me. You know that the mind is the first thing to go." he laughed. "Speaking of the Mandels, how is Dan doing?"

"He seems to be fine." replied Parkes "A little tired and dehydrated, but all in all he's doing well. So did you know that Harry was wounded in the rescue?"

"I heard that while watching CNN. How badly was he hurt?"

"He was shot in the head and is still in a coma. It is still too early to know if he will even survive, or if he does, to what degree he will recover. He just might be in a coma for the rest of his life."

"That's too bad. I didn't know him well, but it is because of his recommendation that I got the ride with the team. To hear this about him is very sad news."

"Yeah, but getting shot is only the half of it. It seems that he was clearly involved in the kidnapping."

"No, Brandon. That sounds totally out of the question to me. How do you know that?"

"One of the kidnappers implicated him during the ransom exchange. They had Harry wearing a wire and Bernstein got it all recorded. It seems that he had run up some fairly hefty debts while gambling in Monaco and decided to cash in on his brothers ransom insurance."

"I see. So, did they get the men who actually carried out the kidnapping?"

"They got 'em alright. Sent those sons of bitches straight to hell." said Parkes.

"Really? Are you sure?"

"Yeah, I went along as Harry's driver. I was right there and saw it all. But what will really blow your away is the fact that Bernstein believes that Silvio Marino was the mastermind behind the kidnapping and has had him picked up by Interpol for questioning"

"Brandon, it is a truly amazing story. It's like something from a novel."

"I know, but Silvio and Christine were found in Zurich, probably depositing the bonds in a Swiss bank, at least that's the story according to Bernstein".

"Well, at least it is all over now. I do thank you for letting me know how things turned out…and please be sure to say hello to Liz and her father and let them know that I have been thinking about them often, OK?"

"Yes, I will do that. You take care of yourself and enjoy your retirement, alright?"

"Don't worry, I will. Good bye, Brandon." he replied with a smile in his voice.

Turning off his phone Henri went to put it back where it belonged. He had been taken aback by what Parkes had just told him and was still marveling at the news.

Opening the valise he noticed the deposit slip from his bank for the two hundred and fifty thousand dollar bonus check that the Mandels had paid him for winning the team championship. It occurred to him that it would be the last payment he would ever receive for driving a race car and that maybe he'd have a copy made and frame it so that he could hang it up on the wall.

After he set the phone back in its inside pocket, he pulled out a large legal sized envelope and opened the flap. He decided that he should count the documents it contained once again, just to make sure they were all still there. As he obsessively counted each piece of paper he thought about what every one of them represented. After he finished counting them and was feeling secure in the knowledge that all twenty documents were there, he closed the flap of the envelope and slid it back into its place.

He shook his head in disbelief as he thought about how things had turned out; Harry was in a coma and all of his Arab cohorts were now dead. That Silvio Marino was currently thought to be the man responsible for the crime was something that he hadn't anticipated.

"I wonder what the odds would have been that I'd end up sitting by a future team mate on a plane flight from New York, at a time when I supposedly should have already been back in Indianapolis?" he asked himself out loud. He felt incredulous that it could have all happened like it did and not cause any difficulty for him in the end.

That he was not a suspect himself was a relief to him, but not at all a surprising. Besides, it didn't really matter what anyone thought. This was Morocco he was living in and he couldn't be extradited.

LeMond sighed deeply and realized that he'd done it. He could finally relax now that he no longer had to risk his life driving racing cars. Ten million dollars in bearer bonds were sitting in his living room and they were all his.

Pleased that his mother was content, now that she was once again, in sunny Morocco, he basked in her approval of his financial coup. The more he reflected on what he had done, the more he became inflated with pride. LeMond smiled as he became completely conscious of the knowledge that retirement would now be much more comfortable than he could have ever imagined.

FINE

Acknowledgements

Thanks to Mark Lewis at Daytona International Speedway, Grand Am driver Ryan Eversley, Airline Captain Lee Brandt, The Super Stars racing series, Mr. Jim Barbour, Geoff Lee, my family and many supporters. Lastly, I thank Vinnie F. who showed me that it could be done.